# Sherwood

Bette Hurst

## Gotham Books

30 N Gould St.
Ste. 20820, Sheridan, WY 82801
https://gothambooksinc.com/

Phone: 1 (307) 464-7800

© 2023 Bette Hurst. All rights reserved.

No part of this book may be reproduced, stored in a retrieval system, or transmitted by any means without the written permission of the author.

Published by Gotham Books (April 13, 2023)

ISBN: 979-8-88775-216-7 (sc)
ISBN: 979-8-88775-218-1 (h)
ISBN: 979-8-88775-217-4 (e)

Because of the dynamic nature of the Internet, any web addresses or links contained in this book may have changed since publication and may no longer be valid.

The views expressed in this work are solely those of the author and do not necessarily reflect the views of the publisher, and the publisher hereby disclaims any responsibility for them.

# Table Contents

Part One .................................................................................. 10
    In the Beginning ................................................................ 11
    Twilight ............................................................................... 12
    Journey through Shadow and Light ................................... 32
    Merry-Go-Round ............................................................... 48
    Clover Time ........................................................................ 67
    Northwest Call ................................................................... 86

Part Two ................................................................................ 104
    April's in the Wind ............................................................ 105
    Melody for May ................................................................ 126
    Crickets' Chorus ................................................................ 145
    Lazy Summer Blues .......................................................... 168
    Flitter the Butterfly ........................................................... 187
    Goblin's Dance .................................................................. 227
    Mummy Case .................................................................... 262

Part Three ............................................................................. 290
    Summer Nights ................................................................. 291
    David ................................................................................. 322
    Afterword ......................................................................... 363
    Figures .............................................................................. 369
    Author Bio ........................................................................ 372

*To Wilbur and Natalie*

*With many thanks to
Helen and Charles,
Ruth and Emilio,
and Kitty*

*Beauty without Truth is mere decoration.*

*Truth without Beauty is lifeless.*

# Part One

# In the Beginning

"I've had this stitch in my side all summer, Dr. Blake," Colleen explained. "I suppose I should have guessed, what with Mom being ill for so long." She paused, bartering for time to think, for time to feel the reality of this new self, for time to hold her feelings of panic at bay. His diagnosis had hemmed her in on all sides.

"I had hoped that the skin test was wrong," she said. "I suppose I thought I was immune."

Colleen felt her tears beginning to flow. She didn't care about hiding them anymore. An invisible barrier now barred the gate to the place where she wanted to be.

"We all feel that way, Colleen, at least in the beginning," Dr. Blake replied. "That's how it is in a serious illness. I think your TB can be cured, but your best hope is Sherwood."

"But that's on the other side of the state! What about school? What about my friends?" she asked desperately.

"Your friends will be waiting for you when you come back, and you'll make new friends at Sherwood," Dr. Blake said, trying to comfort her. He patted her on the shoulder. She had known him all her life. He was close to sixty years old, and his hair had already turned white. Compassion was etched in his lined face. It was the kind of compassion that the experience of suffering teaches a good physician. His blue eyes betrayed his deep concern. Colleen did not want to see what they now saw in the X-ray.

She suddenly hated his white coat, the antiseptic smell of his office, the prescription pad on his desk, and the files of those who had come and gone. She felt utterly alone. She wanted to get up and run, to get out of his office, to go home or to school, to be anywhere but there.

"I don't want to go," she said.

# Twilight

Mr. Reilly's old 1934 Ford slowly made its way up the drive of the Sherwood Tuberculosis Sanitarium. From her improvised bed in the back seat, Colleen could see a gracefully arching canopy of oak branches, which filled the sky and towered above the roofline of the state TB hospital. As the car reached the top of the steep climb, the pale December light cast a mosaic of shadows across the front porches of the hospital. Her father glanced at his watch. It was already eleven o'clock. They were late.

Colleen impatiently pushed the pillows away from the window and sat up straight so that she could see the front of the hospital. Screened porches ran the length of the building. On each porch Colleen could see beds containing patients dressed in robes, scarves, and winter hats. She wondered if one of these porches would become her home and for how long.

The sanitarium sat at the highest point of the wooded grounds. Ravines plunged steeply on either side of the long driveway, and the staff cottages and support buildings were connected to the main hospital by narrow, wooded paths.

As Mr. Reilly scanned the parking lot for a parking space near the admissions office, Colleen stared out the window at the horizon. The scalloped rim of hills blocked the view of the cities, farms, and railroad towns that lay beyond. Over time, the health of the people in many of those towns had slowly worn down. Yet the people had clung tenaciously to the land. They had staked their lives on the coal that was taken out of the mountains and on the railroad that transported the coal to market. Hard work and poverty had created a great belt of TB, which followed the valleys of the Appalachian Mountains all the way to Washington, DC, and beyond.

"Well, Dad," Colleen said, "it's lucky the admissions office parking lot is at the top of the hill. You can coast the car downhill and pop it into gear." They both laughed, but the effort of laughing made Colleen cough.

"The car runs about as well as I do, Dad!" she said ruefully. "You don't suppose it has TB too, do you?"

Colleen studied her father. He was of medium height, and there was just a touch of silver in his wavy brown hair. He looked serious as he gazed at the hospital exterior. Mr. Reilly was normally a cheerful and outgoing man who was always ready to help others. When he looked serious, things were usually quite serious. After years of struggling to feed his family by selling insurance, her father's luck finally changed when he was elected to the town council of Carlton. Nonetheless, Colleen knew that his increased income would barely keep even with the cost of her stay at Sherwood. She could only guess at her father's worries, but she knew she was a big part of them.

Mr. Reilly parked in a spot in front of the admissions office.

Almost immediately, a big-boned, blonde nurse appeared in the doorway and boomed in a German accent, "Miss Reilly? Ve haf been expecting you for the past hour. Please come in out of the cold. You must lie down immediately! I am your nurse, Miss Marthe, and you vill be my patient. Mr. Reilly, you vill haf to sign some forms in the office. You can say good-bye to your daughter on the porch. Colleen, I vill get you a vheelchair so ve can get you upstairs and into bed right away." Before Colleen could reply, Miss Marthe pushed a wheelchair up to her and invited her to sit down.

She then wheeled Colleen into an elevator that took them to the second floor.

Mr. Reilly watched her go and then entered the admissions office. He glanced around the room and smiled at the nurse on duty. He was worried about paying for Colleen's hospitalization, but he tried not to show it. Making ends meet had become a daisy chain of events in which one bad thing always seemed to lead to another.

He believed Colleen's illness had begun when his wife had refused to be hospitalized for TB to avoid straining the family budget. His wife's illness had lasted a year and a half and had exposed the whole family. The cooking and basic household chores had mostly fallen on Colleen and him because his youngest daughter, Katie, had been too young to help. His oldest daughter, Maureen, had already graduated, found a job, and no longer lived with them. His son Elliot had only recently moved home after being discharged from the Naval Air Corps. So the care of his wife had also largely fallen on Colleen and him. They had washed his wife's clothes and had changed her bedding throughout her illness. After each meal, he and Colleen had sterilized his wife's dishes and utensils for twenty minutes in boiling water before washing. He and Colleen had had ample chance to be exposed to her germs.

Mr. Reilly finished registering Colleen and found her on the second-floor porch. He could hear Miss Marthe's German voice booming from beyond a locker room that was between the hall and the porch. He refused to think about how the family would survive if he came down with TB. It ran in his family, too. His sister had died of TB in 1940, having wasted away to a skeleton in a backyard cabin provided for the terminally ill by the health department. He had been declared 4F in 1918 because of TB, and although he had never been treated, he assumed the germ still lay dormant inside him.

"A penny for your thoughts, Dad," Colleen said as her father entered the room. She was already in bed. Her dark brown hair hung in loose, shoulder-length curls that brushed softly against her pale pink robe. Colleen smoothed back a wisp of hair from her forehead and smiled fondly at her father. He was a gentle man, inclined toward deep reflection. He said things that Colleen found more original and sensitive than the things her teachers taught her at school. She felt that he drew his strength from a deep well of happy memories from childhood.

Mr. Reilly smiled back at his daughter. "Sorry, I was just thinking about the car," he fibbed. "Your mom said to tell you that if you need anything, we'll send it in the mail."

*Colleen has grown into a real young lady*, he thought proudly. At fifteen, she was five feet four and stylishly graceful for her age. Her gray-green eyes sparkled alertly. Even dressed in her pajamas and robe, Colleen was artistic to the tip of her toes. The robe hid how thin she had become. A stranger would not have known she was sick, except for her cough.

Mr. Reilly bent over and kissed his middle daughter on the top of her head. "Be a good girl and do whatever they tell you, honey. Then you'll be home before you know it."

"Tell Katie to write, Dad. I want to know what's going on at school, even if I get behind," Colleen replied.

"We'll be thinking of you and missing you," Mr. Reilly said as Colleen clung tightly to him. "By the way, I almost forgot! I've got some knitted hats in my pocket that your mother made for you. And Katie made a pink one," he said as he took out three hats that tied under the chin and fit snuggly like a ski cap. "Your mom wants you to keep your head warm so that you don't lose your body heat through the top of your head when sitting on this porch."

"I'd rather have books, Dad! I can't imagine lying around here all day long—I'll go mad," she said, letting her voice drop so that Miss Marthe couldn't hear. "I've only got the one book Miss Wilson gave me."

"I'm sure everything will work out fine," her father reassured her. "I'll see the school principal when I get home. You just take care now!" He gave his daughter one final hug. "That will have to last until Christmas! And here's a hug from Mom and one from Katie, too!"

Colleen looked up at her father. She wasn't quite ready to say goodbye. "What do we do if this goes on for quite a while?"

"I don't think that's likely, Colleen," Mr. Reilly replied. "Your doctor told us that the average stay is down to about three months. It used to take twenty-six months! Three months is financially survivable, and besides, I'll be able to continue selling insurance at night. If Truman hurries up with his national health care, we won't have to worry about medical bills anymore," he added with some real hope in his voice. Mr. Reilly could see Miss Marthe looking at her watch. "I have to go now, sweetheart," he sighed. *plane*

Colleen smiled and gave her father a long hug. He put on his hat, and with a wave of his hand, he was gone.

There was an eerie silence. The girls in the other beds were quiet, waiting to be introduced. Colleen looked at her hands, which were trembling. Now she knew how the English children felt when they were sent away into the countryside during the German blitz. Only in her case, she had been sent away from her family in the countryside to live on the edge of a strange city where her life was in a different kind of danger.

Colleen listened for the familiar sound of her father's engine catching but heard nothing. *He must be on his way back to Carlton already*, she thought. She felt loneliness settle upon her.

Miss Marthe broke the silence. "You vill be with these four nice girls on this porch, Colleen." Miss Marthe smiled a big maternal smile that seemed to encourage Colleen to feel at home. "The porch has a very nice view of the front lawn, and there is a big lavatory not far down the hall for the five of you. There are men across the hall vith similar accommodations."

Colleen glanced around the porch. Four women were sitting in beds and smiling expectantly at her. The porch itself was bare of any decoration, and the stark outline of the trees in the ravine underscored Sherwood's bleak winter atmosphere. The interior hall was likewise bare and suffused in an eerie twilight, enlivened only by the occasional soft padding of the soles of the nurses' shoes on the linoleum. The porch opened onto a windowless lounge containing lockers that were really only small, open closets. The lockers lined three of the walls, while one low chaise took up the only available corner.

"You vill have your own locker to store your things in, Colleen," Miss Marthe said, indicating an empty locker near the door leading onto the porch. "There are metal ones out in the hall for anything you vish to keep locked up."

Colleen got up from bed and put away her few belongings. Then she stepped back onto the porch, where the screened windows were open to the winter air. Colleen immediately jumped back into her empty bed.

"Good grief, it's cold in here!" she exclaimed as she felt the winter air send a shiver up her spine. "My name is Colleen," she said to a lively looking blonde sitting up in a bed to her left. The young woman was in her early twenties and had flawless white skin and a smile that exposed perfect teeth. She reminded Colleen of the mermaid of Copenhagen harbor, because her silky straight hair gleamed in the noontime sea of light that was washing against the window screens.

How could anyone so beautiful be sick with TB? Colleen asked herself.

"Pleased to meet you, honey. I'm Mandy." Her southern drawl broke the Scandinavian spell she had cast over Colleen. "The lady with the red hair over in the corner is Cleo, but don't get too attached to her because she's decided she's going home! Right, Cleo?"

"Right. Nice to meet you, Colleen," Cleo answered. "I'm just waiting for Daddy to come rescue me out of here—*any day now!*"

Mandy pointed at a woman on the other end of the porch. "And the lady over yonder is Faith."

"Hi, Colleen," Faith said softly. She was a thin and wiry, dark-eyed brunette with a shy smile that communicated a sweet femininity. She looked a little older than Mandy. Colleen liked her instantly.

Mandy continued, "And the young lady right next to you is Laura.

She likes to keep everyone laughing."

Laura looked mischievously at Colleen. "Nice to meet ya, Colleen! My philosophy is, we're here, so let's make the best of it and have some fun!" Laura looked dramatic and worldly for someone who appeared to be only a few years older than Colleen. She had intelligent, dark eyes and the pent-up nature of a thoroughbred racehorse waiting to be let out of the barn. Laura had thick black hair, which she seemed to prefer to leave wildly natural. She was marvelously alive and apparently indomitable.

"Don't forget that there's still hope in this place. There are *men* just across the hall!" Laura whispered so that Miss Marthe wouldn't hear.

"The men might as well live on the other side of the world for all we see of them," Faith sighed.

Mandy turned to Colleen and said, "They keep us real quiet at first, hon. You'll have to stay put and even brush your teeth in bed for a few days. You'll eat your meals in bed too, and you'll cough into these little sputum papers. But pretty soon, they'll let you get up to use the bathroom and maybe even go to the dining room. Some of us are *still* waitin' to be allowed to eat in the dining room!"

Just then, Miss Marthe, who had temporarily left the room, came back in with towels for Colleen. "I heard vhat you said about the men, Laura. Ve must remember that ve are here to get vell. The men are sick too! They are here to rest and get vell, and they vill stay on their side to do that! No exceptions."

"Of course, Miss Marthe!" Laura smiled. Colleen had detected the slightest hesitation before Laura spoke.

Miss Marthe appeared to be trying to ignore Laura, who had pulled out a flannel cap from a pocketed canvas toiletries holder tied to her bed's headboard. She put on the cap and began to sing about going home to where the honeysuckle smelled so sweet.

"You're cute as a bug's ear in that cap, honey," Faith piped up.

Miss Marthe turned her back on Laura. "Colleen, ve vill tie this canvas apron vith pockets onto the head of the bed for you to keep your toilet articles in. If you haf to cough, you must always cover your mouth vith one of these papers, and put the paper in this bag. You must do this every time you cough. Your sputum vill be analyzed for tuberculosis bacilli after you have been under treatment for a vhile. The nurses vill come through every day and take away the old sputum bag for hygienic disposal and put a new one in its place."

"You vill be given lots of ice water to drink each day. It is good for you to drink as much as you can so that the tuberculosis toxins are vashed out of your body. And you must try to eat and gain weight. There is an afternoon rest period from one to three o'clock. After that, a nurse vill come around vith thermometers and take everyone's temperatures." Miss Marthe added, "And, Colleen, you are scheduled for your first pneumothorax tomorrow morning."

Despite the new faces, Colleen suddenly felt all alone with her illness.

She had been sick for months with what she had thought was a persistent, bronchial cough. She had lowered her resistance by swimming during the summer with her friends in the cold water of the Green River.

Colleen remembered one day before the war when her brother dove underwater to catch a fish with his bare hands; nobody believed he could do it. He came up after more than a minute with a fish in his hand, laughing as everyone cheered.

*Of course, he had caught it*, she thought. He could do just about anything he set his mind to. He had caught the fish, but not TB. She had caught TB. For the next three months, she had lain in bed at home, waiting for a bed to become available at Sherwood.

Miss Marthe had disappeared for a while but returned with lunch: hot covered dishes stacked on a cart. The food smelled good, and there was plenty of it.

Miss Marthe left the room, wishing everyone: "*Bon appétit!*"

"Does anyone know how to say *bon appétit* in German?" Laura asked, toasting the others as she lifted the lid off her dinner plate to reveal a piping-hot lunch. Pointing at the slices of bread next to her meat and vegetables, Laura said, "They let us have all the bread we want. They want to fatten us up, just like in Hansel and Gretel!"

Colleen shivered and laughed. "You have a way with words, Laura!"

Laura laughed, completely undaunted.

"So tell us about yourself, Colleen," Laura suggested.

"There's not much to tell," Colleen replied. "I was born and raised in Carlton. Almost all of the men there work for the railroad, but Dad sells insurance and recently became a town councilman. Mom keeps busy raising the four of us, but she also makes arts and crafts for extra income." Colleen paused to consider what else she could say about herself and her family.

"My brother Elliot served in the Naval Air Corps," she said, smiling fondly. "He wants to go to college, study math, and be a college professor one day. He caddies at the golf course, but he hopes that he can go to college on the GI Bill."

Colleen glanced down the row of beds at the faces of the young women she barely knew. She began to feel everything that had been so familiar to her back in Carlton beginning to fade. Her voice sounded like a faraway echo of that life. Her porch mates, however, seemed eager to hear anything new, so Colleen continued.

"My oldest sister loves to play piano. She has graduated and become a secretary, but she still takes lessons in the evenings. My little sister is in junior high. I'm still in high school; I like piano, too. Our house is in a neighborhood that is only four blocks deep and runs right up against the mountains. The railroad tracks and the Green River hem us in on the other side," she added.

"How long have you been sick?" Mandy asked casually.

"I had to leave school in September. Then I lay in bed for two months with a bag of shot over my right lung to reduce its action. It was just a stopgap treatment while I waited for a bed at Sherwood."

Colleen could hear someone coughing in an adjacent room and wondered who was in there.

Faith's bed was closest to the room where the coughing originated. "Miss Marthe didn't introduce you to Sue Ann because she's very sick," Faith whispered. "She's deathly white! That's why they call TB the 'white plague!' Sue Ann's got it bad!" Faith pointed to a small private room adjacent to the porch. "She's in a private room so that she can have total rest. They put her in there when she hemorrhaged. She's not allowed any visitors."

Colleen nodded, wondering uneasily how often patients hemorrhaged.

"On the other hand, if you respond to your pneumothorax treatments," Laura said, trying to steer Colleen's thoughts away from Sue Ann's situation, "they might move you down to the first floor with the ambulatory patients. Sometimes they just plain discharge us. If the pneumothorax works well, your lung will be compressed much more than it was at home. With pneumothorax, many patients heal pretty quickly," Laura explained. "Your sputum should become negative after pneumothorax, if you don't have much infection."

Colleen wondered if her porch mates were responding to treatment, but she didn't want to ask. She felt an eerie unreality creep over her. They all seemed so normal—just a little thin with an occasional cough.

"Exactly what *is* a pneumothorax?" Colleen asked curiously.

"That's when they pump air into your chest to keep your affected lung from fully expanding," Mandy explained. "The air compresses the lung. With the lung resting and the germs getting less oxygen, your body begins to heal up the cavities. Miss Marthe said you'll be getting a pneumothorax tomorrow, so that means you'll be going over to Fluoroscopy. We all go for periodic pneumothorax treatments because the compressed air gets absorbed by the body."

"Dr. Billings is the doctor in charge of Fluoroscopy, Colleen!" Faith said enthusiastically. "He's young and oh so cute, and darned if he isn't married with little kids," she sighed.

"Look here, Colleen," Laura said, seizing the chance to clown around and impersonate Miss Marthe. "I vill explain the concept of pneumothorax vith a simple little demonstration. Now pay attention, Colleen! This is your lung before a pneumothorax." Laura demonstrated by pulling the long tail of the nightcap down over her forehead and making it flap up and down in front of her nose by blowing on it. "You do not vant your lung moving this much! But—*this* is your lung *after* a pneumothorax," she laughed as she made the end of her hat flutter ever so slightly, like the tail of a shy dog. "*That* is the way they try to make us better!" she announced dramatically.

Everyone giggled.

Colleen knew that a fluoroscope could illuminate the moving lungs from any angle a doctor desired, but she had never experienced one. She had never experienced a pneumothorax, either. Her own doctor had diagnosed her with a skin test, a stethoscope, and a chest X-ray.

Colleen settled down for a lunch in bed. The meat and vegetables were piping hot, and the bread was homemade and fresh from the oven. After lunch, Miss Marthe removed the trays and told them it was time to rest.

"You must lie down after lunch for two hours every day, Colleen," she told her new charge, "and be very quiet, even if you don't feel sleepy. Ve vant your body to use all of its energy to vall off the TB bacteria!"

"So, good night, ladies! And sweet dreams!" said Cleo, snuggling under the covers. Cleo was the only one on the porch who had been allowed up for lunch. Colleen looked at Cleo and envied her freedom of movement.

"Good night," Colleen said, finally realizing that she was actually tired from her long trip and the morning's activities. She promptly fell asleep and didn't hear a thing until an afternoon nurse came around to take her temperature, which was 99.6 degrees.

When the rest period was over, Cleo turned on her radio to listen to pop tunes. Colleen zipped her robe tightly up to her neck and slipped two pairs of socks over her feet. She pinched her big toe and took comfort in noting that her feet still had feeling in spite of the cold. The mattress of her narrow bed provided little warmth against the porch's cold air.

Colleen could see that Mandy was reading a book about Charles Lindbergh. Colleen said, "I have an aunt who saw Lindbergh fly over Maine on his way across the Atlantic. Are you interested in flying?"

"Yes, indeed I am! I plan to learn to fly a plane when I get out of here. I've already had a few lessons," she announced.

Colleen was amazed; flying lessons were out of the question on a Reilly budget. Colleen supposed Mandy had access to a little extra money from a rich relative or knew someone at a small airfield, since most Sherwood patients came from families with modest incomes. Her father had told her that only about 10 percent of Sherwood's beds were free, and hundreds of poor patients from across the state were waiting without much hope for a free bed. Colleen doubted that many Sherwood patients had ever taken flying lessons, because patients who could afford to fly would be people who would go to Skyview Sanitarium, which was private. Colleen guessed that Mandy was one of a kind at Sherwood.

"You mustn't have a fear of heights if you enjoy flying so much," Colleen laughed. She had never flown and had never known any woman who knew how to fly. "My brother is a pilot," she offered shyly. "He was in the Naval Air Corps."

"Doesn't he just love flying? I'm thinkin' I might be able to get a job at the airfield to pay for more lessons when I get out of here!"

Mandy exclaimed enthusiastically.

"Sometimes I feel like I'm flying when I play piano," Colleen laughed, trying to keep the conversation going. She knew nothing about airplanes.

"Well, then, you know exactly what I mean," Mandy replied.

Colleen didn't, but Mandy's gumption and daring intrigued her. Colleen tried one more time. "What is it about Lindberg that interests you the most?" she asked, pointing at Mandy's book.

"Well, I like how he wasn't afraid to fly over the ocean, and that he went for the big prize," Mandy said. "But I think I would rather fly over land," she quickly added. "Of course, if I don't get out of here pretty soon, I'll be such an old lady that they'll never let me back in the cockpit. I've been trying to explain that to Miss Marthe."

No one said anything for a moment. Mandy's words, "If I don't get out of here soon," seemed to hang in the air, frozen in time by the cold.

"Cleo, what do you plan to do when you get out of here?" Colleen quickly asked, trying to stay upbeat.

"I'm not sure what I will do," Cleo reflected. She took the pillow from behind her head, fluffed it, and put it behind her shoulders as she tried to get more comfortable. "I used to work in the munitions factory in the early war years, before I got sick. Factory production will probably have slowed way down by now. I suppose women will have to compete with returning vets for jobs. If you've been lying around as long as I have, a person doesn't just suddenly go stand on an assembly line all day. I imagine I'll look for something less strenuous to do."

"What about you, Laura?" Colleen asked.

"Most of all, I'd like to go back and find a very rich man and have his kids," Laura laughed. "I got sick just after graduating," she said. "My parents want me to live with them and get an office job when I'm discharged, but that's too tame for me!" Laura looked at Colleen and added, "I'd like to work for the local newspaper and lead an exciting life. Assuming that I don't meet the man of my dreams right away, I plan to make inquiries at my local newspaper. I'll do anything just to get a foot in the door."

Colleen was intrigued by Laura's two views of her future self: a totally independent working girl or a rich man's wife. It was obviously impossible to be both. Laura struck Colleen as someone who was too impetuous to settle immediately into a life of ease, even if she could find the rich man of her dreams.

Colleen turned to Faith and asked, "What about you, Faith?"

"I took bookkeeping in high school, and I had a job at the local bank," Faith said. "I dealt a lot with the public. They might take me back if they're not afraid of an ex-TB patient. I quit my job when I got sick, and I told my parents not to tell my boss about my illness."

Colleen joined in, a bit shyly, "When I go home again, I want to go back to high school and graduate with my friends. My dad is trying to have some textbooks sent here, so I can keep up with my classwork."

"I've never seen anybody study at Sherwood," Laura remarked gently, so as not to discourage Colleen. "You're probably the youngest patient here," she added. "But the doctors and nurses are really strict about resting. You might just start by setting a goal of going to the dining room. Sometimes patients have relapses and go back on trays, but most patients are eventually moved downstairs before being discharged. You can look forward to a lot more freedom down there, Colleen. And anyway, with Christmas coming, you might not want to have your nose stuck in a book, right, hon?" Laura concluded sympathetically.

Colleen nodded, not sure how she felt about not studying. She stared at the book Miss Wilson, her English teacher, had given her. It was her only connection with school and normalcy. It had a curious title: *Magna*. Yet, in spite of her curiosity, Colleen no sooner began reading it than she drifted off to sleep. The book dropped unnoticed from her hand.

Colleen awoke to the clatter of dishes as the dinner trolley was wheeled onto the porch by a cheerful evening nurse in her thirties. Her voice did not boom like Miss Marthe's. It had a soothing and quieting effect, perfect for an evening nurse.

Through the porch windows, Colleen could see the gathering twilight of the December evening. The sidewalk lamps cast yellow spotlights upon each corner of the front lawn. To Colleen, their cozy glow helped ease a person into the dark and wintry night that would follow. She felt like a bear in its den. *Summer is gone, and this porch will have to be my den*, Colleen thought.

As night fell, a stillness settled upon the ward that was only broken by Sue Ann coughing from time to time. Outside, there was a deep silence in the gloomy ravines. Colleen lay in bed quietly, listening to her own breathing and wondering what the next day would bring. The spotlighted front lawn and the towering oaks spreading their limbs above it reminded Colleen of a three-ring circus tent awaiting the entrance of elephants, bareback riders, and clowns. *Where was the ringmaster?* she asked herself. Who determined when a person could go home? Who declared when the show was over?

Colleen's reverie was broken when she noticed a man leaning against a light pole on the sidewalk below. His hat was cocked at an angle, and it covered a portion of his face. He had pulled the collar of his coat up around his chin against the cold night air. Colleen realized that he had been staring up at the porches at the same time that she had been looking down from hers. When he finally saw her, she detected a flicker of annoyance in his eyes. He glanced away and moved casually out of the light.

She continued to watch him. He was whistling nonchalantly as he walked across the parking lot, but then he looked back at her and changed his course. He took a path that ran along the end of her wing and disappeared in the shadows at the end of the building. As he moved out of the lamplight and was swallowed by the darkness, Colleen could not tell if he had left the parking area, or if he was still out there watching her. He had been smoking a cigarette when she first noticed him. If he was still there, he had put it out.

Because of his furtiveness, Colleen was certain that he was not the ringmaster, but she could not imagine who he might be. If he was an evening visitor, he was a very mysterious one.

Colleen shivered and slid back under the covers for warmth. The evening nurse brought her a glass of water so she could brush her teeth. Earlier in the afternoon, Colleen had been weighed, and the sputum bags had been emptied. Colleen presumed that emptying sputum bags was a dangerous job. She wondered how the staff members protected themselves and whether or not any of them ever caught TB from the patients. Colleen watched the evening nurse perform the rest of her duties but said nothing to her about the mysterious visitor.

A little while later, Colleen heard voices down the hall. A disembodied male voice paused at the door and spoke in low undertones. Colleen saw the evening nurse enter her porch, accompanied by a slim, sandy-haired man wearing glasses. He wore a doctor's gown but seemed very young. His blue eyes glanced alertly at Colleen as he entered.

"You must be Colleen," he said pleasantly. "I'm Paul Harris. I'm interning at Sherwood. There are two of us who help out in the evening. Have you had time to settle in by now?"

"Oh, yes," Colleen replied. "I arrived before lunch. We've all gotten acquainted, and I've met some of the nurses, including Miss Marthe."

"I stop by each evening to see if there is anything that the patients need," he explained.

"My feet are cold!" Colleen exclaimed, surprising everyone and even herself by her vociferousness.

"We have a handyman named Will who has invented a foot warmer for patients who request them. Would you like one?" Dr. Harris asked.

"Oh, absolutely," Colleen replied, without hesitation.

"Do you have any questions for me?" Harris asked.

"That's easy," Colleen smiled. "When do I get to go home?"

"That's what everyone asks," he laughed, "and I don't blame them. We'll see how you take to pneumothorax. Dr. Smith is the one who reads all the X-rays. He'll be the one to make that decision."

So, Dr. Smith is the ringmaster! *Colleen thought.*

"Do you have any other questions, Colleen?"

"Only, why is it so cold in here?"

Paul Harris laughed heartily. "You can blame a Dr. Trudeau in New York's Adirondacks for that. After hearing about the fresh air treatments of the early sanitarium movement in Germany, he decided to do some studies with rabbits. He discovered that rabbits inoculated with TB wouldn't get sick if they were given lots of food in a healthy, outdoor environment. He put other inoculated rabbits down a dark hole without good food, and they quickly became ill. He believed the rabbits down in the hole were living in conditions similar to immigrants living in dark, unventilated tenements, and he concluded that the free-roaming, well-fed rabbits were like people who lived in fresh air and uncrowded conditions. So he built a fresh-air sanitarium in the Adirondacks that was like the healthy environment of the first group of rabbits." Harris concluded, "In addition to his fresh-air treatment, modern medicine has added compression therapy—the pneumothorax treatment you'll be having tomorrow, Colleen."

"I guess I don't have any more questions," Colleen said, feeling like a tired little rabbit in a cold field without a mother or father rabbit.

"Well, then, I recommend that you get a good night's sleep, so that you will be well rested when they come to take you to Fluoroscopy in the morning. I'll look in on you tomorrow evening again, and I'll try to arrange for a foot warmer," he promised.

Harris wished Colleen good night, and he turned away in order to attend to the requests of the other women on the porch. He paused at Cleo's bed and said, "Dr. Smith wants you to continue eating in the dining room, so he can call your daddy soon and tell him to come get you."

"You're teasing me, right, Dr. Harris?" Cleo asked, clutching his arm. "Will I be out of here by Christmas?"

"I couldn't say, exactly. Dr. Smith will decide. He authorizes all of the discharges," Harris replied.

Cleo fell back in bed with a whoop of delight.

Harris laughed, and then he looked serious as he turned to go into Sue Ann's room. "Good night to each of you!" he called out.

Colleen looked over at Cleo; she was rolling around in her blankets, hugging herself in giddy merriment.

"I told you, and nobody believed me!" she exclaimed. "I told you Daddy would be takin' me home soon!"

Laura looked at Cleo, an inspired gleam in her eye. "Now Cleo, since Miss Marthe wants us to gain weight, I want you to have her give you a nice going-away party—with ice cream and cake for everybody!" she added. "We need to celebrate your good fortune properly!"

"If you say so, Laura," Cleo giggled. "Just remember one thing! I'm gonna call Daddy with the good news tomorrow, and I'm going to get out of here so fast that you won't even know I'm gone!" Cleo exclaimed in delight. "There will be only the slightest indentation in my bed where a warm body with long red hair once lay. And you'll say you knew me before I was mysteriously misplaced!"

Colleen lay in bed with the light out, feeling like the cold, motherless rabbit that Dr. Harris had described. The other women had already fallen asleep. From time to time, she could hear Sue Ann coughing in the other room. She doubted that Sue Ann would share Cleo's good fortune any time soon, if at all. She heard the evening nurse go into Sue Ann's room. After a few minutes, she called a doctor from the night desk and told him something in a low voice.

Colleen's thoughts turned away from the others. As she felt sleep begin to steal across her mind, she imagined that she was home in her own bed. She could see the moon shining on the Green River as it glided by Carlton. She pictured the railroad tracks that ran along the main road through town. Colleen loved the slow approach of the night train and the equally slow departure as it passed on, its soft *clickity-clack* a lullaby in the night.

The train passed through the lowlands adjacent to the golf course down by the river. It lumbered past the hayfields where meadowlarks sang in the summer. Its route took it past the floating restaurant by the bridge between Carlton and its twin city, Tylersville. The restaurant was on stilts and had a mechanism that allowed it to rise and fall with the river's stages. It reminded Colleen of a water bug with adjustable legs.

Colleen opened her eyes for a moment, recalling something her brother Elliot had once said. Elliot was a stickler for proper nomenclature of all types. He was an avid bird watcher and had taught her the scientific names of all the birds in their locality, including the meadowlark, whose Latin name was *sturnella magna*. Magna! Was it possible that the heroine of Miss Wilson's book was as musical as a lark? Colleen smiled fondly at the thought of Miss Wilson, her favorite teacher. Miss Wilson knew that Colleen loved music. It would have been like her to find a book for Colleen with a musical theme.

Colleen drifted off to sleep thinking of Tchaikovsky's "Song of the Lark." It was a pretty piece that she had learned to play the previous summer. The plaintive, flutelike song of Tchaikovsky's lark seemed to fill the room. In the haze of Colleen's fading consciousness, the brown and yellow bird seemed to be hiding in one corner and then another, sometimes piping coquettishly from under the bed. It flew out on the lawn and seemed to be singing just for her. Finally, it flew into Sue Ann's room and sang on her windowsill in a minor key.

When it flew away in the night, Colleen could hear its song echo faintly from a faraway place—beyond the hills and the reach of her dreams. The lark was hiding in the secret place where music begins. It wanted Colleen to find that secret place, if she could.

*It wanted her to find the secret place where music begins.*

# Journey through Shadow and Light

When Colleen awoke the next morning, Faith and Mandy were already in the bathroom washing their faces. Laura was still sleeping, and Cleo was in the dining room having breakfast. Colleen heard Faith and Mandy hurry back to their beds when Miss Marthe arrived with the breakfast cart.

"Good *morrrrrning*, Laura!" Faith whispered in Laura's ear. When there was no response from her sleeping porch mate, she tickled Laura's nose with the end of her stocking cap.

Laura awoke and smiled groggily at Faith. "I was just dreaming that there's nothing like a cold night's sleep to get a person going in the morning! Isn't that right, Miss Marthe?" she asked as she stretched her arms over her head and yawned.

Miss Marthe had just come into the room with a fresh pitcher of water. "Ah! It is a beautiful December morning, Laura! There are still many birds around for this time of year. I'm surprised that they didn't vake you up!" she answered cheerily.

Laura looked out across the lawn and listened but heard no warm and cheery chirping. "Would you sing in this cold?" she asked.

The sun had barely begun to penetrate the porch's recesses. There were patches of light here and there as if the sun were uncertain where to place the scant amount of heat. Laura put her hands in a patch of sunlight and rubbed them together briskly.

Miss Marthe placed the water on its stand and then paused at Colleen's bedside to remind her that she would be having a fluoroscopy exam and a pneumothorax right after breakfast. "Ven you come back, Colleen, you vill feel a little short of breath, and you vill vant to lie in bed and rest," she said. "There is a feeling of pressure in the chest, but it is not so bad after a day or two."

Colleen glanced uncertainly at Laura for confirmation.

"It's not anything you can't laugh off," Laura answered, a bit too casually. "We've all been through it lots of times, and we're still here—living proof of Dr. Smith's theory that smothering is *good* for you!"

Miss Marthe looked sharply at Laura. "It is not like that at all, Colleen. Don't you vorry," she said reassuringly.

At that moment, a young black man in his twenties appeared in the porch doorway. He looked over at Colleen and seemed to recognize that she was new. Miss Marthe went over to him, exclaiming, "Ah, Vill, you have come to see us about the foot varmers?"

"Yes, ma'am, Miss Marthe. How many would you like me to make?"

Four hands were promptly raised.

"Vould you be able to make five?" Miss Marthe asked. "One of the patients is still in the dining room."

Will looked around to make sure that there were sufficient electrical outlets. "Yes, ma'am, I could do that."

Colleen watched the young black man as he worked. He was tall and slim and spoke with a French accent mixed with a little bit of Creole. He had a long face with high cheekbones and intelligent, brown eyes. He was broad shouldered and carried his body with an easy lightness that was almost catlike. As he went about the room doing his work, Colleen could see that he carried a small book of poetry by Langston Hughes in his back pocket.

While she ate her breakfast, Colleen thought about Will. According to Miss Marthe, the local newspapers were abuzz with talk about the need for more beds for the state's large number of untreated TB patients. It had been reported that the state legislature was planning a huge expansion in total beds at Sherwood. There were plans for a Negro ward as well. In spite of all that had been written, Colleen had not seen any Negroes at Sherwood except Will, and he was not a patient.

Colleen finished her breakfast quickly and got ready for her fluoroscopy appointment. Her porch mates talked among themselves, but Colleen remained silent, waiting to go. After a while, Miss Marthe took away the trays and came back into the room with a wheelchair for Colleen.

"This morning there vill be a few others ahead of you, Colleen, so you can vatch and see how a fluoroscopy exam is done. Afterward, Dr. Billings vill send you to the treatment room for a pneumothorax, and then you vill come back to rest on your porch. You vill be back before lunchtime, and this afternoon you can rest," Miss Marthe told her.

As Miss Marthe helped Colleen into the wheelchair, Colleen picked up Miss Wilson's book. "I'll take my book with me—just in case there's a long line," she told Miss Marthe.

"If you like to read, Colleen," Miss Marthe replied, "Sherwood has a small library, but vith not so many books yet. Ve must rely on donations. Even so, there might be something you vould enjoy," she added as she wheeled Colleen past the elevator and down a long corridor toward the operating suite.

As she rode along, Colleen told Miss Marthe that she was hoping that her schoolbooks could be sent to her.

Miss Marthe looked skeptical. "Ve shall see, Colleen," she said.

They stopped in front of a darkened room suffused in a greenish light. There were two female patients waiting in wheelchairs outside of the room. Another female patient was standing behind a machine, which displayed her ribs and the organs of her chest. Miss Marthe left Colleen with the patients who were awaiting their turn at the fluoroscope.

Colleen could see a handsome, young doctor seated on a stool. He was holding the fluoroscope. She could see why Faith was smitten. Dr. Billings was tall and well built. He had alert, brown eyes, dark brown hair, and lanky legs. He also had a friendly smile that Colleen found charming, just as Faith had described.

When it was Colleen's turn, he called her name and said, "Don't be shy, Colleen. This machine won't bite. Come on up here and just set awhile."

Colleen's book fell to the floor as she stood up, and she left it beside her wheelchair, intending to pick it up when she was finished. She approached Dr. Billings, studying the fluoroscopy machine curiously. As she stepped behind the fluoroscope, she saw a squat, blue-eyed, muscular man with slicked-back, sandy hair standing in the doorway looking in at her. Colleen saw him look down at his feet as if something on the floor had caught his attention. Colleen continued to watch him, but her view was somewhat obstructed by Dr. Billings.

Colleen thought there was something familiar in the man's demeanor. Then she realized from his careless slouch and the calculating look in his eyes that he was the man she had seen in the lamplight the previous evening. He seemed to recognize her, too. Colleen had no idea how long he had been out in the hall watching. He smirked as if in response to some inner joke, and then he raised his eyes from the floor and looked intently at her. She was certain that he recognized her. He stooped to the floor, never taking his eyes off hers. When he stood up again, he had the cautious, wary look of a thief who is not sure whether his victim fully understands that his hand is already on the thing he covets. Colleen was not thinking about what he was doing. She was thinking about how he did not seem to fit into the surrounding scene.

Too late, Colleen peeked out from behind the machine. The man had her book in his hand! He slowly turned it over, looking curiously at its cover. Then he winked at her, and before she could say anything, he sauntered away, whistling as he had the previous evening.

For a moment, Colleen was stunned by his audacity and familiarity. And in the interval, the man disappeared down the hall. Dr. Billings interrupted Colleen's thoughts and asked her to stand more directly in front of the fluoroscope. She stood where Dr. Billings indicated and mulled over what had just happened. She instinctively disliked the muscular man, and she wondered why he had stood there watching her. Had he been watching long enough to know that the book belonged to her? She stood behind the fluoroscope, perplexed and angry.

Colleen was still thinking about Miss Wilson's book as she was wheeled into the treatment room for her pneumothorax. She saw two nurses in surgical caps, masks, and gowns standing beside a rotund doctor who was wearing rubber gloves and otherwise similarly attired. He introduced himself as Dr. Kurtz in a German accent that was like Miss Marthe's. He had Colleen lie down on an operating table while the nurses arranged clean drapes over her body and a covering for her hair. She could hear the doctor and one of the nurses speaking very quietly in German. Then she felt Dr. Kurtz inject a local anesthetic between her ribs.

"This is a painless procedure, Colleen," Dr. Kurtz said. "But you will feel the pressure of the gas as it compresses your lung. Your X-ray shows you have an olive-sized cavity in your lung, which we hope to squeeze together by keeping the lung as immobile as possible. For about two days, you will feel quite a lot of pressure in your chest and neck until some of the air has been absorbed. During that time, you will be more comfortable lying down."

Dr. Kurtz had a jolly, Bavarian personality. He spoke with a slight lisp, and his eyes twinkled as he worked. He looked directly at Colleen when he spoke to make sure she understood his accented but excellent English. "We will repeat these treatments periodically until the cavity heals up, Colleen. Your sputum will most likely soon become negative, and in a few months you may be able to go home!" he announced merrily.

Colleen nodded that she understood. Dr. Kurtz picked up an

instrument, which could inject the gas between two of her ribs. She heard the sound of the compressed air cylinder being turned on and soon felt as if she could hardly breathe.

"Don't put any more in, please," she gasped.

"We're done now, Colleen. You can go back to your porch and rest," Dr. Kurtz said. "You will feel much, much better in two days, I promise."

An orderly came to wheel her out of the room. Colleen remained silent as she was taken back to her porch and was helped into bed. She didn't want to move.

Faith, with a sheepish grin, told Colleen that Laura had some jokes to tell her. "They really help, Colleen! It deflates the gas if you laugh, hon!" Faith explained softly. "Miss Marthe doesn't approve, but Laura has tried it on all of us," she giggled, "and it works!"

Laura cleared her throat and said determinedly to Colleen, "We all need to be reminded now and then, Colleen, that laughter is *still* the best medicine!" Then for the next hour she told more "little moron" jokes than Colleen could ever have guessed existed.

Colleen felt like an overstuffed sausage from all the compressed air in her chest, and she tried hard not to laugh, but she couldn't help doing so. Laura's steady barrage wore her down. She found herself laughing along with the rest of her porch mates. The more she laughed, the more it pleased Laura. Colleen was grimacing in discomfort. In desperation, she told a joke of her own.

"I think that's enough, Laura!" she gasped. "This will be the last joke. Why did the little moron back out of the bus?"

Everyone laughed gleefully. "We don't know!" they said in a chorus, waiting expectantly for the punch line.

Colleen laughed and said, "Because he was afraid someone would grab his seat."

Mandy guffawed, and Laura looked pleased to have a new joke for her repertoire. "Very good, Colleen!" she exclaimed. Laura studied her and then said, "I can see that you already feel much better."

Colleen silently admitted to herself that she actually felt a little better.

Faith added in a small voice, "Right, Colleen?"

Colleen said, "You know, I really do feel better."

Laura looked pleased and cheerily added, "You'll thank me in the mornin', Colleen." Then she went back to reading a book.

From time to time, Laura looked over and smiled encouragingly at Colleen. Colleen could do nothing but lie in bed and await further improvement. Late in the afternoon, she heard Miss Marthe come onto the porch with Will, who was holding a slatted, wooden cylinder with a light bulb inside it. An electric cord dangled from one end of the cylinder.

"Vill has finished building the first foot varmer," Miss Marthe said, "and since Colleen vill not be able to curl up in a varm ball tonight because of her treatment, I haf decided to give her the first one. Colleen, it vill fit under the blankets at the end of your bed. The bulb's heat vill keep your feet nice and varm," Miss Marthe explained.

Colleen looked dubious, but she extended her feet gingerly down toward the foot warmer that Miss Marthe placed under the sheet, moving cautiously so as not to create more pressure in her chest. The pocket of air down by her feet had already started to warm up. Colleen smiled in delight. Following the pneumothorax and Laura's "cure," the foot warmer was a wonderful surprise.

"Thank you, Will! Thank you very much. I'm sure this will help a lot tonight," Colleen said.

Seeing Miss Marthe reminded Colleen that her book had been taken from the fluoroscopy room. Colleen explained what had happened, and Miss Marthe promised to try to find out where the book was. She thought it would probably be turned in at the library or at one of the nursing stations.

Cleo and Mandy both wanted to know who had taken Colleen's book.

"I didn't get his name, and I have no idea why he took it," Colleen answered. "He winked at me, and I think he knew what he was doing. Somehow, he seemed to know the book was mine. I saw him smoking a cigarette in the parking lot last evening. Maybe he's a staff member," she speculated.

Laura asked what he looked like, and Colleen described him. Colleen thought she saw a look of recognition and apprehension on Will's face, but he said nothing. She wondered if he was afraid to say what he was thinking.

"I have to go back to work, Miss Colleen," Will said. "I hope you enjoy the foot warmer."

Out of the corner of her eye, Colleen could see Laura studying Will with great interest. When he had left the room, Laura said, "I think he probably knows who the thief is, Colleen. I'll try to find out what he knows."

By the end of the second week, Colleen had gotten to know her porch mates fairly well.

None of them, including Laura, had heard anything about her stolen book. Colleen was now allowed to get out of bed to use the bathroom, and she had been sent back for a "refill" pneumothorax. She was becoming used to the routine of life at Sherwood.

Colleen was surprised when she learned one morning that Faith had already been at Sherwood for two years. It didn't seem fair to Colleen that Cleo, who had only been there about four months, would be leaving at the end of the week. Cleo began to chatter nonstop about going home and seeing her boyfriend again. He was a firefighter. Colleen wondered if Cleo's flaming red hair had a subconscious appeal to a fireman. She asked Cleo if she thought that was possible. Cleo just laughed and said firemen were good people, who liked people for themselves and not for their hair.

On the morning that Cleo was to be discharged, she dressed in her street clothes and sat on the edge of the bed, waiting for her father to arrive. She sat there for more than an hour, drumming her fingers impatiently. Miss Marthe came onto the porch and made Cleo sit in a wheelchair, but Cleo continued the impatient drumming of her fingers on the armrests. She listened distractedly to Miss Marthe's final instructions and kept looking toward the parking lot.

"You vill slowly get back your strength, Cleo," Miss Marthe said, "but only if you are careful not to overdo. You vill have to continue bed rest for several more months. That is very important!" Miss Marthe gave Cleo a big hug and told her that she had been a good patient and that she would miss her.

At that point, Cleo's father appeared in the porch doorway. Cleo jumped out of the wheelchair and landed in a heap at his feet. She threw her arms around her father's legs and sobbed, "Daddy, Daddy, get me out of here!"

Her father was a big man with a florid complexion. He picked her up with his two hands, which were strong and gnarled from farm work. Then he said to Miss Marthe, "Well, I guess my daughter would like to go home now."

And with that, he offered Cleo his arm and said soothingly, "After you, my dear." Cleo sat down in the wheelchair, and her father pushed his daughter out of the room, smiling at Colleen as the two departed.

Laura, usually not at a loss for words, sat there popeyed, while Faith cried and said, "Bye, Cleo. Don't forget to write."

From the hall, they could still hear Cleo's sobbing, but she managed a snuffling, "Bye, bye, ya'll," and that was that.

It felt to Colleen as if everyone's emotional floodgates had silently burst and inundated the porch. She contemplated Cleo's empty bed in the corner of the room. The rising waters of their emotions seemed to lap at their own beds, and Cleo's empty bed reminded Colleen of a house stranded on high ground.

*I hope I'm next*, was all that Colleen could think.

There was a long silence, and Laura finally remarked, "Well, she said she'd be gone so fast we'd hardly notice, and I guess she was right."

Cleo's bed remained empty during the week before Christmas, which made the porch seem a bit lonely. Colleen wondered if Cleo was having a merry Christmas with her family. Perhaps her boyfriend had paid her a visit.

Colleen assumed that her friends back home would be going to Mrs. Martin's huge Christmas party. Mrs. Martin was the richest person in Carlton. She had never had any children of her own, so she loved to dress up like Santa Claus and welcome the town's children into her home at Christmas. She made sure every child received a present. Colleen had sometimes helped Mrs. Martin with the party decorations and preparations. It was the biggest Christmas event in Carlton, except for Christmas Day, and Colleen wished that she could be there.

Colleen had noticed that the daily routine at Sherwood did not really change much during the holidays. During this time, she still had not heard anything about her missing book. It upset her that the thief had apparently gotten away with stealing it. As Christmas approached, however, her spirits rose when she saw that Sherwood did its best to make the season bright. The groundskeepers had put up Christmas lights in a fir tree at the top the driveway, and Colleen and her porch mates had all received Christmas packets of toothbrushes and toothpaste from a local church congregation. Since most of her porch mates were poorer than Colleen, she felt guilty when a large Christmas package arrived for her from her parents. Colleen quickly put it in her locker and decided to open it alone on Christmas Day, out of the sight of the others.

On Christmas Eve, Faith surprised her by asking, "Are you going to open your package tonight or on Christmas Day?"

Colleen had been listening to "White Christmas" playing on the radio and was feeling homesick. She looked up and said, "Well, I suppose I could open one present tonight."

"Why don't you do that, Colleen?" Mandy suggested. "Your folks must love you a lot to send such a big box of gifts! My package hasn't even arrived yet! If you open one of your gifts, it will seem more like Christmas to me!" she exclaimed.

Faith and Laura said, "Yes! Go ahead, Colleen!"

Colleen went and got the box out of her locker. She pulled off the brown wrapping paper and found a small present wrapped in red paper labeled, "Merry Christmas, Colleen, from Katie."

"This is from my little sister," Colleen said, sitting down on her bed. Colleen opened the box and held up a fountain pen.

"That's right nice, Colleen," said Mandy. "I guess your sister hopes you'll write to her."

"Well, that would be nice, if I had some ink!" Colleen laughed ruefully.

"My mother sent some cookies," Laura said. "There are enough for us to have some right now. Help yourselves, but don't take my star cookie! I'm saving it for after Christmas dinner tomorrow."

Laura passed the tin down the row of beds. Colleen chose a chocolate ball rolled in confectioner's sugar from the assortment. She could see a two-layer, chocolate-filled, star cookie in the bottom layer of cookies.

Just then, Miss Marthe and Dr. Harris came onto the porch to wish everyone a merry Christmas. Dr. Harris paused by Colleen's bed and said that he had good news for her. Her sputum had come back negative.

"This means if we can get your lung to stay down, the cavity will begin to heal," Harris explained.

"That's wonderful news, Dr. Harris!" Colleen said happily.

"I also have good news for Sue Ann. She's a very lucky girl. Her condition has stabilized, and she can go back to her own bed now. I think we'll move her in the morning, so that she can celebrate Christmas with her porch mates," Harris explained. "I'm going to go give her the good news now."

He started to go into Sue Ann's room, but Laura said, "Wait, Dr. Harris. I have something for Sue Ann."

Laura removed the star cookie from her mother's cookie tin and handed it to Dr. Harris.

"Give this to Sue Ann, and tell her 'Merry Christmas' from all of us," Laura said quietly. "Tell her we hope she feels better soon."

Dr. Harris took the cookie into Sue Ann and soon returned with a piece of paper decorated with four angels drawn shakily in pencil. At the bottom, Harris had written for her, "Merry Christmas! Love, Sue Ann."

"She cried when I told her she could go back to her porch tomorrow," Dr. Harris said somberly. "Evidently, she could hear you laughing and talking all this time; she thought she would never get back to her own porch. I had to warn her that she's not out of the woods yet."

Colleen glanced at the dark ravine beyond the porch and felt a chill run up her spine. The bare trees seemed almost spectral in the moonlight. They clawed the sky and creaked in the light breeze as they reached for the stars. She hoped Dr. Harris didn't notice the look of fear on her face.

The doctor wished them all good night, and then he left to look in on the men's ward.

On Christmas morning, Colleen got up very early and opened the rest of her presents. Her father and mother had sent her a pair of pajamas and slippers. Her brother had sent her long johns! Her older sister had sent her a sweater that she had finally finished knitting after several years.

When Miss Marthe wheeled in the breakfast trays, she brought a sprig of mistletoe. "Not for eating!" Miss Marthe reminded them. "Ve vill hang it in the doorway and see if ve can catch any of the doctors under it!"

Miss Marthe chuckled. The women were scandalized to think Miss Marthe hoped to kiss Dr. Harris, who was ten years younger than she was, or even the venerable and dignified Dr. Smith.

At noon, Colleen's porch mates wanted to know what she had done with her presents, and Colleen said, "I already opened them! You won't believe what my brother sent!"

Colleen went into the locker room and after a few minutes came back wearing only a big grin and her long johns' top and bottom.

At that moment, Dr. Harris popped his head in the door. He stared in surprise and then laughed, "Nice Christmas outfit, Colleen!"

Enjoying the humor of the situation, Colleen pointed at the mistletoe and warned Dr. Harris, "Watch out for Miss Marthe!"

Dr. Harris laughed and blew them all kisses. "That's from all the staff to our favorite porch!" he said, smiling.

When she awoke from the afternoon rest period, Colleen could smell turkey and stuffing roasting in the kitchen down the hall.

Miss Marthe came bustling onto the porch and said, "I haf a special announcement from Kris Kringle himself! Because you haf mostly been very gut," she said, pausing and looking dubiously at Laura, "you may all eat Christmas dinner in the dining room!" Miss Marthe smiled happily. Colleen wondered if she had been saving the news as a surprise all day.

At five o'clock, the women put on their robes, talking excitedly among themselves. As they shuffled along toward the dining room, the men from across the hall joined them. Colleen shyly gathered her robe around her thin body and walked along with a tall boy named Pete. He was classically tall, dark, and handsome, but quite thin. He appeared to be at least eighteen or nineteen years old. What Colleen most liked about him were his musical voice and his intelligent eyes. Colleen was pleased when he sat down with her at the dining table.

There were only two long tables in the small room. Someone had placed them together to make one big table so that they could all sit together. The dining room was cozy and quiet. The lights were low, and Miss Marthe had hung pine and holly wreaths around the room. She had placed some Christmas cards from her relatives in Germany in the center of the two tables as decorations. Colleen felt as if she were in the Black Forest in Germany and Saint Nicholas would soon be coming through the woods on a sleigh.

Colleen discovered that Pete was an excellent conversationalist. They talked together for quite a while.

Although Will had finished his shift, he volunteered to stay and play Christmas carols on the phonograph. He put on a Santa hat and was enjoying the festivities as much as the patients were. When Miss Marthe saw him, she said, "Ah! Vill, you must have some dinner too!"

Dr. Harris placed an extra chair at Colleen's table, and Will looked pleased to be included. He sat down at the table with the patients, and a server soon appeared with a plate of food for him. Dr. Harris and Miss Marthe wished everyone a merry Christmas, and then they went back down the hall together to the nurses' station.

After the meal, everyone began filing out of the dining room. Colleen heard Laura say good night to Will.

He removed his Santa hat and said, "Merry Christmas to all, and to all a *good* night!"

Pete stood in the doorway, obviously hoping that Colleen would walk back with him, but Colleen wanted to savor the moment a while longer. She listened to the sound of ice pellets striking the dining room windows. A sudden flurry had come up, and large, wet snowflakes were sticking to the windows.

She walked over to a window and could see Will walking home alone through the snow. She watched him reach out and catch snowflakes in his hand. Pete came over to the window and said, "What are you looking at, Colleen?"

Colleen pointed outside. Will had stopped under a lamppost and was looking up at the snowflakes swirling in the light. They covered the grass in a thin layer of wet snow, and countless millions more fell out of the dark sky on their journey through shadow and light.

From down below, Will looked up and saw Colleen watching him. He lay down in the thin layer of snow and made an angel. Then he knelt and spelled out *Joyeux Noel!* He bounded to his feet, pointing happily to his handiwork.

"I wonder if he's ever seen snow!" Colleen exclaimed. "This might be his first Christmas in America." Pete peered out into the night to see whether the storm looked like it would amount to much.

"How do I write 'Good night!' in French, Pete?" Colleen suddenly asked.

Pete smiled. There was a circle of condensation on one of the panes. He took her finger and wrote *Bonsoir!* on the window pane.

Colleen frowned and shook her head. "That will look backward out there!" she exclaimed.

Pete rubbed out what he had written. Below his previous words, he wrote *riosnob* on the pane. The letters spelled *bonsoir* backward.

"Is that better?" he asked.

"Perfect!" she exclaimed. "How did you do that so quickly?"

Pete laughed. "I suppose I could say something about symmetry and rotation and all that, but the truth is, I'm a lefty. I used to write like that in first grade until my teacher figured out that she ought to leave me alone and let me write left-handed!" he smiled.

Colleen examined what he had written. "It's better," she said musingly, "but it needs something else!" Colleen drew a snowman with a happy face.

"Now it's perfect!" she exclaimed.

"It's like a Christmas card, Colleen! It's nice of you to send one to Will," Pete said approvingly.

The snowman and the "bonsoir" were now surrounded by a field of snowflakes.

*Pete was right*, Colleen thought. *It looks like a Christmas card.* She looked down and waved at Will.

"He might be feeling lonely so far away from home. He does a lot for us—and at some risk to his health," she said.

Will looked up and waved back to Colleen, pointing at the window to show her that he saw what she had written. Then he turned and walked toward his apartment.

Pete offered Colleen his arm. When they reached their porches, Pete said, "Good night, Colleen!" His voice was deep, resonant, and musical. He paused and added, "And *au revoir*, which means, I hope to see you again, mademoiselle!"

"Merry Christmas, Pete!" Colleen answered gaily. She watched Pete go back to his porch.

Colleen returned to her own porch and sat down on her bed, reflecting on the evening. The rest of the women were already asleep in their beds. She looked through the screen and saw the figure of a man in the parking lot looking up at the porches. He was smoking a cigarette.

*It's him!* Colleen said to herself.

She considered shouting out to the man to give back her book, but Miss Marthe had come in and put out the lights.

*It would have woken everyone up anyway, Colleen sighed to herself.*

The silence of the Christmas night settled over the porch. When Colleen looked out again, the man was gone.

## Merry-Go-Round

At the beginning of January, Dr. Kurtz told Colleen that she would be moved to the ambulatory ward on the first floor. He felt confident that she would respond to pneumothorax.

"You will be allowed out of bed each morning to wash your hair and shower, Colleen," he told her on the morning of her third treatment. "Everyone on the first floor is ambulatory, and you will have a chance to meet more people," he said reassuringly.

Colleen was elated by the thought of more freedom. "Does that mean I can go home soon?" she asked.

Dr. Kurtz had been setting out equipment but now paused. "You are young, and that can mean a quick recovery, Colleen," he said, "but I can't promise you an exact date. It could be as little as a few months. That will depend on how well your lung cooperates. If we can keep it down two full weeks, the cavity will have a good chance to begin healing." Kurtz picked up an X-ray and pointed to the cavity in Colleen's lung. "This is the area we'll be watching."

Colleen examined the X-ray. Her misty gray-and-white lung was floating like a cloud in the darkness of her chest space. She studied the X-ray for a moment more and asked, "How did the cavity form?"

Dr. Kurtz studied the film for a moment. "When TB gets deep into the lung, it is resisted by the body. Mucus cannot bring it out, so the body tries to destroy the bacteria and wall it off. As the body mounts its defense, some of the bacteria and lung cells die. The dead cells and bacteria form a cheese-like substance that eventually liquefies and is coughed up. This leaves a cavity in the lung. We don't want bacteria to get out of the lung and into the blood stream." Dr. Kurtz hurriedly added, "That has not happened in your case."

"You mean, if this goes away, I'll be able to go home?" Colleen asked.

Dr. Kurtz did not respond. He studied Colleen's lung for a while and then said, "The cavity is serious, but not as bad as you might think. There are far worse cases. Unfortunately, pneumothorax by itself works in only 5 percent of early-stage cases, even in young people," he added, glancing up at Colleen. "It's possible that you could develop adhesions that will have to be removed by pneumolysis—perhaps here … or here," he said, pointing to areas in the film where they might develop.

He looked serious as he turned to face Colleen. "Even though the state tries to send us nonadvanced cases like yours, you will meet people at Sherwood whose disease will probably shock you. TB takes on more forms that you might expect. It can spread to various organs and joints, and even to the skin and brain."

Colleen drew back in alarm when Dr. Kurtz mentioned the brain. "Do you think I'll need surgery?" she asked a bit nervously.

"If your lung won't remain compressed so that it can heal, it will most likely be because of adhesions," he explained. "The important thing is that you are here and getting treatment. You are one of the fortunate ones, Colleen," he said, patting her shoulder reassuringly. "Sherwood is too expensive for many patients, and our free beds are limited. Unfortunately, even when a free bed is available, poor patients seldom can afford the travel costs."

"I can understand that. My dad had trouble getting here," Colleen replied. "Our car is old and always breaking down."

"Then you understand that the problem is not just medical," Dr. Kurtz said kindly. "Sherwood has expanded as fast as war shortages have allowed." He looked appraisingly around the room at the modern equipment.

"We lack housing for doctors, and we lack steel to build the new wing for Negroes," he said, his brow furrowed in concern. "Studies have shown that the disease among blacks is usually far more advanced, and blacks receive inadequate care statewide, so Dr. Smith is pushing to get the new wing open as soon as possible. There's also a possibility that expansion will stop altogether if the legislature decides to decentralize TB services and make them geographically accessible throughout the state."

Colleen nodded solemnly. "I hope they work it out so that everyone gets the care they need really soon," she said.

After Dr. Kurtz added more air to Colleen's chest, she was wheeled back to the porch. She was told that an orderly had already moved her bag downstairs. She looked around the porch that had been her home for the past few weeks and wondered what lay ahead for her on the ambulatory ward.

Faith sighed and said, "Colleen, I've been here so long that I feel like a ticket taker on a merry-go-round; all I do is say 'hello' and 'good-bye,' and everyone but me takes a ride and goes home. But I sure do hope you get better soon, and come back and see me before you leave."

"Well, I'll be right downstairs, Faith, so maybe they'll let me come up now and then," Colleen said.

Laura gave Colleen a hug and said, "I sure will miss you, sweetie. We'll stand behind you till your belly's beat blue, like they say back home. And try not to let those first-floor men turn your head!"

Colleen laughed at the wry image of her leading her porch mates into battle while they hunkered down behind her. Nevertheless, she appreciated Laura's somewhat encouraging words of support. She gave everyone a big hug and then sat down in the wheelchair the orderly had provided. "*Auf wiedersehen*, Miss Marthe!" Colleen called out as the elevator doors were closing. Miss Marthe smiled and waved good-bye.

The orderly took Colleen down to her bed on a porch that was adjacent to the administrative offices and entrance. The first floor layout was the same as the one above. The men's porches were on one side of the hall and the women's porches were on the other. The locker arrangement and large, common bathroom for the women were the same. There were five beds on Colleen's porch—just like before—and the same cold air.

Colleen introduced herself to three women who were lounging in bed and talking among themselves, and then she excused herself to go wash up in the bathroom. She walked into the brightly tiled room and saw a woman with long, blonde hair who seemed to be about thirty years old. The woman did not have her shirt on and was getting dressed after taking a shower. Colleen could see a tremendously sunken area of skin beneath part of her rib cage. It was a shocking sight.

Colleen heard someone flush a toilet in the stall behind them. As the occupant pushed open the stall door, it hit the shirtless woman in the hollow below what was left of her rib cage. She cried out in pain. Colleen was stunned, but the woman from the stall seemed unperturbed and just said, "Oh, Geraldine, did I hit you? I'm sorry!"

As Geraldine grimaced in pain, the other woman seemed oblivious and walked right on by and out the bathroom door.

Colleen said to the stricken woman, "I'm Colleen. Are you all right?"

"I'm Geraldine," she replied. "She didn't mean no harm. You're new, aren't you? Where are you from?"

"I've just been moved down from the second floor. I'm from Carlton. Are you on my porch?" Colleen asked. "I'm on the porch closest to this bathroom."

"Yes, ma'am. They gave me 'the rib' because my lung is bein' ornery and won't heal up. They said I'll be here a while."

"Is that where they operated?" Colleen asked, trying not to stare.

"Yeah, they got me good. It was the only way to collapse my lung, they said. Felt like they removed half my rib cage. They don't put you to sleep while they do it, and it's permanent! I'll be this way all my life," Geraldine frowned, pointing at her side.

Colleen stood there mutely. "But you'll get better, right?"

"I hope so, honey," Geraldine said, and she walked out of the room.

Colleen washed her face and looked at herself in the mirror. She muttered glumly to her reflection, "Dr. Kurtz said it would be better down here!" She studied her appearance, trying not to think about Geraldine's ribs. This morning she had brushed her long, brown hair behind her ears and off her forehead. In the hospital, she usually allowed it to fall straight and uncurled to her shoulders. For school, she would always curl her hair and part it to one side, holding it in place with a barrette in the soft styling of the war years.

Colleen tried out her best smile to herself in the mirror, trying to feel pretty. Her green eyes still sparkled, and she saw that her teeth were clean and white. She inspected her gums and tongue while she was at it. She pulled down her lower eyelid, which was pink. "Everything looks okay," she told herself reassuringly. Colleen looked down at her feet. Her pajamas now fell an inch above her ankles. She realized that she was still growing. She examined her pajama-clad figure in the mirror. She looked a little thin, but she doubted anyone on the outside would guess she was pumped full of air! Except at the ankles, her pajamas still fit her, but she was already taller than quite a few of the women. "I'll have to start eating more," she said, giving herself a pep talk in the mirror. "But that should be easy just lyin' around all day, with breakfast, lunch, and dinner the only highlights of my day."

Colleen went back to the porch to lie down. One of the nurses on the floor was a young woman named Victoria. She welcomed Colleen to the first floor and asked her some questions about herself. After they had been talking awhile, she told Colleen that she was both a nurse and a patient.

Colleen was not particularly surprised. Clearly, all of the staff had been exposed to TB. She wondered whether healthy people even applied for work at Sherwood. Victoria was a vivacious brunette in her early twenties, and she had a warm manner that suited the profession she had chosen. She walked gracefully, even in her nurse's shoes. She was so beautiful, tall, and willowy that Colleen thought she must have been a dancer at one time.

When Victoria learned that Colleen liked to play the piano, she told her that there was a piano in the new building. "If you get better, maybe they'll allow us to play a duet at one of the parties, Colleen," she proposed. "There's going to be a party in the new building in a few weeks, and they'll probably let some of us attend. Now that I'm allowed to work part time, I'm hoping they'll let me go," Victoria added with a wistful smile.

"A party sounds really nice," Colleen said hopefully.

"Don't worry if you miss this one. They have them a lot," Victoria reassured her. "They had a party back on Halloween, and some of the patients from this building went," Victoria continued. "This next party will be on Valentine's Day. I suppose they'll have heart cookies and romantic music. Maybe not dancing, but the men will definitely be there too!" she said, smiling. Colleen could easily visualize the pretty nurse dancing gracefully with a handsome doctor or an attractive male patient.

Colleen soon discovered that the patients tended to socialize in the halls, talking in small, mixed groups. She had already met some of the male patients from the porch across from hers. The best place for the women to socialize among themselves was in the ladies' bathroom as they showered, dressed, and styled their hair for the day.

Colleen's porch mates consisted of two older women who constantly talked to each other, Geraldine, who mostly stared out the window, and a young woman named Jeanette, who occupied the bed next to Colleen. Jeanette whiled away her time in bed by telling Colleen about her past and present boyfriends.

Jeanette had worked as a secretary before coming down with TB. She talked freely about her love life and at night whispered confidences to Colleen about the two men she had been dating seriously before she got sick. She couldn't make up her mind between them.

"Joe is a fine dancer and likes to take me places where he can show me off," Jeanette said enthusiastically. "During the day, he works as a mechanic at a garage in town. He just loves to work on fast cars." Jeanette paused to consider her other boyfriend.

"Allen, on the other hand, is quiet and serious," Jeanette said, stretching out the words "quiet" and "serious." "He manages the business office at a lumber yard."

Although at night Jeanette seemed quite sincere about the two men in her life, Colleen discovered that her fidelity did not carry over into the day. Colleen had seen Jeanette and a married man named Cole talking and laughing together.

Cole lived on the men's porch across the hall. Sometimes Colleen would stop by on the way back from the bathroom and briefly watch Jeanette playing cards with Tom, who also lived on Cole's porch. To Colleen's delight, Pete had been moved down to Cole's porch shortly after she had been moved to the first floor. When Pete learned that Colleen was just across the hall, he had stopped by her porch to welcome her. He had seemed very pleased that she was so near him.

Pete sometimes played cards with Tom and Jeanette, while Cole usually just watched from his bed. Cole would sometimes join in, however, and one time Colleen had seen Cole and Jeanette nuzzling their feet together under the table. Colleen couldn't understand why Jeanette wasn't bothered by the advances of a married man. She thought that there was something naively sweet in Jeanette that Cole knew how to take advantage of.

Colleen's mother had recently sent her some ink and stationery to go with her new pen she received at Christmas. Colleen used them to write a long letter to Katie telling her about the new people she had met and about her treatments. She wrote that someone had taken her book, but she asked Katie not to tell Miss Wilson yet because she was hoping the book would be found. Colleen wrote a second letter—in her best handwriting—to her school principal, Mr. Thomas, asking if he would please send the textbooks she needed to finish her studies for the rest of the year. "Just in case," Colleen added.

Colleen longed for a friend of her own age. Except for Jeanette, her other porch mates were considerably older than she was. She missed Laura, Faith, and Mandy, who always treated her as one of them. She wanted to be understood and treated as an adult. A friend of her own age would understand that. She felt that Pete was the only one who treated her as an equal, but he was at least four years older than she was. She wondered if he felt alone, even though adult conversation came easily for him. He was cultured and intellectual, but his seriousness and intelligence set him apart from the others. She wondered if he was looking for acceptance, too.

The bathroom was a social place, but when it was empty it also served as a refuge from the endless prattle of her two eldest porch mates. Colleen got up to use the bathroom. She entered one of the stalls just as the two older women from her porch came into the bathroom. She could see the women through the crack where the door joined the stall. Their breasts hung full and drooped halfway down their chests under their pajamas in spite of their thinness. She could hear them gossiping about two people down the hall who were an "item." They stopped talking when Colleen came out to brush her hair. They remained silent, watching her and waiting for her to leave, as if she were too young to hear what they were saying. Colleen decided to make a stand.

"Hey, you can say 'item' in front of me," Colleen said lightly. She tried to stare them down with a friendly smile and pretend she was one of them. It didn't work. They stood there in silence, staring at her, and so she left.

Colleen went back to bed and pulled out her stationary. She wrote a quick note to Laura, asking if she had heard anything more about the whereabouts of Miss Wilson's book.

A few days later, Laura sent a note back to Colleen. Will had told her that the man who took Colleen's book was most likely a former patient who had become a handyman at Sherwood. Will had also told her that the man had a reputation as a Don Juan. It was rumored that he met female patients on the roof for trysts. He had bragged about his conquests to some of the maintenance staff. Laura wrote, "Will thinks you should stay away from him! He might try to seduce you!"

Laura had added a postscript to her note that said, "Will told me that this fellow seems to have a grudge against him. I think Will's afraid of him. He said that the fellow is very hard to work with and that he is secretive and not very well liked by the staff. They call him the Handyman. He thinks of it as a badge of honor with women. Beware!"

Colleen blushed. Her name had never before been connected with the word *seduce*. She was concerned for Will, too, and it made her even more determined to find out what had happened to her book. She reminded herself that the Handyman might have thought the book had been left by mistake on the hall floor. But if that were the case, why had he winked at her? Colleen frowned in frustration.

Colleen glanced at the two whispering women at the far end of the porch. By the look on their faces, their conversation was for no else to hear—Colleen least of all. Geraldine looked sympathetically at her but said nothing and looked back out the window. Colleen looked out the window, too, because she had nothing to read and no one to talk to about all these things.

One morning, Victoria came onto the porch to tell Colleen that Dr. Kurtz had decided to perform pneumolysis surgery on Colleen. He planned to remove the adhesions that were binding her lung to her chest wall and keeping it inflated. The surgery was scheduled for the next morning. Victoria answered Colleen's questions and seemed pleased by Colleen's interest in the details of the procedure.

"Not many patients ask as many questions as you do, Colleen. You've got a really good head on your shoulders. You should consider a career in the medical field," she said, smiling in a friendly and admiring way.

Colleen smiled at the unexpected compliment and replied, "Thanks, Victoria. If the surgery makes me better, maybe we'll get to play a duet together after all."

Victoria eagerly agreed. It seemed to Colleen that Victoria might one day become her friend and not just her nurse.

As Victoria was about to leave, a brunette in her thirties dressed in vivid floral pajamas came onto the porch and greeted Colleen.

"Mind if I interrupt you two with some news?" she asked.

Victoria turned to Colleen and said, "I take it you know Greta?"

Colleen nodded. Wisps of hair hung down around Greta's ears from a loosely-tied French knot. It looked as if she had slept that way. Colleen knew Greta from the ladies' bathroom. This morning Greta was brimming over with excitement.

"Colleen, they gave me some good news for a change. I'm goin' to the Valentine party this weekend!"

Victoria looked up with interest.

"That's great!" Colleen said, grinning. "What are you going to wear?"

"That's what I come to ask you about," Greta replied. "I have a black dress with long sleeves, but it needs somethin' more."

Colleen tried to picture Greta in her black dress for a moment. "Tell us about the dress. Maybe we can think of something," Colleen suggested.

"It hangs loose, but it swirls way up to here when I cut a rug!" she replied merrily, pointing to a place well up her thigh. "And I have some low-heeled black shoes that are good for office work, sort of plain an' all, but great for dancin' in."

Colleen felt herself relax as she thought about the party. She enjoyed getting dressed up for church socials. At home, she liked looking at the latest fashions in the newspaper advertisements. She was an excellent seamstress, and she could sew a dress or suit and make it look store-bought.

"How about a scarf or maybe a brooch?" Colleen asked.

"I didn't bring nothin' extra. The dress and shoes are all I've got for as long as I'm here," Greta laughed, not bothering to conceal her own poverty.

Colleen had a black-and-white scarf, which she thought would look pretty with Greta's dress.

"My mom always said that if we all share, we'll get by fine and dandy," Colleen said as she rummaged through her locker for the items she had put away. "I think I brought something that will go with your dress," she called back to Greta.

"How about this?" Colleen asked as she came back onto the porch. She extended her dress scarf to its full length so that Greta could see its design.

"Why, it's beautiful, Colleen!" Greta cried in delight. "You're just too sweet!" Her eyes sparkled. "Thank you so much! I'll bring you back the scarf an' a cookie, too. I promise."

"Who around here decides which patients go to the party, Greta?" Victoria asked.

"You would have to ask at the nurses' station," Greta answered.

Victoria hurried out of the room. In a few minutes she returned, all out of breath.

"You asked to go to the party, didn't you, Victoria?" Greta said, grinning.

Victoria nodded.

"I knew it! You two are a pair. The grass don't grow under neither of your feet."

Victoria smiled and then looked at Colleen and, changing the subject, said, "I never asked you, Colleen. What kind of work do you do?"

"I still go to high school," Colleen answered quietly, so that the two older women wouldn't hear.

Victoria was amazed. "Why, sweetie, I thought you were at least eighteen. An' here you're still in high school. You're much more mature than other girls your age!" she exclaimed.

Colleen glowed with pleasure and looked triumphantly at the two gossiping women. For the first time since she had been at Sherwood, someone had made her feel like an adult. Then Colleen remembered Pete. Like a true gentleman, he had also held open the doors to the adult world for her.

Actually, Colleen felt that some of the staff had tried to adjust to her in-between status, but they didn't seem to always know how. One of the nurses had even gotten the notion that she was an orphan. She had fussed over Colleen and treated her like her own daughter, but when she discovered that Colleen had parents, the nurse quickly shifted back to a professional relationship.

"I'll go try on Colleen's scarf and come back later to find out what you'll be wearin' to the party, Victoria," Greta said as she headed back to her own porch.

Colleen settled back into bed. "Thanks for the kind words, Victoria!" Colleen said to the young nurse, who had already started to leave the porch.

Victoria whirled around in surprise. "Why, Colleen, you're not a bit like anybody on this floor, except maybe Pete. I'll have to introduce you two."

Colleen laughed. "We've already been introduced—twice! I met him upstairs at the Christmas dinner, and then Jeanette insisted on reintroducing us."

Colleen was scheduled for pneumolysis surgery early the next morning. She went to bed worried about the surgery. As she lay in her bed, she reminded herself that Dr. Kurtz seemed unconcerned about the procedure. He had cauterized lung adhesions hundreds of times.

She tried to relax by recalling Schubert's waltzes. She mentally fingered one of her favorites, almost aching with the desire to be back home at the piano. She fell asleep telling herself that the compression therapy would work better once the adhesions were removed. Maybe then, she really could go home.

Early the next morning, she was taken to the treatment room. Dr. Kurtz and his nurse, Miss Kirsten, spoke together in German as they organized the surgical equipment. Colleen guessed that Dr. Kurtz was about thirty. He spoke perfect English and rarely used German around patients, but from time to time, he and Miss Kirsten would lapse into their native tongue. Dr. Kurtz's German often sounded soft and sweet and reminded Colleen of the great tenderness found in the music of Schumann and Schubert. Yet, when his words sounded clipped and guttural, they reminded Colleen of a Wagnerian Norseman. The thought of Dr. Kurtz in an operatic, horned helmet made her smile.

"You are happy this morning, Colleen!" Miss Kirsten said approvingly. "That is *gut!*"

As Dr. Kurtz and Miss Kirsten prepared for the surgery, Colleen watched and listened, wondering if they were refugees from Germany. Ten years ago, in 1936, Dr. Kurtz would have been about twenty years old. She wondered if he and Miss Kirsten had escaped just before the war broke out.

Colleen reflected on what she knew of the Hitler era and its effect on the German people. She remembered that Miss Wilson had written on the blackboard one day: *"One must cultivate one's garden."*

Miss Wilson had directed Colleen's class to remember the quotation as they prepared a theme on fascism and democracy based on another quote from Voltaire: *"Anyone who has the power to make you believe absurdities, has the power to make you commit injustices."*

Miss Wilson had suggested that they try to explain the rise of fascism in Germany in terms of the duty of a free press to inform belief and to expose evil. She asked them to explain the difference between molding belief and truly informing. They were to compare the provisions of the First Amendment to Hitler's censorship of books.

Colleen had written that she thought many people were capable of fooling themselves, either out of fear or self-interest or from too much trust in authority. In her essay, Colleen had compared the Nazi attitudes toward Jews to the American attitudes toward Negroes. She noted that Negroes and Jews were still discriminated against in America. She said Voltaire would have called such attitudes *absurdities* because they were based on lies that people perpetuated in order to justify their privileges. Colleen believed that the German people had allowed Hitler to cultivate their prejudices and fears after their defeat in the previous war and the economic collapse that followed it. She tried to show that American Negroes had been demeaned, used as slaves, and even killed, in much the same way that Hitler had treated the Jews. She wrote that racist attitudes had been manipulated by politicians for selfish and undemocratic purposes, and many people in both countries had gone along with the lies.

Miss Wilson had written a note by her grade that said that Colleen's composition was very well written, but that Colleen had left out a discussion of Hitler's power to censor, as well as a discussion of the book burnings. She said that she had hoped students would discuss how Hitler had burned books and stifled opposition speech after destroying the Reichstag. Her note to Colleen concluded with, "Goebbels understood Voltaire's warning, and he used it for evil purposes. He got the German people to believe that life could be good without the right to read and write freely or to speak the truth about injustice, which is the ultimate absurdity!"

Colleen thought guiltily of her missing book. Miss Wilson's words seemed to apply to her present situation. Colleen realized that she should have spoken up when the Handyman took her book, but his daring had taken her by surprise, and he had walked off with it before she could even speak out. Of course, it would be harder to walk off with a person's rights than a person's book, Colleen mused. It had taken time, coercion, and unanswered lies in Hitler's case. She wondered what the Handyman was really up to, but she was forced to admit that she had no way of knowing—at least, not yet. It might be nothing at all, but she doubted it.

Dr. Kurtz broke into Colleen's thoughts by asking her to lie on her side with her arm over her head. Then Miss Kirsten draped her so that only her face remained uncovered. Colleen felt the injection of the local anesthetic, and then she heard the clinking of various instruments. She waited anxiously.

Dr. Kurtz said they were ready to begin. "Are you comfortable, Colleen?" he asked. "You mustn't move during the procedure."

Colleen promised that she would lie still.

When the surgery began, Colleen lay quietly on her side as Dr. Kurtz and Miss Kirsten worked together over her. The surgery took longer and was more painstaking than a pneumothorax treatment.

Many minutes passed in silence, and then Colleen exclaimed, "I smell burnt feathers!"

She heard Dr. Kurtz laugh from behind her. "No jokes, please, Colleen. This is painstaking work."

She lay still for several more minutes, her arm uncomfortably over her head. Then she protested, "I wasn't joking about the feathers! What *is* that smell?" she asked in alarm.

"That was the last of your adhesions," he said. Colleen heard Dr. Kurtz sigh in relief. "Yours were very easy to remove. There were no complications."

Colleen also breathed a sigh of relief, because the procedure was over and hadn't hurt.

After the surgery was completed and Colleen had been undraped, Dr. Kurtz said, "I think all of the adhesions are gone, Colleen, and I think you will begin making good progress now. He bent kindly over his youngest patient and asked, "How do you feel?"

"As usual, I guess," Colleen answered. "I'd like to go back to the porch and rest now."

When Colleen got back to her porch, Victoria came in to tell her that she had gotten permission to go to the Valentine's Day party.

"Well that's just wonderful, Victoria," Colleen said, still tired from the surgery.

"I'm just thrilled! I'm going to wear a red dress and high heels." Looking guiltily at Colleen in bed, she added, "Why couldn't we have a quiet party over here, too?"

"Personally, I'd just like to get my schoolbooks, even if it means studying on Valentine's Day," Colleen said.

"Well, over in the new building they have crocheting and crafts. So that's a possibility for you, if the books don't come," Victoria told her. "Even some of the men crochet over there," she added, smiling.

"Now that would be too cute," Colleen said, picturing men crocheting while talking about sports.

On Saturday evening, Greta and Victoria came onto Colleen's porch to show her their dresses. Both women looked very pretty. Victoria had found some heart earrings to wear, and Greta was wearing Colleen's scarf.

Colleen asked them to twirl around to show off their dresses, and she told them approvingly, "You'll be the belles of the ball!"

Colleen watched as Victoria and Greta were taken in wheelchairs to the waiting van. She heard the heavy, outside door open and slam shut as the women left the building.

The party was being held in the basement of the new building. As the van drove away, Jeanette began describing the last time she had gone to a dance with Joe. Colleen fell asleep halfway through the story.

At eleven o'clock, Greta came onto Colleen's porch, crying and carrying on. Jeanette turned on a light, and Colleen could see Greta's tear-stained face.

"I got terrible news. Victoria collapsed tonight at the party, and they took her away to a private room. She was havin' a wonderful time, just playin' the piano and bein' the life of the party and all. She had everybody singin' along. An' suddenly she just clutched her chest and fell onto the floor. They took her away on a stretcher and came back and told us her lungs had collapsed. Both of them! It looked real, real serious. She was unconscious and white. No blood, but she looked real bad." She leaned against Colleen's bed to steady herself and catch her breath.

"It might have been too much singin'," Greta said quietly. "She just looked real scared and surprised all of sudden, like somethin' real bad had gotten ahold of her insides, and she just called out, 'Help me!' Those were the last words I heard her say before they took her away." Greta started crying again. She sat down in a heap on the visitor's chair in the corner.

"Do they think she'll die?" Jeanette asked almost inaudibly.

"They're not sayin' a word," Greta answered. "I thought you should know right away. I'm goin' back to bed, because I'm real tired and don't feel too good." Greta said good night and went back to her porch.

For a moment, Colleen's mind flashed back to Faith's description of Sherwood as a merry-go-round. On the Sherwood carousel there was a pale-white horse, which no one wanted to ride. The riderless horse went round and round as the music played. If, by bad luck, you bought a ticket and were forced to choose the pale horse, it would carry you helplessly away into the woods and ravines around Sherwood.

Colleen remembered her Uncle John's face when he was dying of pneumonia. It had been pale and beaded with sweat. She had been just five years old then, and her mother's silence about her brother's death had provided Colleen with a small inkling into the hidden world of adult emotion. It was only a fleeting glimpse, like a blurred memory of watchful parents that a child might recall from a merry-go-round ride.

Victoria hovered briefly between life and death after the dance. A nurse told Colleen that Victoria's parents had been summoned immediately.

When Victoria died, her parents had left without talking to anyone.

Later that day, Greta came over to Colleen's porch to talk. "I guess you've heard by now," Greta said.

Colleen nodded silently.

Greta said in a flat tone, "I saw her parents leave. Her father took her mother out to their car, and then he came back for Victoria's suitcases.

"When I was a little girl, I had a dog I really loved," Greta said tearfully. "When he was old, he got sick. One day, he came over to me and squeezed my arm real hard with his two front legs. I didn't know a dog could hold on so hard with just paws and legs; he was askin' for help, but there was nothin' I could do except pet him. He just fell back and lay on the rug like all the hope and life went out of him because I couldn't help him. He didn't crawl away or nothin' 'cause he was so sick. My parents took him to the vet, and the vet said my dog's liver had gone bad an' that he needed to be put to sleep.

"That night I had a dream that me an' my dog had got on a train that followed the edge of a lake," she continued. "At the first stop, my dog got off. When the train started up again, I was real desperate, tryin' to get the conductor to stop the train, but the passengers just said, 'Don't worry, lady, your dog will be waitin' for you when the train comes around again.' When the train came around to that stop, my dog wasn't there. I knew I would never see him again."

She paused and then said slowly, "An' what I want to know is, how could anyone bear somethin' much, much worse, like the death of a child?"

The room fell silent. Greta's words had even temporarily silenced the gossiping old women.

Colleen thought bitterly of Faith's merry-go-round. Victoria had bought a ticket and gotten the pale horse. Death had snatched her away. Death, a "now-you-see-life, now-you-don't" grotesque magician in a long black cape and a mask with unreadable eyes—a barker in a sideshow who fooled you into taking a ride when you ought not to.

Victoria had paid her money. Death shrugged indifferently and pointed to the pale-white, riderless horse as Victoria looked in vain for a different horse to ride. Victoria had mounted that pale horse and the carousel had spun faster and faster. Then time ran out. She had bought the ticket to ride because she loved life and she loved the carousel's music.

Colleen could not comprehend Victoria's death. She lay back quietly in her bed, her thoughts confused and fluid. Victoria had been perfect. She had been a good friend. She had trusted life's magic and music; but Death had bided his time, knowing Victoria would come to him through them. In spite of her name, Victoria had not been the victor.

Colleen wondered if she just did not have the right words, as Miss Wilson might say. Then she realized that this time Miss Wilson might be wrong. There were some things for which there were no words.

# Clover Time

By the end of February, the days had noticeably lengthened. The sunlight was no longer pale, wan, and sickly. It reached down into the depths of the shadowy ravines and glittered off the trunks and branches of the trees that grew there. It refused to be denied access to all but the deepest recesses of that nether realm. The sunlight felt warm and life-giving. Colleen and her porch mates still shivered during breakfast, but by noon they basked in the promise of spring.

Hospital romances began to grow as wildly as the burgeoning nature all around them. Jeanette began to visit with Cole whenever she could, and she would occasionally set up a table so that Colleen and Pete could join them in a game of cards. Although Cole flirted constantly during the card sessions, Jeanette's exact relationship with Cole remained a mystery to Colleen. She couldn't tell if there was more heat than lightning in their flirtation.

Cole was a man who liked to keep his ear to the ground and was a veteran people watcher. He claimed that detecting hospital romances kept him busy and "out of trouble." In the spring, he found it a challenge to keep up with all of the romances.

According to Cole, one of the female patients had been placed in a private room down the hall because she was not well. She had a boyfriend who was very popular with the staff and patients. Cole had deduced from a few conversations overheard in the men's bathroom that a doctor had found the young woman in bed with her sweetheart.

Cole said she was rich and used to getting her way. Nevertheless, the boyfriend had been sent off the hill when they were caught together. According to Cole's sources, the young woman had threatened to sign herself out.

"I guess she lost that battle because she's still in her room," Cole snickered. "Doc Smith don't put up with no shenanigans—*if* he finds out," he laughed, with a knowing wink toward Jeanette.

Colleen guessed that the young woman had no choice but to remain at Sherwood because she was too sick to leave. Colleen knew that the rules had to be followed because they were designed to save lives, but her romantic side wanted the romance to be able to continue.

One morning a patient named Muriel came down the ward's dark interior corridor, her high heels clicking in time to a pop song she was humming to herself. Jeanette peeked out the porch's doorway when she heard the approaching footsteps and announced excitedly, "Here comes Muriel, and my, oh my, has she dolled herself up!" Colleen knew from the way Muriel talked in the women's bathroom that she was experienced with men. Her sexuality was second nature to her, and she talked openly about the men she had known.

As Muriel was passing by, she poked her head inside the porch to say hello to Jeanette. Colleen thought that Muriel looked simultaneously cute and tough. From her bed, Colleen studied Muriel's outfit and hairstyle trying to figure out which parts looked tough and which looked cute.

Muriel crossed the hall to Cole's porch. Without bothering with chitchat, Muriel announced to everyone, "Hi, y'all. I got a pass! I'm goin' to town to have a friendly look around at the nightlife!"

Cole and Jeanette had by then come out into the hall. Cole had been eying Muriel's outfit with interest. Cole and Jeanette looked at each other, and they both laughed, but Colleen didn't see what was so funny. Pete looked away and said nothing.

"Don't anybody wait up for me," Muriel called out as she clicked out the door and down the hall.

That night, as Colleen slept, she had a dream about a large mansion that had been built alongside the ocean. It had a long front veranda, which faced the sea. The first floor patients were sitting in rocking chairs, bundled in blankets and watching the sea. Colleen dreamed that she was playing Debussy's *Clair de Lune* on a grand piano in the mansion's enormous living room. Through an open window, Colleen could see the moon rising, and there were low storm clouds scudding along the horizon. Just outside the window, the patients rocked silently in time to the waves. Colleen knew the Debussy piece by heart and felt that it was the most beautiful music she had ever learned to play.

In her dream, Colleen could see two ballet dancers on the beach. They were Jeanette and Cole, but in her dream they were both in perfect health and showed no signs of tuberculosis. Lightning flashed in sheets behind the clouds on the horizon, and a breeze swirled restlessly through the trees. As Cole and Jeanette danced to Colleen's music, the first floor patients continued to rock in their chairs and stare at the sea. They seemed oblivious of the weather, the music, and the dancers. Only one patient rose to his feet and tried to dance to the music, but he could not. He sat down, tired and defeated.

Jeanette performed graceful arabesques and leaped effortlessly into Cole's arms. She seemed like a piece of shimmering cloth draped effortlessly in his strong hands. Cole leaped high into the air, his taut muscles gleaming with perspiration in the moonlight.

When the storm had passed farther out to sea, all was quiet. Colleen looked down the beach, but Cole and Jeanette were gone. The patients had fallen asleep in their chairs. The ocean was now utterly calm, sparkling with moonlight.

At the conclusion of the piece, Colleen rolled the final chord as she always did and felt stunned by its evaporation into the moonlight. Overwhelmed by the beauty of the moment, she sat hunched over the piano keys, her long brown hair flowing down her back in cascading waves.

At seven in the morning, Colleen awoke to the annoying strains of the same pop music that had been playing on the radio for the past week. Perhaps it was because of her dream, or perhaps it was because of the homogenized daily routine of the hospital, the long hours spent in bed in mindless chatter, and the total lack of educational stimulation, but Colleen suddenly decided that she had to call the radio station and request that they play *Clair de Lune*.

She walked down the hall and placed a call to the radio station from the nurses' desk. To her surprise, she got hold of the show's host, Jumpin' Joe Jackson. Colleen told him she was a patient at Sherwood and asked him if he would consider playing classical music in addition to the pop and country and western music he usually played. Jumpin' Joe seemed to hesitate, but he said he would consider it.

"What would you like to request, Colleen?" he asked politely.

Colleen requested *Clair de Lune*.

She went back to her porch and listened to the *Jumpin' Joe Show* for a while and wondered why love inspired such a wide variety of insipid songs. She detested beginning her morning with country and western music. She much preferred to start the day with music with zip, such as the jazz of Ella Fitzgerald or songs by Louis Armstrong or Nat King Cole. At least they made a person feel like getting up and moving. In Colleen's view, whiling away the time listening to songs with titles like "I'm Tired" or "All Alone in the World" or "Long Time Gone" was depressing therapy for TB patients. Even though Colleen complained, the two older women on her porch tuned in Jumpin' Joe every morning, bright and early. Colleen usually headed for the bathroom when she could no longer stand it.

Three days later, Jumpin' Joe read Colleen's request on the air. Jeanette came running into the bathroom.

"Colleen, come quick! They're gonna play your *Clair de Lune*! He read your name on the radio!"

Colleen sat down on the sink and listened. She could hear the beautiful piano music. No one was saying a word on the porch. The older women seemed stupefied. Jeanette was grinning from ear to ear. "It's right nice, Colleen!"

There was a ten-second pause after the final chord. Colleen felt her ears get red. She knew it was a non sequitur in the programming, and she wondered whether Jumpin' Joe would make a joke of it. The silence continued; it seemed that Jumpin' Joe had thought better of saying anything while he changed records on the turntable. Then suddenly the sounds of the Andrews Sisters singing "Her Bathing Suit Never Got Wet" filled the room. The two older women turned up the song extra loud as if to purge the radio of the classical music. Colleen sat very still on the bathroom sink, fervently hoping that no one else at Sherwood had heard her name mentioned on the *Jumpin' Joe Show*.

Jeanette, however, had totally enjoyed the musical interlude. "Colleen, that was the loveliest music they ever played on *Jumpin' Joe*," she said dreamily.

Jeanette started humming the theme and dancing around the bathroom. "I could almost hear them French loons singin' in the moonlight." She twirled back toward Colleen excitedly, "An' did you hear how Jumpin' Joe put a nice respectful pause between your music and the rest of the regular music? I'll bet he thought it was swell!" Jeanette paused and added, "Colleen, you ought to put in another request, right away!"

Colleen felt better when she saw that Jeanette had enjoyed the music. She spent the rest of the day feeling a little conspicuous, but no one mentioned the *Jumpin' Joe Show* to her either in the hall or in the ladies' bathroom. Of course, not many people at Sherwood had radios, but Colleen hoped that her request would encourage others who had been listening to put in similar requests. She decided she would follow up on Jeanette's advice by sending Jumpin' Joe another classical music request right away.

The next morning Colleen awoke to Jumpin' Joe's usual medley of pop and country and western. She was about to go into the ladies' bathroom when she heard Jumpin' Joe mention Sherwood's "musical wars."

Jumpin' Joe was replying to someone who had called in to deride the use of classical music in the programming.

"It seems," noted Jumpin' Joe, "that not all the residents at Sherwood love classical music. Yesterday, we received a message from 'the second-floor girls' requesting that we no longer play classical music. Well, second-floor ladies, I want you to know that I'm going to defend Colleen's right to love classical music. So, Colleen, never you mind, and keep the requests coming. Now here's a tune the second-floor girls specifically requested this morning."

Colleen could not believe her ears. Was this another one of Laura's jokes? Colleen got out her pen and quickly wrote a note to Laura asking her why she didn't like *Clair de Lune*.

By noon, Laura replied, "We have no idea what you are talking about! *Clair de Lune's* a song, isn't it?"

Colleen dispatched another note asking if Laura had heard the *Jumpin' Joe Show*, and whether she knew anything about a group of second-floor girls who might have complained about her request.

Laura wrote back, "This may take a while, but I'll try to find out who it was. The new building also has a second floor." It was signed, "Laura, future investigative reporter."

Meanwhile Colleen had walked down the hall to the nurses' desk and called the radio station. Jumpin' Joe answered immediately. He laughed when he heard Colleen's voice on the other end of the line.

"I thought it might be you," he said.

Colleen requested that he play Robert Schumann's "Traumerie." She also thanked him for standing up for classical music on his program. "Not everyone would have done that. I know it sounded a little different, but I play the piano, and it's hard not being able to play and listen to classical music here at Sherwood like I used to at home."

Two days later, Jumpin' Joe played Schumann's "Traumerie," and "the second-floor girls" countered with a claim that the classical music was interfering with their right to stay current with popular music.

Laura had a pretty good idea who the protesters were, but Colleen had already decided the whole thing wasn't worth a public battle.

When Laura found out that Colleen had capitulated, she was irate. Her short note to Colleen read, "We could have made them at least identify themselves, Colleen. You gave up too easily! I was hoping to start a hospital newsletter with you as the subject of my first editorial." It was signed, "Laura, future editor and publisher."

Colleen doubted that Laura would have uncovered a hotbed of opponents of classical music at Sherwood, but she was glad to hear that Laura would stand behind her till her "belly got beat blue!"

Colleen wrote a thank-you note back to Laura saying, "Laura, you will make a great reporter someday. You have a nose for news and the fighting spirit that it takes. Thanks for trying!"

Laura immediately wrote back to Colleen, "Thanks for the compliment, Colleen. That's real sweet of you. Jumping right into controversy suits me fine. Just give me the truth, the whole truth, and nothing but the 'who, what, where, when, and why'!"

Not too long after the "musical wars" had subsided, Laura sent a note to Colleen, which mentioned that she and Faith were doing much better and that they might be moved downstairs or over to the new building in a month. Laura had also heard that reporters from the magazine *Focus on Health* would be coming to Sherwood to do a story on the advances being made in the treatment of TB.

"They want to know if there's going to be a cure for TB and an end to the need for prolonged sanitarium care. According to Dr. Kurtz, a New Jersey scientist named Dr. Waksman has discovered a mold in the soil that might kill TB." Laura's note concluded with, "Do you think we'll get a chance to talk to the reporters?"

After the musical wars, Colleen's only desire was to escape further notoriety, but one morning, one of the nurses came into the porch with a dozen red roses for Colleen. The two older women became instantly interested in Colleen for a change, and they came over to inspect the huge bouquet. Colleen picked up the card tucked inside the wrapping.

Colleen read it aloud to the two women. "It says, 'From Your Secret Admirer.'"

"Who's that, Colleen?" one of them asked eagerly.

Colleen was mystified by the message. She had no admirers, and the only two men she knew well were Cole and Pete. Colleen wondered if Pete could have sent the roses. But as she thought more about it, she decided that Jeanette and Cole were probably the ones.

Colleen reasoned that Jeanette might have talked Cole into sending them because of the musical wars fiasco. It seemed to Colleen that Jeanette might have felt partly responsible because Jeanette had urged her to make the second request. But when Colleen asked her porch mate if she had sent the roses, Jeanette looked genuinely surprised and replied that she wasn't the one.

"I like you, Colleen, but not to the point of being 'your secret admirer!'" Jeanette laughed.

In spite of the flurry of excitement caused by the musical wars, Colleen's routine settled down into regular trips for fluoroscopy exams and pneumothorax, with the usual uncomfortable bed rests afterward. Because she was young, her lung was very elastic and required frequent treatments to keep it compressed. Colleen stayed in bed nearly all of the time, because it was the only thing to do if she wanted to get better.

Colleen's daily routine changed slightly when a middle-aged nurse named Miss Hawkins began to work on Colleen's ward after Victoria's death. Miss Hawkins was intelligent and seemed to know a lot about tuberculosis. Colleen and she had a common bond in that both of them had been Rainbow Girls, which was a sister organization of the Masons. Colleen had always liked the idea that Mozart had been a Mason. Since Miss Hawkins was planning a weekend trip back home, she asked for Colleen's home address. Colleen's parents lived not far from where Miss Hawkins was going.

"If you like, Colleen, I'll give your parents a call on my way back and let them know you're doing well," she promised.

Colleen was delighted. She gave Miss Hawkins's hand a squeeze. "You're too sweet! My parents will love to hear from you."

As Miss Hawkins began removing Colleen's sputum bag, Colleen asked, "Did you see my roses, Miss Hawkins? They're from a secret admirer," she added shyly.

Miss Hawkins inspected the bouquet of roses and exclaimed, "Why, Colleen, you're a lovely young lady, and this doesn't surprise me a bit. I hope he came around and identified himself!"

Colleen shook her head. "I have no idea who it could be." Suddenly Colleen remembered the man who had taken her book. "Unless ..." Colleen's voice trailed off in a troubled way.

Miss Hawkins looked quizzically at Colleen. "Unless what?"

"Oh, nothing," Colleen laughed, trying to hide her unease. "I suppose it might have been Pete if he heard about the musical wars." However, an image of the squat, sandy-haired man flashed through Colleen's mind—as well as Laura's remark about seduction.

As they were talking, Colleen heard the sound of a ladder being erected in the hall, which was followed by the tapping of a hammer. She listened to the voice of the person who was working. He was talking to the janitor.

Suddenly, Colleen heard a cry of pain, followed by cursing. A moment later, she saw the sandy-haired man walk by her door. He was looking at his thumb and muttering to himself. He stopped when he saw her, looking annoyed that she had overheard the incident. He put down the ladder he was carrying and walked into the room. Obviously recognizing her, he said, "So, we meet again—" His eyes fell on the roses and the enclosed card, and he added, "Colleen."

"How do you know my name?" Colleen responded. She was trying to think of a way to bring up the subject of her book.

"You're the girl who watched me from your porch. I saw you in the lamplight," he answered. He projected the same swagger that she had first noticed in him.

"You're the one who took my book, aren't you?" Colleen said boldly. "I saw you in the hall outside the fluoroscopy room."

The man looked surprised and wary. "I don't know what you mean," he said, a bit roughly.

He glanced at Miss Hawkins. "I don't know anything about a book. I'm too busy keeping the place from fallin' down. It isn't my fault if people are always losin' things and leavin' stuff lying around the halls where a fellow can trip on it. Somebody has to keep order around here!"

He started to walk away, but Colleen said, "You didn't explain how you knew my name!"

He had turned around as if to go, but then he stopped. His cheek muscle twitched in irritation at Colleen's accusatory tone, but he smiled suavely and answered, "I read it on that card by the roses, Colleen."

Colleen felt he had deliberately used her first name again in order to regain the upper hand.

"I'll look around and see if I can find that book of yours," he continued. "It's probably around here somewhere. No tellin' where it will turn up! I'll get it back to you when I find it."

He looked at his thumb, which evidently felt better. He gave them a thumbs-up sign and then a cocky grin. "Are you the young lady who likes to request songs on the *Jumpin' Joe Show*? Her name's Colleen, too." He smiled at her, knowing he had caught her by surprise. He was obviously enjoying himself.

Miss Hawkins stared at the two of them. There seemed to be some unspoken cat-and-mouse game going on, but she wasn't sure why.

Colleen said nothing.

The man left the room, picked up his ladder, and started back down the hall, whistling nonchalantly. There was a silence, and then he called over his shoulder, "I'm sure your book will show up eventually—Colleen!"

The whistling faded as he continued down the hall, and with it, Colleen's hope that her book would soon be recovered.

"What was that all about?" Miss Hawkins asked in astonishment.

"I don't know ... yet," she said.

"Well, I have one request, regardless of who sent you those lovely roses," Miss Hawkins said, unaware of Colleen's thoughts. "Could I have a slip from one of them? I'd like to start up a bush from it if I could. We have a small rose garden at the nurses' residence, and those roses are especially beautiful."

"You can have *all* of the roses, Miss Hawkins!" Colleen exclaimed loudly, hoping the Handyman could hear her, if he truly was her secret admirer.

Miss Hawkins looked startled. Colleen promised to save a rose for the thoughtful nurse. She wrote her parents' address and phone number on a sheet of paper, which Miss Hawkins put away carefully in the skirt pocket of her uniform.

After Miss Hawkins left the porch, Colleen lay in bed thinking about her secret admirer. Colleen wracked her brain trying to think of possible admirers. She even thought of Jumpin' Joe, but then ruled him out.

Colleen's only clue was that the Handyman wasn't telling the entire truth. He *had* taken her book, she mused. She had seen him do it. Colleen remembered Will's warning to stay away from the fellow.

If he is a fox on the lookout for unwary chickens, *she reflected*, he certainly has access to the chicken coop. *She would have to outfox the fox to get her book back.*

Since it was a fluoroscopy morning, Colleen put on her robe and slippers. She soon forgot about the Handyman and Miss Wilson's book. Across the hall, she could see Pete getting ready to go for a procedure in the treatment room. By the time Colleen was wheeled into the fluoroscopy room, there were four patients ahead of her. Pete was already draped and on the treatment table. She could hear him talking to Dr. Kurtz.

In the darkened fluoroscopy room, Colleen watched each of the women ahead of her being examined. The murky green glow was more suited for Halloween than for a fine spring day. Women's heads peeked above the machine as a reminder of the individuals attached to the body parts on display. For a moment, Colleen wondered what "the rib" would look like in the fluoroscope, but she pushed the thought from her mind.

When it was her turn to step behind the fluoroscope, she heard Pete cry out from the treatment room. She saw Dr. Billings give a worried look in the direction of the cry, but he continued what he was doing with Colleen. He asked Colleen to rotate a bit so that he could see her affected lung from a better angle. Colleen heard Pete cry out a second time. Dr. Billings quickly finished with Colleen and turned off the fluoroscope.

"Your nurse will be right along to take you back to your porch, Colleen. You just wait here. I'm going to go see if they need me in the treatment room," he said.

Colleen nodded in silence, wondering what was happening in there. When Miss Hawkins arrived with a wheelchair, Colleen told her that Pete had cried out and that Dr. Billings had gone to help, leaving her to wait by herself. The treatment room door was now shut.

Miss Hawkins frowned and said, "Don't worry, Colleen. They are both very experienced doctors, and they will know what to do if there is some kind of problem. They'll probably bring you back up after lunch for your refill."

After lunch, Colleen checked to see if Pete had been brought back to his porch, but there was no sign of him. Cole came over to ask about him, and Colleen told him what she had overheard. Cole looked surprised. "He seemed fine this morning," he said with a shrug.

Jeanette looked concerned and said, "Colleen, you can ask Dr. Kurtz about him when you go back up for your refill."

About twenty minutes later, Miss Hawkins came onto the porch to take Colleen upstairs. Miss Hawkins told Colleen that Pete had been moved into a private room, because he'd had a small hemorrhage during the pneumolysis.

"He's still growing like a weed, which is natural for a young man of his age, but he hasn't been eating enough to keep up his strength, which is why we try so hard to get all of our patients to gain weight, Colleen," Miss Hawkins said gravely.

Colleen thought about Pete's appearance for a moment. He was indeed thin, but nevertheless quite handsome. He had piercing brown eyes and thick black eyebrows, curly black hair, aesthetically high cheekbones, and a well-formed mouth and chin. He had dramatically good looks. He might have been perfect if he were not so thin. Colleen resolved to start eating something extra at each meal and to get Pete to do the same when he was released from the private room.

Dr. Kurtz said nothing when Colleen was wheeled into the treatment room. Miss Kirsten also seemed more subdued than usual. They talked to one another in German again, and Colleen waited patiently for the inevitable uncomfortable pressure. When they were done, Dr. Kurtz patted Colleen's hand and said, "You are a good girl, Colleen. I hope your friend Pete will have a quick recovery. He is a very nice young man. He likes you and thinks you are different from the other women on the ward."

Colleen glanced up in total surprise. "He told you that?" she asked. Colleen felt herself blush.

Dr. Kurtz smiled a cupid-like smile. "You would be surprised what patients tell their doctors, Colleen," he said, without further elaboration.

As she lay in bed back on the porch, Colleen mulled over the possibility that Pete was her secret admirer. She would be delighted and relieved if he was.

Cole came over to confirm that Pete was down the hall in a private room. "They say he's not as bad off as the original rumor," Cole relayed. "He may not be a goner."

Colleen flinched at Cole's bluntness, but she didn't reply because she was full of compressed air. She lay there, immobile, worried about Pete, but she didn't feel up to talking to anyone about it.

Jeanette could see that Colleen was upset, and she offered to bring her something to read from the nurses' desk. When she returned, she offered Colleen a crumpled, day-old newspaper.

"It's all they had," Jeanette apologized.

Colleen glanced at the headlines. On the front page, there was an article about Churchill's "Iron Curtain" speech in Fulton, Missouri. Colleen shook her head. It hadn't even been a year since the atomic bomb had ended the greatest war in history. Now the world was again dividing into hostile camps.

Colleen tossed the paper aside impatiently. She didn't want to read about divided places like Berlin, Korea, China, or Europe. She just wanted to know that there were peaceful corners of the world where people were friendly and always happy to help one another. To Colleen, this was the simple and logical goal for mankind, despite the newspapers' attempts to convince readers that violence in the world was a normal state of affairs.

Colleen believed that Roosevelt had been right in saying that there was "nothing to fear but fear itself." She wanted to believe that the bad times were over and that good times would bring about Roosevelt's dream of his four freedoms: freedom of speech, freedom of worship, freedom from want, and freedom from fear—"everywhere in the world."

*It is a simple prescription for paradise,* Colleen thought. So what would stand in its way?

She thought of Miss Wilson again, who had once asked her in private, "Do you suppose God looks down on us and thinks we're a bunch of monkeys?"

Colleen looked over at Jeanette, who was reading the newspaper Colleen had discarded.

"Jeanette, do you suppose God looks down on us and thinks we're a bunch of monkeys?"

One thing Colleen really liked about Jeanette was her imagination. No question was too strange or too silly. Jeanette took every question in serious, childlike stride.

"Well, I don't rightly know. Joe has a laugh that is sort of high-pitched, like an excited chimpanzee. Mind you, it's his only fault. The first time I went to dinner at his parents' house, I realized that his whole family laughs like that, and don't you know, when they all get to laughin', they *do* sound like a troop of startled monkeys!" Jeanette paused a moment to reflect on this new concept. "Why do you ask, Colleen?"

"Oh, I don't know. How do *you* laugh, Jeanette?" Colleen was starting to feel very silly and much better.

"Well, I guess I sort of go, *heh heh heh*, and sometimes, *hee hee hee*." Jeanette started to laugh in earnest. "You see?" she giggled.

The two of them got to laughing so hard that Geraldine joined in too, but she had to stop because her rib operation made it harder to laugh.

"That's no fair, ya'll. You've got all your ribs!" Geraldine spluttered.

Then the two older women started to laugh. There was nothing like a good laugh at nothing at all. At the peak of the laughter, Miss Hawkins came onto the porch to see what was so funny.

Jeanette by now was holding her sides in pain from laughing so hard. "Nothing, Miss Hawkins. We're laughin' at nothin' at all!"

Colleen added, "We're just practicing, Miss Hawkins!"

Miss Hawkins looked amused. "Well, I'd like to see how you'd laugh if you really had something funny on your minds!" Everyone went into another gale of laughter. As Miss Hawkins left the room, she reminded them that they would have to stop laughing during the rest period.

Jeanette called out, "We will, Miss Hawkins, but right now we're havin' more fun than a barrelful of monkeys!" There was another peal of hysterical laughter.

When the weekend was over, the doctors allowed Pete to return to his bed on the porch. He was on strict bed rest, and the nurses brought him extra snacks and checked his water intake frequently. When he seemed a little better, Colleen and Jeanette were allowed over to wish him a speedy recovery.

"You two are my best friends besides Cole," Pete said gratefully. "It's always good to have friends, especially when the going gets a little tough."

Cole cleared his throat and said with a quavery voice, "We're real pleased you're still with us, Pete. You gave us a little scare for a while."

"Hah! I gave myself a big scare—and Dr. Kurtz, too, I think!" Pete replied. "But it doesn't seem as if I'm much worse. At least the adhesions are gone."

"Good for you, Pete!" Colleen said kindly.

Pete placed his hand on top of Colleen's. "Thanks for coming over, Colleen." Colleen looked at his long fingers. His hand was huge compared to hers. If he grew to fit the hand, he would one day be a very tall man. He was already over six feet tall. Colleen pulled her hand away and patted Pete on the shoulder. "I want us to make a pact and each agree to put on at least ten pounds, okay?"

Pete smiled at her, sensing her unspoken thought. "That's a good idea, Colleen, but you needn't worry," he said. "I'll be just fine."

Miss Hawkins came back a day late from her weekend trip. Her aunt had gotten sick, but she had still managed to call Colleen's parents on the way home.

"Everyone is doing fine, Colleen," Miss Hawkins said happily. "Your older sister is planning a wedding for June, and your younger sister likes all her teachers. Your family wanted to know all about your progress, Colleen, and if you like it here; I told them you're an excellent patient and doing well. The biggest news is that your brother has been accepted into college. He'll start in the fall, and he's going to visit you at Easter so that he can see you before he leaves for school."

Colleen was very excited for her brother. "Where will he go to school?" Colleen asked.

"He's been accepted at Northwestern University outside Chicago, and they've awarded him a mathematics scholarship," Miss Hawkins said. "He can also take advantage of the GI Bill. Your father is bursting with pride about it."

"No one's ever gone to college in my family before, not to mention on a scholarship," Colleen said excitedly.

"I have other news," Miss Hawkins said, turning to everyone on the porch. "In case you haven't heard, reporters from *Focus on Health* are coming to Sherwood tomorrow to do a story about tuberculosis. They may come into this building and take pictures and ask questions."

There were twitters here and there like songbirds awakening at dawn's first light. The two older women began tugging at their pajamas and adjusting their covers. Colleen wondered if Laura had already figured out a way to accompany the reporters on the story, and she was worried that Laura might mention the musical wars. After lunch, Colleen wrote a note to Laura reminding her not to say a word to the reporters about her.

The reporters arrived the next day, shortly after breakfast. Colleen could hear them coming down the hall. She poked her head out the door and looked down the corridor. She could see a photographer with a big flash camera and two women reporters dressed in suits and hats. They were coming down the hall toward her porch. Mrs. Smith, the director's wife, was conducting them on a tour of Sherwood. Colleen ducked her head quickly back inside the doorway.

Colleen decided it would be best to avoid the reporters, if possible. She went to her locker to get her robe and slippers. She quickly combed her hair while trying to figure out what to do. She heard the reporters coming onto her porch. They asked Geraldine if she would tell them about her rib surgery. Geraldine went into a few of the details, but she wouldn't show them her missing ribs.

"You don't want a photo of that, sir, believe you me," she said to the disappointed photographer.

It seemed to Colleen that if the reporters had known to ask about Geraldine's ribs, they might also know about the musical wars. The last thing in the world she wanted was to have her parents read her name in a story about the musical wars that might be carried coast to coast in a national magazine. Colleen stood very still, waiting to hear whether or not anyone would mention the *Jumpin' Joe Show*.

The cameraman tried several times to convince Geraldine that he wouldn't show her face in the photo, but Geraldine held her ground.

The younger reporter pointed to the lounge and asked to see it. Colleen was still trying to get her second slipper on, but when she leaned against her locker, she lost her balance and upset a tall, skinny jar of olives whose lid must have been loose. Colleen had eaten a few of the olives before breakfast and had intended to finish the rest by lunch. To her dismay, the olives rolled into the middle of the floor.

When Colleen heard the reporters moving toward the door of the lounge, she sat down on the sofa, trying to look casually unconcerned. The reporters did not seem to notice her. Mrs. Smith was waiting out in the hall. Only the photographer smiled as the group came into the room. It seemed to Colleen that the green olives with their red pimento fillings resembled eyeballs rolling around on the tile. They seemed to be peeking up from the floor in terror, betraying their secret knowledge of the musical wars to their interrogators.

Without even looking around, the two lady reporters strolled across the lounge, tramped through the olives, and exited into the hall, oblivious of Colleen's guilty look. The cameraman, more visually alert, noticed the olives immediately and walked carefully around them, giving Colleen a friendly smile. The two reporters stopped briefly to poke their heads onto Cole's porch. Colleen breathed a sigh of relief. The *Jumpin' Joe* incident would not be talked about around the nation's dinner tables, including her family's dinner table.

Suddenly Colleen felt much better about the "musical wars." Classical music on the *Jumpin' Joe Show* was a small thing to have hoped for, but a good thing, even if it had only happened twice. She was glad she had spoken up for classical music. Laughing at her self-consciousness, Colleen rose from the sofa and called to the reporters from the lounge doorway, "Don't forget to tell about Pete's recovery!"

The two reporters and the photographer had already started following Mrs. Smith down the hall. They looked back at Colleen in surprise, and then they disappeared around a corner and were gone. They took whatever knowledge they had of a future cure for TB with them.

Too late, Colleen realized that no one had asked the most important question of all: if there was a cure for TB, when would it come to Sherwood?

# Northwest Call

Colleen's brother Elliot arrived at Sherwood on Good Friday. When Colleen spotted him coming up the drive, her heart skipped a beat. She watched as he paused at the top of the drive to catch his breath after the long climb, and she saw him pick some wildflowers at the edge of the asphalt. He studied the great expanse of porches, looking for Colleen's porch, and when he spotted her, he waved excitedly and shouted that he was coming right in.

Colleen went into the lounge and waited for her brother. In a few minutes, she heard him coming down the hall with Miss Hawkins. Elliot entered the lounge with a big smile on his face and kissed Colleen on the cheek. "How are ya doin', Colleen?" he asked as he pinned a few of the wildflowers under a barrette in her hair. "There! You look great!" he said enthusiastically, without waiting for her answer. "Life at Sherwood must be treatin' you right."

"I'm happy as a clam to see you, that's how I am!" Colleen exclaimed. "But how in the world did you get here?"

"I thumbed rides," he smiled. "The driveway is a lot longer and steeper than it seems at the bottom, I can tell you! There's a guy who's willin' to take me as far as Lockwood today, if I'm back at the bottom of the drive in an hour. He said he'd go eat his lunch while I visit with you. I can't even stay for lunch, but I just had to stop off and see you."

Elliot sat down beside Colleen and said to her enthusiastically, "You look much better than the last time I saw you! I do believe you've grown an inch or two!"

"They keep telling us to eat, so I do!" Colleen smiled, feeling pleased that Elliot thought she looked well. "It's a fine sanitarium, Elliot. I told everyone you were in the navy. I can't wait to hear what you've been doing since you got out!" Colleen said excitedly.

"I spent part of the fall applying to colleges. I guess Miss Hawkins told you about the scholarship. I'm going to start in September. I had an interview, but I never thought they'd want to give me money. Guess what, though? While I was at Northwestern making arrangements for a room, I met a sociology professor from the West. He was real interested when I told him about you bein' at Sherwood. He said that TB is bad among the Indians in the Dakotas. Their TB hospitals are not much more than places to go and die. The food's inadequate, and they have to work and take care of each other. He also said that Negroes in the big city TB hospitals are mistreated, and that's assuming they can get in."

Colleen nodded and told Elliot about the proposed Negro wing, the delay in construction, and the debate about whether to centralize or decentralize TB services across the state.

They talked awhile about news from Carlton. Then Colleen told Elliot about the friends she had made at Sherwood, and especially about Laura, Faith, and Mandy, but also about Jeanette, Cole, and Pete. Elliot laughed when Colleen got around to telling him about the musical wars and the mysterious "second-floor girls."

"Don't tell Mom about that!" Colleen laughed. "You can tell her that when the *Focus on Health* reporters were here, we heard that there might be a cure for TB. It's some sort of antibiotic. We don't know when it will come to Sherwood."

"That's great news!" Elliot exclaimed.

Colleen turned to a different subject. "I have a favor to ask of you, Elliot," Colleen said. "I still haven't received any schoolbooks, and I don't want to get so far behind that I'll never catch up with my class. Could you look into it for me when you go back? Mr. Thomas hasn't answered my letter." Colleen sighed.

"Maybe they think you'll be able to catch up this summer at home," Elliot suggested. "Or maybe there's no point in sending you books in the middle of the semester," he said, trying not to stress his last thought. Colleen was not to be dissuaded.

"Well, maybe you and Dad could force a decision out of them. It's not right that they don't even answer my letters!" Colleen said indignantly.

"I think Dad might have tried already, but as you say, no one has answered your question." Elliot agreed to follow up when he got home.

Elliot changed the subject by telling Colleen about Maureen's upcoming wedding. Elliot said that she planned to have the reception at home, in the event that Colleen would be home by June. They talked awhile about other news from home and about Elliot's impressions of the university.

Elliot glanced at his watch, and then he jumped up from the sofa. "I hate to leave so soon, Colleen, but I've got to be goin' now if I don't want to walk back to Carlton. There's plenty of traffic going east and west during the day, but I'd like to avoid hitchhiking south at night," Elliot said, grabbing his jacket and his hat.

"I'm so glad you came!" Colleen exclaimed.

Elliot took Colleen's hand and said, "I would say I'll stop by on the way out to Chicago, but I'm sure you'll be home by then," Elliot said reassuringly. "And like you say, this is a good place."

Colleen gave her brother a hug. She didn't want to look at him because she knew she would cry. "Good-bye, now, and thanks for comin'," she said, her voice cracking.

"Not 'good-bye,' Colleen, but 'see you soon'," Elliot said, and he kissed her on the cheek.

When Elliot left, Colleen watched him walk down the drive as far as the first bend, where he disappeared from view with a jaunty wave. "See you in June, Colleen!" he called out.

After her brother left, Colleen went back to bed. As she lay in bed thinking about her brother's visit, her thoughts were interrupted by the sound of voices coming from a supply room just up the hall. She recognized Pete's voice. When Miss Hawkins came by a few minutes later, Colleen asked her what Pete was doing.

"A shipment of books from one of the local charities arrived today," Miss Hawkins said as she started taking everyone's temperatures. "He was so restless for something to do that I just had to let him go look at them for a few minutes."

"Could I go, too?" Colleen asked. "I can't settle down after Elliot's visit. A book to read would really help."

Miss Hawkins hesitated, and then she agreed to let Colleen go. "But for just a few minutes!" she added.

Colleen felt elated. Here was an opportunity for her to read something other than a day-old newspaper.

Colleen walked past the ladies' bathroom and arrived at the supply room where she saw Pete sitting on the floor. He was surrounded by some open boxes and a few dozen books. Colleen looked into the nearly empty boxes. Only a small stack of magazines remained in the one nearest her. The pitifully small number of books that were scattered around the floor wouldn't even fill a small bookcase.

"Is this it? Where are the other books?" she asked, her hope quickly fading.

"If you were on a desert island, Colleen, you might think these books were manna from heaven," Pete said as he began arranging them by author. "Want to help?"

"Sure, why not?" Colleen replied.

Colleen picked up a small, hardback book from the nearest open box. "Well, speaking of a desert island, here's a good book for people stranded on one," Colleen joked. "It's *Robinson Crusoe*, and there are two more by the same author, including *Journal of the Plague Year*. Colleen handed the three books to Pete. "You can put them under "D" for Defoe," she said.

Pete examined the cover of *Journal of the Plague Year*. "I've read this one," he said. "My mother was a librarian, and she was always after me to read different books—before she died of TB, that is."

"When was that?" Colleen asked quietly.

"About a year ago. She never had a chance," Pete said, not looking at Colleen and trying to keep his voice steady. "She had miliary TB. It kills quickly."

"I'm sorry," said Colleen. "That must have been a terrible shock."

"It was," Pete answered. "I've still got my dad though. My mom recommended this one because I'm interested in medicine," he said modestly. Pete began thumbing idly through the book. "Would you be interested in hearing about the plague year?" he asked, obviously hoping that she shared some of his interests.

"Sure," Colleen answered.

"The bubonic plague that Defoe described took place in London in the mid-1600s," Pete began. He told her that it started innocently enough with a few cases in one end of London, but it soon spread to different parts of the city, and people started being afraid. In a few months, it began spreading so wildly that the city had to quarantine the sick by boarding up families in their houses. The death rate was high and victims died quickly. Family members under quarantine sometimes escaped out back windows at night and fled into the countryside, leaving sick relatives to die alone in their houses.

Colleen interjected, "They put my aunt in quarantine too, in a shed by herself in the backyard when her TB was incurable. But my relatives didn't run off and abandon her the way the Londoners abandoned their relatives."

"Yes, well, during the plague year, Londoners did try to flee into the countryside. They were turned back by country people who were afraid of the plague," Pete continued.

"In America, TB patients used to move west to hike and lead an outdoor life, especially in the mountains," Colleen observed. "Nobody turned them back the way the country people in England turned back plague victims. I remember hearing about TB patients who were urged to go west by doctors. When they got there, they were taken in at rooming houses, but sometimes they *did* have to hide their TB to get a room. Some lived, and some died. It wasn't a perfect solution. At least that's what Dr. Kurtz said."

"Well, during the bubonic plague, they couldn't go west because England is an island," Pete reminded her with an unruffled smile. "Just about everyone died who caught the plague. At the height of the *black* plague, which is what we're talking about, people were buried in mass graves in deep pits in the church yards. The death carts dumped the bodies into the pits in layers and covered them with dirt, awaiting the next night's layer of dead. Some infected people even threw themselves in alive because the swelling of their lymph nodes was unbearable. Healthy people were afraid that at any moment they would be the next victims. Colleen, are you listening to this?"

"Of course!" Colleen replied. "It's somewhat different from our situation at Sherwood, that's all. Sometimes people at Sherwood have no idea that their deaths are near. TB smolders inside the lungs, and it can creep up on you. That was true in my friend Victoria's case. She seemed fine, and she was looking forward to a wonderful time, but she died instead."

"That was a terrible thing," Pete said solicitously. "Well, death was everywhere in London during the plague year, and there were no dances. Dancing would have been suicidal, because bubonic plague strikes very quickly." Pete made a heroic effort to regain his thoughts. "Colleen, it's hard for me to tell you about the black plague with you interjecting stuff about TB," he sighed.

"Sorry," said Colleen. "TB is called the *white* plague, by the way!"

Pete was a good musician and used to following many piano parts, but the counterpoint of Colleen's narrative was making his head swim. He felt as if he were trying to follow a complicated fugue whose parts didn't quite fit.

Pete ran his fingers through his hair, trying to remember the thread of the conversation, and then he said, "Colleen, conversation is like music! The parts have to go together. We should be talking about one thing at a time."

Colleen sat still, eagerly awaiting the rest of the story. "I know that, Pete. I play the piano," she said encouragingly.

Pete studied Colleen with renewed interest. "So do I," he said. "Well, as I was saying, Defoe hoped that God would spare him from the bubonic plague because of his prayers and repentance. He searched the Bible for passages that seemed to guarantee his safety. But for insurance, he saw a doctor, went to church, and took medicine whenever he went out into the streets," Pete continued.

"We don't have church services at Sherwood, and we don't go out in the streets! There are no guarantees of safety, either. We have to say our *own* prayers of repentance. At least Defoe could go out and about!" Colleen exclaimed.

Pete had to laugh, but then he said, "Colleen, you're trying to picture this in terms of Sherwood. There were no 'Sherwoods' back then! There were only plague houses and burial pits. Their only protection was to avoid exposure. The better-off people laid up provisions, but the poor had to go out daily and risk infection. When they bought bread, they disinfected their coins with vinegar. Even so, the poor would often be found dead in doorways as they tried to make their way home. The farmers from the countryside started selling food from the edge of town, because they didn't want to die. They were afraid of the contagion of the crowded city."

Pete looked up, half expecting another of Colleen's interjections. Her eyes had the eager look of a schoolgirl.

"What is it, Colleen?" Pete asked.

"The fresh air of the countryside is no protection, no matter what Dr. Trudeau said about the studies in the Adirondacks!" Colleen asserted quietly, realizing that she was again treading on the holy ground of Pete's thoughts. "I got sick in Carlton! We have plenty of fresh air and countryside there!"

Pete was determined to finish his description, despite the differences between the "black" plague and the "white" plague.

"Colleen, I'm getting to my concluding thought. This is important!" he said in exasperation. "The most amazing thing is that at the height of the plague, people sat side by side in churches regardless of social status, and they forgot all their class differences. They prayed together for deliverance from their sins. They considered the bubonic plague to be a sign of the wrath of God. But when the moment of danger was past, they forgot their deliverance and went back to their old divisions!" Pete concluded.

"We sit side by side in our beds at Sherwood, but we're pretty much alike here," Colleen observed. "The better-off folk are all over at Skyview. It's a private sanitarium. You have to be able to afford it," Colleen said wryly.

Pete laughed. "You're incorrigible! May I ask what you have concluded, if anything, from what I've just told you?" Pete asked, his eyes twinkling in amusement.

"I've concluded that I'm very glad this is the 1940s and not the 1600s, even if I have TB," Colleen said.

"Do you think you'd be interested in reading the book?" Pete asked.

"Well, yes, I would be interested in knowing what it was like to live through something like the bubonic plague, I suppose," said Colleen.

"I found it interesting because of the public health aspects," Pete added. "When I get out of here, I'd like to be a missionary doctor and do what I can to improve public health in the poorer countries of the world. I'd especially like to help little children. After that, I'd like to retire on a mountaintop. With a little luck, I'll live long enough to do all that!"

Colleen stared at Pete in total amazement. He had his whole life worked out.

"What about a wife?" Colleen asked, curious to know whether Pete had that worked out too.

"Well, she'd be the kind of woman who wanted those things too," Pete mumbled shyly, looking up at Colleen with interest.

Colleen blushed under his penetrating gaze. She was about to ask Pete if he was the one who had sent her flowers when Miss Hawkins bustled in from the hall. "Are you two still in here? It's dinnertime!"

Pete took the copy of *Robinson Crusoe* for himself. "Living on a desert island isn't that different from living on a mountaintop," he laughed, "so maybe I'll learn a thing or two from Mr. Crusoe. What do you say, 'Friday,' shall we go to dinner?" Pete said to Colleen as he offered her his arm.

"Call me Ishmael," she joked as she tossed a copy of *Moby Dick* back into one of the boxes. Colleen took Pete's arm as they began to walk back down the hall.

"Ishmael was the sole survivor of an ill-fated whaling expedition," Pete said somberly, pausing to study Colleen intently. "Everyone else perished when the white whale destroyed their vessels."

"I haven't ever read *Moby Dick*," Colleen said. "It was just a joke."

On Easter morning, Miss Hawkins informed everyone that some children from "down the hill" would be coming up in the afternoon with Easter eggs for the patients. Colleen had not seen a child in more than three months.

Colleen's thoughts turned to her memories of Easters in Carlton. Because of the narrowness of the valley in which Carlton was situated, her neighborhood church had been built on a steep hillside. It was a small church, but it seemed to have both the moral and physical high ground because of its imposing position atop the highest hill in her neighborhood. Stone stairs curved up the hillside to the church door. When Colleen would stand at the base of the stairs and look up, the church's spire seemed to reach all the way into the clouds.

As she lay in bed this Easter morning, she imagined her neighbors all dressed up and expectantly listening to the pastor talk about the resurrection. He had once said during a sermon, "One day we will look back and think of all of this as a bad dream." He was referring to heaven, Colleen had supposed.

But Colleen refused to think that life was just a bad dream. Her parents were liberal in their interpretation of religion, and they had always encouraged her to think for herself. If Colleen misbehaved, her mother would simply tell her to go upstairs and look at herself in the mirror to inspect her guilt.

Colleen thought about Pete's description of the people of the plague year. They didn't know that the plague was connected to human commerce and carried in the holds of cargo ships by rats and fleas. When the plague had run its course, the people had taken it as a sign that God approved of them again. They didn't know that the plague lay dormant in its carriers: rats and fleas or the straw of thatched-roof cottages. Pete had said that the people of London had gone back to their old ways and their old divisions. They had gone from what her pastor would have called one bad dream to another. Pete had not been shocked by the plague; what shocked him was that the people had gone back to their old ways. Nothing had been learned. Colleen had seen the amazement in his eyes.

At three thirty in the afternoon, three little girls came along the sidewalk and stopped outside of Colleen's porch.

They were carrying a basket of pastel, cooked eggs as well as some chocolate candies. They stood there silently, not knowing what to say. Finally, one of the little girls said, "These are for you."

Colleen had noticed that one of the little girls had a basket of her own with three little rabbit finger puppets sewn into the bottom. Colleen said to her, "Hi there! I'm Colleen. Could you show me your basket of rabbits?"

The little girl put the three middle fingers of her right hand into some holes on the underside of the basket and made the rabbits wiggle around and peer over the edge of the basket.

Jeanette immediately fell in love with the bunnies. "They are just too cute and precious!" she exclaimed.

"Do your rabbits have names?" Colleen asked.

"This one is Flopsy, and this one is Mopsy," she said, indicating the two brown ones, "and this one is Peter," she said, making the white rabbit move. "He gets in trouble a lot. He tries to get out of the basket, and his sisters have to keep him in."

It occurred to Colleen that Pete was like the white rabbit in the little girl's basket. Sherwood was quickly becoming a basket that was too small for him. It would be impossible to confine his restless intellect indefinitely. Miss Hawkins had already tacitly acknowledged this by allowing him to go to the supply room for books.

"Could you show me how the bunnies move?" Colleen asked curiously. The little girl turned the basket upside down and showed Colleen which finger moved which rabbit.

"You didn't tell us your names!" she said to the girls.

They looked at each other and said their names, which were Rose Marie, Darlene, and Rachel. Jeanette, Geraldine, and the others asked them about school and what they did for fun. They looked through the screen shyly, telling the women about their favorite games as they took in the details of the porch.

"Could I have a look at the rabbits, too?" Jeanette asked the girls. They nodded and held the basket as close to Jeanette as they could through the screen. Jeanette's eyes filled with childlike wonder.

"You could also call them Joy, Norm, and Hap," Jeanette suggested, with tears in her eyes, "because you give us *Joy*, and you make us feel *Normal*, and you bring us *Happiness*."

Rose Marie smiled very sweetly as she continued to hold the basket to the screen. "I'm glad they give you hoppiness!" she said solemnly to Jeanette.

The little girls said they had to go back to the nurses' station to meet the rest of their group. They would leave their eggs at the nurses' stations as presents for the patients. The women thanked them for coming.

"You're welcome!" they said as they scampered away like little rabbits.

"Come again!" Geraldine called after them.

The women laughed and talked awhile, buoyed by the fact that some part of the world outside Sherwood had come to their doorsteps.

Later in the afternoon, Colleen settled down to read more from Defoe's journal. The book was actually quite good, and by dinnertime she was surprised to see that she had read nearly a third of the book. After dinner, she stayed up until bedtime and read some more.

In the morning, Miss Hawkins told Colleen that Dr. Kurtz had scheduled her for a second surgery to remove more lung adhesions. It was scheduled for the following day, so Colleen decided to finish reading her book while she was comfortable. By late afternoon, she had finished.

On her way to the bathroom, she stopped to tell Pete that she had finished the book.

"How did you like it, Colleen?" Pete asked eagerly. Cole looked up and seemed interested too.

"It was so good that I almost finished it in one reading, but I think Defoe should have included the London fire to make it really good," Colleen added. "Would you like to read it?" she asked Cole.

"Thanks anyway, Colleen, but I'm not much of a reader," Cole said.

Colleen turned back to Pete. "Have they moved those books over to the new building yet? I want to get something else to read before I go for a pneumolysis tomorrow."

Pete said he didn't think the books had been sent over to the library yet. When Miss Hawkins came back onto Colleen's porch with some fresh pitchers of water, Colleen begged the nurse to let Pete and her go back for more books.

"You two are becoming bookworms!" she exclaimed. "In fact, you're the only patients on this floor who have ever asked for books."

"Maybe nobody knows the books are there," Colleen suggested. Miss Hawkins agreed that Colleen was probably right. Normally, they were taken over to the library within a few days.

Miss Hawkins went and got a key to the closet and returned to tell them that the books were still there. "Just five minutes, and then right back to bed, Colleen," she warned.

Colleen crossed the hall and told Pete that they could pick out more books if they wanted. When they reached the supply closet, Colleen dropped her book back into the box it had come from and began examining some of the other books. There was a long poem by Helen Keller called *Song of the Stone Wall* in one of the boxes. Colleen read some of the passages and was impressed by its beauty. It read like a poem written by a sighted person.

Colleen closed her eyes in thought and then opened them and said to Pete, "Someone donated a book by Helen Keller. What would you do if you were blind and deaf, Pete?" Colleen asked.

Pete looked at Colleen in surprise. "If I were a child in that situation, I think I would find life almost unbearable," Pete replied. "I imagine I would feel trapped inside myself, until someone helped me find a way out."

Colleen thought of the little girls who had visited them on Easter Sunday. They were full of life. She couldn't bear to think of an innocent child trapped alone in silence and darkness. It seemed so absurdly cruel. The thought of Miss Sullivan's work cheered her, however.

"Helen Keller and Anne Sullivan shared a secret language of the fingertips," Colleen added. "Miss Sullivan showed Keller that she could *live*, and not simply exist. What a wonderful moment that must have been for both of them!" Colleen exclaimed.

Colleen was quiet a moment, and then she asked, "Do you think TB will leave us handicapped when we leave here, Pete?"

"It depends on how badly we have TB and on what treatment we receive; most of us will probably be okay," Pete replied cheerily. He seemed undaunted by his illness. "What do you think you'll do when you leave here, Colleen?" he asked.

"I hope to finish school. I've already lost one year," she replied. "I can't get any answer from my high school principal about having my books sent up here."

Something in the way Pete was looking at her made Colleen remember the roses.

She decided that Pete wouldn't mind if she asked, so she just said bluntly, "Were you the one who sent me roses, Pete?"

Pete looked surprised and nonplussed. "No, I didn't, because I don't have any extra money," he replied. "Not that I wouldn't have liked to," he said, after an embarrassing pause.

Colleen sat frozen in thought. She had half expected Pete to answer yes. If Pete had not sent the roses, she could think of no one else who might have except the Handyman.

"Why the frown, Colleen? I hope I didn't offend you," Pete said kindly.

"Of course not, Pete, you're a perfect gentleman. I was thinking about someone who might *not* be one," Colleen said.

She described what had happened to Miss Wilson's book and what Will had said about the Handyman. Colleen looked around the nearly empty storage closet. "We have so few possessions here at Sherwood. I should have spoken up on the spot when he took it! For him to take my book and then wink and swagger away as if it were an even exchange was too much."

"You'll get to the bottom of it, I'm sure," Pete said, and smiled reassuringly.

They continued to look through the rest of the books. Pete had already read most of them.

"Here's one for adults only," he said, laughing. "It's *Madame Bovary*. I can't believe someone donated it. It's about an adulteress and the meaning of love and fulfillment."

Colleen didn't reply, wondering if Pete thought she was too young to read it.

"How old are you, Colleen?" Pete asked curiously.

"I'm going on sixteen. I'll be sixteen very soon. On May 26, to be exact!" she said firmly. "How old are you, Pete?"

"Nineteen," he answered. "And by the way, you are old enough to read about Emma Bovary's love life if you want to!" he laughed.

"How old were you when you got sick?" Colleen asked.

"I got sick right after I graduated," Pete answered. "I received a draft notice, but they turned me down when they found out I had TB."

"How will you go to college without the GI Bill?" Colleen asked, remembering Pete's grand plan to become a missionary doctor and retire on a mountainside.

"Oh, there are scholarships from churches and other institutions," he replied.

They went back to sorting the books. In one box, Pete found a small collection of poetry, a few books of religious readings, and several Bibles. Old editions of the *Saturday Evening Post* were stacked together in another box.

"What will you read, if you've already read most of the books?" Colleen asked Pete.

"I'm sure I'll find something in here," he said optimistically.

Colleen and Pete finished sorting through the rest of the books and then began to put them back in the boxes in alphabetical order. Pete scooped up *Moby Dick* and a few old issues of the *Saturday Evening Post*. Colleen had already decided on Mark Twain's *A Connecticut Yankee in King Arthur's Court*.

She looked over at Pete, who was now studying the cover of *Moby Dick*. He seemed completely oblivious of her, lost in contemplation. She looked over his shoulder at the dust jacket. She saw a great white whale breaching the surface of the sea and the face of an old man dimly outlined in the clouds. A ship was plowing through the waves toward the behemoth.

Pete looked at her and pointed to the book. "Melville thought he had written a very wicked book, Colleen. *Moby Dick* is an incredible journey into the nature of spleen. Ishmael says that at the beginning of the story."

Colleen looked puzzled. "What's spleen?" she asked.

"It's our anger with God for our own situations," Pete replied. "Captain Ahab blamed God for all the suffering in the world since the fall of Adam. He also blamed God for allowing Moby Dick to bite off his leg. He thought of Moby Dick as the mask over the face of a malevolent God. He didn't understand that love has nothing to hide and *never* wears a mask—and that only love itself is purely beautiful! Ahab's spleen did him in, and it took the rest of the crew with him, except for one man."

*He didn't understand that love never wears a mask*

"And that man was Ishmael?" Colleen asked.

Pete nodded.

While they waited for Miss Hawkins to come back, they read each other the first pages of their books, trying to decide which one started out better.

Toward the end of the week, Colleen had made some headway into Twain's novel. Dr. Kurtz had told her to take it easy and stay in bed as much as possible as she recovered from her surgery, but when Colleen got to the part about the mother of the Germanic language, she laughed so hard that she thought surely most of the air had come out of her compressed lung. Jeanette wanted to know what was so funny. Colleen did her best to explain, and then Jeanette asked if she could borrow the book for a moment. She marched across the hall to Pete and Cole's porch.

"Will you take me up to the broom closet so I can pick out a book too?" she asked Pete plaintively. "I want to have some fun too! I want to read something like this!" she exclaimed.

Cole looked over at Jeanette in total alarm. Cole's *raison d'etre* was to be Jeanette's knight in shining armor. Cole believed that Jeanette's *raison d'etre* was *not* to be anyone else's damsel in distress.

Cole looked over at Pete furtively. "There could be danger in there," he said casually, if not preposterously. "*I'll* take you up to the broom closet, Jeanette," he said.

Pete looked over at Cole as if to say that some things never changed, and he went back to reading the *Saturday Evening Post*.

# Part Two

## April's in the Wind

At the beginning of April, Miss Hawkins informed Colleen that she and Pete, as well as a few others from Colleen's floor, were to be moved by van over to the new building. Colleen couldn't see the new building from her porch, and Cole's usually reliable sources only knew that it had three stories and that it had been built off by itself toward the rear of the sanitarium property.

Colleen gathered her things together, and on the following day, a van took the first-floor patients down to the new building. The van driver circled behind the hospital and pulled into a lot next to a large brick building with a green, pointed roof. When Colleen was wheeled into the building, the first thing she saw was a central atrium containing the nurses' station. Halls extended in four directions off the atrium. A short hall connected the van lot to the nurses' station. The dining room was just off this hall and overlooked the parking lot. The smell of lunch emanated from the kitchen, and Colleen could hear the kitchen staff working behind closed doors.

To Colleen's delight, sunlight poured in from all sides of the atrium, creating a very cheery effect. A nurse named Miss Jackson hurried over from the nurses' station to take Colleen to the west wing. She led Colleen down a hall lined with lockers and then through a door onto a screened porch. Colleen glanced around and saw that her new ward contained eight beds. There was an empty bed for her in the middle of the row. At the end of the ward, Colleen could see a solarium that accommodated five more patients. There was an additional porch, which projected off the bath and shower area in front of the nurses' station. Miss Jackson told Colleen that the east wing was a mirror image of the west wing, and that it also housed women. There was a small women's ward on the second floor as well.

Because the nurses' station faced the front porch, the nurses could see the outdoors as they worked. Colleen had noticed an elevator to the second and third floors located behind the nurses' station. Miss Jackson told her that the men's wards were all on the second floor and that there was a library up there as well. The third floor, she said, housed interns and a few ambulatory patients who were well enough to work full time. Colleen assumed that Pete had been taken to a porch somewhere on the second floor.

After Miss Jackson helped Colleen settle comfortably into her new quarters, Colleen looked through the screen at her new surroundings and saw a large lawn bordered by a path that wound its way along a wooded hillside. The path led to the nurses' and doctors' residences. Another walk led in the opposite direction toward the main hospital building—back to Cole, Jeanette, and Miss Hawkins. Earlier in the morning, Cole had told Colleen that he had heard that first-floor patients were being sent to the new building for recovery.

As Colleen looked out upon the open space of the vast lawn, she felt a surge of freedom. The grass was a lush, spring green, and there were wild flowers in bloom along the edge of the wooded path. There were no gloomy ravines on this part of the hill. There was only sunlight and spring. School seemed far away, a nearly unreal and fading memory. *This* was her new reality. Colleen decided that she would start anew and somehow make the most of her recovery time. The library would be the place to start, she told herself.

It was nearly lunch time, and Colleen was about to introduce herself to her seven porch mates when, to her great surprise, she heard the unmistakable, booming voice of Miss Marthe in the hall.

"Laura, you must go back and get ready for lunch," Miss Marthe remonstrated.

"I just want to say hello to Colleen. I'm on my way to lunch!" replied the other unmistakable voice.

Colleen laughed out loud with joy.

"I'm in here, Laura!" Colleen called out, knowing full well she was disobeying Miss Marthe.

Laura poked her head in, and spying Colleen, smiled happily and said in a whisper, "I'm in the east wing solarium. So is Faith."

"Will I see you at lunch?" Colleen asked, still astonished.

"That depends on where you sit!" Laura replied and ducked back into the hall before Miss Marthe could say anything more.

Colleen called out to Miss Marthe, but the nurse was following Laura back down the hall. Feeling quite elated, Colleen introduced herself to the woman in the bed to her right. The woman's name was Edith. She seemed very distinguished, and Colleen was not surprised to learn that she was a teacher. Colleen guessed she wasn't more than fifty. She was very attractive, and her medium-length brown hair had only a touch of gray.

"Who's your friend?" Edith asked Colleen.

"That was Laura. We were together for a while back in the main building. They must have moved her over here recently. I didn't know she had been moved," Colleen replied.

Farther down the row, a teenager with a friendly smile said, "I'm Annie. I'm pleased to meet you, Colleen. This here's Charlotte," Annie added, pointing to the next bed down the row.

Charlotte smiled wanly. "They pumped air into my abdomen this morning. It's a little hard to talk." Charlotte was a blue-eyed, dishwater blonde. Colleen guessed that she was about thirty. Her skin was sallow, and there were dark circles under her eyes.

Charlotte's peritoneum procedure had forced her diaphragm up into her chest so that it would compress her lungs as the pneumothorax was supposed to do. Dr. Kurtz had told Colleen that the peritoneum approach was taken only when the pneumothorax technique failed. One end of Charlotte's bed had been elevated.

"I imagine they pumped you pretty full of air, then?" Colleen asked.

Charlotte nodded.

Another lady introduced herself as Virginia. "I've got TB in the joint of my big toe and in the rest of me, too," she murmured uneasily.

Colleen gave her an understanding smile, trying to seem friendly and upbeat. Colleen surmised that Virginia's TB had broken out of her lung and into her bloodstream, where it must have traveled to her big toe. Virginia was also blonde and blue-eyed, and she was very fair. Colleen had heard a rumor that blondes with fair complexions healed the least well from TB, that redheads were in between, and that brunettes were the best healers of all. Dr. Kurtz said it wasn't so.

As Colleen uneasily considered the fact that TB could spread to a toe, Miss Jackson appeared in the doorway with some lunch trays. Colleen got up to go to lunch just as a protracted howl unexpectedly pierced the quiet.

Colleen plugged her ears. *"Weeeeeeeeeeeeeeeeeeeeeoooooooh, Weeeeeeeeeeeeeooooooooooooooh!"* rang out from the upstairs porch, creating a din loud enough for all of Oakton to hear. The music of Eddie Arnold's song, "Cattle Call," reverberated across the lawn and beyond, toward the other buildings. Colleen wondered if Dr. Smith could hear it in his office.

A middle-aged lady called out from the corner, "This is Wanda, and I've had enough of Eddie for today, Thank *yooooooooooooooooh!*"

There was a sudden silence and then lusty male cheers and a round of applause from above for Wanda's rendition of Eddie Arnold.

"That's how Bret and friends call us to lunch," Wanda explained to Colleen. "You can count on it every day at noon. It's their favorite radio program, and it always starts with Eddie Arnold crooning his cattle song. It sorta reminds me of hog callin'."

"Bret, you get yourself down to the dining room right now!" a pretty blonde in her late twenties shouted at the ceiling. "That boy has a wild side that needs some taming!" she exclaimed. As she bustled past Colleen, she grabbed Colleen's arm and said, "I'm Dolly. Let's go to lunch. It smells good today. It smells like black-eyed peas!"

As her porch mates filed out for lunch, Colleen noticed that the woman in the bed on her left had not spoken. She was pale and listless and made no effort to get up for lunch. Nor did Edith or Virginia.

Edith sighed and said, "We three get room service."

By the time Colleen joined the rest of the patients waiting for lunch, the dining room doors had already been opened. People were sitting at six different tables. Colleen found a seat at Laura's table. She could see Pete looking over from another table full of men.

Pete waved and called out, "Hi, Friday!"

Laura glanced at Pete and asked, "What's he talking about? He's cute."

"That's Pete. He's a good friend from the old building. You met him at the Christmas party, but you must have forgotten. He wants to be a doctor someday," Colleen replied. "We've been reading library books we found in the old building. It sounds like he's still reading *Robinson Crusoe*," she said.

Laura looked over her shoulder at Pete, who was still looking at Colleen. She finally seemed to remember him. He glanced away when he realized Laura was looking at him again. There were times, Colleen thought, when Laura completely lacked social inhibition. Her friendly frankness was unapologetic.

Laura leaned toward Colleen and whispered, "If he would put some weight on, you two would make a very cute couple." Laura turned around for one last look.

"Laura, please …" Colleen frowned.

"Well he's staring over here, so what's wrong with having a look?" Laura replied.

Pete began picking at his food, aware that he was probably the subject of their conversation.

"He's interested, Colleen, or haven't you noticed? If you actually *looked* over there, you could see it in his eyes!" Laura observed as she turned back around and resumed eating her salad. "You two would probably have very tall children," she added, causing Colleen to choke on her water.

Colleen laughed, stealing a furtive peek at Pete, who was now resolutely not looking in their direction. "We'll see about that," she said.

"He has very kind eyes, Colleen," Faith added. Faith was the only one who had observed the entire scene without moving.

"Speaking of men," Colleen said, trying to change the topic, "which one is Bret? I mean the one who plays Eddie Arnold on the radio just before lunch."

Hearing his name, a young man at the end of the table looked over at Colleen. "Did someone mention my name?" he asked.

Bret had green eyes and curly, sandy hair. His smile was warm and friendly. Lean, but broad-shouldered, he radiated a masculine strength that obviously appealed to the women patients. He was surrounded by the prettiest girls in the room. There was a gleam in his eye that suggested a quick mind, but what else? Colleen couldn't define it. He was dressed in a robe and pajamas, and he wore a small, silver cross on a chain around his neck, suggesting an inner, spiritual strength. Colleen could not fathom why a young man like this would entertain folks by playing Eddie Arnold at train station decibels. He seemed like a contradiction in terms that needed explaining.

Colleen looked up and said, "I did. I was just wondering who it was who liked to play Eddie Arnold at noon." Colleen felt his eyes taking her measure. "I'm new here," she added, a bit self-consciously.

Bret smiled. "I know," he said as he picked up his chair with a smooth and assured movement and placed it in between Colleen and Laura. "Well, I'm the Bret you're looking for. What's your name, if ya don't mind my askin'?"

"Colleen Reilly. It's nice to meet you," Colleen said, meaning it.

"These are my friends, Laura and Faith."

Laura deliberately looked over at Pete and said, "Pleased to meet you."

Faith said, "We met yesterday."

"I remember," Bret said softly. "You two are residin' in the solarium in the east wing, right?"

Laura nodded distantly, remaining ever loyal to Pete. She gave a disapproving look at Colleen, which clearly said, *Do not forsake Pete!*

"So, where are you from, Colleen?" Bret asked politely.

"I'm from a little town called Carlton, on the east side of the state. You've probably never heard of it," Colleen answered.

"Oh, sure I have! I used to live in Clarksburg, about thirty miles from there," he said.

After asking Faith and Laura where they were from, Bret asked Colleen how long she'd been at Sherwood, what ward she was on, and how she liked it so far. He then excused himself to get back to his friends.

"Right nice to meet you, Colleen," he said as he took his chair back to the circle of women.

When lunch was over, Colleen went back to her porch for the rest period. At three o'clock, Nurse Jackson came to refill the water pitchers and to check temperatures. She was an efficient woman, and her energy was contagious. When she straightened the bedding, she would karate-chop the pillows as she tucked them under the spreads. Her hand was firm on the pulse, compared to some of the nurses who barely touched Colleen's wrist. She was short and sturdy, and she was younger than Miss Marthe—perhaps twenty-eight. If Miss Jackson hadn't become a nurse, Colleen thought that she would have made a cheery camp counselor.

Shortly after five o'clock, Colleen saw a tall girl dressed in a shirt dress coming along the sidewalk from the old building. Colleen saw her enter their building. In the morning, Colleen saw her walk over to the hospital again.

Colleen had so little else to do that the young woman's comings and goings were like a small mystery in her otherwise monotonous life. She pointed her out to Edith and asked, "Do you know who that is? I saw her in the dining room last evening."

Edith looked over and said, "Oh, that's Claire. She lives up on the third floor. She's Pop Smith's private secretary. You ought to meet her, Colleen. You two probably have a lot in common. She has a piano up in her apartment. She entertains at some of the parties, too. She's quite accomplished."

Colleen looked wonderingly at the retreating figure. She decided to try to meet Claire at dinner some night.

After breakfast, Colleen went to wash her hands and face in the women's bathroom. Wanda was already there. She had taken out her false teeth and was applying adhesive to them. Her grin was like a Halloween pumpkin with no teeth.

A pretty young woman with freckles, apple cheeks, and a turned-up nose was talking to Wanda. Her long, blonde hair was pulled back from her forehead, but the rest of her hair was a mass of curls that hung below her shoulders. When she laughed, her cheeks, eyes, and even her perky nose all joined in the laughter. Colleen had to laugh too, when Wanda made a friendly, but toothless, attempt at "Nice fair weather we're havin' today."

Wanda smiled, unconcerned about her toothless diction. She turned and said, "Abby, stop laughin' for a while. I want you to meet my new porch mate, Colleen. She got moved over here from the old building. Colleen, this here's Abigail, but she goes by Abby."

"Pleased to meet ya, Colleen," Abby said merrily. "When did you arrive?"

"On Wednesday," Colleen said.

Abby pointed to her teeth. "Mine are false too," she said. "They had to replace mine because I've had so many bronchoscopies. Every time they push one of those awful tubes down my throat, they promise me it's the last time! It feels like I'm swallowing the Brooklyn Bridge."

Colleen refrained from asking for details.

"Where are you from, Abby?" Colleen asked, changing the subject.

"I'm from Hinkley, down in coal country. My daddy was a miner. He was killed in a mine accident. Where are you from?" she asked.

"I'm from Carlton. Hinkley's way down south, isn't it?"

"Umhumm," Abby responded. "Most people know about it because of a famous coal strike there. The miners were starved into goin' back, in spite of the union. My dad used to talk about it a lot when I was growin' up."

"The coal trains still pass through Carlton on their way out of the mountains," Colleen responded. "My dad sells insurance, but a lot of Carlton people still make a livin' off the railroad and the coal traffic."

"Well, it's surely a different way of life in this place." Abby yawned and raised her arms to the ceiling in a huge stretch. "I've been here almost a year now, an' the best thing to do is to keep busy. I've been thinkin' about learning to crochet. There's a big Italian guy upstairs named Emile. He's been crocheting things for his wife and sending them home to her. He said I should take up the hobby."

Colleen looked interested. "Where does he get his yarn and crochet hooks?" she asked.

"He has a catalog," Abby replied. "He told me that he learned to crochet from it. His wife sent it to him. Would you be interested?"

"Maybe we could all do that. We could borrow Emile's catalog and order yarn and needles," Colleen suggested.

"Well, hon, Emile's easy to spot in the dining room. He's *way* over six feet tall and gentle as a lamb. He'd take triple helpings if the kitchen staff would let him," Abby laughed. "They can't seem to fill him up.

We can ask to borrow his catalog at lunch."

At lunchtime, Colleen and Abby found Emile and asked him if he would lend them his catalog. He smiled amiably and agreed to bring it down with him at dinner.

"Itsa nice catalog. I'ma makin' a nice scarf for my wife," he said happily. "If you do it, you can make yourselves some pretty things. You justa start with somethin' easy, and then maybe you'll wanta try something harder," he said enthusiastically.

Abby and Colleen thanked him and went to sit down with Laura and Faith. Pete had already joined them. Colleen introduced Abby, but Abby already knew Laura and Faith. Pete introduced himself as a friend of Colleen's.

"Would anyone be interested in learning to crochet?" Colleen asked. "Emile will lend us his catalog."

"I'd like that a lot!" Faith said enthusiastically. "I used to knit all the time at home."

Pete was reluctant to be left out and said, "Well, why not? Emile seems to take a lot of pleasure in it. You can count me in too."

At dinnertime, Emile brought the catalog over to Colleen's table. Colleen thanked him and passed it around to the group. The photos of scarves, hats, purses, doilies, and blankets were colorful and attractive. Directions came with whichever item was ordered.

Colleen put the catalog in the pocket of her robe as she eyed her dinner plate. "What is this?" she asked Laura, crinkling up her nose in displeasure.

"It's lamb stew, can't you tell by the smell?" Laura laughed.

The meals were served family style, but no one seemed to be helping themselves to much of the stew. Colleen did not like the flavor of the meat or the broth, but she ate all the vegetables. There were some disgruntled remarks about the taste of the lamb. When Colleen went to scrape her plate, she noticed that virtually no one had eaten the lamb. The stew lay in lumpy piles in a sea of broth in the garbage can. Colleen thought the lamb was almost as bad as the black-eyed peas they had served for lunch, which was the worst thing she had ever tasted.

Since the plates were first dipped in sterilizing pans before going into the kitchen for washing, a kitchen worker named Skippy was watching all the lamb being dumped as he oversaw the sterilization pans. Skippy was a good-natured black man who was always laughing, but he wasn't laughing now. "That's a passle of lamb going unet! Pop Smith won't like that!" he observed.

Colleen heard Bret exclaim behind her, "This is a *mutton mutiny*. No more lamb!"

A few of his friends began to take up the chant, "Mutton mutiny! No more lamb!" Heads popped out of the kitchen to see what the fuss was all about.

Evidently the "mutiny" got back to Dr. Smith because at lunch the following day, he came into the dining room to make a short speech about the continuing shortage of meat.

Dr. Smith started his speech by admitting that he hadn't always liked lamb. "As you know," he said, "we try very hard to get the best food we can, but there are continuing shortages even though the war is over. Our budget only allows us to buy in bulk, and we must take what is available at any given time. Since lamb is quite nutritious and digestible, it's actually very good for you. I'm asking you for your own health not to throw it away on nights when it's served. I hope you will all support the kitchen staff's efforts to make the best meals possible under the circumstances."

Everyone remained silent for a while, but then someone had the temerity to call out, "But it tastes *baaaaahd*, Doc!"

Everyone laughed, including Dr. Smith. He cheerfully replied, "We'll try to avoid lamb, but I can't promise you it won't show up on the menu now and then. In a few more months, meat ought to become more plentiful," he finished.

Afterward, a few patients came up to Dr. Smith and told him they appreciated his explanation. He was well-liked by the patients and affectionately referred to as Pop Smith. Colleen filed out with her group. She gave Dr. Smith a friendly smile, and he smiled back. Dr. Smith had a high forehead, and he wore wire-rimmed glasses, which gave him a very intellectual air. The eyes behind the glasses sparkled with intelligence, warmth, and dignity. They seemed to see all and understand all, missing nothing. Colleen thought he looked a bit like President Truman, only taller and darker.

Colleen went back to bed for the evening. She copied the order form and filled in the crocheting items she needed in the blank provided. Sherwood had an account with a needlework store that allowed the nurses to place orders by phone. The orders were immediately filled and sent out COD the same day. She asked the evening nurse to give the form to Laura and then to Pete on the second floor. Before bedtime, Dr. Edmonds and Dr. Collins strode into Colleen's ward.

Dr. Edmonds asked Colleen how she felt and asked a few medical questions.

Dr. Collins was obviously popular with the women in the ward, and Colleen could hear Annie joking with him at her end of the row. The outlines of Annie's breasts could be seen clearly under her thin nightclothes. Annie seemed unconcerned. Dr. Collins made some remark about everybody looking real well tonight and joked about the lamb mutiny in the dining room. He said, "I wish *ewe* a good night, Annie, and *ewe* and *ewe* and *ewe*, too. "*E-w-e*, get it? Ha, ha!" he laughed.

Dr. Edmonds, however, did not even smile. He was stern and all business.

In the morning, Colleen waited by the front door and was able to catch Claire before she left the building for work. Colleen introduced herself and told her that she also played piano.

Claire said, "Why, you'll have to come up for a visit, if they'll let you! I have a grand piano and tons of sheet music. I wouldn't mind if you used it while I'm at work. In fact, since tomorrow's Saturday, why don't you see if you can come upstairs after the rest period and try it out? I leave my room unlocked."

Colleen was delighted and quickly agreed.

Colleen spent Friday resting and finishing Twain's *Connecticut Yankee in King Arthur's Court*. The ending was not what Colleen expected.

At lunch, Colleen told Laura about the book and asked her if she wanted to read it.

Laura said it sounded good, and Faith said she would read it after Laura. They spent the rest of the meal talking about knights and medieval times and wondering how a knight of the roundtable would react to the modern age of atomic bombs, tanks, and other weapons. Faith wondered if people got TB in medieval times. Pete said they got the plague. Colleen could see that Bret was listening.

Colleen awoke on Saturday morning thinking about Claire's grand piano. She had never played one. She *needed* to play the piano—and a grand one, at that! On her way to lunch, she watched the nurses as they worked at their station. Feeling a bit like Eve in the Garden of Eden, Colleen guiltily realized that the nurses were too busy writing up reports to notice which of the patients were using the elevator.

At three thirty, when the rest period was over, and the nurses were busy writing their reports, Colleen walked slowly toward the ladies' bathroom, casually pressing the elevator button as she entered the atrium. She had brought a book in case anyone questioned her reason for being up. If asked, she would say she needed a nurse to return it to the library for her. The elevator doors opened quietly and almost immediately. For a brief second, Colleen paused, thinking she would surely be caught. When she realized that none of the nurses had noticed the sound of the elevator doors opening, Colleen quietly stepped inside.

She rode the elevator up to the second floor to find Pete's ward. Her heart was pounding. She discovered a men's ward and a women's ward, just as Miss Jackson had said. There were also private rooms along the back with very sick patients. Colleen saw a priest enter one of the private rooms.

Colleen stood in the doorway of Pete's ward and caught his eye. She silently motioned for him to come out in the hall. Pete sat up and rose uncertainly out of his bed. Bret appeared to be asleep. No one else seemed to notice her.

"I'm going up to Claire's apartment on the third floor. She invited me to play her piano," Colleen whispered. "I just want to return a book to the library."

"Can I go, too?" Pete asked.

"We could get in trouble," Colleen replied.

"Let's get rid of your book and then go on up," Pete whispered. Pete led Colleen to a small room with bookcases built into the walls. The shelves had been painted white. There was an empty counter where books could be checked in and out, but there was no librarian.

Colleen laid the book on the counter.

"You don't mind if I go upstairs, too, do you?" Pete repeated.

"Are you allowed up for an hour?" Colleen replied.

"No, but I'll bet you aren't either!" Pete said.

"You're right, but I'm not the usual suspect when it comes to breakin' the rules, so I hope I can get away with something just this once."

"I'll just say you needed an audience if we're caught," Pete said with a nervous smile.

Pete and Colleen were surprised to see that Claire had left her apartment door slightly ajar. She had left a note indicating that she had been called over to the hospital to help Dr. Smith. It also said, "Help yourself to some cookies. I left some music on the piano if you want to play. Just close the door, and no one will mind. Dr. Edmonds is over at the hospital today, and I don't know where Dr. Collins is."

Colleen and Pete went in and sat down together on the piano bench. They each helped themselves to some freshly baked cookies.

"Yum!" Colleen exclaimed. "Peanut butter cookies. Somehow I feel like Goldilocks!" Colleen laughed, taking two of the cookies.

"You mean because we're not allowed to be up here?" he asked, chewing his cookie happily.

Colleen nodded.

"I just feel excellently full," Pete replied.

Colleen looked around. A fresh April breeze was blowing gently through the open window. In addition to the piano, the room was furnished with a day bed and two stuffed chairs with calico prints. Next to the window, there was a mahogany dining table with fold-down sides. Claire had set a vase of wildflowers in the center of the table. There was a small kitchen alcove and bathroom. The apartment was not very large, but it was cheery and inviting.

Pete stood up and said, "That was a delicious interlude. It would be perfect if the cookies were followed by some beautiful music. Won't you please play something for me?" Pete took another cookie and went and sat down in one of the stuffed chairs.

Colleen looked dubious. "It's been a long time since I've played, Pete," she said.

"If I had my violin, we could play a duet," he said, smiling encouragingly from his chair.

"That's a hard instrument!" Colleen acknowledged. She turned around on the bench and ran her fingers in an arpeggio over the keys. Claire had left a stack of music on top of the piano.

"Oh, look," Colleen exclaimed. "Claire left out a copy of *Clair de Lune*. There's a note on it. It says she was pleased to hear *Clair de Lune* on the *Jumpin' Joe Show!*" Colleen laughed.

Pete set down his milk, and Colleen handed him the note.

"*Clair de Lune* is a beautiful piece!" Pete exclaimed. "I haven't heard it played in a long while. Can you play it?"

"I learned to play it last summer," she answered. "I taught myself. It's beyond what my teacher would have assigned me, but I kept at it."

Colleen studied Claire's beautiful piano, looking solemn. "I think of music as the secret language of the fingertips. It's *still* very mysterious and magical to me! On the first night I was here, I had a dream about a lark hiding in the secret place where music begins. I suppose I was afraid I would never find it."

"I was the kid in the choir who always bobbed around when he sang," Pete reflected. "So I guess the beat is where music begins for me. That's why we *dance* to music, don't you think?" he said laughingly as he jumped out of the chair, pulled Colleen to her feet, and began waltzing her around the room.

"You see, when I learn to play a song," he said teasingly, "everything has to fit into the beat. That includes the notes and phrases." Pete whirled her around several times. "And the fingering and dynamics as well!"

Pete dipped Colleen with a flourish, which made her groan as the air in her chest further compressed her lungs. "Music doesn't come alive without its heartbeat!"

Colleen thought his eyes looked feverish.

"It's a bit like the little Russian dolls that all fit neatly into one another, don't you think?" he laughed.

Colleen was trying to catch her breath, but she smiled at the thought of uncorking all the little dolls to discover a hidden lark.

Then she said, "Rhythm is just fractions, after all. There's no mystery about that ..." Her voice trailed off in thought. "The notes are unequivocal and indicate specific places on the keyboard," she added, trying to convince herself that she could do it.

"Which can be identified by touch," Pete interrupted. "You can always figure out which notes you have under your fingertips and tell yourself the composer means *that* sound when you hear something new and different. No mystery there!"

"Fingering is just fingering ..." Colleen mused to herself.

"There are only five possibilities. No mystery there, either!" Pete agreed. "So have you talked yourself into playing yet?" Pete asked, his eyes smiling merrily as he held her at an arm's length and studied her.

"It's just that when I play for someone, Pete, I try to show that my soul understands the beauty of the music—and that it's not a stupid and clumsy sort of soul," Colleen said shyly. She felt insignificantly small around Pete's intellect.

Pete looked at Colleen in a way she had never noticed before.

She thought for a moment that he wanted to kiss her, but that was forbidden because of the risk of infection. He ran a finger down Colleen's cheek. "You would be beautiful even if you played chopsticks," he said.

"Wouldn't I, though?" Colleen joked, not exactly sure how to acknowledge the compliment. She sat down hard on the piano bench and placed *Clair de Lune* on the music rack. Pete's obvious affection had caught her by surprise, and she was fighting to regain her inner composure.

"Bach said it's just a matter of being able to follow two parts and then three parts and so forth," she said, trying to refocus on the music.

"Who would know better than Bach?" Pete said encouragingly as he sat back down.

Pete settled back into the easy chair, obviously fatigued. Then he held up both of his thumbs. "Just don't forget these little guys, Colleen," he said. "Those beautiful, long arpeggios in *Clair de Lune* wouldn't be possible without thumbs!" Pete held up his right thumb and joked, "You're number one, pal!" He looked over at the last of

Claire's cookies. "Besides, without thumbs how could I consume so many cookies so quickly?" Pete reached for the last cookie on the plate. "Do you mind if I take the last one?"

Colleen smiled at Pete fondly. "Help yourself! And you're right about *Clair de Lune*. It has lots of difficult arpeggios, but if a player piano could play it, I guess I can too!" she declared.

Pete sat up, surprised by Colleen's observation. "Are you saying that if a player piano can play a tune, then music isn't a secret language after all?" he asked.

He paused, looked seriously at her, and said, "Aha!" like a medieval monk discovering a simple truth while copying the classics by candlelight. Pete said nothing more for a moment, studying the wavering flame that was Colleen, charmed by the young woman who had slipped so unexpectedly into his sanctuary.

"Then how do we account for its secret magic?" Pete continued, never taking his eyes off Colleen. "Mozart could compose a complicated work in his head and then jot it down without revisions at the parties he gave! He could hear it *and* write it. Let's see a player piano do that!"

"But he had absolute pitch!" Colleen exclaimed.

"He had more than that," Pete replied.

Colleen said nothing. It was probably true that perfect pitch could not account for Mozart's creativity. Besides, she mused, there were other great composers who did not have perfect pitch.

"When I was a little boy, my mother gave me a music box," Pete said. "I still have it. It plays 'Twinkle, Twinkle Little Star.' When I was further along in piano, she gave me a copy of Mozart's variations based on the same theme. They're easy to follow because "Twinkle, Twinkle Little Star" is so simple and familiar, and yet they are very beautiful. Have you ever heard them?"

"No, but I would like to," Colleen replied, greatly interested.

Pete smiled mysteriously. "Perhaps that can be arranged."

"You know," Pete said wistfully, "last year, before I got sick, I thought all the pieces of my life had fallen into place for me. I thought I had a chance to make something of myself. I could play piano and violin, and I was good at math. I thought that maybe I could be another Albert Schweitzer. My math teacher was even teaching me calculus after school. I had won a scholarship to a prestigious school up in New England, and I was planning to become a doctor. Then disaster struck. Mom got sick and died, and I came down with TB, too. I had to cancel my college plans and turn down the scholarship. My mother died, never realizing that I wouldn't be able to use the scholarship."

"That must have been a terrible disappointment for you after the death of your mother," Colleen said, feeling Pete's obvious pain.

"Sherwood obviously isn't what I was expecting in my future, but it's not such a bad place to be—especially since I've met you, Colleen," Pete answered.

Colleen studied Pete's lined and haggard face. At times, it contained a sadness that reminded her a little bit of Abraham Lincoln. Pete also had Lincoln's thick, black eyebrows. She felt as if she were seeing Pete clearly for the first time.

"Whenever I get discouraged about a hard piece of music, I just tell myself that nothing good comes easily, Colleen," Pete said earnestly. "I think Albert Schweitzer got it right. Every good thing begins with a certain reverence. That is true about music, too."

Pete was quiet for a moment. "Schweitzer says that God is like a pure and distant melody cutting through the noise of the world's busyness. Music in all its forms tells us, 'This is your goal; this is why you live. Just listen, and you will find that all the parts count.' We have to live in harmony with God's melody at all times. We get so busy constructing our own parts that we forget to listen for it, Colleen, but Schweitzer says, 'Happy is the man who listens!' To me, the piano is like a temple that teaches us what it is to truly listen. Sometimes, when

I'm playing, I feel as if I'm reaching for a million, faraway stars, and the grand staff is the Milky Way. But most of the time, I'm back on earth, tending my sheep—always counting them and listening."

"That is a beautiful way to describe God," Colleen replied softly.

"Michelangelo painted a picture on the Sistine Chapel in Rome that shows God giving Adam life," Pete continued. "It shows God reaching out to Adam's *hand*—as if He gives life through the hand. What we do to heal others and to create a beautiful world counts with God, even if we can't *do* much in a place like this, don't you think, Colleen?"

"Of course it matters!" Colleen responded. "Especially in a place like this. Life and death matter to God." Colleen took a deep breath, trying to concentrate on playing the piano. "Let's just hope my piano playing shows the same level of respect as Schweitzer's and that you'll still want to be my friend after you hear me play!"

Colleen turned back to the keyboard and played a few scales to warm up. "And by the way, now that I know you can play," Colleen laughed self-consciously, "you can be the guinea-pig maestro next time."

Colleen looked down at the sea of white and black keys. "I *think* I can do this! Here goes!" she exclaimed, and she began to play.

In the middle of the piece, Claire entered the room and sat down quietly.

When Colleen had concluded, Claire and Pete both applauded.

"That was very pretty, Colleen!" Claire said enthusiastically. "You can hear it in the stairwells."

"Bravo, Colleen!" Pete seconded.

The happy moment was fleeting. Miss Jackson had appeared in the doorway, totally red-faced and not at all her usual smiling self.

"*What* are you two doing *up* without permission?" she thundered.

Claire looked up in surprise at the irate nurse. Claire had long auburn hair and serene blue eyes, but her eyes showed that she had deduced she was harboring fugitives from medical justice.

"I'm sorry, Miss Jackson, I invited Colleen up for just a moment to try out the grand piano. She had never played one. Don't you think she plays beautifully?" Claire asked timidly.

The efficient nurse was not to be dissuaded.

"Both of you need to go back to bed *at once*," she said. "Neither of you is ready to be up for an hour yet. You may have caused yourselves irreparable harm."

Miss Jackson turned and told them to follow her. She also said she was going to enter the episode into their charts and inform Dr. Kurtz.

Pete grinned sheepishly at Colleen and Miss Jackson as they rode down to the second floor in the elevator. "Will you be coming to dinner tonight, Colleen?" he asked.

"Oh, yes. I'm quite tired, but happy," Colleen replied almost inaudibly.

As the doors opened and Pete stepped out, he said to the air and to no one in particular, "If I go insane from boredom and lack of a good friend, will I be cured?"

"We will have to find something quiet for both of you to do. Perhaps crocheting," Miss Jackson said to both of them as the doors closed on Pete's back.

"Perhaps crocheting," Colleen sighed.

# Melody for May

After Miss Jackson discovered them in Claire's apartment, Colleen avoided Pete, and Pete avoided Colleen. Both were very careful to stay in bed whenever possible. Dr. Kurtz spoke to both of them about the need for constant bed rest, and he warned them that any kind of exertion could cause a hemorrhage. They agreed not to go up to Claire's apartment again.

Pete was surprised to learn that Bret knew about his adventure with Colleen.

"I saw you two sneak on the elevator," he laughed. "Never thought you had it in you, Pete! Nor Colleen, for that matter! You were doin' real good till the music started comin' down the stairs. I started countin' to myself to see how long it would take Miss Jackson to get up there. To say she's a righteously efficient nurse doesn't capture her essence. No, sir, she's a race horse! You should have seen her runnin' up the stairs! Too bad I couldn't have added a little Eddie Arnold music to the mix!"

"And then what would have happened?" Pete laughed.

"Well, then she would have had two fires to put out!" Bret replied enthusiastically. "My daddy taught me to be a student of human nature. He always said that if we don't see ourselves without the fairy tale rouge and makeup, we'll never grow up. Nurse Jackson is more than a nurse, and I'd like to know what the *real* Miss Jackson is all about. These are things we should know if we are going to entrust our bodies and minds to her care. Besides, if we don't laugh, what else is there to do around here, anyway?"

Pete looked inquisitively at Bret. He considered him bright and imaginative. Pete presumed that Bret was as restless and bored as he was. He had quickly discovered that Bret was a born iconoclast and full of shrewd observations about the staff. Yet when Bret finally settled down at night, he could talk equally well about philosophy or sports and the latest news events. Pete scowled. He had noticed that Colleen could usually be found talking to Bret before the dining room doors opened for meals.

Bret looked at Pete a bit slyly. "So, what did you and the fair Colleen do up in Claire's apartment, if I may ask?" he asked casually.

Pete looked back equally slyly at Bret. "We ate peanut butter cookies and talked about music, if that's what you want to know! But I learned something."

"What's that?" Bret asked.

"Well, Colleen's a good dancer, for one thing! She was hesitant to play piano for me, but she actually played a difficult piece quite well. She's not completely sure how she plays, but she's well on her way. Her older sister is already an excellent pianist."

Pete fingered a small music box he kept by his bed. He glanced over at Bret to see if he was still listening. "I also found out that Colleen's still learning to trust. She's very shy about her skills. In fact, she's shy about a lot of things."

Bret looked up with the same gleam in his eye that Colleen had first noticed about him. "Is that right?" he asked.

"I think I'll give her this music box for her birthday next week," Pete said. "I've asked my father to send me the sheet music to Mozart's variations on the 'Twinkle, Twinkle Little Star,' which is the song the music box plays."

"How old is Colleen, did you say?" Bret asked.

"She'll be turning sixteen," Pete answered.

"She seems older than that to me." Bret said nothing more.

"I think we should all learn to just relax and crochet!" Emile exclaimed enthusiastically. "There's no point in makin' the mountain outta the molehill. We're here, and we might as well enjoy it."

"You and Miss Jackson!" Pete answered with a sigh. "She wants

Colleen and me to tend to our knitting. No piano playing allowed."

Colleen, meanwhile, had discovered that many of the first-floor women had decided to send away for crocheting supplies. When Colleen's order arrived, she lay in bed and looked at the instructions. Edith helped her get started, and Colleen was able to begin a small doily. She lay on her back for an hour, crocheting. She found, to her surprise, that it was very relaxing.

When Miss Jackson came in to check temperatures, Colleen thanked her for the idea of crocheting and apologized for going up to Claire's apartment. This seemed to smooth the waters, and Miss Jackson left smiling happily. Later on, when Miss Marthe brought in a fresh pitcher of ice water, Colleen asked her if she would mind taking Pete's crocheting supplies upstairs to him. Their orders had arrived in the same package.

"Ach! He is a vonderful young man! I heard vhat happened, Colleen. Miss Jackson is not so hard-hearted as you think! Ve know how difficult it is for you to lie in bed for so long. You are both young, and you do not understand the reality of death."

Miss Marthe took the crocheting supplies upstairs to Pete, but paused in the doorway to the men's porch. Pete, Bret, and Emile were discussing the fact that Jackie Robinson had become a player on the minor-league Montreal Royals baseball team.

"He's playing second base," Emile said. "He's a doin' just fine. The French Canadians love him very much."

Pete asked, "If he does well, I wonder if they'll sign him up for the major leagues next year?"

Bret reflected, "Well, he would get a lot of moral support from black folks, if that happened. They're following all his games on the radio. You have to wonder how he'll be received by whites when his team plays in the South, though."

Emile added, "What if Montreal and Jackie Robinson play down in

Louisville for the Little World Series Championship in October? The Colonels are red hot this year!"

Miss Marthe came into the room. "In that case, I vould hope that he vould be better received than Jesse Owens vas by Hitler in Germany! Hitler vould not shake Mr. Owens's hand at the 1936 Munich Olympics because Jesse Owens vas not of the Aryan race. Hitler left the stadium so that he vould not have to shake the hand of a black man who had von so many gold medals. It spoiled Hitler's superiority feelings! Hitler's defeat should be a lesson to the vorld!"

The men looked up in surprise. They had never heard Miss Marthe talk about Hitler or the war.

Miss Marthe said nothing more about Jackie Robinson. "Your crocheting supplies haf arrived, Pete," she said. "Colleen sent them up to you. She says perhaps you can make something varm for this vinter like a scarf or hat."

"Why, thanks, Miss Marthe!" Pete said. "Emile is going to teach me. He's an old hand at this. He says there's nothing to it."

Miss Marthe smiled. "Vell, most of the vomen find it very relaxing, so I hope you vill too," she said. She handed Pete the materials and removed an empty pitcher of water. "I vill be back soon with some fresh ice vater."

On the following morning, Miss Marthe came onto Colleen's porch with some news. Colleen was to be moved. Colleen shot a glance at the girl lying in the bed next to her. Colleen presumed she was being moved because TB had spread all through the girl's body. Colleen looked guiltily away, hoping the girl had not noticed her looking at her.

"Where will I be going?" Colleen asked. She had barely settled into her new surroundings. She glanced around at her porch mates.

"Ve are moving you to a bed on the porch vith Laura. Faith, Abby, and Julie are also there. Julie is about your age, Colleen."

Edith, Wanda, Annie, and the rest of the women all looked disappointed.

"I vill help you get your things together so that ve can move you right away. I haf already told your friends that you are coming," Miss Marthe said.

"What did they say?" Colleen asked.

"They vere very happy, of course!" Miss Marthe responded.

As Colleen was wheeled onto the porch, her former porch mates made a great fuss over her return. Julie looked at Colleen curiously, because she hadn't realized there were any other young women patients at Sherwood.

Laura was lying in the last bed at the far end of the porch by the left-side screen, and Faith had the bed next to Laura. Colleen's bed was in the middle. Abby was to her right, and Julie was sitting up reading in the last bed on the right side of the porch.

Colleen introduced herself to Julie. Julie was a cute girl with dark-brown eyes, jet-black eyebrows, and thick, brown hair that she pulled off her high forehead into a long pony tail. Her eyes sparkled with animation. When she spoke, her voice was musical and high. She too was from a small town. Her father was a grocer.

Shortly before noon, they walked as a group to the lunchroom. The patients always shuffled slowly down the halls, slightly bent over like marching penguins because of the air in their chests. When she reached the dining room, Colleen joined her porch mates at one of the longer tables. Emile, Pete, and Bret filtered in after a few minutes. Charlie, a lanky blond man in his mid-twenties, sat down beside Abby on her side of the table. Charlie always sat next to Abby whenever he could, and the two were best friends. A few other women patients took seats at the far end of the table.

Colleen glanced out the window and saw a man carrying some garden tools cross the parking lot. He set them down, hooked up a hose, and then proceeded to water a small garden outside the east corner of the dining room. He looked in and saw Colleen watching him. He moved away from her view, with a backward glance at Colleen. Colleen nudged Laura in great excitement.

"He's the fellow who picked up my book in the hall outside the fluoroscopy room!" she exclaimed. "He's outside working in the garden. You know, the Handyman!"

Laura looked over but saw no one.

"He stepped out of view when he saw me!" Colleen exclaimed.

"Maybe he thinks you're nosey," Laura suggested.

"Laura, he's the man that Will said I should stay away from!"

"Well, it looks like he's saving you some time and effort by staying away from *you*," Bret joked.

"Then how will I get my book back?" Colleen asked.

"Maybe he just wanted to be cooler in the shade," Faith suggested.

"Maybe he's my 'secret admirer' and a strange one, at that!" Colleen exclaimed uncomfortably. Colleen described the card and the roses she had received and the fellow's contradictory behavior.

Bret looked at Colleen in surprise. "You wouldn't be the Colleen who requested *Clair de Lune* on the *Jumpin' Joe Show* by any chance, would you?" Bret asked disbelievingly.

Colleen stared back at Bret. "Don't tell me *you* sent me the roses?" she asked incredulously.

Bret smiled to himself, remembering the episode.

"When I heard Jumpin' Joe play *Clair de Lune* during a program of pop music, I just had to call in with that 'second-floor girls' protest. It was just too funny, Colleen!" Bret exclaimed, shaking his head and laughing. "I just wanted to see what my imaginary Colleen would do! Then I felt guilty, so I sent you the roses a few days later. Sorry, Colleen, but the Handyman's not your 'secret admirer.' I am!" Bret finished, blushing as everyone stared at him. "In my own defense, now that I've met you, I must admit that I have excellent taste."

Laura rolled her eyes. Colleen stared in disbelief, her assumptions dashed, even if she still instinctively disliked the Handyman.

"In my opinion," Bret observed, "the Handyman can have his gardening. I'd rather be out in the sun takin' care of horses and ridin' them as fast as they'll go."

Charlie reached around behind Abby's back and pulled on Julie's ponytail. "This here is the cutest little filly at Sherwood, Bret," Charlie teased, admiring her long hair.

Bret looked at the pretty young woman appreciatively.

Colleen asked, "Have you ever been to the Oakton Stakes, Bret?"

Bret turned to Colleen. "No," he replied, "but we had two horses on our little farm, and I worked one summer at one of the big horse farms for extra money. I've been around horses most of my life. When Pop couldn't afford to modernize the farm, he sold out two years ago. When we moved to Lockwood, we had to sell the horses."

"My brother promised to take me to the Oakton Stakes when I get well. It must be exciting to see the horses flyin' along the rail and pounding down the homestretch. Piano playing is pretty tame in comparison!" she exclaimed.

"Music just looks like a bunch of ants on the page to me!" Abby exclaimed. "I'd like to see a real horse race sometime, too."

"Racing can be pretty hard on horses," Pete interjected. "My father's a vet. He's against the sport. He said horses shouldn't be raced when they're adolescents because it ruins their joints."

"Well, Colleen, when we finally escape this place, I promise to take you and Abby to the races," Bret answered, ignoring Pete's objections. "We'll take your brother along too."

Pete smiled thinly, glancing over at Colleen.

There was a lull in the conversation. Colleen saw that the Handyman had removed the hose and gone off to do some other work.

When Colleen returned to her porch after lunch, she noticed storm clouds gathering on the horizon. In a short time, the sky turned dark and threatening. The awnings began to flap as the first stirrings of the unsettled air gave warning of the approaching storm. When Miss Marthe came onto the porch to change the water pitchers, she looked worriedly toward the west. "It is a good thing that ve haf the awnings!"

Colleen settled into her bed for the customary rest period, but she slept restlessly, tossing and turning to the sounds of the gusting wind and the torrential rain.

She dreamed that she, Pete, and Bret were caught suddenly in a storm along a lake. Bret was walking along the shore. She was in a small boat, and Pete was swimming. It quickly began to rain so hard that she could not see the shore beyond the curtain of driving rain. Waves started crashing against her boat and threatened to swamp it. She could hear Pete calling for help as he struggled to swim back to shore, but she no longer had any idea where he was or even the direction of shore. She listened and called for Pete, but there was no answer. Suddenly, she saw a hand grab the side of the boat. Bret was in the water, struggling to get into the small boat. She was afraid the boat would sink.

Bret pulled himself over the side, grabbed the oars, and began to row toward shore. She shouted, "Where's Pete?" But Bret couldn't hear her because of the wind. It was only when they got to shore that they found Pete's body, which had washed ashore. Bret said, "I couldn't save you both."

When she awoke, Colleen felt shaken by her dream. The foot of her bed was damp, and she realized that the storm had been its most likely cause. Her dream quickly receded into the mist rising from the river of puddles left by the storm on the outside walk. She felt a bit groggy after her fitful sleep, but she began to revive in the cool, sweet air that had followed the storm.

Abby pulled out a Sears and Roebuck catalog and began to thumb through it until she found the dress section.

Looking over Abby's shoulder, Colleen pointed to one of the pages of the catalog, which showed a pretty pink dress with smocking and short sleeves. "That would be nice to wear into Oakton, when I go to the doctor at the beginning of June," she observed. "Dr. Kurtz thinks I'm too thin and that my hormones are unbalanced. He wants me to have progesterone shots."

Abby looked over at Colleen. "We could all stand to put on a little weight, don't ya think?" she asked. Then she said, "Tonight's a toasting night! We'll have milk and cinnamon toast before bed, and Mr. Olsen will probably come up the hill and take photographs, as he usually does on Wednesdays. He has a photography studio down on the highway."

"Do you think that if I gain a few extra pounds I could attract Bret's attention?" Colleen asked shyly.

Laura sighed. "You might be interested to know that yesterday morning Marietta was playin' around with some dolls she has on her bed. As I passed by her porch, she had the boy doll's arm around the girl doll, and she was sayin', 'Look, this is Bret!' Then she made the boy doll kiss the girl doll," Laura quipped.

"How would Marietta know?" Colleen retorted.

Faith answered, "If you ask me, Bret's just a great guy who likes a good laugh. Besides, Marietta told me that Bret went up on the roof a while ago with some family friends who brought a movie camera during a visit. She said he was clowning around with the women the way he always does, but she didn't say he kissed anyone!

"I've heard that he's quite devout," Colleen added in Bret's defense. "Do you think he would take more of an interest in me if I were Catholic?" Colleen asked.

Laura and Faith both groaned. Colleen looked at them, surprised by their reaction to an innocent question.

Julie interjected, "I think he's interested, all right, and so is Pete!"

Colleen blushed and said nothing more.

After dinner, as Miss Marthe was setting up the toaster and milk glasses, Colleen watched some men from the custodial staff walking along the sidewalk on their way back to their apartments. She saw Will, who had made foot warmers for them, trailing along behind. He had replaced a gutter on their porch that week. From a distance, he seemed to be trying to walk and juggle something, but Colleen couldn't see what it was. As he came nearer, he paused and then went around to Laura's side of the porch, laughing and talking excitedly to three tiny kittens that were clinging desperately to his shirt. The handsome Negro was grinning from ear to ear.

"Look, Miss Marthe, one of the resident cats had a litter of kittens! I brought three of her babies for everyone to see," he said, grabbing one by the scruff of the neck. He gently stroked the struggling kitten, and it settled down happily in the palm of his hand. "This one is going to be a very nice cat when he's grown. In my native Haiti, we had one just like him. You can hear his little *moteur* purring all the time. Listen, Laura! You can hear the *ronron*." He held it up to the screen. Laura listened hard, and a soft smile spread over her face as she tried to pet the kitten through the screen.

"Could the kittens come on the porch for a while, Miss Marthe?" Laura pleaded.

Miss Marthe nodded in agreement. "Perhaps ve can give them a saucer of milk," she replied as she concentrated on filling each glass. "If you go around to the front door, Vill, I vill let you in.

Will put the other two kittens in his shirt pockets for safer keeping and trudged off toward the front of the building, still holding his favorite in the palm of his hand.

Miss Marthe came back after a few minutes. Will followed her onto the porch. He placed each kitten on the floor, and they began to prowl around. Will's favorite one began to play with the hem of Laura's bedspread. Laura reached down and pulled the kitten onto her bed.

The kitten was mostly black, but he had a white bib and three white paws. "How did you lose the mitten on that front paw?" Laura asked the kitten.

"I'll just wait outside while the kittens play, Miss Marthe," Will said. "I'll come back when you want me to take them outside again. There are some boxes that I can sit on next to the screen on that side of the porch." He pointed toward Laura's bed.

"Mr. Olsen vill soon be here, and then you can take the kittens outside," Miss Marthe said kindly. "I vill just go and find a bowl they can drink from. Perhaps you could help by serving the milk to everyone, Vill."

Miss Marthe left the room to search for a bowl, and Will served each of the women a glass of milk and a plate for the toast. Then he excused himself and left the porch. After he had come around the side of the building, Colleen could hear him stacking some wooden crates. His face soon reappeared outside the screen. He put his fingers up to the screen, scratched against it, and the kitten immediately pounced. Laura laughed, catching the kitten as it bounced off the screen.

Colleen noticed that Will was not alone. On the sidewalk behind him, the Handyman stood staring and scowling at Will. Unaware that he was being watched, Will began to scratch on the screen, trying to get the kitten's attention. Night was approaching, and he was mostly in the shadows, except for the light that fell on his face and hands through the screen.

"Hey, black boy! What do you think you're doin' there? Spyin' on them pretty white girls?" he snarled.

Startled by the voice behind him, Will lost his balance and fell off the boxes. He jumped up quickly to face his accuser. Miss Marthe had already come back onto the porch and had heard what the Handyman said. Bristling, she said icily, "Vill had my permission to come onto this porch! He is vaiting to complete a job for me."

The other man squinted into the bright porch light at Miss Marthe and then glared menacingly at Will. "That's a mighty strange way to wait," he sneered. "It's after hours, and you don't belong there," he muttered. He backed away from the light and fled.

"Perhaps you can take the kittens back now, Vill. I don't vant you to get into any trouble. It was a very nice of you to bring them by. I vill bring them around to the front door for you," Miss Marthe said.

Laura looked very upset. She pressed the black-and-white kitten to her cheek. "I don't see why Will can't sit there and visit with us if he wants!" she protested hotly. "This little kitten is just too sweet. He's not like the other two. He looks like he's dressed in a little tuxedo! He's not meant to be a mouser! I'd like to keep him and take him with me when I go home!" Laura stroked the kitten and then buried her face in its fur. The animal was purring and nearly asleep. "What do you say, Miss Marthe?" Laura asked.

"Ve cannot keep cats on the porch, Laura! I vas probably wrong to let the kittens come inside. Perhaps Vill could bring the kitten here from time to time. You could vatch it grow up until you are ready to leave," Miss Marthe replied.

Will was listening intently to Miss Marthe. He looked over at Laura, awaiting her reaction. Laura looked hopefully toward Will. There was a silence on the porch, and then Will replied in a guarded voice, "I could do that if Laura was willing, ma'am."

Before Miss Marthe could say anything, Laura replied, "Please bring him by whenever you like, Will!"

Will nodded and then turned away from the screen and went around to the front door. Miss Marthe gathered up the cats and the bowl of milk. Darkness was descending as Mr. Olsen's booming laugh announced his arrival on the hill.

The next morning, Miss Marthe came onto the porch and told Abby that she would have to go over to the main building for another bronchoscopy. Abby's face turned ashen.

"Why do they have to do this to me, Miss Marthe? Don't make me go!" Abby wailed desperately.

Miss Marthe tried to soothe her, but Abby would not be consoled. She put on her robe and slippers, with a resigned sigh.

She turned to Miss Marthe and pleaded, "No one should have to go through this, not even the poorest of the poor, which I guess I am! It's not fair! How would you like to have a huge piece of metal rammed through your vocal cords and down into your chest, while being suffocated, and then have some awful chemicals sprayed into your lungs?"

Miss Marthe tried to reassure Abby that it would soon be over, but Abby was not deceived. Miss Marthe couldn't think of anything else to say, so she silently helped Abby into the wheelchair.

Julie said nothing, but her eyes were huge with alarm.

Faith murmured, "Don't cry, Abby, it won't help."

Colleen said, "Tell them you don't want it done anymore, Abby!"

Laura added emphatically, "And clench your teeth like you mean it!"

Laura's last remark elicited a small smile from Abby.

"They take out my false teeth before the procedure, ya'll. Do you think my bare gums will scare them?" Abby asked glumly, but she waved a forlorn "V" for victory sign as Miss Marthe wheeled her off the porch.

After Abby had been taken to the main building for her bronchoscopy, Miss Marthe returned to Colleen's porch with a note in her hand that she gave to Colleen. Colleen opened the folded card and read the note inside.

*The note said:* Meet me on the roof on Wednesday, after dinner. I may have found your book. Come alone.

The message was unsigned. If this was a message from the Handyman, why hadn't he signed it? Colleen felt a slight shiver go up her spine. She put the note in her pajama pocket.

Colleen lay in bed for an hour, worrying more about Abby than the mysterious note. Today was Colleen's birthday, and Abby's bronchoscopy had started the day out all wrong. The mysterious note had made things worse. Within an hour, however, Miss Marthe reappeared, pushing an ecstatic Abby in the wheelchair.

"They didn't do anything to me!" she told everyone. Her cheeks and eyelashes were still wet with tears of relief. Her hair was fluffy and curly, not matted and rumpled the way it usually was after the procedure.

"Can you believe it? No more bronchoscopies! They just called me over to tell me that they wouldn't be doing it to me anymore! Put me back in bed, Miss Marthe!" Abby said ecstatically.

The women all made a fuss over Abby's good fortune. After a while, they got out their crocheting needles and talked idly. When Colleen said that Abby's good news was the best birthday present she could get, they made a fuss over Colleen as well. Then out of sheer relief, Abby took a long, restful nap before lunch.

At eleven forty-five, the patients began shuffling down the hall toward the dining room. Colleen could see Pete and Bret standing together, waiting to be let in for lunch. Pete had a box in his hand, which he was showing to Bret. When Colleen approached, he quickly slid the small package into his robe pocket with a nonchalant smile.

"Hi, there, Colleen!" Bret sang out. "And how old are we today?"

"Sixteen!" Colleen exclaimed, surprised that Bret knew it was her birthday. Colleen felt ebullient, because she thought sixteen sounded much older than a mere fifteen. She felt as if she was at last catching up with the rest of them.

"And never been kissed?" Bret added inquisitively. Pete shot him a disapproving look.

"Happy birthday, Colleen," Pete said.

"Thanks, Pete! And I was kissed lots when I was a baby, Bret!" Colleen retorted.

"I stand corrected," Bret said, stepping aside to let the women go in first. Pete darted in front of Bret and sat down at Colleen's right just as Bret took the empty chair on her left. Laura arched her eyebrows from across the table. Abby still looked as if she were floating on a cloud. Bret and Pete sat looking at Colleen and at each other over Colleen's shoulders.

Charlie cocked his head toward Abby. "What's gotten into you, Abby? Are you ladies brewin' moonshine down on your porch and not tellin' us?"

"She had a nice, long nap this morning, Charlie!" Laura laughed.

Charlie suggested, "I think it was a nice, long nip! Where are you hidin' it, Abby?"

Abby laughed. "There's no moonshine, Charlie. They just told me I'm done with bronchoscopies!"

"Oh, that's swell news, Abby!" Charlie exclaimed.

When the food had been put on their tables, Colleen filled her plate with chicken, potatoes, and vegetables. It was a tasty lunch, which made her birthday more festive. To her surprise, she saw a small box beside her napkin. A large envelope with her name on it lay beside the box. On the other side of her plate there was an irregularly shaped bundle, wrapped loosely in newspaper and tied with a cord. Colleen moved the envelope out of the way so as not to splash it with food. "What's this?" she asked the two men, who were sitting there with pleased looks on their faces.

"Open them, and find out, Colleen!" Laura exclaimed, unable to conceal her curiosity.

Colleen suggested that they eat first. "They made us a nice chicken dinner, and it would be a shame to let it get cold," she explained.

Julie was not very hungry, and she was nibbling unenthusiastically on a drumstick. Abby looked at the uneaten chicken and said, "Julie, honey, if my poor ole mom was here, she would pick that bone clean! You should eat up!"

"It all starts to taste the same when you've lain in bed long enough to kill your appetite," Julie complained.

As soon as everyone had finished, Colleen opened Pete's present. She looked curiously into the small box and saw a silver music box in the shape of a piano. She located the key and wound it a few times. The music box began to play "Twinkle, Twinkle, Little Star."

"It has a faraway sound—just like the music you were telling me about in Claire's apartment, Pete!" Colleen exclaimed, looking at Pete with wonder.

"It was made in a town near Strasbourg, France, where Schweitzer grew up," Pete explained. "Open the envelope, Colleen. You'll find something inside that goes with the music box."

Colleen opened the large envelope and pulled out some sheet music by Mozart.

"These are the variations on 'Twinkle, Twinkle, Little Star' that you told me about!" Colleen exclaimed.

Pete pointed to the French title. "They're called, '*Twelve Variations on Ah! Vous Dirai-Je, Maman.*' Mozart wrote them for his mother."

Colleen turned the title page and looked through the twelve variations. Pete said, "The first one is really simple. It's written in quarter notes like the children's song. See, Colleen? Then Mozart begins the variations. Some of them are grand and almost operatic."

Colleen looked at the last pages, admiring the intricacies that such a simple tune could produce in the mind of a genius.

"You can learn to play them when you get home, or even here, if they ever let us get out of bed!" Pete said.

Colleen looked at the birthday greeting Pete had written in pencil across the top of the music. It said, "Until you find your lark, will a music box do? Love, Pete."

"What a perfectly unexpected and beautiful present!" she exclaimed. "Is this the music box your mother gave to you? I really shouldn't ..."

Pete looked so crestfallen that Colleen simply said, "Thank you, Pete, for such a wonderful present."

Colleen turned to the other package beside her plate. "Is this from you, Bret?" she asked.

"Why, yes, Colleen, I believe it is," he replied, with mock surprise.

Colleen shook the package and could hear the tinkling of a small bell inside the newspaper wrapping. She pulled on the cord and the newspaper wrapping fell off. Inside was a horse made out of crocheting yarn. Bret had somehow found a jingle bell, which he had tied to the horse's neck.

"If we can't go to the Oakton Stakes, why not bring the horses here?" Bret joked. "I call him Sea Biscuit."

Colleen read the note on the card that Bret had attached to the horse. It said, "Sea Biscuit was the little horse that nobody respected until he beat the superior competition. He put his heart into it and won." He shot a quick look at Pete.

"Thanks so much, Bret. You shouldn't have!" Colleen exclaimed.

"It was really Miss Marthe's idea. She suggested that I make a yarn doll for my mom. When Pete said your birthday was comin', I made this little horse instead. Happy birthday! And many happy returns of the day," Bret said warmly.

"Thanks, Bret! The horse is very cute. His eyes look so hopeful!" Colleen exclaimed.

Pete cleared his throat and stared at Bret. There was a flicker of distrust in Pete's dark-brown eyes.

"I'll keep both of these presents in the pockets of my bed," Colleen said. "Thank you both, very much!"

When dinner was over, the patients began to file back to their porches. Colleen and the rest of her porch mates left almost immediately, but Pete and Bret remained seated. Bret stretched his legs out comfortably under the table and said, "That was a nice party for Colleen, wasn't it?"

"Yes, it was. I think she enjoyed herself," Pete agreed. "She's growing up. She's not the uncertain girl she was back in the old building."

"She liked the music box very much, I think," Bret said.

"I've had that music box since I was a child, but I want Colleen to have it now," Pete answered.

"Why is that?" Bret asked.

"Music enchants her, for one thing. I also want her to remember me when we finally get out of here. Maybe I'll go look her up when we've both recovered," Pete said, watching Bret to measure his reaction. "I gave her the sheet music because she's interested in composition. That's where her passion lies."

"She's a great girl," Bret answered, "but don't forget that opposites attract. There's more to romance than a common interest. Like they say, variety is the spice of life." Bret casually looked over at Pete to judge his reaction.

"Is that why you promised to take her to the Oakton Stakes?" Pete asked.

"Well, why not? She said she would love it. She said she admires the power and beauty of horses."

"Maybe, but she's still too young to pair off with anyone around here!" Pete declared, a bit heatedly. "We're all too old for her."

"Well, I think we should let Colleen figure that out," Bret suggested, with an unperturbed smile. "As you say, she's not a young girl anymore."

"You don't agree that she's too young?" Pete queried.

"I think you should trust the woman you love," Bret replied.

Without another word, Bret got up and left Pete alone with his thoughts.

That evening Will returned with the black-and-white kitten. Miss Marthe allowed Will and the cat to come onto the porch again, and while he was there, Colleen showed him the mysterious, unsigned note. Since Colleen wasn't allowed to go upstairs anymore, she asked Will if he would be her substitute. Will agreed to help her.

"I don't know who the note is from," Colleen explained, "but I think it may be from the Handyman, the fellow who took my book from the hall."

Will seemed eager to help Colleen but was disturbed by the daring tone of the anonymous note.

"You should not ever go up there alone at night, Miss Colleen!" Will exclaimed. "There wouldn't be anyone around if you needed help at that time of night. The custodial staff would all be at home by then. The Handyman probably won't like it when he sees that you sent me, but I think he will give me the book. If I tell him that you saw him take it, I don't see what other choice he would have than to return it."

Colleen thanked Will and gave him the note. After a short visit, Will left with the kitten. Colleen looked out into the darkness and saw the light of a cigarette glowing not far from the pile of old boxes stacked by the screen near Laura's bed.

# Crickets' Chorus

On the first day of June, Colleen awoke to birdsong and the sweet smell of newly cut grass. As soon as breakfast was over, she returned to her lounge and dressed in a pretty, pink shirtdress that she had borrowed from a woman on the second floor. Colleen put on her best shoes, combed her hair, and then applied some lipstick. She moved her toes inside her high-heeled pumps, enjoying the sensation of her feet inside leather. It felt dressed up merely to be wearing shoes.

Miss Marthe came in to tell Colleen that the cab had arrived to take her to the doctor's office in Oakton. She handed Colleen Dr. Kurtz's note to the doctor, which Colleen tucked inside her purse. There was another note in her purse as well, which she had received from a married patient named Bill the previous evening. Bill's note asked if Colleen would buy him a carton of cigarettes. He had enclosed five dollars. Colleen hadn't wanted to do it since he shouldn't be smoking when he was so ill and he had a family to think of, but she didn't want to tell him no. She had sent him word that she would buy him a carton of cigarettes if there was a drugstore near the doctor's office.

Miss Marthe took Colleen's things and helped her into a wheelchair. When they reached the front parking lot, Colleen saw that the cab was already waiting. The driver opened the door for her cheerfully and helped Colleen into the back seat. Miss Marthe gave him the address of the doctor's office in Oakton.

"You haf an eleven o'clock appointment, Colleen," Miss Marthe told her. "I know the doctor. You vill like him, I'm sure. Enjoy your day out!"

Colleen was unfamiliar with Oakton and was relieved to hear that Miss Marthe liked the doctor she was being sent to see. As the cab descended the long driveway, Colleen opened her window. "I'm used to a lot of fresh air!" she said to the driver.

"No problem, miss," he replied. They reached the bottom of the hill and turned onto the main road to Oakton. As they came into the center of the city, Colleen caught glimpses of elegantly dressed mannequins in storefront windows. She also saw young mothers pushing babies in baby carriages, a sure sign the war was finally over.

The cab driver finally stopped at a two-story building on a busy street. "This is it, miss!" he said. Colleen thanked him and paid her fare. She entered the narrow building and took an elevator to the second floor. The doctor's office was opposite the elevator, and there was only one other office on the corridor.

A nurse looked up from the desk and smiled pleasantly when Colleen entered the waiting room. Colleen told the nurse who she was and looked around. There were several young pregnant women sitting in the chairs. Colleen felt like a fish out of water. She took a seat and waited to be called.

After about fifteen minutes, the nurse took Colleen's temperature, pulse, and blood pressure. She weighed Colleen and then escorted her into the doctor's office. Dr. Stevens read Dr. Kurtz's note and asked Colleen some questions. After examining her, he drew some blood. He said he agreed with Dr. Kurtz, and he reassured her that her hormones would come back into balance as she continued to improve and gain weight. The he wrote down some instructions for Dr. Kurtz.

Colleen tucked the instructions inside her purse and, with a sigh of relief, left the doctor's office. She looked down the short corridor and saw a balcony with a wrought iron railing. The sun was streaming in the balcony window. Colleen walked to the end of the hall and peered over the balcony rail, trying to see if there was a drugstore nearby. The passing traffic made her a bit dizzy. She steadied herself and then bent over again, this time leaning as far out as she dared.

She heard the other office door open, and then two voices shouted in unison, "Don't!" Colleen looked back in total surprise and nearly lost her balance. Two nuns, one tall and willowy and the other short and plump, were hurrying toward her, their eyes the size of goose eggs.

"I'm all right!" she said. "I just felt woozy for a moment. I needed a breath of fresh air after the seeing the doctor. I was looking for a drugstore," she faltered, not exactly certain why they were continuing to stare. "It's still early. I have plenty of time," she said, nonplussed by their solicitude. "I need something ... for a friend," she finally added.

The nuns nodded as if they had saved her from a terrible fate. "We know how it is, my dear girl!" one of them said very piously as she looked back toward the obstetrician's office. They smiled knowingly at one another.

The three rode the elevator together down to the first floor. The nuns kept smiling in obvious satisfaction at having saved Colleen from a terrible fate. When they got to the lobby, the taller nun said, "There is a drugstore about half a block down on the other side of the street. Perhaps you will find what you need there." The shorter one quickly added, "Never forget, my dear, that God knows your every need!"

Colleen looked down, trying to avoid their gaze and finally said, "I know." Then she hurried away before they could say anything else.

She crossed the street in the middle of the block without looking back at the nuns and entered the drugstore. Colleen glanced around the empty store and saw a young clerk not much older than herself working behind the counter. She walked up to him and asked to use the telephone, and then she added in an offhand manner, "Oh yes, I would also like a carton of cigarettes." She gave him the brand name Bill had asked for.

The clerk looked Colleen up and down, trying to guess her age. He finally said, "You're a little young to start smoking, aren't you? Does your mother know you smoke?"

Colleen answered quickly, "I can't. I have TB. It's for a friend."

The clerk drew back in surprise.

"Please, he's dying of TB. It's his dying request!"

"Well, in *that* case," he said sarcastically. Nevertheless, he handed her the cigarettes. Colleen thanked him, and then the clerk pointed down the street. "There's a public phone down on the corner. Keep the cigarettes in the bag until you leave here."

Colleen gave the clerk Bill's five-dollar bill, received change, and rushed out of the store before the clerk could change his mind. She nearly collided with the nuns who had by then caught up with her. The bag dropped to the ground, and the carton of cigarettes fell halfway out. Colleen made no attempt at an explanation. "Excuse me, please! I'm in a hurry!" she exclaimed as she again rushed off, feeling like an exceedingly fallen woman. She heard the taller nun say to the shorter one, "Act in haste, repent in leisure!"

When she reached the corner, she saw a phone booth and pulled out a card on which Miss Marthe had written the telephone number of the taxicab company. Colleen dialed and got the dispatcher. He asked where she wanted to be picked up. "I'm at the drugstore," and she told him the name she had read over the door.

The dispatcher responded, "Miss, there are at least five of those in Oakton. Which one is it?" Colleen looked down both streets and saw nothing but bustling crowds of people coming out of their offices for the lunch hour. It seemed to Colleen that she was on the corner of Busy and Busier. Her head pounded, and she was hungry and tired. She looked up and read the corner signpost. "I'm at Melville and Wilkes. Could you come quickly, please?"

The dispatcher told her that a cab would be there within ten minutes. Colleen sighed and sat down on a street bench. Behind her was a small, city park. An elderly black man was standing at a bus stop near the intersection. He looked tired and worn out, although it was only noon. When the bus arrived, he got on at the rear door and took a seat in the back of the bus. The white people on the bus sat talking in their seats at the front of the bus. They paid no attention to him. The old man looked out the window at Colleen and nodded his head wearily. Colleen thought about the kitten that Will had brought them out of friendship—or perhaps out of simple compassion.

She suddenly recalled the image of a group of destitute black men in a history book photograph of New York City during the Depression years. The image of their poverty had remained with her as something that was deeply wrong and unfairly beyond their control. The conditions were much worse than anything she had known in Carlton.

Colleen asked herself how a person could truthfully say that he or she didn't know about such things. She knew that poverty and segregation were wrong, and she presumed others knew that too. The problem was that most people were too "busy" to look at what was going on around them to think about who counted and who didn't. This kindly old man on the bus simply didn't count. He was a missing puzzle piece that no one seemed to notice—even though the picture had a great big hole in the middle of it.

Colleen had almost completely forgotten about the world's busyness; life at Sherwood had begun to take on a timeless quality. Sherwood had given her a new perspective on things but not a completely right one, she realized—at least not until Will had come into the picture.

Colleen could not help thinking about a fellow patient who had called Colleen's long legs "aristocratic" one night in the dining room. The same woman had approached Colleen one morning in the ladies' bathroom. She seemed fixated on the fact that Colleen was caring and considerate despite her good looks. "You could be really stuck up if you wanted, but you aren't," she had said.

Colleen had been surprised by the remark, which she considered very odd. There was something craven and obsequious in the old woman's rodent-like eyes. Colleen had studied her for a moment, and then she had asked, "But why would I do that?"

The woman had looked befuddled, and Colleen had turned away without another word.

As Colleen looked at the old man seated at the back of the bus, she knew that "aristocratic" long legs didn't "make" a man or woman any more than their clothes or the color of their skin did.

Colleen thought about how kind Will had been to all of them. She looked into the old man's eyes, but he self-consciously turned away from the window.

As the bus pulled away from the corner, Colleen saw the nuns walking up the sidewalk toward her. She wanted to avoid speaking to them again, so she closed her eyes and pretended to be resting. Colleen glanced up as the nuns passed, but they seemed not to notice her. She shut her eyes and kept them closed until she could no longer hear their voices. She supposed they felt they had done their best with such a wild young woman. She obviously no longer counted as something for them to do today. With her eyes closed, the nuns ceased to exist for Colleen too. When Colleen finally opened her eyes, she watched the nuns cross the intersection, and then they were gone. They had passed into someone else's picture puzzle in a different part of the city.

The taxi had pulled up in front of the doctor's office, so Colleen walked back down the street with the bag of cigarettes tucked under her arm. She carefully folded the top of the bag so that the cab driver would not see the contents. She knew she shouldn't be taking Bill the cigarettes. It *was* a somewhat wild and crazy thing to do, she had to acknowledge.

Within half an hour, Colleen was back at Sherwood, and she was in time for the last part of lunch. She walked down to the dining room and found her porch mates still eating. Bret was keeping them company, although he had already eaten and had taken his plate and utensils back to be washed. There was no sign of Pete.

"How was your trip to Oakton?" Laura asked.

"It was nice to get out and see the city, even if it was just to go see another doctor!" Colleen replied. "I bought some cigarettes for Bill."

Bret looked at Colleen with a surprised look on his face. "Bill's family is here today for a visit," Bret said. "His kids are out on the lawn playing. They aren't allowed inside. They put Bill in one of the private rooms. His wife looked pretty worried when she came upstairs to our ward."

Colleen nodded. "I can't believe he wanted cigarettes in his condition!"

Colleen looked around, noticing that Pete was not there. "Where's Pete? Didn't he come to lunch today?" she asked.

"He came, but he ate quickly and went back upstairs," Laura answered. "We thought it was because you weren't here. You don't suppose there's any connection, do you?" she quipped.

"Not really," Colleen rejoined. "He looks tired sometimes. I worry about him, that's all."

Bret nodded in agreement.

Pete at that moment was taking the elevator up to the third floor. He stepped out of the elevator, looked around guiltily, and then paused in front of Claire's apartment door. He was about to knock when Dr. Edmonds came out of his own apartment. He looked surprised to see Pete.

"Well, hello, Pete! What brings you up here? Not another piano recital, I hope," Edmonds joked.

"Actually, I thought I had left some music in Claire's apartment," Pete replied.

"Why would you need music?" Edmonds inquired a bit suspiciously.

"It was a birthday gift to Colleen," Pete mumbled, wondering if he was being convincing.

"Well, Claire's probably still at work in Dr. Smith's office, since today is Wednesday. She sometimes leaves at noon on Fridays to go visit her fiancé and his family on the weekends. She's going to be married, you know," Edmonds observed.

"Who's the lucky guy?" Pete asked, eager to change the topic of conversation.

"He's a sailor. Real nice guy! Quite a bit younger than Claire. They're crazy about each other," Edmonds replied.

"That's swell, Dr. Edmonds!"

"She usually leaves her door unlocked because nobody ever comes up here but Dr. Collins and me. We could try to see if the music's in there," he said, testing the doorknob. The door opened easily. Pete could see the beautiful grand piano through the open door.

"That's okay," Pete said. "I'll wait until the next time she comes down to the dining room. There's no hurry."

Pete went over to the elevator and pushed the button.

"Hold the elevator for me, Pete!" Dr. Edmonds exclaimed. "I almost forgot my bag."

Pete waited impatiently by the elevator, his plan in temporary limbo.

Dr. Edmonds went back inside his apartment and picked up his doctor's bag. The two men stepped into the elevator together. Pete got out quickly at the second floor without saying another word.

When the elevator opened at the nurses' station, Dr. Edmonds saw Colleen crossing the atrium. He strode over to her and told her that Pete had been looking for her music. Although she knew that the Mozart variations were tucked safely away in her bed pocket, she replied that Pete had mentioned to her that he was looking for them. They were a birthday present, she explained, and to her relief Dr. Edmonds seemed satisfied.

"Happy birthday, Colleen!" he said cheerily as he took his leave to go over to the other building.

Pete did not return to bed when he got out at the second floor. He waited by the elevator and pushed the button for the third floor again. When he reached the third floor, the elevator doors opened, and he peered out to make sure no one was around. He quickly strode across the landing and knocked on Claire's door, but there was no answer. He called her name, and there was still no response.

Pete turned the knob and continued to knock on the door as he opened it. The apartment was silent and dark. Pete entered and walked quietly to the piano. He shuffled through the music and found a Chopin waltz that he especially liked. He set it on the music rack and began to play. When he had finished playing the piece, he replaced the music in the middle of the stack. Beads of perspiration stood out on his forehead. He sat still on the piano bench, deep in thought. He played a few phrases over again and then got up slowly, steadying himself against the piano top. Pete thumbed through the music to see what else Claire had in the stack. There was an impressive selection from Bach to Rachmaninoff. Pete was ecstatic.

"Good girl, Claire!" he whispered to himself, and then he left as quietly as he had come.

By five o'clock that evening, Will had finished work and was climbing the stairs to the roof of the new building. He wasn't sure what he should say to whoever had sent the note to Colleen about her missing book. Expecting to find the Handyman waiting on the roof, he looked up at the closed door at the top of the stairs and hesitated. He listened and heard nothing.

He climbed the stairs quietly and then warily opened the door to the roof. The slanting rays of the sun caught his eyes and temporarily blinded him, but in that brief moment, he saw the silhouette of the Handyman against the sky. There was a look of disbelief on the Handyman's face, which quickly turned to rage.

"Colleen sent me. I came for Colleen's book, if you have it," Will said as pleasantly as he could. "She will be very pleased to get it back."

The Handyman had his hand in his right pocket. The other pocket bulged, revealing the outlines of a rectangular object. He said nothing, but his eyes smoldered with hatred.

"Colleen sent me," Will repeated, holding out his hand, but still smiling.

"Why didn't she come herself?" he asked. The hand in his pocket never moved.

"She's not allowed out of bed," Will replied.

"But she's allowed to have cats and black men pay her visits?" the Handyman snarled. "You can just tell her that I don't have her book, boy! Who do you think you are?"

The Handyman's hand began to stir restlessly in his pocket. Suddenly, there was a glint of a pocketknife as his hand flashed out of his pocket. Will drew his own hand away instinctively, but he was too late. The blade caught the side of his hand. It had obviously been kept keenly sharp, and Will's hand began to bleed. Will grimaced and stepped back, drops of blood falling profusely at his feet.

"Let that be a warning to you to mind your own business!" the Handyman sneered as he pushed Will aside and fled down the stairwell. Will pulled a handkerchief from his pocket and wrapped his hand in it. He waited a few minutes before he also left the roof.

As it was Wednesday, the evening had been scheduled as a toasting night. Will brought the kitten again for Laura to see as he had promised. The young man sat quietly on the stack of boxes, holding the kitten up so that the women could admire it. He placed it next to his cheek and joked, "It looks a little bit like me, don't you think?"

After a while, the women went back to talking quietly among themselves, except Laura who was nearest the screen. Colleen could hear Laura and Will talking, but she could only hear snatches of Will's words. After a while, she heard Will telling Laura about his childhood in Haiti.

Then Colleen heard Laura ask him, "So how is it different here?"

Colleen couldn't hear Will's answer because he had lowered his voice. She saw him point to a blood-stained bandage on his hand.

Colleen watched as Will opened his book of poems by Langston Hughes. He began to read from it in a low voice. Colleen heard Laura ask him to read some more, and Colleen wished she could hear what the poems were about.

When they had finished their toast and milk, Miss Marthe weighed everyone. She was especially pleased with Colleen's weight. "You haf gained seven pounds since you've been at Sherwood, Colleen! Keep up the good vork!" Miss Marthe removed the trays and left the porch to put the scales back in a closet.

Julie had borrowed a radio from someone so that she could listen to a favorite radio show. After it ended, the station started playing boogie-woogie music. Colleen tapped her toes, and Julie suddenly jumped out of bed. "Come on, Colleen!" she exclaimed. "Let's cut a rug. We're fit as fiddles!"

Colleen needed no further encouragement. The two young women began to jitterbug for all they were worth. Colleen didn't know many moves, but Julie did. Her big black eyes sparkled as she passed Colleen under an arm and around her back. "That's it, Colleen!" she exclaimed.

As Colleen danced by the screen, she saw Mr. Olsen, the photographer, laughing merrily as he watched the girls. He raised his camera and quickly snapped a picture in the gathering dusk. "Hah! Caught for posterity! Wait until Dr. Edmonds sees this! Shall I send copies to your parents to let them know what a nice vacation you girls are having up here?"

Julie and Colleen jumped back into bed. "You wouldn't!" they laughed. "It was just this one time!"

Mr. Olsen came onto the porch. He quickly spied the tray that Miss Marthe had left out for him. He rubbed his abdomen and sighed. "You, too, can pack on a few pounds if you continue to eat cinnamon toast!" Will had been about to leave, but he sat back down to watch what Mr. Olsen was doing.

Mr. Olsen ate his toast, but didn't touch the milk. Instead, he offered it to Colleen. Colleen declined because she was full.

"Give it to me, Colleen. I'm still thirsty," Julie said.

"I think I will call the photo, *The Dancers*," Mr. Olsen teased them. He offered to take a still picture of Julie. Julie smiled shyly as he snapped a photo.

Then Mr. Olsen spied Will through the screen. "Who's this?" he asked in surprise. Then he saw the perfectly marked kitten and exclaimed, "Ah! What a gorgeous animal! Animal shots are hard to come by at Sherwood. Come in, young man, and bring your pet!"

Will glanced uncertainly at Laura. Laura explained that Will was one of the maintenance men at Sherwood and that he brought the kitten around every week so that the women could see it grow up. Miss Marthe had come back onto the porch, and she invited Will to bring the kitten in.

"It's quite all right, Vill." She turned to Mr. Olsen. "Do you think you could get some nice pictures of the kitten for us? Laura vould like to keep him as a pet vhen she goes home. Vill is taking care of him for her. It vould be nice for her to haf some pictures of him vhen he vas small."

"If Will could help me with the lights and calm the animal until I'm ready to shoot, that will be no problem," Mr. Olsen said agreeably.

Will brought the kitten onto the porch, squinting in the bright light. He paused by Colleen's bed and whispered, "The Handyman claimed that he doesn't have your book, but I'm certain he had it in his pocket! He cut me with his knife when I asked him for it!"

Colleen gasped in dismay.

Will turned to face Mr. Olsen and held up the kitten for him to see. "Where would you like me to put him, Mr. Olsen?" Will asked, wincing as the kitten struggled to get comfortable in his injured right hand.

"Over there on the end of Laura's bed, please," Mr. Olsen

suggested. Laura pulled up her legs under her, and Will placed the kitten on the end of the bed. He scratched its ears, and it began to purr. It was soon fast asleep.

Will helped Mr. Olsen set up two lights. When the camera flashed, the kitten sat up. Mr. Olsen took another quick shot, and it darted off the bed.

"Mind if I take your picture, Will?" Mr. Olsen asked. He had Will stand over by the screen at the end of Laura's bed. Colleen heard something move beyond the porch screen, and then Mr. Olsen snapped the picture.

"I'll bring these back next week," he said. "I think that is enough for now. Sorry to be so late tonight! You were a big help, Will. Maybe you can help me with the lights and set up when I come on Sundays. There's usually plenty of work because of the visiting families."

Will thanked him and said he would be glad to help. He gathered up the kitten.

"By the way, Will. What is the kitten's name?" Mr. Olsen asked.

Before Will could reply, Laura said impulsively, "His name is Langston Mews! Right, Will?"

"That's a fine and distinguished name, Miss Laura," Will laughed. He scooped up the playful kitten and left without another word.

"Good night, Will. Thanks for bringing him by," Laura said appreciatively. "And sleep tight, Mr. Mews!" she added. The cat meowed a good night.

"Ach! He is a talking cat! Mr. Mews is a very special little fellow!" Miss Marthe laughed. "I haf cats myself, but none of them can talk!"

The following morning brought a thunderstorm before breakfast. The wind gusted strongly as the storm passed, and the awnings flapped wildly and barely kept the women dry. By noon, the sun had come out, but the day was unusually cool for June. Colleen put on her robe and started walking toward the dining room for lunch. She stopped at her locker in the hall and pulled out a pair of socks from one of the drawers. Her locker was on the end of the hall and adjacent to the atrium. The contents could easily be seen by passing patients. It was the least private locker on the hall.

A voice behind Colleen said, "Boo!" It was Bret. Colleen jumped and turned around to face him.

"Must you do that?" she asked him sternly, in mock anger.

"It got rid of your hiccups last time, didn't it? You sounded kind of drunk walkin' down the hall that way, as I recall," Bret reminded her, teasing Colleen about a night a few weeks earlier.

"You're always the gentleman, Bret! I don't like people peeking at my underwear, that's all," Colleen answered.

"What makes you think I'm interested in your drawers, Colleen?" Bret asked innocently.

At that moment, Pete walked by on his way to the dining room. He heard what Bret said, paused slightly, and then kept on walking. Bret blushed at the unintended pun. He looked at Colleen and broke into a hearty laugh. Colleen looked at Bret and burst out laughing, too, because he was such a bright red. She watched Pete walking down the hall, knowing he could hear them laughing together.

Colleen and Bret followed Pete into the dining room and sat down. Colleen found an empty chair next to Laura. Bret sat next to Pete at the edge of the group. Laura told everyone about Mr. Mews and how she planned to take him home with her. Pete looked up with interest and smiled. He was obviously an animal lover.

"I wish I could see him!" he exclaimed. "That's awfully nice of Will to bring him around in his spare time."

"Last night he told me about growing up in Haiti," Laura said. "The rest of his family is still there, except for one brother who lives in Chicago. Will read a few of his favorite poems by Langston Hughes to me. They were good."

"I noticed he carried a book by Langston Hughes in his back pocket the first day we met him," Colleen recalled.

"He's quite interested in books and writing," Laura added. "He said he'd like to work someday for the big Negro newspaper, the *Chicago Defender*. He speaks French and knows Haiti, and so he's hopin' they could find a use for that. That's his dream, anyway. He said there's a lot of poverty and political unrest down there that ought to be written about. The ruling whites and part-white people have most of the wealth."

"I thought Haiti was an all Negro country," Abby said.

Pete spoke up and said, "My mother had a childhood friend who lived for several years in Haiti. He told her that when the French came after Columbus, they imported African slaves to work their plantations. Sometimes they had children by their female slaves. When the slaves revolted, Napoleon tried to put them down and failed. Haiti became the first black republic, but the French still dominate it, with the help of the US Marines!"

Bret began to make something out of his napkin when he heard Pete mention Napoleon. At first, Colleen thought it was a paper boat, but when Bret was done, he put it on his head like a hat. Then he stuck his hand inside his robe and started humming "La Marseillaise."

Bret reached for the desserts, which had been placed in the center of the table. "Well, Napoleon got his "just desserts," and I think I will get my dessert—or should I say my desserts, since none of you seem interested!"

Eight hands reached simultaneously toward the center of the table as the group rushed to beat Bret to the apple cobbler.

After finishing her dinner, Colleen returned to her room. She fell asleep promptly and heard nothing for two hours. Toward the end of the rest period, she was awakened by a loud bell, which sounded three times.

"That's the emergency bell! Someone must be dyin'," Faith said mournfully. "I've only heard it two other times, an' that's what happened."

Within an hour, word got around that a patient named Hank had hemorrhaged to death in front of his porch mates on the second floor. It was Bret's and Pete's ward.

Pete and Bret came to supper that night looking ashen and upset. Neither had ever seen anyone die at Sherwood, although they both knew it was always a possibility. When Colleen had seen Hank at his last fluoroscopy session, he had looked sallow and tired, but she had not imagined that he would die.

Pete said, "It was over very quickly, and it was very bad. He was very frightened and struggling for air. There was nothing anyone could do. Emile called the nurse, but Hank was beyond help."

No one said anything for a while. Charlie, who was a rib patient, said, "They do everything they can for us, even take out our ribs, but sometimes it catches everyone by surprise. They're sending Tom out for a lobectomy in Oakton next week, by the way."

Nobody said anything more about Hank. After a while they talked about other things in subdued tones.

Colleen returned to the porch and thought about her own situation. Her sputum had been negative for many months now, but her lung refused to stay down. Dr. Kurtz was considering pumping even more compressed air into her chest. Colleen wondered how she would be able to breathe if he did that. He said he would have to check with Dr. Smith. The problem was that Colleen's lung simply would not stay down long enough to close the cavity.

It is too elastic and healthy, *Colleen thought uneasily.*

Colleen didn't want a surprise like the one Hank experienced. She lay down quietly in her bed, feeling her breath going in and out shallowly. She longed to run and breathe deeply, the way she had done as a little girl. What a foolish chance she and Julie had taken by jitterbugging! Colleen thought about the fruit trees that blossomed every spring in the backyards of her neighborhood. She wished that she could inhale deeply and breathe in their sweetness, but one spring had already come and gone. How many more would pass until she could breathe freely again? Dr. Kurtz had no definite answer for her.

Abby's piping voice penetrated Colleen's thoughts. "Colleen, listen to me," she said, trying to get Colleen's attention. "Pete is planning a skit for the Halloween party in October. He wants to play the Mozart variations so that you can hear them. There's a *Butterfly* Etude by Chopin that he wants you to play while I dance as a butterfly."

"That sounds great!" Colleen exclaimed, excited by the idea of a Halloween party. "Would I have to dress up as Chopin?"

"You could be a lady from that era, Colleen!" Abby suggested. "I want to be a butterfly dressed in a black gown with sequins and diaphanous wings and wear a hat with little antennae," Abby said, imagining herself in such a costume. "What do you think, Colleen?"

"I think blondes have all the fun!" Colleen exclaimed. "They always look beautiful in black!"

"Really?" she said, beaming. "Sewing on sequins will give me something to do. Bret thinks you should play the *Moonlight* Sonata so that I can turn into a *moth*. Can you imagine me turning into a moth after playing a beautiful butterfly? I told him nothin' doing! That boy has a twisted sense of humor!"

"What's Bret going to be?" Colleen asked, hardly daring to imagine what Bret might come up with.

"He hasn't said. He wants it to be a surprise," Abby said with a giggle. "Pete also wants you to play the *Minuet in G*. He said it's the one by Beethoven. He said you would know it."

Colleen nodded. She had learned that piece and it was fairly easy for her to play.

"Maybe I could be Martha Washington or somebody from that time period," Faith volunteered.

"In that case, I could be George Washington and dance a minuet with you, Faith," Laura suggested.

"Is there something I can be?" Julie asked, feeling overlooked and forgotten.

"Can you juggle?" Abby asked. Pete says he wants to include a piece called "The Juggler." If you can't juggle, you could clown around with the juggling."

Julie's large black eyes sparkled. "That's perfect. I'll do it!" she exclaimed.

"Now all we have to do is get Pop Smith's permission," Laura added uncertainly.

As Laura was speaking, Colleen heard a mewing sound and saw Will outside the screen. He called to Laura from the sidewalk, "Look, Laura, you must see how Mr. Mews is learning to go for walks with me," he said, smiling and pointing to the kitten out in the grass. "He is almost as smart as a dog."

Laura looked at the kitten running in the grass. "You'd better catch him, Will. It looks like he's out for a run—not just for a walk," she laughed.

Will caught the kitten, who was romping through the grass after lightning bugs. Will waved good night to them. "I must be going back to my room. I will see you next Wednesday when Mr. Olsen comes."

The women wished him a good night and went back to talking quietly among themselves. Laura watched Will and the kitten until they disappeared from view.

On Sunday afternoon, Mr. Olsen arrived at Sherwood with his camera and lights in tow. He crossed the parking lot and looked for Will, who was supposed to meet him at the main entrance. Will was standing on the front sidewalk, involved in what looked like a one-sided tirade by a man Olsen had never seen before.

Mr. Olsen heard the fellow say, "You're just using that cat to get on the porch with the lady patients! You wouldn't mind cuddlin' in their laps, just like that cat, I'll bet. That cat's livin' out your dream! But you ain't got no call bein' in a white woman's bedroom at night like that. You Frenchies may think it's okay, but it ain't done in America, see? It ain't *natural* not stickin' with your own kind. You must think people can't see through them screens, or maybe you just think you're different because you speak French! Well, you ain't! You're an uppity foreigner who doesn't understand that he ain't white and he ain't special." The Handyman turned to walk away and snarled over his shoulder, "This is your last warning, black boy!"

He sauntered down the sidewalk, nodding deferentially as he passed Mr. Olsen, and then he entered the hospital. Will said nothing and looked a bit embarrassed when he realized Mr. Olsen had overheard what the man had said.

"What an unpleasant fellow!" Mr. Olsen exclaimed. "I asked you to help me, Will, because I know how highly Miss Marthe thinks of you. When I told her I needed an assistant, she suggested that you might like to learn photography on the side. If you have some spare time, perhaps you could come to my studio in the evenings. I can show you something about cameras and developing. My wife would like to spend more time doing other things now. I could really use an extra pair of hands in the dark room. What do you say? Are you interested?"

"I am most interested, Mr. Olsen, and I thank you very much," Will replied. "Don't worry about that guy. He doesn't know what he's talking about. Miss Laura wants me to bring the kitten around so that she can see it, and I only go on the porch when Miss Marthe asks me to do so."

"Well then, good! You could help me in the evenings each weekend and, of course, on Sunday afternoons. We can start today. Let's go in, and I'll show you how to place lights and a little bit about *f*-stops.

There's a family visiting today who has requested a group photograph. They're right here on the first floor."

Will helped pick up some of the equipment and started down the sidewalk with Mr. Olsen. "That is where I met Miss Laura and Miss Colleen," Will said, pointing to the upstairs porch. "I made some foot warmers for them out of cylinders and light bulbs," he said shyly, eager to convince Mr. Olsen that he would be a capable assistant.

"I'm sure the women appreciated them last winter," Mr. Olsen said as he opened the door and held it while Will carried in the rest of the equipment. Mr. Olsen pointed down the hall to a porch on the right side. "It's down there," he said. "Let's get to work!"

On Wednesday, Will brought Mr. Mews for a visit as usual. He said nothing to Laura about the ugly incident over the weekend, but he told her he had a part-time job with Mr. Olsen. Laura was thrilled. Will sat on the boxes and fed a small piece of his sandwich to the kitten. Will picked up Mr. Mews and put the kitten in his lap when he had finished eating.

"Why do you suppose that some people do not treat each other as well as they treat their pets?" Will asked.

Laura looked startled. "Well, I suppose a pet is content with simple things like food, a warm place to sleep, and fitting into the family," she said. "Human beings are more demanding and judgmental."

Laura placed her fingers against the screen and tried to get Mr. Mews to play. Will unconsciously placed his fingers against the screen, lost in thought. Laura could feel his fingertips through the screen. She had never touched a black man before.

"And why do some individuals treat people who are different badly?" Will persevered. Will moved his fingers to a different place on the screen, but Laura followed with hers. Will looked at her hand thoughtfully, but he kept his fingers against hers.

"I suppose there could be a lot of things that make a person mean,"

Laura replied.

"What do you think makes a bully?" Will persevered, deeply interested.

"I suppose a parent or his friends might admire his power and encourage it, rather than teaching him to get along," Laura said. "They might tell him some people are zeros and that it's okay to hurt them, or he might live in a country where he has the right skin color, or religion, or the right amount of money so that he simply *can* be a bully!"

"And why do you think people bully people who are of a different race?" Will persevered.

"Because they can't imagine that it's possible for everyone to be happy! They're ignorant and frightened and can't see that people are people," Laura said quickly. "They're lost in the herd and follow a bad shepherd. They don't follow Jesus. Is that what this is all about, Will? You don't think I'm like that, do you?" Laura asked anxiously.

"No, Miss Laura, you clearly are not." Will took his fingers away from the screen.

Laura said quietly, "Put your fingers against the screen one more time and listen to me." Will hesitated and pressed his fingers against Laura's again. "There are screens between people, Will, because something has made them sick. It's never healthy for there to be screens between people," Laura whispered.

"Does the bully know that, Miss Laura?" Will asked. "Does he know that he is sick?"

"I don't know," Laura answered, peering out into the darkness. "You'll have to ask the Handyman when he shows up some night. That's what this is about, isn't it?"

Will nodded his head and quietly told her what the Handyman had said to him on Sunday.

Will waited awhile for Mr. Olsen to appear, but Miss Marthe came out onto the porch and said that he would not be coming tonight. "He asked for you to come down to his studio, instead of meeting him here, Vill," Miss Marthe said. She gave Will a scrap of paper with Mr. Olsen's address written on it. "It is not far from the bottom of the driveway," she added. "It's on the left. You vill see his sign."

Will said good night and left to put Mr. Mews back in his room before starting down the hill to Mr. Olsen's studio.

As he walked toward his room, he listened to the crickets singing in the night.

*They are listening to one another and trying to understand the circle of their community*, he thought. Then Will thought of the Handyman, and the metallic chorus of the crickets in the night suddenly sounded like dull, pocket knives opening and closing upon themselves.

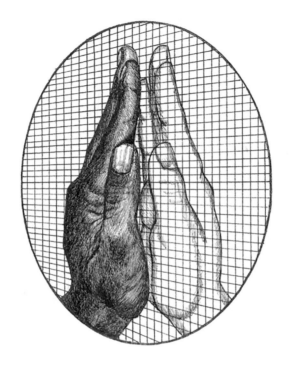

*It's never healthy for there to be screens between people.*

# Lazy Summer Blues

When Will entered his apartment, he immediately placed Mr. Mews in a basket with the two other kittens, which were sleeping soundly. He put on a light jacket and cap because of the unusually cool weather and stepped back out into the night air. The moon was on the wane, and only a few stars were visible in the cloudy night sky.

As Will set out for Mr. Olsen's studio, he met Skippy coming down the path. Will had gotten to know the dining hall worker while working on a stopped kitchen drain in the new building. Skippy had spent the evening at a local pub and was in a jovial mood. He looked at Will, put an arm around him affectionately, and began singing, "Sometimes I feel like a motherless child!" Will said good evening to him and tried to get by, but Skippy grabbed Will by the arm and sang an encore. "Don't you know that song, Will?" he asked.

"You go inside and have a nice cup of coffee, *mon ami*," Will suggested. "You should get out of this chilly night air!"

Skippy nodded and headed for the door. He entered his apartment, and Will could hear him fumbling around with some pots. Skippy sang out lustily, "Sometimes I feel like an eagle in the air!" There was a loud crash as some pots crashed to the floor from an overhead cabinet. There was a pause, and then Will heard, "Sometimes I feel like a mournin' dove!" There was a longer silence and then, "Long way from home!" Will heard Skippy grumbling as he picked up the pots and put out the lights.

Will took a shortcut across the lawn and headed toward the main hospital building. He followed the path, which skirted the east end of the hospital and ended at the parking lot. The lights had already gone out on most of the porches, but he was still able to see by the lamplight in the parking lot.

He started down the long, steep drive. Overhead, he could hear the wind blowing wildly though the tops of the trees. It was very dark, and he stayed in the middle of the drive, trying to avoid the edges of the ravines.

About halfway down the driveway, Will thought he heard footsteps behind him. He paused and listened. Will walked a few steps farther and felt something hard hit him on his left shoulder. Will watched a large rock skip along the side of the driveway and hurtle away into the darkness of the ravine. He quickly whirled around and saw the figure of a man running back toward the hospital.

"You!" he yelled after the fleeing figure. The man paused, did not turn around, and then ran out of sight. Will rubbed his bruised shoulder. The rock had barely missed his head.

Will listened as the sound of the man's footsteps faded into the night. He wondered whether he should turn back or continue on. He thought that ambush was possible in either direction because his assailant might not be alone. Will started down the hill again, running as fast as he dared in the pale moonlight.

By the time he reached the bottom of the driveway, he was panting and out of breath. He waited as a few cars passed by, and then he crossed the road. The light from an old 1930s' roadhouse and gas station illuminated one side of Mr. Olsen's Victorian-style house. A sign in his front yard advertised his photography business.

Will waited as an attendant filled up a car with gasoline at the roadhouse. After the attendant went back inside and the car had pulled away, Will looked around to make sure he was not being followed. Then he walked on down the road. He reached the Olsen house and climbed the front porch stairs. He looked back down the road. No one was there. There were lights on in the living room, and Will could see Mrs. Olsen sitting in a chair listening to the radio and knitting. She looked up as Will rang the doorbell, and then she rose to answer the door.

"You must be Will!" she exclaimed. "I'm Roslyn Olsen, Jim's wife.

Please come out of the chilly night air. My, but it's cool for this time of year." Mrs. Olsen was an attractive woman with dark hair that hung loosely to her shoulders. She was slim and seemed much younger than Mr. Olsen.

"I'm very pleased to meet you, ma'am," Will said, taking off his cap.

"Jim is downstairs in the dark room. I'll let him know you're here," she said. She disappeared down the kitchen stairs, and Will waited. A studio opened off the living room. Inside the studio, Will saw lights and a camera mounted on a tripod. There were boxes covered with rugs as well as a trunk containing hats and other props. The walls were a very soft pink, and dark green floral drapes framed the windows.

Mr. Olsen came into the room and greeted Will cordially. "I'm so glad you want to learn to do this, Will," he boomed. "I really need the help!"

"It will be my pleasure, Mr. Olsen. I would like to learn a profession," Will replied.

"You won't mind being around the chemicals and working in the dark most of the time?" Mr. Olsen asked.

"Oh no, sir," Will replied.

"Good!" he exclaimed. "Let's go down and get right to it then! Afterward, Roslyn will make us some tea, won't you, my dear?"

Mrs. Olsen nodded pleasantly. "As soon as the two of you are ready," she replied.

Mr. Olsen led Will downstairs, and they entered his dark room. After Will's eyes adjusted to the low light, he saw a row of liquid-filled trays, which were lined up in succession. A few prints were submerged in the last tray. There was an enlarger along the wall and a closet in the corner where Mr. Olsen loaded his film into his camera.

Mr. Olsen explained what the chemicals did in the various steps of printing. Then he began making prints of the film he had shot the night Will had brought Mr. Mews onto the porch. When they got to the photo of Will, Mr. Olsen said, "What's this?"

The two men bent over the newly made print. The camera's flash had caught the shadowy figure of a man standing on the edge of the light cast from the porch. The man's hostile expression was unmistakable. Will remembered the Handyman's snarling threat and Miss Marthe's defense of his own presence on the porch.

"Why, this is the same man who insulted you on Sunday," Mr. Olsen exclaimed.

"He is the very one," Will agreed. "He ..." Will hesitated a moment and then continued, "He accuses me of desiring the white women on the porch. He twists what he sees, and he falsely attacks my intentions. Now he is trying to frighten me." Will told Mr. Olsen what had happened as he came down the driveway and how the Handyman had cut him with his knife on the roof of the new building.

Mr. Olsen looked at the wound on Will's hand and said, "This is serious business, Will. I think I'll drive you back to Sherwood tonight. In fact, I'll drive you back and forth from now on until we get to the bottom of this."

Will thanked him, and then the two men finished printing the rest of the film. Mr. Olsen explained the reversal of dark and light in the negatives and the restoration of true white and black in the prints.

"This is the only way for whites and Negroes to change places and see themselves in a new light, eh Will?" Mr. Olsen exclaimed, looking at the Handyman's blackened face in the film negative.

"Black or white, he is still the same man!" Will exclaimed.

Will studied the darkened features of the Handyman. "A photograph does not always show the inner man, except perhaps in the expression of the eyes and eyebrows," he observed. "And sometimes in the way the body is carried and in the turn of the mouth. Sometimes, everything is hidden by a false smile. That is when a man is most dangerous."

"And what does this picture tell you, Will?" Mr. Olsen asked.

"It tells me that this man did not know he was being observed," Will replied. "It shows me that under the cover of darkness, he has a secret self. He has two selves, but I believe that neither of them is under his own control. His has forfeited his true self, and perhaps it has been lost forever to the control of others. He thinks that by stealing my dignity, he can increase his own. I do not understand how a man can sell his soul for the perverse pleasure of hatred. I can understand his fear. At heart, he is a coward. Even so, I cannot understand his strange pleasure."

Will said nothing more.

Mr. Olsen showed Will how to make prints from the negatives. He made a test strip while Will watched. Will was very interested in the transformation from negative to positive and wanted to know more about the chemistry. Mr. Olsen went and found a booklet about the photographic process for Will to take home and study. Will took it upstairs with him when they were through for the evening.

As it was very late, Mrs. Olsen made some chamomile tea and served some bread and jam with the tea. Mrs. Olsen asked Will about his life in Haiti and all about his brothers and sisters.

"I have one older brother in Chicago," Will said. "I would like to go and visit him this year. It has been a long time since my last visit there."

Mrs. Olsen had relatives in Chicago, too. The two of them compared notes about the busy city. When they had finished their tea, Mr. Olsen rose and told his wife that he would be driving Will back to Sherwood. He did not mention what had happened. Will thanked Mrs. Olsen for the tea and bread and wished her a good night.

As the two men rode up the driveway, Mr. Olsen suggested that Will tell Miss Marthe what had happened to him in the driveway that night. "Someone on the staff should know about these things, in case there's any more trouble," he said.

Will promised Mr. Olsen that he would tell Miss Marthe. Mr. Olsen told Will he would meet him next Wednesday in front of the new building. "Let's see if my presence and a car ride to and from my studio will be of any help. Perhaps it will scare him away," he said, trying to sound unworried.

Will furrowed his brow in thought. "It might be better if I just stay away," he said.

"Nonsense," Mr. Olsen said.

Will got out of the car and crossed the parking lot. Mr. Olsen watched as Will went down the path along the side of the building, and then he turned the car around and drove back home. As he began to descend the hill, he saw a man on the side of the driveway strike a match and light a cigarette. He had his hat drawn over his face. The flash of the match had illuminated his face for only an instant. By the time he reached the bottom of the hill, Mr. Olsen realized who it was. Mr. Olsen smiled to himself in grim satisfaction, glad that he had offered Will a ride.

The week passed uneventfully for everyone. There were no more deaths. On Wednesday night, Will brought Mr. Mews for a visit and then left in Mr. Olsen's car. He watched for the Handyman through the car window as they went down the drive, but he saw no one.

Also on Wednesday, Colleen made a new friend in an older woman named Marguerite. She preferred to be called Daisy, the English translation of her French name, which she found pretty but too formal. Colleen had met her while waiting for the dining room to open. When Colleen found out that Daisy was Catholic, she told her that she wanted to learn more about Catholicism. Daisy was pleased by Colleen's interest and suggested that she meet with a priest who sometimes came to Sherwood to minister to seriously ill patients.

Colleen made arrangements to meet the priest, and a few days later she met with him in the library. The priest asked Colleen about her religious background and why she wanted to study Catholicism.

Colleen said that a friend had inspired her interest.

"He's a patient here at Sherwood," Colleen explained, preferring not to mention Bret's name. "Marguerite and I have been talking about religion, too. She suggested that I see you."

"I see," said the priest. "I will give you a book, which you can study, and a rosary, which you can use in prayer. The next time I come, I'll try to answer any questions that may arise in your mind as you study the catechism."

Colleen thanked the priest, grateful that she did not have to tell the whole truth about her interest in Bret. She felt a slight twinge of guilt as the priest shook her hand and thanked her for their talk, which he said he had greatly enjoyed.

Colleen saw Pete look up in surprise from his bed when Colleen and the priest left the library together. He smiled and waved. Colleen hid the rosary in her pocket and then poked her head into the doorway of the men's porch.

"What's up, Colleen?" Pete asked. "I hope no one is sick at home!"

"Oh, no, my family is well. Since we don't have services here, I felt the need to talk to a clergyman, that's all. They sent a priest."

Pete looked disappointed. "I thought you and I could talk freely about such things."

Colleen returned to her porch and opened the catechism. She spent the rest of the afternoon reading. When it was time for dinner, she walked down the hall to the dining room, lost in thought.

By the time Colleen reached the atrium, she could see that the dining room doors had not yet opened. She joined Daisy and told her about her meeting with the priest. Daisy was pleased that Colleen been studying the catechism. "He said to write down any questions I have so that we can discuss them next time," Colleen confided. "I already have a question," she added.

"What is it, Colleen?" Daisy asked curiously.

Colleen hesitated. "Well, I was just wondering whether the world's religions are all variations of one universal religion. Something Pete said made me think that." Colleen was thinking about Pete's concept of God as a pure and distant melody. "You know, like variations on a beautiful theme. There might be many ways to understand God, depending on a person's experiences," Colleen said.

Daisy looked at Colleen thoughtfully. "The Catholic Church has teachings that are considered infallible, Colleen, but our missionaries' experiences help add to our understanding of God. I suppose you could say they help us hear God's voice through new melodies."

Colleen could see Bret approaching. He came over quickly to the two women when he saw Colleen. "How are the two most beautiful women at Sherwood doing today?" he asked, looking at Colleen.

Colleen laughed. "We were just talkin' about religion, Bret."

Seemingly inspired by the idea, Bret stared at the locked, dining room doors and commanded, "Dining room, give us this day our daily bread!"

Skippy came over to the doors and looked out at Bret through the glass panes. "Mr. Bret, you goin' to get fed just as soon as we finish puttin' it out!" he exclaimed.

Bret sniffed the aroma of roast chicken wafting from the dining room and said to Daisy, "Seek and ye shall find manna in the desert of the Sherwood dining room!"

"Bret, if you were in the desert, all the women would be waiting on you and bringing you your manna," Daisy joked good-naturedly, but she half meant it.

Seeming to take this last remark as a compliment, Bret responded by putting his arms around both women. "It is better to give than to receive! I'll just leave you two ladies to your philosophical pursuits," Bret said as he withdrew to join Emile.

Pete had joined the gathering crowd by now, and he came up to

Colleen and said, "Bret really believes what he just said, you know."

"What do you mean?" Colleen asked.

"Let's just say, he loves everyone as he loves himself," Pete laughed, but not unkindly. Skippy opened the dining room doors, so Pete said nothing more as everyone filed in.

During dinner, the conversation seemed to drift aimlessly. Only an occasional breath of air wafted through the open windows. Despite the oppressive July heat, Bret was in high spirits, and he wasn't about to let his companions' torpor ruin his dinner.

He stared around the room at the sea of wilting and perspiring people. His high spirits began to sag. He felt too good to be dragged into the undertow. He looked at Charlie, who was sitting across the table from him. Charlie was picking at his food. Pete was slumped on one elbow, and Emile was mopping the perspiration from his face as he gulped down large quantities of iced water.

"It'sa hotter than southern Italy in August!" Emile complained.

Faith and Laura were fanning themselves with their napkins. Colleen eyed Bret as he clicked his knife against his water glass and announced, "Will this meeting please come to order?"

Julie sat up alertly and said, "What do you want to talk about, Bret?" Then she yawned as widely as a cat.

Bret's eyes gleamed. "There was a message left at the nurses' station in the atrium. God called, and he said he wants us to 'Wake up!'" he shouted. "We're supposed to call back."

The entire dining room looked up. "You go answer it, Bret!" someone suggested. "It's for you!" There was general laughter, and Bret frowned in irritation. He felt the tide of boredom returning, and he knew he was being sucked into it. It was a feeling he could not tolerate.

"Just take a good look at us!" he exclaimed in a quietly disgruntled tone. "We sleep through lunch, and then we sleep through the rest period. That's so that we can get up and sleep through dinner so that we have a good night's sleep." Bret pointed out the window in exasperation. This is *Sherwood*, for heaven's sake. We're sleepin' our lives away! That's *our* forest. Where have all the merry men and maidens gone?" he asked.

Everyone groaned.

"It's too hot to do anything but sleep, Bret," Charlie said. "We'll eat, drink, and be merry later. It's ninety degrees in the shade, but you can go out there if you want. We're all too hot to stop you," he added with a laugh.

"Daisy and I were talkin' about religion just now," Colleen said, hoping to steer the subject onto religion and hoping it didn't overstep the line of dinner etiquette. She was eager for an answer to the question she had posed to Daisy in the hallway. "Since Bret raised the question of sleeping and dreaming our lives away, here's a question that ought to wake us up. Do you suppose all religions express a universal dream of mankind?"

Bret stared at Colleen as did the rest of her tablemates.

"Well, Colleen, if I remember my Genesis rightly, things got off to a pretty bad start when Adam and Eve chose the snake's dream," Bret said as he ran his finger around the top of his glass, seeing if he could make it ring. "Maybe trying to be as smart as God is mankind's universal dream."

Colleen tried to ignore Bret. "It has to be a dream that works, Bret. And anyway, everyone dreams at night, so dreams must be important. What if our dreams and the dreams of the world's religions are just variations on a universal dream? What would that dream be?" she asked, thinking of the catechism book the priest had given her.

"Eve thought bein' as smart as God would work for her! And for Adam too!" Bret reminded her.

"What do *you* think, Colleen?" Faith asked, trying to ignore Bret.

Colleen thought a moment and said, "Well, if we treated each other in the spirit of the Golden Rule, wouldn't that be the dream of every religion?"

"Personally speaking, my only dream is to get off the Sherwood merry-go-round," Faith sighed. "Then I think I could be happy forever! I'd *never* sleep again. I'd live my life till I dropped."

"It'sa not so bad here," Emile said. "You can always crochet something lovely and share it with someone like your wife!" he smiled. "Life is justa like crocheting! Sharing your crocheting is justa like spreading Jesus's mustard seed."

"What if you can't afford your dream?" Abby asked. "My mom has been dreamin' for years about havin' enough to eat, and it never seems to happen, no matter how hard she works."

"And what if someone's nightmare drags you into it, too?" Laura asked, thinking about Will and the Handyman. "Didn't the German Jews have dreams? Why did their dreams have to go up in smoke in Hitler's crematoria? Didn't their dreams count?"

Pete finally said, "When a monster like Hitler has a vicious dream and the means to carry it out, he has to be stopped before it's too late. That happened in France when Zola exposed the Army's treachery during the Dreyfus affair. Zola saved an innocent man, and along with him, he saved the honor of France. Sometimes one man doing the right thing is all it takes."

"That's what the Nuremburg trials are all about. I wish I could be there to see them!" Laura exclaimed.

"Hitler tried to destroy *God's* dream with the 'Final Solution'," Pete said. "I wonder how far down the chain of command they'll go at Nuremburg and where they'll finally draw the line between the merciless and the merciful."

"Hitler's dream of a master race appealed to the worst in the Prussian spirit," Laura said angrily, still thinking of Will and the Handyman.

"Hitler obviously didn't fear God's judgment!" Colleen exclaimed. "I wonder what his last thoughts were when he took cyanide in his bunker."

"The Allies were closing in on him. Maybe there was no time to think," Bret suggested.

"Maybe he said, 'Nuts!' justa like General McAuliffe at the Battle of the Bulge," Emile said, grinning.

"The Allied bombing must have taught him a final lesson about the reality of raw power," Laura said.

"And the reality of mothers and children going hungry," Abby said sadly.

"Maybe *sturm und drang* were the only two things he *ever* understood," Charlie added.

"I think he only heard the pounding of his heart," Faith said.

"And the solitude and guilt of his 'Final Awareness'!" Julie exclaimed.

"I wonder if God's melody seemed very, very far away to Hitler in the total dissonance of defeat," Pete asked softly. "*Sturm und drang* means shock and awe. Awe is supposed to be reserved for God."

Then Colleen added, "He must have thought war and violence could drown out the voice of God!"

"Or he thought he could *be* God, which is the sickest dream of all," Bret said quietly.

Daisy had been following the discussion with interest from her end of the table, but it had begun to make her head swim. She pushed back her chair and said, "Well, the wages of mercy and the wages of sin are a lot to think about. Although they're pretty obvious in Hitler's case. I have a slight headache. For now, I think I'll go back to bed … and sleep," she laughed.

Colleen felt upset. She hadn't meant to open a can of worms or to frighten Daisy away.

After Daisy left, everyone began to eat again, this time with gusto. A feeling of peace and calm settled over the table as the memory of war passed.

Colleen looked up from her meal when she heard Abby turn to Pete and say, "I'm going to ask Miss Marthe for some sequins and gauze for my Halloween costume. They must have material left over from last year." Abby had visualized her costume down to the last detail. It had been on her mind ever since Pete first suggested doing skits for the Halloween party.

"Dr. Kurtz is going to inject 750 cc's of air into me the next time I go for pneumothorax," Colleen added. "I don't know if I'll be up to playing piano with that much air in me, Pete," she said, not too optimistically.

Pete was dashed by Colleen's comment, but not defeated. He again outlined his plan for the skits. He emphasized that Colleen's piano piece was not difficult. "You won't have to pound the keyboard, Colleen," he reassured her. "The question, of course, is whether Pop Smith will allow us to attend. If we go ahead and make our costumes, maybe he'll consider it a *fait accompli*. I'm sure you'll be fine, Colleen."

"Having a chest full of air is better than having rib surgery, Colleen. You don't want to end up like me," Charlie reminded her.

Colleen sighed. "I know, and I'm sorry they had to do that to you, Charlie. It's just that I've missed an entire year of school so far, with no end in sight. I'm beginning to understand how hard it is to grow up on a sanitarium porch."

Colleen looked at Pete and remembered his forfeited scholarship and his mother's death. "We've all lost a lot," she corrected herself. "I'm sorry. I guess I've got a bad case of the lazy, summer blues," she sighed.

After they had finished dinner, Colleen walked to Daisy's porch and stopped briefly to chat with her. "I was hoping we would get back to my original question about religion, but we ended up talking about other things. You didn't mind, did you?" Colleen asked.

Daisy studied Colleen for a moment. "Your friends are very different," she said. "A group of us meet on Sunday before the dining room opens for lunch. We talk about religion in a more structured way. Why don't you join us some time so that we can discuss your questions?"

Colleen thought that would be interesting, so she quickly agreed to join Daisy's group. She said good night to Daisy and returned to her porch.

On the following morning, a van came to take several patients over to the main hospital for another round of fluoroscopy. Colleen got into the van reluctantly. She was not looking forward to having so much air pumped into her chest. It was a hot July day, and the van was quite warm, even with the windows open. Miss Marthe looked flushed and tired. It had been a busy morning for her.

The fluoroscopy room felt cooler and was a welcome relief from the heat. Colleen stepped into the dimly illuminated room, which was shrouded in the eerie, green glow of the fluoroscope, and she saw that Dr. Edmonds was sitting in front of the machine instead of young Dr. Billings. Colleen was a bit disappointed because she enjoyed Dr. Billings's boyish charm. Dr. Edmonds was always so businesslike. Colleen stepped in front of the screen, and he examined her lungs. "They're still not staying properly compressed, Colleen."

"How is the cavity in my lung?" Colleen asked.

"Somewhat better, I should say," Dr. Edmonds answered. "When you go over to the treatment room, you can talk to Dr. Kurtz about it."

Colleen entered the treatment room and found Dr. Kurtz patiently waiting. He gave her a warm smile. He told her that she was doing well, but he felt it would still be a good idea to increase the amount of compressed air.

Colleen lay down on the treatment table with a sigh. "Let's go ahead and get it over with, then," she said unhappily. Then she remembered Dr. Billings. "Why wasn't Dr. Billings working the fluoroscope today, Dr. Kurtz?" she asked.

Dr. Kurtz's expression quickly turned from jovial to a look of concern. "He's very sick, I'm afraid, Colleen. They've moved him into a private room. That's never a good sign. He's been in there for a week. I haven't heard the exact diagnosis."

"Could it be TB?" Colleen asked. Dr. Billings seemed too young and healthy for that.

"He was exposed to the machine's radiation, of course. He was also exposed to a lot of sick patients. We will just have to wait and see."

Colleen heard Dr. Kurtz turn on the gas, and then she felt the pressure in her chest. It was about as much as she could bear. When the procedure was completed, Dr. Kurtz said, "I hope this will hold down your lung, Colleen. I've given you a large volume of gas, but it may do the trick. We shall see."

Colleen didn't say a word. She couldn't. The van came for her, and she sat silently in her wheelchair on the way back to the new building. She was glad to get back into bed, and she rested for the remainder of the morning, intent on keeping her breathing steady. At lunch, she walked listlessly down the hall to the dining room. She sat quietly throughout the meal, only picking at her food. Bret offered to walk her back to the porch after lunch. It was the highlight of an otherwise bleak day, which stretched on for another three days until Colleen felt she could breathe more freely again.

On the second day after Colleen's treatment, Abby volunteered to go up to the library and pick out a book for Colleen to read while she recovered. Abby was now allowed up for one hour a day. She had already gained back most of her weight, and her mood was bright because the bronchoscopy treatments had been discontinued. However, when she returned with a book in hand, her eyes were round with horror.

"You won't believe what I just saw!" Abby exclaimed. "Somebody jumped off the roof! I saw him falling through the air outside the library window. He landed in some empty bottles near the trash bins in the parking lot. He was moanin' and hollering for help." Colleen could hear an ambulance siren in the distance.

"I think it was Mr. Perkins! I just couldn't look. Here's your book, by the way, Colleen. When I stepped out of the elevator, I heard a big commotion in the atrium, so I figured they knew what was goin' on. That must be the ambulance comin' for him right now!"

"He's on the same porch as Bret, Pete, and Emile!" Faith exclaimed.

Julie's eyes were huge. "He's an old man. How could he survive a fall like that?"

"Maybe he didn't fall," Laura said solemnly. "He shouldn't have been up there at all. He might have gone up there deliberately."

"He might have slipped," Abby suggested, totally horrified.

"They didn't sound the emergency bell, so maybe he'll be all right," Colleen said. "Maybe Bret and Pete will know what happened."

As they walked down the corridor to the lunchroom, Abby asked Colleen, "Why would he jump into all that glass? It must have cut him up badly."

Laura stared at Abby. "I think the sudden stop would be worse, Abby!"

When they got to the dining room, a crowd had gathered in front of the doors. Everyone was talking in subdued voices about what had happened. Laura pulled Colleen aside and said, "I have other news for you, Colleen."

"What could possibly top somebody jumping off the roof?" Colleen asked.

Laura lowered her voice and said, "Emile told me Bret has a crush on you."

Colleen raised her eyebrows in surprise. She didn't have time to reflect on Laura's news, however, because the doors of the dining room opened, and everyone began to file in.

Colleen sat down next to Laura, Faith, and Julie. Bret and Emile soon came into the dining room, but Pete was nowhere to be seen.

"Where's Pete?" Laura asked.

"He said he'd be down in a little while. He was feeling a little tired today," Bret replied. "Maybe it was all the excitement. It seemed to drain him. I guess he's okay."

Abby anxiously asked, "How's Mr. Perkins?"

"Miss Jackson said he was pretty banged up, but he'll pull through. They took him to the hospital. He was depressed because a nurse gave him the cold shoulder two weeks ago. He had a crush on her, despite the difference in their ages. This morning he said that he felt old and washed up. Lonely, I guess," Bret mused. "He felt like he was never going to get out of his bed again. He must have figured the roof was the only way out."

"The poor man!" Abby exclaimed. "I couldn't look after I saw him in a heap in the parking lot."

"Maybe he thought that if he jumped, somebody would care," Faith said. "Maybe he thought jumping would get the nurse's attention again."

"Maybe he thought he was Superman!" Emile exclaimed. "When I was a little boy, I jumped off the barn one time justa trying to fly. I broke my leg!"

"Maybe we shouldn't speculate on someone else's pain," Laura said.

At that moment, Pete came into the dining room and sat down at the edge of the group. He looked tired and drawn, Colleen thought. He didn't say much during the meal and only looked up occasionally at Bret or Colleen. After lunch, Bret walked with Colleen as far as the atrium elevator, while Pete followed slowly at a distance.

"Colleen, sometime I'd like to talk to you alone about Pete. Maybe we could meet somewhere private."

"You don't mean up on the roof do you?" Colleen asked.

"Well, that's a possibility. Sure, why not?" Pete had caught up with them, so Bret stopped talking. Colleen walked back to her porch, wondering what Bret had to say about Pete that was so private.

On Sunday morning, Colleen joined Daisy and a few other women who were standing together in a group near the dining room entrance.

"Good morning, Colleen!" Daisy exclaimed enthusiastically. "We were just talking about faith and hope."

"What do you mean?" Colleen asked.

"Oh, just that God is forgiving and loving, that everyone has to accept the cup that God gives him to drink from," another woman said rather piously, "and that God will never give us a burden that is too hard to bear."

Colleen thought that they must have been talking about Mr. Perkins. She said nothing until the conversation turned to other topics. After a while, they talked about Paul's meaning of the gifts of faith, hope, and charity. They talked about what it meant to see through a glass darkly. One of the women wondered if Mr. Perkins viewed life in that way.

Colleen thought of what Laura had said about not speculating on another person's pain and said nothing.

Meanwhile, Laura had spotted Will in the atrium. Will was pacing back and forth, waiting for Mr. Olsen, and he did not see her come up behind him.

"How are you, Will?" she asked. He looked up and smiled with pleasure.

"I am very well, thank you. It is nice to see you walking around. You look healthy that way," he said.

"How is Mr. Mews?" Laura wanted to know.

"He is growing so quickly now, Laura! He's hardly a kitten anymore. There is just one thing," he said, his forehead wrinkling in concern. "I might not be able to bring him around from now on."

"What do you mean?" Laura asked. "Why not, Will?"

"The Handyman speaks harshly to me every time he sees me. When we work together, he makes remarks about you and me. He has suggested certain things. Yesterday he warned me not to bring Mr. Mews onto your porch any more. He said, 'I wouldn't do that if I were you.' I think he would like to get me fired if he could, but I don't think he will succeed at that. He is not clever enough, but he may try to harm Mr. Mews or me in order to frighten me away."

"He can't do that. You've done nothing wrong, Will. You should tell Miss Marthe, right away!" Laura replied.

"That is what Mr. Olsen suggested, too," Will answered. "I cannot prove anything, unfortunately, and nothing can be done in your country without proof. He is a sly one, the Handyman. He leaves me no other choice than to wait for him to act or to stay away from your porch."

"Please don't stay away, Will. We enjoy seeing you and Mr. Mews so much!" Laura answered unhappily. "All of us do. And I would like to hear more of your poems."

"I am sorry if I have worried you," Will said. "Everything will be all right, Laura."

At that point in their conversation, Mr. Olsen came into the atrium with a packet of photos to show Will. Laura went back to the porch and wondered whether she would see Will on the following toasting night.

## Flitter the Butterfly

Miss Marthe came bustling onto Colleen's porch one afternoon with some sheer fabric and a box of sequins, which she handed to Abby. "These vere left over from last year's Halloween party, Abby," she said. "Perhaps you can make butterfly vings out of them."

Abby wiped beads of perspiration off her brow and inspected a remnant of sheer material that Miss Marthe had found.

"I can make lovely wings out of this, Miss Marthe, and sequins will add to the effect!"

Abby pulled at her curls, which were matted around her ears because she had lain on her side during the rest period. It was a stiflingly hot August afternoon. The heat wave had burnt out the grass in many places on the front lawn. The awnings only provided partial shade on the porch, and the glare of the sunlight forced Abby to squint as she looked at Miss Marthe.

"You'll need something to stiffen them, Abby," Laura pointed out. "Will might know where to find the right kind of wire."

"Are there any wigs in storage?" Laura asked Miss Marthe.

"Why don't you just braid your hair and powder it?" Faith suggested. "Isn't that what George Washington did?"

"Abby and I made some summer pants cut off at the knees that could pass for riding pants, Laura," Colleen suggested. "Wealthy men like George Washington wore white stockings in those days. I'll bet that Miss Marthe would lend you a pair of nurse's stockings."

"I hope you're not suggesting that the nurses look like George Vashington, Colleen!" Miss Marthe exclaimed.

"Only if you braided and powdered your hair, Miss Marthe!" Laura teased. Then she added, "I wonder where I can get hold of a long jacket fitted at the waist to go with the cut-off pants? Do you suppose anyone has a jacket like that?"

Julie added, "I have to be a clown juggler. I need a baggy costume and a silly hat."

"What about Emile's big slippers and pajamas and maybe a night cap?" Faith suggested. "I'll bet that would work! You could paint your nose and cheeks with lipstick."

"The kitchen staff might even let you use pie tins to juggle with, Julie," Abby suggested. "Speakin' of pies, wouldn't a big piece of lemon meringue pie and some iced tea taste wonderful right now?" Abby asked. "It seems like I'm hungry all the time! I *must* be getting better!"

As the women discussed their favorite summer foods, Abby put away the sequins and sheer material, anticipating that it would take Will a few days to find some suitable wire for her butterfly wings. She took out a pad of paper, sketched the details of her costume, and then held up the drawings for everyone to see. She had drawn a long, black dress, and beside it a side view of the dress and wings. The wings were covered in sequins. "Do you think I should wear a little black mask?" she asked. "Butterflies have black faces and bodies, don't they?"

While the rest of the women discussed the details of their costumes, Colleen picked up the book that Abby had checked out of the library for her. It was a copy of *Madame Bovary*. Colleen looked curiously at the cover. It showed a demure woman whose dark brown hair was pulled back in a bun. The bodice of her long dress buttoned primly at the neck. Her dark eyes held a hint of some brooding mystery. All the rest of her seemed provincial and ordinary. She didn't look like a woman of flaming passions, Colleen thought. She didn't even look like a social butterfly. Colleen glanced again at Abby's sketch, which seemed so delicately innocent, and she wondered what could have caused a woman like Emma Bovary to dare to dream such wild dreams.

Colleen was still thinking about Madame Bovary as she walked toward the dining room at noon. Her thoughts were interrupted when she saw Bret waiting impatiently by the elevator. He pulled her out of the passing crowd and whispered, "Eat quickly and meet me on the roof. I'm going to skip dinner. I ate some stuff Mom sent me from home. I told Pete I wasn't hungry. He thinks I'm still in bed."

Colleen nodded, not understanding why they had to meet on the roof. "I'll eat as quickly as I can."

Colleen entered the dining room and found Pete and Emile sitting with her porch mates. Pete looked up and smiled at Colleen when she sat down. Colleen began eating her dinner as quickly as she could without speaking to anyone. Laura noticed and said, "I suppose all that talk about pies made some of us pretty darned hungry."

Colleen laughed. "I just want to get back to my book. It's really good," Colleen said, trying not to draw attention to herself.

"What are you reading, Colleen?" Pete asked.

"*Madame Bovary*," Colleen replied.

Pete looked surprised. "That's an amazing book. She gets herself, her husband, and her child into a terrible predicament. She was amazingly obsessed with passion and sex."

Julie looked up innocently. "Why?"

"She was of the Romantic School, with a capital *R*," Pete said, smiling. "You'll love it, Colleen."

Having bolted down her food, Colleen exclaimed, "Sounds good!" Then she rose and said, "If you'll excuse me, everyone, I'm going back to bed," and she left before anyone could ask her any more questions.

Colleen walked through the atrium and took the elevator to the third floor. Claire's door was shut, and there were no sounds coming from behind it. Colleen's heart beat faster as she remembered that she had promised Dr. Kurtz not to go to Claire's apartment anymore. She slowly climbed the stairs to the roof.

When Colleen reached the top of the stairs, she was out of breath. She stepped onto the roof and found Bret peering over the ledge. He pointed down to the parking lot and quipped, "Mr. Perkins was either a brave and desperate man, or else he had no depth perception!" Bret stepped back from the edge with a queasy look on his face.

Colleen laughed. "I'm not a fan of heights, either."

Bret sat down in the sun, leaning his back against the stairwell door. "Have a seat, Colleen. You look tuckered out."

Colleen sat down next to Bret. The sun was hot and she was perspiring from the effort of climbing the stairs. "So what's the big news about Pete?" she asked.

"Well, for one thing, Pete doesn't seem very well to me," Bret said. "Also, I've seen him take the elevator to the third floor several times during the past month. Last week, I waited about five minutes and followed him upstairs. Sure enough, I heard him playin' Claire's piano. When he got back to the porch, he claimed he had gone to the bathroom to wash up after lunch. He went to Claire's apartment after dinner that day, too. My hunch is that he does the same thing every weekend when she's away. I just wanted to warn you in case he tries to drag you along. I wouldn't like to see anything happen to you, Colleen," Bret said.

Colleen was shocked. "He had a small hemorrhage over in the old building, and he has dark circles under his eyes again," she said pensively. "I know he loves to play the piano. It's almost as if he can't live without it."

"Well, perhaps you should tell him it's not worth riskin' his life over, if that's the case. I can tell by his expression that he doesn't completely approve of me, so I'm not goin' to say anything. I think what's driving him has something to do with you, Colleen. I can't figure him out."

"Why do you think he doesn't approve of you, Bret?" Colleen asked.

Bret flushed in embarrassment. "Oh, you know. My appreciation of the opposite sex, some of the pranks I've pulled ... that sort of thing."

Bret lay back in the sun and thought. He didn't say anything for a while, and Colleen began to wonder what was really on Bret's mind.

He finally said, "I think that in our situation, laughter is the best medicine. Don't you agree, Colleen?" He looked intently at Colleen and tried to judge her reaction. "I like you, Colleen," he added, almost shyly. "Is there anything wrong with that? I know what Pete thinks of me, but you're different from those other girls."

"We all enjoy your company, Bret!" Colleen exclaimed, self-consciously keeping her reply in the plural. "Pete likes you, too, even if he doesn't admit it."

Bret rolled over on his side and looked seriously at Colleen. "Let me tell you a story that may explain why I wanted to meet you up here. It's sort of a shaggy-dog story," he laughed.

Colleen lay down, too, smiling in amusement and thinking that Bret had another joke for her. "Well, what is it?" she asked curiously.

Bret's eyes twinkled briefly, but his mouth did not smile.

"Well," Bret said as he settled more comfortably onto his back, "we have a big dog at home. His name is Bud. He looks something like that big cloud up there with the tail. See it, Colleen?"

Colleen studied a cloud that looked something like a running dog.

"Bud is smart and gentle, and a good work dog, too. He was king of the hill on our farm, until my father decided to get a Boston bull terrier," Bret laughed ruefully. "That little bull terrier was always getting into scrapes with dogs twice his size, including Bud."

"One day my father gave Bud an old soup bone," Bret continued. "He probably had forgotten that Bud loves to bury bones. When the little bull terrier came up the back stairs out of the basement and saw that Bud was about to bury that bone, it was too much for him. He wanted the bone. He came up the stairs, never takin' his eye off old Bud. Bud never took his eyes off him, either. When the terrier got to the top and made his move for the bone, Bud tore into him like he was going to kill him. I could hardly separate the two of them. They wouldn't stop fightin' because each thought he was right! Bud wanted to bury his treasure, and the terrier thought it was a waste of a perfectly good bone!"

"What has that got to do with Pete?" Colleen asked curiously.

Bret looked at Colleen. "I told Pete that story, and I said I thought both dogs were right. Then I added that it's the same with people because you can't tell who's wrong when the fightin' starts. Each side thinks they're right or else they wouldn't be fighting. I asked him what he thought about that."

"What did Pete say?" Colleen asked.

"He said it's *always* wrong to fight because we're not animals. He said that's what's wrong with the world."

Bret sighed. "I made the mistake of suggestin' that the real world doesn't work that way. I agreed that we're smarter than dogs, but I pointed out that we're no angels. I said maybe we're a little too smart for our own good. I didn't mean to imply *he* was too smart for his own good, but maybe it sounded that way!

"Pete looked at me with an odd look on his face. Then he told me that a philosopher named Pascal had felt the way I do—that we're higher than the animals, but lower than the angels. Pete said Pascal made a famous wager about God. Pascal figured that if God and heaven *do* exist, believing in God will get a person into heaven. On the other hand, if God *doesn't* exist, there's no heaven and hell to worry about. Pascal decided that we might as well believe in God *just in case* God exists."

Bret paused and added, "Pete said it was a 'heads-you-win, tails-you-don't-lose' kind of faith. He told me the universe doesn't work that way, and it's no good gambling on the odds. He called it a lukewarm kind of faith, and he said he couldn't live his life that way."

Bret laughed. "I asked him, 'What about Bud and the bull terrier?' But Pete just answered, 'You pulled them apart, didn't you?' Then he suggested that I take up the piano, and he even offered to give me some lessons on Claire's piano!"

Bret had a hurt expression on his face. "I don't think a person goes to heaven just because he *says* he believes in God, Colleen. I was just askin' an honest question."

Bret looked upset, and then very concerned.

"I doubt that anyone can keep him away from that piano, Colleen, except maybe you," he said.

Bret fingered the cross on the silver chain that hung around his neck. "I felt a little insulted about his 'lukewarm faith' remark, Colleen, so I didn't say anything after that," Bret finally added. "But I *felt* like tellin' him that if he keeps on playing Claire's piano, he's heading for a big fall. He'll likely hemorrhage again. I'm sure he *knows* that Colleen, but he doesn't seem to care. I just don't want him draggin' you down with him!"

Bret's description of Pete's recent activities had upset Colleen. "I'll try to talk to him, Bret," she promised.

Colleen let Bret help her to her feet. They rode the elevator back to the second floor in silence. When the doors opened, Pete was standing by the elevator. He looked surprised to see Colleen and Bret together, but he said nothing. Bret stepped out of the elevator, and Colleen and Pete both watched him get back into bed. Bret waved cheerily to Colleen from his bed as she briefly held the elevator doors open. As the doors shut, Pete kept his eyes on hers, but he said nothing.

Since the next day was Sunday, Colleen decided that it was very likely that Pete would again go upstairs to play Claire's piano. She ate quickly again, and there was no sign of Pete. She quickly excused herself and took a piece of fruit, some carrots, and a chunk of cheese from the table as she walked out of the dining room.

Colleen took the elevator to the third floor without even stopping at the second floor to see if Pete was in bed. When the elevator doors opened, she could hear someone playing Claire's piano. Colleen listened awhile to the flawless playing, and then she opened the door a crack and saw Pete in profile. He didn't notice her because he was totally absorbed in the music. Colleen said nothing. When he finished, she tapped lightly on the open door.

"Mind if I come in? I brought you some lunch!" Colleen said.

"We're not supposed to meet this way!" Pete said with a smile. "But please come in. I suppose Bret told you I was up here."

Colleen couldn't hide her surprise. "What makes you think that?"

"Isn't that how he got you to go up on the roof with him yesterday?" Pete asked. "Don't you remember? We met when you were coming down."

There was no deceiving Pete, and Colleen did not wish to do so, anyway. "He's worried that you'll exhaust yourself, Pete," Colleen said.

"He thinks I'm cracking up," Pete said. "He's worried that I'll drag you along in my madness, but I haven't. It's none of his business that I come up here."

"I brought you some lunch," Colleen said, changing the subject and handing him the food. Pete placed the napkin of food on top of the piano.

"Thanks, Colleen. That's wonderful of you," Pete replied. "I was just finished anyway. Now I won't have to hurry down to the dining room, and we can talk." Pete bit into the chunk of cheese. "This cheese is almost as good as Claire's peanut butter cookies," he said, showing Colleen the big bite he had taken out of it. "I was hungry!"

Colleen smiled, remembering the catastrophe with Miss Jackson.

"We had fun until Miss Jackson arrived, didn't we?" Pete asked.

Colleen laughed, feeling no guilt whatsoever about their previous adventure. She was standing at the left end of the grand piano keyboard, and she could see that Pete was playing from his own copy of the same Mozart variations that he had given to her on her birthday.

Pete drummed his fingers on the piano top, lost in thought. "I've been thinking about the lark in your dream, my mother's music box, and your 'secret language of the fingertips'," he said.

"What have you figured out?" Colleen asked curiously.

"I've been thinking that music must be very close to language for musicians who have been trained in sight singing," Pete said. "The question is, what kind of language is it?"

"My mom can sight-sing very well," Colleen replied. "My grandmother could sight-sing, too. She told me that there used to be traveling musicians who would stay awhile in a town and give nightly lessons. They were social occasions, and many people turned out for them to learn to sing together and to have a good time. They sang out of books with different-shaped note heads for *do*, *re*, *mi*, and so on. Mom says it's too bad people don't do that anymore."

Pete nodded understandingly. "A Hungarian composer named Kodaly has been doing a similar thing behind the Iron Curtain. He's teaching the children of Hungary how to follow simple melodies by understanding hand signals for notes in the scale. The children take to it quite readily." Pete showed Colleen the hand signals and watched her as she imitated him.

"A rock, for *do*," Colleen repeated to herself, curling her hand into a ball as she tried to remember the signals. "Then an inclined plane, for *re*; followed by the hand held level with the floor for *mi*. For *fa*, the forefinger points down toward the floor. The signal for *sol* is a vertical wall—a partial stop. Next, an arch or bridge for *la*; and finally, the forefinger points up, for the leading tone, *ti*. Then you're back to *do*, the rock!" Colleen exclaimed. "The symbols form a little staircase!"

"So there you have the keys of the kingdom, Colleen!" Pete held out his hand clenched in a ball, for the note, *do*. "Upon this rock something very great has been built!" he joked.

Pete wasn't sure Colleen had heard him because she was still practicing the hand signals. Pete pushed back the piano bench and stood up for a moment. He lifted Colleen's chin with his forefinger and stared at her. "I'm making puns, and you're not laughing!" he laughed.

"I know, but this is more interesting!" Colleen said with an innocent grin.

Pete sighed as Colleen went back to memorizing Kodaly's hand signs.

"It's the language of God, Colleen," Pete said in a very serious voice. "George Sand understood that when she heard Chopin playing."

"You're saying there's a light at the top of the staircase, aren't you?" she asked, this time looking up and trying to prove that she really was still listening to him. In reality, she was also thinking about what Bret had told her on the roof about Pete.

Pete watched as Colleen went through the hand signals one last time. "There must be a part of the brain that has no need for words and is fascinated by pure melody, harmony, and rhythm," he marveled.

Pete fell silent as a bird began to sing outside the window. "Who knows, maybe it all started with birdsong!" he exclaimed.

"I once saved a bird that was caught in our backyard feeder," Colleen said, satisfied that she understood the hand signals. "I found him hanging upside down by one of his claws, which had caught in the clasp. I had to hold him in my hand to release him, and he didn't even struggle. I think that he had almost given up hope. When he flew away, he looked back at me from a tree for a long while. Then he began to sing. I think I restored his hope! Maybe music makes us feel that we can fly away and escape all our problems," Colleen observed.

"If I could, I would fly out that window right now and never come back!" Pete exclaimed passionately. "We could fly away together, Colleen," Pete added. "Want to go with me?"

"Maybe someday, Pete," Colleen said, surprising herself with her answer. She said nothing more, and they both continued to listen as the bird sang in the tree. Then Colleen said, "Do you think that a bird understands that music can be like moonlight?"

Pete sat back down. He patted the piano bench and said to Colleen, "Come sit down beside me, Colleen, so you don't tire yourself."

Colleen took a seat beside Pete on the piano bench. He reached for Claire's stack of music and removed a collection of Bach fugues as well as a copy of Debussy's *Clair de Lune*.

Colleen asked, "When the bird in my backyard sang after I released him, do you think that I was just confusing my feelings with his?"

"That's probably a big part of what happens when we listen to music," Pete replied. "If only we shared those feelings more often, the world might be a better place!"

Pete listened again to the bird singing outside the window. "He may not know it, Colleen, but he has discovered melody and rhythm. His little song contains the possibility of a symphony in just a few notes."

"It's like Beethoven's Fifth Symphony, in miniature," Colleen added as she listened to the pretty motif floating through the window.

"Birds are highly musical creatures," Pete observed. "A flock of birds synchronizes its movements as if in response to music!"

Colleen touched the piano keys. "I only know that when I discovered music, I *had* to keep going until I understood it. Do you suppose the little bird outside the window feels that way, too?" she laughed.

Pete smiled appreciatively. "You have a lot of music in you, Colleen!" He studied the Bach fugue a moment, and then he said, "Just look at these two compositions, Colleen. What could be more different? And yet they are both utterly musical. The language of music is a hybrid of math and poetry, but it contains phrases and themes the way language does."

Colleen nodded, wondering vaguely what this had to do with her lark, Pete's music box, and a secret language of the fingertips. She was beginning to tire as the rest period approached.

She finally said, "When I play a piano piece, I want to know what it *says*. Does that make it a language?"

Pete wiped away the perspiration that had beaded up on his forehead. Colleen thought Bret was right. Pete looked exhausted.

"Helen Keller learned to hear through her sense of touch, Colleen. Her brain learned to make the necessary connections without actually hearing or seeing anything. Her sense of touch along with her mind's ear and eye sufficed. How else could she have done it? Music creates imagery and meaning, with the fingers as a secret guide, perhaps. Maybe that's what you meant by a secret language of the fingertips, Colleen."

Pete pointed to the last line of *Clair de Lune*. "This final and beautifully drawn-out chord might be a clue to the meaning of music, Colleen," he said. Pete played the concluding arpeggio and exclaimed, "There is something in a final cadence that gives us hope that all things resolve and work out in the end! Even when the melody just floats away and dissolves into nothingness as it does in *Clair de Lune*."

The notes of Debussy's final arpeggio reminded Colleen of her dream of *Clair de Lune* following the *Jumpin' Joe Show* debacle. Only one of the patients in her dream had actually been stirred by the music. Although Cole and Jeanette had danced as Colleen had performed the music, they had seemed to respond more to the storm of their emotions than to the music. Then they had disappeared at the final chord as if in a cloud of smoke—as if the spell could last as long as the music played, but no longer. Debussy's music hadn't seemed to resolve anything for the patients in her dream, either. They had neither seen Cole and Jeanette's dance nor heard the piano music. They had felt nothing as they rocked endlessly in their chairs, absorbed in their own thoughts and concerns. She was about to say this when Pete interrupted.

"Even a modern piece as brutal as Stravinsky's *Rite of Spring* has logic and order, Colleen, but it forces the audience to hear in new ways. It's so wildly discordant that it takes getting used to. At its debut, it created a kind of madness in the audience that resulted in a riot. Stravinsky dared to show them what he believed were the primitive, hedonistic roots of human nature. He dared to base his music on total dissonance. The audience took it as a philosophical and auditory insult, both to themselves and to music."

Pete played an E major chord with his right hand while playing an E-flat major chord with his left hand. The jarring dissonance caused Colleen to clench her teeth and laugh, "I can understand their reaction!"

*At least no one rioted in my dream when I played "Clair de Lune,"* Colleen thought to herself. Indeed, no one had even budged from their rockers!

Pete studied the keyboard, oblivious of Colleen's thoughts. After a moment, he added, "So the final cadence, or lack thereof in Stravinsky's case, may be at the heart of the language of music. The final chord provides a feeling of hope and release that people expect from music. That obviously didn't happen at the debut of *The Rite of Spring*," Pete added wryly, "even if it did release a lot of pent-up feelings!"

But Colleen was not completely listening to Pete. She had reentered the world of her dream. In her dream, she had slumped over the piano after she played Debussy's final chord. She tried to recall how she had felt. Had she been overwhelmed by the beauty of the final chord, or was it only emotional exhaustion, or maybe a longing to be accepted into the adult world of Cole and Jeanette? What had she really felt? Perhaps all three, she decided.

"But a chord progression and a final cadence without melody are meaningless, lacking in form and grace," Pete mused, completely unaware that he had lost his audience. "In music, the emotion and beauty of each part are completely out in the open, creating a harmonious whole.

"Ordinary speech is quite different, Colleen. Words can be used duplicitously. In ordinary conversation, thoughts and feelings are often held back and kept hidden. It all depends on the individuals involved."

Colleen laughed. "You make conversation sound like a game of poker."

"Sometimes it is, when the stakes are high and the players are rough customers!" Pete observed.

"But each musical note is more like a valued flower in a well-kept garden, Colleen," Pete quickly added. "I imagine that Kodaly wants every child to sing so that children can feel that way about life and about themselves."

Colleen looked surprised by this last remark. "Are you saying that music allows a child to bloom and be a part of a beautiful whole, and this gives him hope?" she asked.

"The world doesn't give every child hope, Colleen," Pete said. "But music can! One question remains, however! What *is* the ground out of which such a beautiful garden grows?"

Colleen had never thought of music as being hopeful; she had always thought of it as being merely beautiful—perhaps unattainably so. Pete watched Colleen as she stood up and walked across the room to the open window.

It was a hot day, and through the open window Colleen could see cumulous clouds in the west that reached high into the sky. It looked as if it would storm by evening. "If music gives us hope, how do you account for its discordant and sad elements?" she asked, turning to face Pete.

"There's nothing unlovely about sadness, longing, or repentance, Colleen," Pete replied, looking surprised by Colleen's question. "Many beautiful pieces are written in the minor mode. There's *nothing* beautiful in the lies and vanity that cause suffering. As for discord, most theorists say that discord provides grist for the forward movement of the melody."

Colleen leaned across Claire's table and placed her face in the sun. By now, she had grown used to living behind screens and in the open air. In spite of Claire's wonderful piano, she felt confined by the apartment's walls. She took a deep breath of the summer air, but she remained silent. She still felt that the element of discord in music was a flaw in Pete's theory. It was like the little bacillus of TB. Its existence didn't fit the beauty of the whole.

"What about the Handyman?" she asked. "Where does he fit in all this?"

"He doesn't feel the music of life anymore, Colleen. To him, the noise and dissonance of life are normal. He doesn't understand the most essential thing: that we all need to move from dissonance to resolution. He'd rather live with that tension—for some reason known only to him, I suppose."

*She felt that the element of discord was a flaw in Pete's theory. It didn't fit the beauty of the whole.*

Colleen left the window and took a seat on the floor beside the piano bench.

She looked up at Pete and studied his profile. He had begun to play one of Haydn's more spirited sonatas. He stopped for a moment, clearly exhilarated, and said to Colleen, "It's like walking in another man's shoes, isn't it? If I'm clever enough, I can hear exactly what Bach, Beethoven, or Mozart heard—their dreams, their hopes, everything. Words alone can never express the whole man, Colleen, or the things that inspire him and move him to action. It's the music within that stirs us and makes us who we are and what we can be."

When Pete had finished speaking, he was quiet for a long while. Finally, he began to play from memory Robert Schumann's "Perfect Happiness." Halfway through the piece, he paused and said, "All of us keep within us memories of happy times, Colleen, scenes from childhood and the like, which we carry throughout our lives as our own secret Garden of Eden. There are private hells, too, I suppose, but they have nothing to do with music. They need tending, lest they overwhelm our ability to listen!

"I imagine that if we got to know the Handyman better," Pete added, "we might find out that he was never offered any hope as a child. He'll try to destroy Will before this is all over, because he's become an outsider like Cain in the Bible. The melody of God is very far away from him now. He's cut off from his inner melody. His racial rivalry with Will goes far deeper than simple male rivalry over a woman."

Pete sighed and began to play some more lines of the Schumann piece. "This piece is a scene from Schumann's own childhood, I imagine. We resurrect emotion in music, but the older and sicker we get, the more remote that beautiful possibility sometimes seems. Despair often fills the vacuum. At that critical point, we sometimes forget that death isn't the end; it's just a deceptive cadence. The beauty that we create lives after us."

Colleen looked at Pete and simply said, "We'll both get well, Pete."

Pete stirred uneasily, and then he said, "Let me give you an example of what I mean about hope and music. After the First World War, a large portion of the German population gave in to their economic despair and their sense of national defeat. Thugs roamed the streets looking for people to blame. Hitler felt the same way, but he saw a way to use that despair for his own purposes."

Pete frowned, thinking of Europe, which was now in ruins. "After the First World War, the German people were hoping for a happier time, but it no longer seemed possible to too many people. The music was going out of them! Hitler came along like a pied piper playing an evil, twisted tune full of false hope. Many Germans listened to it and forgot about the spiritual beauty of Bach, the egalitarian spirit of Beethoven, and the sweet gentleness of Schumann. They forgot the joy of listening for *every* voice, which is the real lesson of Bach!"

Pete said this with a passion that startled Colleen. She found herself again wondering what Miss Marthe and Dr. Kurtz had experienced before leaving their homeland. She wondered why so many Germans had failed to foresee the coming disaster.

"The guards tore the Jewish children from their mothers' arms, gassed them, and then called themselves superior. What was so superior about that?" she asked indignantly. "Their terrible vanity made them blind and deaf to the Jews' cries of pain!"

"They did to the Jews what they wouldn't have done to themselves," Pete exclaimed in disgust. "But not everyone was deceived. Men and women like Schweitzer still recognized the spirituality of listening for the beauty of *every* note!"

"Hitler didn't remember that pride goes before a fall!" Colleen added.

Pete frowned. "A spiritually blind and deaf nation is a dangerous one—to itself and to the world—especially when it's armed to the teeth and willing to risk everything in a vain cause."

Pete moved down to the floor to sit next to Colleen. Colleen found it cozy to sit on the floor after having been confined to a bed for so long. The piano loomed over them like a cathedral, an endless cavern of human emotion in whose heart of steel strings Pete found hope. Pete put his arm around her and drew her closer to him.

"Sigmund Freud had to escape the Nazis, Colleen, because he was Jewish," Pete said, looking earnestly at Colleen. "Toward the end of his life, he wrote that if civilization failed to provide cleanliness, order, and *beauty*, people would revert to primitive urges and taboos. He should have considered the alternative possibility. Under such circumstances, we may become automatons following a dictator to the brink of destruction."

Pete was silent a moment, lost in deep thought. "Freud placed pleasure and pain at the center of the universe—as well as our need to control them. Some Germans fled from the pain and ugliness caused by Nazi Germany. They feared for their lives, and they feared the German madness. Who could blame them? Those who remained were forced to live in a state based on ruthless efficiency and racial purity. Hitler and Mussolini kept the trains running quite efficiently, while Hitler just as efficiently dispatched the Jews to the gas chambers. Theirs was a society of perfect cleanliness and order, but without real beauty. Some clung to the old music. What they heard was the last vestige of civilization. Mussolini *admitted* that he wanted the world to fear Italy rather than be 'charmed by its guitar!' He tried to steal Italy's soul, and like Hitler, he reaped the whirlwind."

"And so the music went out!" Colleen said, her eyes round with the horror.

"The Germans who managed to escape knew one thing, Colleen. Hitler was dividing and conquering the people, from themselves and others." Pete's eyes were filled with consternation. "He should have been stopped before it was too late! It was as if a witching hour had been reached. Too many Germans refused to look in the cracked mirror of a society gone bad, because then they would have to face the music! Or lack thereof!" he exclaimed. "The same thing is happening in this country in the way we treat blacks, but we don't admit it."

This sudden outburst startled Colleen, who had been trying to follow Pete's ideas with her eyes closed. She opened them and saw that Pete was staring at her.

"There is music in all creation, Colleen. There is music in movement, form, and even in color. Renoir said that the color red sang to him. There is music in Will, too, in his blackness, and in the suffering of the Jews and other minorities. Hitler couldn't admit that. Their deaths meant nothing to him."

Colleen nodded her head in agreement.

"They say that when we die, our hearing is the last thing to go," Pete continued reflectively. "Freud didn't believe in God. I think that is wrong. I think that when we die, our own melody is at last in harmony with God's melody. We merge into it.

"Shakespeare had Hamlet say as he was dying, 'And the rest is silence.' Do you agree with him, Colleen? Do you think that our memories end when we die and that our music dies with us?" Pete asked, looking intently at Colleen. "Do you believe that the rest is silence?"

Colleen looked worriedly at her friend. "Of course not! The good that we do goes on, but so does the evil. I think two other things, Pete. I think that since I will die one day, having my soul united with God's melody would be a lovely way to conclude it, but we also have to think about today and the rest of our lives. You're overdoing by coming up here, Pete. You might have another hemorrhage," Colleen said quietly.

Pete just smiled, ignoring Colleen's warning. "I come up here because listening is the hardest thing to learn to do truly. Music keeps us from listening to our own foolish despair.

"Besides," Pete added softly, "you're suggesting that by coming up here, I'm living my life at *tempo rubato*! You think that pretty soon I'll have to make up the stolen time. Isn't that true, Colleen?" he asked.

"I don't know," Colleen said, almost inaudibly. "I only know that I would like to see you become a doctor someday and help people, like you said."

Pete stared a long while at Colleen. "But we can't let time drive our decisions, Colleen!" Pete exclaimed. "There *is* a rhythm to our lives, but Schweitzer was right. We have to set aside our busyness and listen to the melody of our lives. Life is more than a metered, unstoppable river of time. That's probably what Freud realized. He *admitted* that we die without beauty, even if he didn't fully understand its implications! Music isn't just an experience; it's a way of life, a way of listening, and the portal to that secret garden within. We're not caught in a current of time and circumstance. We *can* make time flow more beautifully. It's up to us. Music reminds us, when we forget, of all that life can be."

Pete stood up and took his place at the piano again. He found a collection of Chopin waltzes and opened it to one of Colleen's favorites. He flashed Colleen a happy, boyish smile over his shoulder as he began to play. "I'm wading in the water, Colleen! I'm telling you, the water's fine. You should come on in!" he teased.

Colleen tried hard not to laugh, but Pete's unabashed love of music was infectious. She listened to the Chopin waltz, allowing herself to be immersed in the beauty of Pete's playing.

"Besides," Pete continued with a flourish of his right hand as he struck the last chord, "Chopin said that the *singing* hand may deviate from the tempo, Colleen."

Pete swung around on the piano bench and stared a bit defiantly at Colleen. "Chopin said that it's only the accompaniment that must keep strict time, Colleen. And if a person can't sing, what good is life? So you see, I have Chopin's permission to deviate—if not Miss Jackson's," Pete concluded, giving Colleen a reassuring smile.

"But, Pete, Chopin *died* of TB!" Colleen cried out in exasperation.

There was no reply. Pete had already turned back to the keyboard. He began to play Chopin's "Prelude in B Minor."

Colleen stood up so that she could look over Pete's shoulder as he played. The repeated notes in the right hand sounded like the ticking of a clock. The subdued and melancholy melody occurred in the bass clef and was played by the left hand. Colleen felt that the haunting melody might not have come from a hopeful place in the human soul, but it did seem to come from a place deep within it.

As Colleen listened, she realized that Chopin had managed to separate his melody from time by allowing it to be heard over and against the steady, insistent ticking of the notes in the right hand. Chopin had indicated that the piece was to be played *sotto voce*. The hauntingly simple melody was pure and distant, like the tolling of a church bell in the night. Pete was playing the melody very softly, but he was playing the ticking of time even more softly. Colleen suddenly understood how Pete might feel that God was like a pure and distant melody cutting through the busyness of the world. She thought that music might be like a prayer to Pete, and perhaps his prayer was that the world would learn to hear truly.

The prelude was not long, and Pete quickly finished it.

"It's a very simple piece," Pete said, pointing to the first line of music. "In the right hand, you can hear Chopin's awareness of his mortality whispering to him in those short, repeated phrases."

Pete played the sixth, seventh, and eighth measures again and added, "In this part, Chopin seems to be singing with death in the right hand, but the voice of God in the left hand can still be heard. Time has temporarily dropped away, and in its place, there is only anguish and pain. In the closing measure, we again hear God's voice and the endless ticking of time. The solitary, middle note in the last chord captures Chopin's feeling of being caught between time and eternity. He captures this in the double rests at the end of the composition, but there is resolution even in that silence. The mind's ear hears the tonic chord repeated, Colleen!" Pete exclaimed. "But it is only in the mind's ear."

"And that final resolution is the most important thing to you, isn't it, Pete?" Colleen asked.

"Awareness of it is what separates us from the animals," Pete said.

"But is it more important than the good that we do for each other, right now?" she asked. "How can we accomplish something good if we don't live?"

Pete looked up at Colleen and didn't answer her question. He merely said, "If Chopin didn't already know he was dying of TB, he must have had some intimation of it. You can hear it in this prelude."

Pete seemed to be trying to come to grips with Colleen's implied criticism of his visits to Claire's apartment. "Nevertheless, Colleen, Chopin kept on playing and writing. If we go through life without hope, constantly avoiding pain or seeking our own petty pleasure, what good have we accomplished, even if we live to be one hundred?"

Pete looked frustrated. It was the first time Colleen had ever seen Pete even slightly angry. He peeled the banana that Colleen had brought him, took a bite, and said, "Did you hear me playing the Mozart variations when you came in?"

Colleen nodded. "They're very pretty. It's such a lot of beauty from such a simple theme. Imagine creating all that from 'Twinkle, Twinkle, Little Star'!" she exclaimed.

"They're a good place to start thinking about variation and the design of melody, Colleen," Pete suggested.

Pete hummed the original tune as he played the first of the Mozart variations. "You can hear the core melody and chords in each of the variations in the back of your mind, even when Mozart switches to a minor key," he said. "Variation and improvisation are possible because we compare and remember."

"And also because we can think of similar, but new ideas," Colleen added.

Pete smiled, pleased that Colleen understood.

"I wonder if Laura truly understands music?" Pete mused. "She said the arts are like fiddling while Rome burns. Well, she should consider Picasso's *Guernica*. That's speaking truth to power, too! Picasso wouldn't let the world forget the horrors of fascism."

"Laura told me that journalism is supposed to comfort the afflicted and afflict the comfortable," Colleen said in defense of Laura. "She believes in God, art, *and* the First Amendment."

Pete laughed and said, "True enough!" Then his expression grew more serious. "Colleen, music is an integral part of you! You mustn't forsake it for something else … or someone else." Pete's last words were added almost inaudibly. He looked into Colleen's eyes for an answer.

Colleen suspected that the "someone else" was Bret. It was nonsense for Pete to think that Bret could come between her and music. In fact, she thought of Bret as an unfinished symphony, but she said nothing.

There was a somewhat guilty silence and cautious truce between them.

Pete rose shakily from the piano bench. "Do you mind if we sit down and rest for a while, Colleen?" he asked. "I'm more tired than I realized." Pete took a chair by the window. Colleen drew her chair closer to Pete's.

Pete let out a long sigh. "That feels better!" he said. "Say," he laughed, "did I ever tell you about the French poet named Baudelaire? We were speaking before about music as a garden, and it reminded me of his poems." Pete seemed anxious to change the subject from Bret.

"What about him?" Colleen asked curiously as she nibbled at a carrot.

"My high school English teacher told me about him. I ended up writing a paper about his poems. He believed that other poets had already exhausted the best topics, so he deliberately chose the topic of evil! He called his poems *The Flowers of Evil*. He felt everybody was a puppet of Satan. He pointed out the nastier and petty aspects of human nature. He also thought the middle class were a bunch of bored hypocrites who were aloof to the desperation of the poor and to artists like himself. Unfortunately, the devil was always triumphantly lurking around Baudelaire's temple of beauty. His theory of art was that the senses could combine in unusual ways and transport us to other realms, but his portal to the Infinite was probably opium."

Colleen sat quietly, still worried about Pete's health. "Don't forget to eat your carrot, Pete!" As soon as she said it, she knew it was the wrong thing to say.

Pete laughed. "Don't you see, Colleen? He had it all wrong. In the *real* world, there are plenty of people who lead good lives and make it a better place, like Miss Marthe and Dr. Smith. They *tend* their gardens. Unfortunately, many Germans didn't. They felt *nothing* when the Jews were being taken away. Baudelaire was wrong. There are plenty of people who don't shrug and say, 'Oh, well, there's nothing we can do because we're all puppets of Satan!' They understand the musical ties that bind us naturally to one another. They know that we don't have to be puppets on strings, dancing to phony music!"

Pete hesitated, and then he added, "There's a bit of the world's boredom and despair in Bret, too, but it's not from intolerance or stupidity," Pete said, looking down and flushing self-consciously for having criticized his rival. "At heart, he's *too* much of an idealist. I think he's very sensitive to everything he's seen at Sherwood, but he covers it up with pranks and romances. Which of us, Colleen, do you think is the true realist?"

"Maybe those labels describe both of you, for all I know!" Colleen exclaimed heatedly. "Can't you see that Bret's behavior is his way of dealing with life in a TB sanitarium? Under normal circumstances, none of us would lie in bed all day. The two of you just react differently to the necessary discipline and regimentation, that's all. Bret is *very* concerned about what might happen to you if you keep coming up here!"

"At any rate," Pete continued, embarrassed at having mentioned Bret, "only a few of Baudelaire's poems offer much hope. He thought the world had no use for a poet who spoke plainly about evil. He wrote that we *all* jump at Satan's bait to relieve the monotony of our corrupted existence. In one of his poems, he admitted that his own garden was full of holes, and he was right! At heart, he was bored by the world's dreary corruption. He was always looking for something better, or at least new. He never found it.

"He misunderstood silence as the indefiniteness of all things, and he blamed God for that silence and rebelled. He forgot that silence is a necessary part of listening," Pete said, looking at Colleen and studying her.

Pete said nothing more, and Colleen could feel the silence between the two of them. It was palpable. She could feel it, hear it, and even see it in the gulf she sometimes felt lay between them.

"Do you think Baudelaire was like Madame Bovary?" Colleen finally asked, deliberately ignoring what Pete had said about Bret. She hadn't finished Flaubert's book, but she had read enough to see where it was heading. "Emma Bovary said it would be *boring* to be married to Jesus! Maybe Baudelaire was bored in the same way that Emma was!"

Pete laughed. "Baudelaire was a lot smarter than she was. At least he recognized depravity and corruption for what they are. She dressed it up and made it seem like a fine thing. A mere *child*, like Helen Keller, knew more about goodness and beauty when she learned how to communicate than Baudelaire learned in a lifetime of describing the horror of humanity. In the end, we have to discover what beauty and goodness *really* are, or we are cooked! We have to learn how to listen to one another."

"You mean, otherwise we *are* just puppets on strings?" Colleen asked.

Pete suddenly looked very upset. "We're all fools until we understand the reality and beautiful potential of time. We're always forgetting the most important things."

Pete sat back in the chair to get more comfortable. "When I was a little boy, whenever I had trouble learning a piano piece, my mother would encourage me by saying, 'It's still just notes to you. When you learn to listen correctly, you'll play it perfectly.' She said that music is a special language that is in us from the start and never leaves us entirely. But we must give it a chance, and be patient with it, listening for each voice as we would in ordinary language—until the music *speaks* to us and we can understand its ever-changing forms. She said when that happened, I would feel happy that such a thing could be in me and in others, and I would know that this world was meant to give delight and not sorrow."

Pete coughed. He quickly covered his mouth and glanced over at Colleen to see whether she had noticed. He looked upset and exhausted.

"Pete, you've got to stop coming up here!" Colleen exclaimed, remembering her purpose in being there. "It's too hard on you!"

Pete frowned. "The staff seems to think they can keep us happy and occupied with activities like crocheting. Meanwhile, the most important needs like religion, beauty, and love—" he said, looking searchingly at Colleen, "are being ignored as if they have nothing to do with healing. I know about Dr. Trudeau's studies in New York's Adirondacks, but we're not like rabbits down a hole. I can't believe that sitting at the piano on Sunday for twenty minutes each week is any worse than sitting at the dining table three times a day, seven days a week! They keep telling me that the rest period is supposed to be healing, but I lie there and go crazy. I'm very pleased you came up here, by the way!" he added, smiling affectionately at Colleen. "Bret says I don't know how to talk to women, yet here you are! He still has a few things to learn about the intelligent ones, I think!"

Colleen smiled at the compliment. "Bret's a great guy, but he's an expert on women only if sheer volume of experience counts!" she replied. Colleen pulled her chair alongside Pete's. "You look tired. Let me massage your shoulder blades a second. Maybe that will help you relax."

Pete obliged happily. "Ahh! That feels excellent! I think you should become a nurse, after you become a musician of course, and run away with me when I finish medical school someday. You have a healing touch.

"Do you want to know my other reason for coming up here, Colleen?" Pete asked, with his back turned to her so that she could continue to rub his back.

"Of course," Colleen said. She had begun to sense the futility of trying to convince Pete not to play Claire's piano anymore.

"The doctors and nurses assume that we have family to go back to and that the thought of home will buoy us up. I don't have a mother to go home to, Colleen. I come up here to try to remember her in music." Pete's voice cracked. "When she died, I didn't want to live anymore. The thought of suicide was tempting. I stopped eating. The doctor told me that surviving children sometimes get the same symptoms as those of a dying parent. He said it happens because the child is trying to understand death. But my illness became real. It made me realize that if I died of TB, my dad would be left to carry on all alone."

Pete smiled wanly, remembering that painful period. "So, I had to go on. I had already decided that I wanted to be a doctor, but the only thing that kept me sane during that bad time was the concept of music. My mother had wanted me to become a pianist. After her death, I realized that I'm more like my dad. She's been gone a year now, and I accept the fact that she'll never come back. The unbearable longing is over, but the sad look on her face will always haunt me."

"What about your father, Pete?" Colleen said gently.

"I think he has recovered, somewhat. He finds his job satisfying and useful because he can be with people and their animals all day. I think my mother didn't want to die because she felt that she would never know what happened to me. I saw the look on her face. She was afraid I would get TB. If she could only have known that I'm not afraid to die! After she died, I tried to live each day like my father."

"Then, don't you think you should keep her music box, Pete?" Colleen asked, thinking of Pete's birthday gift to her.

"No. I want you to keep it! The Mozart version is titled, '*Ah, vous dirai-je, Maman!*' That means, 'Oh, Let Me Tell You, Mother!' There is so much that I will never get to tell her, except through the piano. She wanted me to be able to play music the way she could. Perhaps the music box will inspire you, too! I have no more use for it. The piano is all that I need now."

"I'll bet she was the best mother ever!" Colleen exclaimed.

"Do you remember the story of Pandora's box, Colleen?" Pete asked.

Colleen nodded, wondering why Pete had asked.

"When Pandora opened the box, she let out all of the world's troubles. She wasn't supposed to open the box, but she did," Pete said.

"I don't see why the girl is always blamed!" Colleen half-joked. Colleen stopped rubbing Pete's back in order to rest her hands awhile, and Pete glanced at her over his shoulder.

"When Pandora looked in the bottom of the box, what was in there, Colleen?" Pete asked.

"Hope!" Colleen quickly replied. Colleen resumed rubbing Pete's shoulders. She could feel the tension going out of him.

"When my mother read the story aloud to me, I thought that hope was actually music. I believed that Pandora quickly closed the box so that the music wouldn't escape. In my child's mind, I imagined that she had invented the music box. I told my mother, and she just laughed. She bought me a real one and showed me how it worked. So then, I wanted to learn how to play the piano. Then she said that God gave us two hands—one for healing, through harmony, and the other to give delight, through melody. She told me always to remember that hope and delight are the same things, and that I would always find them in music and in people who feel the music of life—like you, Colleen."

Colleen continued to rub his shoulders, but she leaned over and said, "I think that's the nicest compliment I've ever had, Pete."

Pete looked up at Colleen and smiled. "I mean it, Colleen. Now that I'm no longer a child, music has become less magical and mysterious to me. I've come to understand rhythm and harmonic progressions, phrase structures, cadences—the theory of music. I finally understand the alternating feeling of completeness and incompleteness that music conveys, but the genius of melody eluded me for a long while. Its meaning seemed beyond my grasp.

"But one day I found the definition of *Muse* in the dictionary. The original Greek concept of Muse was a combination of song, memory, and meditation. The Greeks understood that music is more than mere pleasure, Colleen. They understood that the qualitative is hidden in the quantitative. I realized that with pleasure and pain as our only guide, a certain cruelty and wildness sets in. The gardens of our lives go to seed. That was when I realized that Schweitzer was right about music. I figured out that the Golden Rule, understood in the language of music, is this: We can make our time on earth beautiful by healing and giving delight—or we can waste our time making the world a lying and violent place, and die anyway.

"For the first time I understood Schweitzer's words, 'God is like a pure and distant melody, and *happy* is the man who listens'!" Pete exclaimed.

"It was as if I had found a flower in a war zone," he added. "I felt at peace with myself at last. I realized that words often deceive, but a flower never lies. I threw away my copy of *The Flowers of Evil* and poured my soul into the piano. When you told me about your dream, I knew that music is very important to you!"

"Do you mean my dream about the lark and the secret place where music begins?" Colleen asked, bewildered.

Pete nodded. "That's why I gave you the music box, Colleen. I wanted to give you Hope, in the way that my mother gave it to me. There is no lark in the music box. It's a machine. The lark is in you, Colleen. It's the gift of hearing truly. It's a simple thought, but it makes all the difference."

There was a long silence. After a while, Colleen felt Pete relax all over. His head fell forward. "I think I'm falling asleep," he mumbled. "It's not the company!" Colleen tried to turn him around so that he would not fall out of the chair, but he had already toppled over to one side, overcome with fatigue. She caught his slumping body and eased him back into the chair. She let him sleep. He was quite handsome in his sleep. All the strain had gone out of his face. After about five minutes, Colleen heard Dr. Edmonds outside in the hall. There was a tinkling of keys and then she heard the door shut. Colleen nudged Pete gently, and he awoke with a start.

"Dr. Edmonds is next door. We need to get out of here!" Colleen whispered.

Pete seemed unperturbed. His nap had refreshed him, and he seemed back to his cheerful self. "Don't worry about Dr. Edmonds! He has no idea I've been coming here." Pete chuckled to himself. "I guess it was wrong to presume on Claire's hospitality, but she did invite you up here to use the piano anytime. We'd better get going, because I'm never sure when she'll come back on Sunday evenings."

Pete and Colleen walked silently to the door, opened it a crack, and hurried across the landing and down the stairs to the second floor.

Colleen saw Bret, smiled, and waved cheerily. Pete got into bed without a word of explanation. Colleen went back to her porch, wondering what Bret and Pete would have to say to each other. On the way back, she remembered that she had failed to push her chair back into place. Claire would instantly realize that someone had been in her apartment. She would start locking her door. There would be no way that Pete could secretly go back to Claire's apartment again, even if he wanted to.

Laura looked up when Colleen came onto the porch. She said nothing, but Colleen guessed that Laura was suspicious by the curious look she gave her.

Later in the evening, Will stopped by with Mr. Mews so that Laura could see him. When Colleen asked him what had happened between him and the Handyman, Will looked down and seemed not to want to talk about it.

He finally said, "When I asked him for the book, he took it as an accusation. I could see that he had something in his pocket. It was probably your book, Miss Colleen. Perhaps he'll try to contact you again somehow."

"Let him!" Colleen said angrily. "He's enjoying this game, but two can play."

Will looked distressed, but he stayed for a while and read some poems to Laura. The rest of the women wanted to hear them, too, so he read aloud some of his favorites as clearly as he could so that everyone could enjoy them. He read one called "The Negro Speaks of Rivers," which reminded Colleen of what Pete had said about the current of time. This particular poem by Langston Hughes spoke about the Negro's place in time and history. It spoke of ancient dusky rivers and of the Negro having known them all. It spoke of what the Negro had experienced along those rivers.

Colleen watched Laura as she stroked Mr. Mews and listened quietly to the music of Will's voice. Will seemed to understand that

Laura's soul was becoming deeper, like the rivers in the poem. After about a half hour, Will excused himself and took Mr. Mews back to his apartment.

On the following Wednesday, Colleen received a letter from her parents. They had decided to take her brother to college in their car, and they planned to stop by Sherwood en route to Chicago in order to visit Colleen. Colleen reread the letter to make sure of the date. The letter said they would arrive on the first weekend in September, which was only two days away.

Colleen had at last finished reading *Madame Bovary*. She felt that Emma's story was like a Cinderella story gone horribly wrong. Emma was like a Cinderella who couldn't face the pumpkins and mice after the ball. Colleen thought that the swirl of the dance that Emma had been caught up in was like the merry-go-round that Faith had described and Victoria had ridden. But in Emma's case, it had led to her spiritual death and suicide.

Bret had said that one must see the world without fairy tales and rouge, but Colleen felt that the reality people create is sometimes hard for them to accept. Emma had not seen the ball for what it was. Her downfall began with a waltz, a flirtation, and a glimpse of "high" society—and with her headstrong belief that she had a *right* to more. But it was the music that had probably most seduced Emma's artistic nature, along with her vanity.

She had not perceived that music could be used falsely as a veneer for a sordid and corrupt lifestyle or as a façade for a venal social class; nor had she allowed herself to believe that her own sense of beauty could be prostituted, along with her body and soul in the process. Most importantly, Emma hadn't understood that there would come a time when the music would stop, and it would be midnight. When midnight finally came, she couldn't face the darkness. There would be no more balls. Instead of accepting the pumpkins and mice, she chose rat poison. With dismay, Colleen realized that Emma had chosen a private hell over an imperfect heaven because she thought that she understood and could control the merry-go-round. Her vanity had allowed her to believe that she could control the hell that she had created.

The next two days passed quickly for Colleen, and on Friday afternoon, after the rest period, Colleen awoke thinking how nice it would be to see her parents and brother again. She lay in bed thinking about her brother for a while. Then, out of the corner of her eye, she thought she saw something move on the lawn. She looked out through the porch screen and saw a black shadow in the grass. She got out of bed, and to her surprise, she saw Mr. Mews lying on his side, panting and seemingly in distress.

"Laura! Come over here!" Colleen called to her worriedly.

Laura got out of bed and joined Colleen by the porch screen. "What is it?" she asked, and then her eyes fell on the sick cat. "Oh my gosh! How did he get out of Will's apartment? Will would never leave Mr. Mews outdoors without water on a hot day like today!"

Laura left the porch, and without asking permission, she went out a side door and followed the path around to the front of the building. It was odd to see Laura out on the lawn. Laura, too, seemed to become aware of her sudden freedom. She looked around appreciatively at the expanse of lawn and then bent over Mr. Mews. She picked up the panting cat in her arms and said, "I'll be right in, Colleen, and I'm bringing Mr. Mews. Would you please see if Miss Marthe can get him an ice bag and a bowl of water? Maybe he'll take a drink!"

Colleen walked down the hall a short way and ran into Miss Marthe, who had already met Laura in the hall and had found a hot water bottle, which she had filled with ice. Laura came onto the porch shortly with Mr. Mews and laid him on her bed. Miss Marthe put the ice pack against the cat's groin, and the cat did not move. Then Miss Marthe went and got some ice chips, which she put on a saucer and offered to the cat. Mr. Mews weakly lifted his head and began licking the ice. Laura stroked his head. "I vill take his temperature. I haf cats of my own, and I know how to do it."

Mr. Mews did not like the thermometer, but Miss Marthe was able to keep it in. She saw that the cat's temperature was well above normal for a cat. "Vhen he stops panting, ve can probably remove the ice pack. Ve should find Vill right away so that he can take Mr. Mews home."

Within an hour, Will had been located and sent for. He came down the sidewalk hurriedly and through the screen saw Laura sitting on her bed with Mr. Mews. Mr. Mews lifted his head in recognition but quickly lay back down in exhaustion.

"Please come in, Vill," Miss Marthe said. "Mr. Mews seems much better now, but ve think he should be put in a cooler place right away. Laura found him out on the lawn about an hour ago. He vas very hot and dehydrated."

"Thank you, Laura! I think I know how he got out of my room!" Will said angrily.

Within a few minutes, he appeared in the porch doorway and quickly crossed the room. He picked up Mr. Mews, who curled up happily in his arms. "You see, he is an extraordinary animal, Miss Laura. He knows who his friends are, and he knew where to come when he felt in danger. He must have been out in the heat all day."

"I gave the Handyman my key so that he could return your book, no questions asked. He claimed he could not give the book to me immediately, as he didn't have it. He said he would check in the library and see if it was there. He claimed he could not remember taking it from the hall as you described. He must have deliberately let Mr. Mews out as soon as I went to work. He probably hoped he would run away, the scoundrel!"

Will began to hum a lullaby to the cat. Mr. Mews closed his eyes. "I will take him back to my room now and let him rest," he said.

As Will was leaving, Mr. and Mrs. Reilly arrived along with

Colleen's brother Elliot. They paused to pet Mr. Mews.

"What a fine cat you have there, young man!" Mrs. Reilly exclaimed.

"He almost didn't have one, Mom!" Colleen exclaimed. She explained what had happened. Will backed shyly out of the room. As he left, he called across the porch to Laura, "Don't worry, Miss Laura! Mr. Mews will be fine now!"

Miss Marthe looked very angry. "There is something I must do!" she said, and she left the room with no further explanation.

"Well, Colleen, it looks like you had some excitement around here today!" Mr. Reilly exclaimed.

"It will be all right, I think," she replied. "Will has been boarding Mr. Mews for Laura. She plans to take Mr. Mews home with her when she leaves here. So! How was your trip up here?" she said brightly, trying to sound as if all were well.

"We're packed to the gills because I have a bunch of stuff to take to Northwestern with me," Elliot said. "But we made it up here in good time. We even had time for a picnic lunch along the way. It's swell to see you again, Colleen," Elliot said, bending down and giving Colleen a hug.

"Let me hug my daughter, will you, Elliot?" Mrs. Reilly said, hurrying over to Colleen. She gave her a long hug. "It's so wonderful to see you, Colleen," she said.

Then Mr. Reilly gave the two of them a bear hug. "These are two of my four favorite women in the whole world! Colleen, you look wonderful! You've gained weight and look so much better!"

"Where's Katie?" Colleen asked.

"She's home with Maureen and her new husband. She has a bad cold! We thought it best not to bring her," Elliot said. "She'll be fine in a week."

They talked together during the hour before dinner, and then they left Colleen so that she could go eat. They promised to come back in the morning before they left for Chicago. Colleen tried to put the episode of the cat out of her mind, but Laura sat very glumly through dinner, clearly worried about Will and Mr. Mews.

Laura finally said, "I'm certain Mr. Mews didn't just happen to escape when the Handyman went into Will's apartment. He hates Mr. Mews! He hates Will even more!"

"If he thought my book was lost, he should have returned it to the library," Colleen said. "I think he just wanted to get my attention. He held it up and winked at me when he picked it up."

When she got back into bed, Colleen lay there wondering when and where the missing book would finally show up. Colleen had asked Pete and Bret to look for it in the library when they had a chance. She doubted the Handyman would ever admit to taking it after all the fuss he had made about Will being on the porch. It seemed more likely that he would never give back the book.

Late in the evening, Will appeared again outside the women's porch. He was clearly agitated. He asked for Colleen in an urgent voice. Colleen came over beside Laura's bed, wondering what could have brought him there so late at night. Will turned on a flashlight and showed the two women a note written on a crumbled piece of paper. He explained to them that he had heard something thrown against his windowpane. When he had gotten up to investigate, he had found the note outside his door. Will read the note to them, and it said:

*Frenchie:*

*You've been causing a lot of trouble around here. It's time you found out that you can't get away with it any more. You've been tellin' tales about whites stealin' books from the hospital. A smart foreigner like you ought to know he can't get away with making false accusations in a white society. You and that cat have used up your nine lives! Both of you had better be out of here by sundown tomorrow, if you know what's good for you.*

"I couldn't sleep, Laura," Will said, with a frightened look in his eyes. "I've packed my bag. I will leave in the morning. I just wanted you to know what happened. I will try to get to Chicago somehow. I have a little bit of money saved. It is enough for a bus ticket. The man who wrote this note will find a way to carry out his threat, and he has the advantage of knowing where and when. He may have friends who are willing to help him. I will write to you when Mr. Mews and I get to Chicago safely."

Colleen felt this couldn't be happening. These were things she had heard about but had never experienced. Laura began to cry.

"Don't cry, Miss Laura! I will bring Mr. Mews back when you are ready to leave here," Will said gently.

"It's not that, Will. I just don't think you should be forced to leave when you've done nothing wrong. Why should you be made the scapegoat for another person's twisted thinking? Running away will let him think he can get away with it anytime he pleases."

"It will take more than one black man standing up to a man like him, Laura. You see, he is bold because he does not feel alone in his hatred. It will take many black people arising together with dignity against this kind of behavior to prove to him that whites cannot treat us like animals. As long as a creature like him can roam the night, a black man is not safe in white society. I will be safer in Chicago, Miss Laura."

"But—" Laura began. Will interrupted her.

"Justice will be achieved someday in the way I have just described, Laura. On that day, things will begin to be different. I must go and get some sleep now. Good night."

"Wait, Will!" Colleen exclaimed. "Don't go just yet. My parents can give you a ride to Chicago. They're leaving in the morning. There's room for you in their car! You saw how much they liked you and Mr. Mews!"

"We'll pass through small, country towns," Will said. "What if the car breaks down? I think your parents would be putting themselves in great danger by taking a black passenger with them. There are not many places that would welcome a black man dining and staying overnight with whites. There are towns in which blacks are not allowed after sundown."

"They could buy food along the way," Colleen suggested. "You could all eat in the car. They wouldn't mind, I'm sure." Colleen was beginning to feel desperate because Will's efforts to help her had precipitated the crisis. "Please let me ask them!" she exclaimed.

Again, Will looked down as if Colleen had asked him for an impossible favor. Finally, he looked up at her and said, "I do not wish to be inhospitable to your kindness, Colleen. I would gratefully go with your parents if they could get me and Mr. Mews out of here quickly and safely."

"I'm glad, Will," Colleen said, breathing a sigh of relief. "They'll be here at seven o'clock. Why don't you have your suitcase and Mr. Mews ready in the front parking lot by then? Put Mr. Mews on a strong leash! I'm sure they will take you to Chicago."

"I will be waiting there, Colleen. Tell them I would be most appreciative. Good night!" Will turned and directed his flashlight down the path and into the darkness. There was only the circle of light and the darkness beyond. He quickly departed. Colleen went back to bed, and she could hear Laura tossing and turning for a long while.

In the middle of the night, Colleen heard Laura get out of bed and leave the porch. When she came back, Colleen sat up in bed.

"What is it, Laura?" Colleen whispered.

"I asked the night nurse to call Miss Marthe first thing in the morning and tell her that Will is leaving."

In the morning, Colleen's parents were shocked to learn about the chain of events that had turned Will's life upside down. They were anxious to help when they found out that Miss Wilson's missing book had precipitated the crisis.

"Of course we'll take him, Colleen!" Mr. Reilly exclaimed.

"We can rearrange the car trunk when we get up to the parking lot," Elliot seconded.

"I'll volunteer to hold Mr. Mews, so that Will knows we don't mind having the cat along," Mrs. Reilly added.

After they had visited awhile, Mr. Reilly stood up and looked at his watch. We'd better get going, or Will may think we decided to leave without him!" he reminded everyone.

"Tell him to write us as often as he can," Laura said.

"Tell him we'll miss him and that he's the best handyman we've ever had. Oh! And tell him that we'll tell Mr. Olsen what happened! Maybe Mr. Olsen could send Will a letter of reference!" Colleen exclaimed.

As Elliot and Colleen's parents were preparing to leave, Miss Marthe entered the porch. She was wearing a sundress dotted with little flowers. It was her day off, and everyone was surprised to see her at the hospital.

"Yesterday, I made an appointment to see Doctor Smith about vhat has happened to Vill over the past two months. Then I received a phone call that he is leaving. Many people died in my homeland because of such nonsense!" Miss Marthe said. "It is time to remember vhat harm comes from living vith lies! I am going to see Dr. Smith this morning. I am sure he vill set things right because he is an honest and good man!"

Miss Marthe left the porch without saying another word.

## Goblin's Dance

"Where are we, Elliot?" Mrs. Reilly asked. They had been on the road for many hours, and Mrs. Reilly was beginning to feel hungry.

"We're still a long way from Indianapolis," he replied. "The town Will told us about is up ahead. We could stop there for lunch if you like." Will had given Mr. Reilly the names of lodgings and restaurants along their route that were listed in the *Green Book*, a guide for Negro travelers in America. The book provided the names of lodging places and restaurants where Negroes were welcome.

Mr. Reilly turned off the highway and followed the town's main street for about a half mile. He spotted the family restaurant he was looking for down a side street and parked in front of it. He went inside and asked the waitress if the restaurant had any objection to serving Negroes. It did not, so he signaled for the family to come in. He placed an order for chicken sandwiches, soup, and coffee. A few of the customers looked up in surprise when they saw Will walk in with a white family. The Reillys sat down at a table with Will and waited to be served.

The waitress brought them their food and said nothing when she saw Will. They all ate in silence awhile, and then young Elliot began talking about his plans for his first year at Northwestern. The family listened with interest, while Will said nothing and ate his sandwich. The restaurant patrons around them remained silent and seemed to be listening to their conversation, so they quickly finished their meal and left.

"Was it me, or did you feel as if we were in a goldfish bowl in there?" Mr. Reilly asked ruefully.

"Now, Elliot, it was a nice restaurant, and the food certainly was good," Mrs. Reilly laughed nervously.

Will had saved a piece of his sandwich for Mr. Mews. When they got back into the car, he offered it to him. Mr. Mews eagerly ate it. After he had eaten the treat, he began to groom himself.

"This town is not so bad," Will observed as they pulled away from the curb, "but there are other towns where I may not be welcome, Mr. Reilly. We will have to be careful. Before the war there were plenty of towns that banned Negroes after sundown." Will paused for a second and wondered if he should say anything more on the subject.

He decided that the Reillys were open-minded people, and so he added, "Your dollar bill proclaims, 'In God We Trust,' but in many towns in America, white people do not trust the Negro after dark. Your finest Christian neighborhoods in the north won't allow Jews to live in them, even though Jesus was a Jew. I cannot understand your American Christ, nor can I place my trust in such an unloving God."

Mr. Reilly looked back at Will in the rearview mirror. He looked startled by Will's passionate reference to an American Jesus. "Are you a Christian, Will?"

"I am a Haitian Catholic," he replied.

Will petted Mr. Mews awhile and then continued. "Do you know that Negro jockeys are not permitted to ride in the Oakton Stakes? They used to, and they used to win. So they were barred. Just a few years ago, your American baseball commissioner would not hire Josh Gibson from the Negro Leagues, even though the Pittsburgh Pirates wanted him to play for them. The Canadians have allowed Jackie Robinson to play with the Montreal Royals, but how do you think he will he be treated if he ends up playing an American team in the Little World Series?"

"The newspapers say he always conducts himself like a gentleman," Mr. Reilly responded.

Young Elliot interrupted and said, "The real problem, Dad, is that the newspapers never describe white fan behavior as *ungentlemanly*."

"I am glad you see this, Elliot," Will said. "Do you know that

Negroes are excluded from good jobs and from decent homes even when we save our money? The military doesn't want us commanding its white soldiers, and white workers don't want us taking good jobs. There are two countries in America, Elliot, and they are separated by a color line. How can we be integrated if we can never cross this color line?"

"Were you happy at Sherwood, Will?" Mrs. Reilly asked.

"Yes, I was happy there," Will reflected. "I was given many opportunities, and I was treated well. Dr. Smith and Miss Marthe were very good to me—as were your daughter and Miss Laura. Mr. Olsen is the only white man who has ever offered to help me, except you, Mr. Reilly. Miss Laura trusts me to take care of Mr. Mews for her. I must find a way to take him back to her someday."

Will was silent for a long while. Mrs. Reilly wanted to hear about Haiti, so Will talked for quite a while about his relatives and about Port-au-Prince, where he had grown up. Mrs. Reilly had never been to a Caribbean country. They talked at great length until Mr. Reilly noticed that they were short of fuel.

"We'll have to stop at the next town for some gas," he observed.

When Mr. Reilly pulled into the gas station, he noticed a car containing several young white men. They stared at Will, and one of them in the front seat reached over and honked the horn. "Come on out here, Ed, and take care of your Negra customer!"

A muscular man appeared in the doorway of the station and saw the Reillys. Then he saw Will in the back seat. He came over to the driver's side of the car, and Mr. Reilly said through the open window, "Would you fill it up, please?"

The attendant looked undecided and didn't say anything for a moment. Then he began filling the tank. The youths in the car started whistling and telling Ed to hurry it up. The driver revved his engine several times as if he wanted to race.

Mr. Reilly paid the attendant, and then he asked to use the bathroom, which was at the side of the building. The attendant pointed to the back of the building. "If your friend there wants to go, there's one out back for coloreds," he said curtly. "I'd appreciate it if you'd hurry it up and be on your way. He's bad for business!"

As the two men got back into the car, they saw the four youths watching them. Mr. Reilly reached into the glove compartment, found a cap, and put it on Will's head.

"You can drive a car, can't you Will?" he asked nervously.

"Yes, sir," Will replied. "I sometimes drove a truck for Dr. Smith."

"Good! Then from now on you'll be my chauffeur, just in case anybody asks!" Mr. Reilly told him. "You have business reasons for travelin' with white folks, at least until we clear this part of the country, okay?"

Will saluted Mr. Reilly. "Yes, sir!" he replied.

Will took a seat behind the wheel, while Mr. Reilly got out and sat in the back next to his wife. Elliot moved to the front passenger seat, beside Will. When everyone was settled in comfortably, Mr. Reilly told Will to drive on toward Indianapolis.

As Will pulled out onto the road, he heard the driver of the carload of youths rev his engine again. He could see that the occupants were smirking and enjoying themselves. The driver began to follow Mr. Reilly's car. Will drove very carefully, well below the speed limit. The other driver began blowing his horn impatiently. As both cars were approaching the main road, Will felt a tap on the rear bumper.

"He's trying to make trouble, Will! Slow way down, and signal them to pull by us," Mr. Reilly directed.

Will did so, but the car did not pass them. It again bumped them, only harder. Will had trouble controlling the car. He sped up, and the other car did the same, again striking them in the rear. The driver suddenly pulled around them and slowed way down. Will slammed on the brakes. It was then that Will saw a flashing red light in the rearview mirror.

The driver of the other car sped away, but Mr. Reilly saw him pull off about a hundred yards farther down the road. Instead of pursuing the other car, the policeman motioned for Will to pull over. Will saw the car with the youths make a U-turn and come slowly back down the road.

The driver pulled up in the other lane and leaned out of the car. He complained that Will had struck his back bumper and had tried to force him off the road.

"Back at the gas station I heard that there was a Negro travellin' with a white family," the policeman stated. "I just wanted to find out what his business was in town and how long he planned to stay."

"We're on our way to Chicago, officer," Mr. Reilly answered quickly. "We'll not be stayin' the night. This man is my chauffeur. My son's on his way to school up there."

"Ask him why the nigger was sittin' in the back of the car, if he's a chauffeur!" the driver of the other car snarled.

The policeman looked puzzled. "Is that so?" he asked.

"My chauffeur ate something that didn't agree with him at a restaurant a while back, officer," Mr. Reilly explained. "We had to switch drivers for a while because he was sick. I thought it was best that I drive until he recovered." Mr. Reilly said this with an unruffled air. "He felt better after he used the restroom back at the gas station. We appreciate the hospitality, and we'll just be on our way now, if you don't mind."

"And what's this about you bumpin' their rear bumper?" the policeman asked. He walked around to the rear of the youths' car. "There ain't no sign of nothin'. Are you boys pullin' my leg again?" he asked indulgently.

Mr. Reilly remained silent, thinking it best to say nothing about his own bumper.

The other driver looked angry. "Ain't you gonna arrest him?"

"I cain't arrest him if there ain't no damage, Johnny. It's just your word against his. Why don't the four of you just find yourselves somethin' else to do while I accompany these nice folks out of town?" he suggested.

The driver appeared frustrated and looked at the others to see if he should say anything else. One of the two youths in the back seat just shrugged his shoulders.

I'll follow you as far as the road to Chicago—so that you, er, don't get lost," the policeman grunted. "You boys skedaddle!" The driver of the other car revved his engine one last time and took off without another word.

As the police officer walked back to his car, he inspected the bent bumper on the rear of Mr. Reilly's car. He came back alongside Will and peered into the back seat at Mr. Reilly. "Say, did you know your bumper's all smashed up? You'd better stop off at Indianapolis and have it looked at on your way to Chicago." He looked at Mr. Reilly to see what he would say. He had an unfriendly grin on his face. He had obviously figured out what had really happened.

Mr. Reilly just said, "Why, thank you, officer. I'll be sure to do that!"

The policeman paused and said to Will, "What's your name?"

Will looked frightened and replied, "William."

The policeman straightened up, looking displeased. "William what?" he asked in a rough tone.

Will didn't know what to say, so he said, "William, the chauffeur."

The policeman seemed to be enjoying himself. "William, the chauffeur, what?" he repeated patiently, like a cat playing with a mouse.

Will was afraid the policeman would ask him for a chauffeur's license. He replied desperately, "William, the chauffeur, *sir*!"

Although the policeman had wanted Will's last name, this last answer seemed to please him. "That's more like it!" he said, and he got back in the police car.

He motioned for Mr. Reilly's car to move on. Will drove for another mile with the police car right behind him. When Will finally turned onto the road north, he saw in the rear mirror that the policeman was no longer following him.

"He is gone, Mr. Reilly. Would you like me to keep driving?" Will asked.

Mr. Reilly suggested that Will keep driving until they reached Indianapolis. "We'll have to stop for a while and have the bumper looked at," he sighed. "Perhaps we can find a place to stay overnight."

Will said he knew of a boarding house that would take all of them. Mr. Reilly looked vastly relieved. The next two hours passed uneventfully. When they got to Indianapolis, Mr. Reilly left the rest of the family at the boarding house and then drove off to have the bumper repaired. He came back at dinnertime with a new bumper.

The owner of the boarding house was an elderly black woman. She took Mr. Reilly upstairs to his room. Mrs. Reilly was lying on the bed reading a book. Elliot and Will were in the adjacent room talking. The proprietress offered a meal at six o'clock. It would be served family-style in a large dining room on the first floor.

The family had an excellent meal and retired early. It was decided that they would get up at seven o'clock, have breakfast, and get into Chicago sometime after rush hour.

After a delicious breakfast of hot cereal and bacon and eggs, they packed up the car again and drove on to Chicago. As they approached the windy city, traffic became very heavy. Mr. Reilly asked Will where his brother lived.

"He lives on the south side of the city, Mr. Reilly," Will replied. "Chicago is a very big place. If you don't want to get lost, it would be best for you to leave me at the Loop. From there, I will be able to take the train and then a bus to my brother's apartment."

"How can you carry Mr. Mews and your suitcase?" Mrs. Reilly asked worriedly. "You'll need another pair of hands!"

"I have a small carrier for him," Will explained, "but it is an old one. He knows how to get out of it. If he were to escape, there is the chance that he might run into the street."

"Why don't you let me keep him for a week?" young Elliot suggested. "I'll be staying on the estate of a man who has hired me to help him sail his boat and to be his gardener in exchange for room and board. I could bring Mr. Mews to you next weekend, before school starts. It's right on Lake Michigan. Mr. Mews and I could even go for a walk around the property every day. I'm sure I can find someone with a car who would drive me to your brother's place."

Will smiled happily. "That would be most helpful, Elliot. I gratefully accept your offer!" he exclaimed.

When they found State Street, the business area was already crowded with shoppers. Mr. Reilly was able to find a parking place on a side street. When Will opened the car door, the sounds of the elevated trains frightened Mr. Mews. He jumped onto Will's head and clung so tightly with his claws that Will cried out in pain. Elliot pried the terrified cat off Will's head and held onto him firmly. "I've got his leash, Will, don't worry!" Elliot exclaimed.

"As you can see, Mrs. Reilly, it is a very good thing that Elliot has offered to take him," Will replied. "Mr. Mews is used to the quiet of a TB sanitarium. He is terrified of the noise of the city."

Mr. Reilly got out of the car and helped Will with his suitcase. He shook his hand and wished Will well. Will came around to the sidewalk and reached through the cracked window in order to pet Mr. Mews one last time. "*A bientot*, my little friend!"

Elliot reached through the window and took Will's hand in both of his hands. "It's a pleasure knowing you, Will," he said warmly. "I'll see you with Mr. Mews next weekend."

Will wrote down his brother's address and phone number on a piece of paper and handed it to Elliot. "I will be looking for work during the day, Elliot," he said, "but you can call me any time after dinner." Will thanked Mr. and Mrs. Reilly for their kindness and then turned and walked down the street toward the elevated train. They watched him until he disappeared into the crowd.

Mr. Reilly sighed. "I hope he will find a good life here!"

He got back into the car and drove down the street. Then he made a turn toward Lake Michigan. The beautiful canals in this part of the city reminded Mr. Reilly of pictures he had seen of Paris. *Perhaps the Parisian ambiance will make Will feel a bit more at home*, he thought. He had never been to the south side of Chicago. He guessed that it was poor. He doubted that it looked like Paris.

They drove along Lake Michigan toward Evanston, but young Elliot kept looking back at the city skyline through the rearview mirror. He ignored the sparkling blue water that stretched northward for three hundred miles to the Straits of Mackinac. He also ignored the sailboats, bicyclists, and sunbathers who were enjoying its magnificent beauty. He was worried about how Will would adjust to life on the south side after having lived in the fresh air and green hillsides of Sherwood for so many years.

As Mr. Reilly pulled up to the gate of the estate, Elliot pointed out the refurbished carriage house where he would be living. He was expected, and he had been told that his apartment would be open for him when he arrived. As they drove up to the carriage house, Elliot enjoyed a fleeting image of Will, Mr. Mews, and himself living alone together in the main house. He pictured the three of them being served dinner each night by the butler.

Elliot looked at his employer's elegant home, which was a rambling Victorian mansion with several porches and a graceful entrance. There was a light on in a first-floor room. Gorgeous flower gardens edged the walkways. It would be a lot to take care of, but Elliot enjoyed outdoor work. The elderly owner was a pleasant man, and he had been impressed that Elliot had a scholarship in mathematics.

Elliot looked all around him and guiltily realized that he would be living in splendor. He wondered if Will had yet reached his brother's apartment on the south side. Elliot thought of the two countries Will had spoken about, and the color line that divided them. He thought the color line must be like a river. It would have a source, just like the Mississippi. Perhaps it began in these wealthy estates and trickled past small enclaves of the Negro bourgeoisie. Perhaps it broadened, fed by many tributaries, creating widening expanses that separated white office and factory workers from Negro hospital workers, domestic workers, and sharecroppers. As it flattened out into the canyons of urban ghettos and into the deltas of other bypassed landscapes, it would ultimately pass by the homeless and unemployed. If there were indeed two countries in America, Elliot concluded that it would mean that America had never ceased to be Lincoln's "house divided against itself."

"Elliot!" Mrs. Reilly exclaimed, jarring him from his thoughts. She was out of the car and had already opened the trunk while Elliot had been lost in his thoughts. "Aren't you going to give your father a hand with these suitcases?" she asked.

"Just a minute, Mom!" he answered from the front seat. Elliot petted Mr. Mews and then took him into the refurbished carriage house, holding the cat tightly to his chest. Elliot quickly closed the door with one hand, and Mr. Mews sprang happily from Elliot's loosened grip. He landed in one bound on the windowsill and immediately began to groom himself.

Elliot opened the window so that Mr. Mews could bask in the sunlight. "Welcome to Chicago, Mr. Mews!" he exclaimed.

Mr. and Mrs. Reilly spent two more days in Chicago and then

headed back for Carlton. On their way home, they avoided the town where Will had been stopped by the policeman, because they were afraid of being asked about their missing chauffeur. They decided to surprise Colleen with another visit on the way home. When Mr. and Mrs. Reilly came through the doorway of Colleen's solarium, Laura was the first to spot them.

"Colleen," she said, "look up from your crochetin' and see who just walked in!"

"Mom! Dad!" Colleen exclaimed.

Her mother came over to her bed and gave Colleen a big hug. "We just got in from Chicago. We thought we should stop and let you know we all got there safely. Elliot has a dandy place to stay right on Lake Michigan, Colleen. I hope he remembers to go to class. He even gets to help sail a boat with the man he'll be working for. Imagine that!"

"I'd never bother with school except in winter, in that case," Colleen laughed. "Did Will find his brother all right? Tell me all about it."

Miss Marthe brought in two chairs for Colleen's parents. She stood listening beside Laura's bed because she too was curious to know what had happened to Will.

Colleen's parents took turns describing the events of their trip. Colleen laughed hard when her father got to the part about Will masquerading as the family chauffeur. "Good thinking, Dad!" she said approvingly. "But how did you make them think we're rich with that old car of ours?"

Mr. Reilly looked startled. "You know, I never even thought about the car! I was too busy thinking about those boys in the other car. Maybe the cop had never seen a chauffeured car before. Anyway, he believed me," he chuckled. "Those hoodlums didn't believe Will was a chauffeur, but they got caught in their own lie about their bumper."

Mr. Reilly gave Laura the piece of paper with Will's address and phone number in Chicago. "My son will be taking Mr. Mews back to him this weekend," he added. "Will hopes to find a job soon. You can write to him at that address."

"You'll never guess what happened while you were gone, Dad," Colleen said excitedly. "Bret and Pete found Miss Wilson's book in the library! They saw the Handyman go in there on Sunday. He didn't appear to have my book, but when Pete and Bret went into the library, they found it lying in a corner on the floor behind the check-out desk. It had been thrown very hard against the wall. The jacket was torn and some of the pages were crumpled."

"That's not all, Mr. Reilly," Miss Marthe added. "The Handyman has left Sherwood for good! Dr. Smith called him to his office today. He vas very upset that Vill left Sherwood because he vas afraid. Dr. Smith told the Handyman that he vouldn't tolerate any more racial incidents at Sherwood. He told him he vould make him do all the maintenance in the new Negro ward as soon as it is open, and that this vould teach him how to behave properly toward his fellow man. Vhen Dr. Smith told him that he vould be fired if there vas even one complaint from any of the Negro patients, the Handyman quit—just like that!" Miss Marthe snapped her fingers.

"Now that I have Will's address, I'll be able to write to him and tell him that Dr. Smith hopes he'll come back," Laura said enthusiastically. "Mr. Olsen wants him to come back too. If he doesn't return, Dr. Smith said that he will write him a letter of recommendation. Mr. Olsen will do the same."

"Well, Laura, you'll have to be sure to tell him all that!" Mr. Reilly exclaimed.

Colleen's porch mates appeared to be enjoying the visit as much as Colleen. Everyone wanted to hear all about Elliot's new place and about her parents' visit to Chicago. Her parents had saved money by staying with Elliot. Mrs. Reilly told them that they had greatly enjoyed going to the art museum. They had walked along the beach at Northwestern University and had seen some of the buildings where

Elliot would have his classes. Laura was alarmed when she heard that Mr. Mews had been frightened by the noise of the trains.

"I'm sure Mr. Mews will be very happy in his new apartment, Laura," Mr. Reilly reassured her. "Will took wonderful care of him here at Sherwood. Under his good care, Mr. Mews has become a very sociable and adaptable animal. Mr. Mews sat on all of our laps during the trip."

As it was nearing the lunch hour, Mr. and Mrs. Reilly decided to get back on the road. After they had kissed Colleen good-bye, she listened as they went down the hall, talking about happy things.

She was on her own again, and she realized that it was the beginning of another school year. She wondered what it would be like to sit in a classroom again. Sherwood had become an interesting side stream in which one could drift aimlessly and timelessly. There was no curriculum. There were no requirements or tests at Sherwood. One crocheted. One made friends. One looked forward to being fed. A person could easily be lulled into complacency by the endless drifting. It seemed to Colleen that only Bret, Pete, and perhaps Mr. Perkins had ever truly thought about rocking the boat.

After about a week, Colleen received a note from her mother. She asked for a picture of Colleen. "It's for the school yearbook," she had written. Colleen had several photos that Mr. Olsen had taken of her. Many were in black and white, but there was also a color photo she especially liked. It was a close-up, and she looked happy and healthy, and not like someone with TB. She put it in an envelope along with a letter to her mother, and on the way to lunch, she left it at the nurses' station for Miss Marthe to mail.

At lunch, Pete and Bret were discussing a male patient named Frank. "They've moved him into one of the private rooms, Colleen," Bret said. "It doesn't look good."

Frank died at the end of the week, but not before Colleen went up to his room for a brief visit. On her way up to the second floor, Colleen thought about her first night at Sherwood, and about Sue Ann's fear that she might die alone in a private room. She wasn't sure what she would say to Frank.

Colleen stepped quietly into Frank's room, and she saw immediately how pale and weak he was. She was taken aback, because she had always liked Frank. He had never been much of a talker, but he had always been kind and shown an interest in her. She said she just wanted him to know that she was thinking about him, and she tried to cheer him up by telling him the good news about her family's visit.

Frank's eyes were feverish, and he didn't say anything at first. Then he finally asked her, "Have you any good news for *me*, Colleen?"

Colleen's stricken silence filled the room. She finally said, "I didn't want you to feel alone, Frank."

"Thank you for coming, Colleen," he said, but it was in a very weak voice. Then he asked, almost crying, "Why haven't they told me that I'm dying?" He turned and faced the wall.

"I'll call a nurse, Frank," was all that she could think to say.

Colleen found a nurse and told her about Frank. The nurse rushed into Frank's room.

Colleen went back to her porch and thought about Frank's two questions. She lay down, feeling exhausted. Frank had asked her if she had any good news for *him*, but she had only talked about her family. All the while, Frank had been wondering why they hadn't told him that he was dying. He had turned and faced the wall because he had known there wouldn't be any more good news for him. He had come to the end, and the end was a blank wall.

Pete had tried to convince her that death was not the true end. He had called it a *deceptive* cadence. He had told her that death doesn't belong to God's eternal nature, and that death is only the ugly consequence of nature's chaos and brutality. In her heart, Colleen wanted to believe that, because she wanted to believe that even though the miracle of life is fragile and can't last in the barbaric world outside of God's Eden, we can still make life better, with God's help, by *listening*. Isn't that what Pete always said? But she also knew that she had failed Frank because she hadn't told him that life matters to God. She had said that to Pete the first time they had gone up to Claire's apartment. But she hadn't told Pete or Frank that their goodness mattered to *her*, too, and this was a grievous failing that she now rued. The problem was that she hadn't known how to respond to the pain in Frank's voice. It had frightened her. She thought again of Victoria on the carousel and of her mother's reticence about her Uncle John's death. Colleen knew she had gone to Frank's room hoping to find a way to make death perfect and beautiful, when in fact, it never could be. It was what it was.

Nevertheless, she felt that Pete's philosophy of life and death was true, and the sad truth was that life *is* like a music box winding down. But even though it fades away, it is still true and beautiful to the last note. She had thought Frank wouldn't have understood if she had said something like that. It came too close to the horror of the silence and lonely pain of approaching death—and it would have sounded corny. She thought bitterly that all philosophy sounds corny in the end. In the end, all words fail us.

No, she should simply have said to Frank that it mattered to her that he was in pain, and that she would heal him if only she knew how. But she didn't say that either, because she didn't want to say that there was no physical hope. Then she realized that she should simply have said that Frank mattered to her, and that no further explanation was necessary. Just simply that he mattered. Instead, she had realized one terrible fact standing there and listening to Frank's pain and sense of abandonment. And that fact was that no one should die alone and forgotten in a private room facing a meaningless blank wall.

The truth was that she had been *afraid* of Frank's pain and his feeling of already being dead and forgotten while still alive. She had been deathly afraid. Wasn't that the word people used to describe what she felt? She had been frightened by his futility and his lost hope that family, friends, or God still cared. She was afraid to say good-bye, because she didn't really understand what that meant, and she hadn't known how to say it. She only knew that Frank did not want to say good-bye alone, and he was right. To say good-bye to no one made no sense whatsoever.

When she had gone to Frank's room, she had not expected to find out that death could take away all hope, and so she had fled. Instead of telling him that his friendship mattered to her and had given her hope, she had remained silent. She had been afraid, like a young child on a carousel who had lost sight of the ever-watchful parent—the caring and good parent, but above all, the fearful and protective parent. Lost and afraid in the whirl and blur of the carousel, she had seen the riderless pale horse, and she had not known how to say good-bye to Frank.

As Colleen and Abby were eating dinner the evening after Frank's death, they saw Dr. Kurtz quickly cross the parking lot. He was carrying a pan draped with a white cloth. Two nurses accompanied him. They were not talking, and they were very businesslike. All three of them got into a van and drove off toward the other building. Abby nudged Colleen with her elbow. "What do you suppose is under that cloth?" she asked in a very subdued voice, her eyes round with apprehension.

"It looks like it might be a medical specimen," Colleen answered.

"Do you think it could be Frank's lungs?" Abby asked almost inaudibly.

Colleen had no answer, and furthermore, she didn't want to know the answer. A day later, a rumor circulated that Frank's lungs had been autopsied. The mere thought of having no lungs, dead or alive, filled Colleen with a suffocating horror.

Toward the end of the month, the newspapers began carrying news of the upcoming Little World Series between the Louisville Colonels and the Montreal Royals. The first three games were to be played in Louisville, Kentucky. The newspapers were abuzz about Jackie Robinson. He was Montreal's second baseman, and he was the International League's leading hitter. He was the first Negro in history to play in postseason baseball.

By Saturday night, Pete, Emile, and Bret were glued to the radio. The first games were to be played in Louisville. They listened until late in the evening as Louisville rallied in the ninth, but came up short with a final score of 7–5. Robinson didn't get a hit, but he made a great play in the outfield.

"Did you hear that some of the black fans had to watch the game from rooftops when they ran out of tickets?" Emile asked. "Good for Jackie for not folding under the pressure of the booing! They shoulda have let him alone! He's a great player! His batting average this year was .349!"

"You're right, Emile, but how about Jim Gleason's attempted double steal in the second inning?" Bret said. "The Colonels put up a good fight."

"Montreal has a great home-run hitter in Les Burge," Pete observed. "That may spell trouble for Louisville. He got two home runs in one game!"

They lay awake for a while, rehashing the game. In the morning, they woke up thinking about the second game to be held that afternoon. Bret said he thought the Louisville team could win. Emile bet Bret his desserts for a week that Jackie Robinson and the Royals would win the series. Bret bet similarly on Louisville.

By the end of the week, Emile was proven right. The Royals won up in Montreal, and their fans booed the Colonels because of some of the fans' bad manners toward Jackie Robinson when he had played down there. As Colleen entered the dining room following the Montreal victory, she saw Emile proudly arranging his two desserts in front of him. As she sat down at the dining table, she heard Emile say to Bret, "Let thisa be a lesson to you, Bret! Never, ever bet against the underdog in America!" Emile's Italian eyes glittered with immigrant pride, his faith in the American dream fortified by two helpings of apple pie.

Bret looked hungrily at the pie. "I think that Jackie really proved the old line that goes, 'It's not whether you win or lose, but how you play the game that counts!'"

Emile looked very happy with Bret's concession and said, "Jackie Robinson turned the other cheek, justa like Jesus said! And you know what, Bret? Ita worked!"

On the way back to their porches, Pete asked Colleen if she still wanted to play piano for the Halloween party. "That piece is really simple, and we could practice it just one time up in Claire's apartment this weekend!" he suggested.

Colleen shook her head and looked at Pete's tired face. "I don't think you've recovered from the last time we were up there, do you?" she asked. "Don't you remember how tired you were?"

Pete pulled his fingers through his hair and looked at the ceiling in exasperation. "Don't worry, I'm fine!" he exclaimed. "I haven't been up there for a while."

"Are you sure?" Colleen asked disbelievingly.

Pete didn't answer. "Then it's a deal?"

"This is the last time," Colleen warned him.

They agreed to meet up in Claire's apartment during lunch on Sunday.

When Colleen got back to her porch, Laura was writing a letter to Will. "Miss Marthe said that Mr. Olsen and Dr. Smith want to include letters of recommendation with my letter, just in case Will needs them right away," she said. "They will go out together in the afternoon mail."

Colleen lay down in bed with a sigh. It was a beautiful mid-October day. She thought about Will and Elliot in Chicago. It seemed very far away. "It's hard to believe Will is gone. I imagine he's glad to have Mr. Mews back again, at least," Colleen said.

"I miss them both," Laura replied. "If Will doesn't come back by the time I recover, I'll go up north and try to find him." Laura did not elaborate, so Colleen left her alone to finish writing her letter. She drifted off to sleep and slept through the entire rest period.

On the following Sunday, Colleen waited for everyone to go to lunch, and then she took the elevator to the third floor. When she stepped out of the elevator, Pete was already there. He was pacing the landing, looking very upset.

"We're locked out!" he exclaimed.

Colleen remembered the chair she had forgotten to put back in place. "Oh, no!" she exclaimed. "She's figured out that someone's been coming in! I forgot to put my chair back before we left. I meant to tell you, but I forgot."

Pete was nearly distraught. "We can't be shut out! She promised that you could use her piano!" he shouted.

"Shh! Dr. Edmonds will hear!" Colleen warned him.

Pete glanced toward Dr. Edmond's apartment. There were no sounds coming from within. "I think he's over at the hospital," he said.

"Well, we might as well go to lunch," Colleen suggested.

Pete tried the knob one last time. It didn't budge. "How could you!" he shouted at the door. Claire's apartment was as silent as a tomb.

They went back to the dining room and entered separately so as not to arouse suspicion. Laura looked up and said, "Oh, good! We were wondering where you were. We were just discussing the Halloween party. Faith doesn't have a part."

Pete was still glum about being locked out of Claire's apartment, but he told her there were lots of songs in the book that could be used as skits. He suggested Tchaikovsky's "Waltz of the Flowers." Claire could easily play it. He also suggested that Faith round up some of the rest of the female patients so that they could be dancing flowers. This appealed to Faith, and she said she would do it.

Pete was quiet throughout the meal and didn't participate in the general conversation. He left without saying another word. As Colleen was leaving the dining room, Bret pulled her aside and asked, "What's wrong with Pete?"

"Claire locks her door now. He can't get in and play the piano," Colleen answered. "I left a chair out of place when we were up there the last time. She must have figured out that someone's been coming in."

"That's a tough break for Pete, but someone has to stop him before his health completely falls apart," Bret observed.

Pete got even worse news from Miss Marthe the following morning. It had been decided that both Pete and Faith were not well enough to attend the Halloween party. Faith was despondent. Pete took it philosophically.

As Pete and Colleen were walking to the dining room, Colleen broached the subject of the party. Neither she nor Laura knew how to dance a minuet, which their parts in the Halloween skit called for.

"It won't matter, Colleen. No one will know the difference if you two dance a waltz," Pete said. "Besides, Halloween is a silly holiday. It's not worth worrying about," he added, trying to hide the wistfulness in his voice. "Psychologists would tell you that dressing up like ghosts and goblins is just acting out the death wish."

Colleen could not fathom his mood. "What do you mean?" she asked, a bit surprised by the remark.

"Let's just say that Halloween is a season of masks—not to mention fairy princesses!" he added with a laugh, glancing at Colleen. "Unfortunately, some people hide behind masks all year round, like the Handyman. You are the marvelous exception, Colleen. You never wear a mask!" he exclaimed.

"Then you don't think I have an inner fairy princess?" Colleen teased him.

"I like you just the way you are, Colleen!" Pete hesitated as if there was something important that he wanted to say to her. After a moment, he sighed, unable to find the right words.

"My plans for the party didn't work out exactly as I had hoped," he sighed. "Sherwood's highest authorities have spoken on the subject. I can't go, and that's final. I was wrong to think they would let me go," he said regretfully.

"Dr. Smith and Dr. Kurtz are just being careful, Pete," Colleen said as gently as she could.

They walked along for a while, Pete obviously trying to conceal his disappointment. "Doctors are always on the alert for the worst possible turn of events!" he exclaimed. "Freud did the same thing; he looked for the worst, and he found it."

"Freud called the human race 'homo sapiens *lupus*,'" Pete exclaimed. "Rub our fur the wrong way, and out pops the inner wolf!"

"You mean that deep down we're like werewolves?" Colleen asked incredulously. "What a spooky thought!"

"Well, only when the conditions are right and it serves our purposes. Freud didn't believe in the Golden Rule, either. He said it's foolish to trust the wolf in other people—or in ourselves! Do you agree with that, Colleen?" Pete asked earnestly.

Colleen shook her head. "Maybe he was scared by a wolf when he was a little boy," Colleen suggested. "I'll bet Bret would say it was the fairy tales that did it!" she joked.

Pete stared hard at Colleen when she mentioned Bret. "Freud had another terrible idea, Colleen. He called the wolf within the 'death instinct.' He doubted it could be overcome," Pete said.

Colleen studied Pete, trying to fathom his mood. "Maybe we should ask Dr. Kurtz if he's ever seen the death instinct in any of our X-rays.

He could project its image onto the dining room wall during the Halloween party. That would give us a good scare for Halloween!" She laughed, but the thought sent a shiver up her spine.

Pete laughed. "I suppose Dr. Kurtz would have to know where to look."

They walked along in silence until Pete said, "I can't believe Dr. Kurtz wants us to stop playing Claire's piano!"

Colleen looked sharply at Pete. "We were better off not knowing about the piano, Pete. If we don't want to die, therapy is our only hope."

"The best therapy for you and me is Claire's piano, but it's locked up in her apartment now," Pete lamented. "Dr. Kurtz told me that crocheting can calm the most turbulent artistic spirit. He asked me if I really wanted to die in the cyclone of a Beethoven sonata, and he warned me again to stay away from Claire's piano. He said that included you, too."

"Claire must have said something to him!" Colleen exclaimed.

"I reminded him that Beethoven's artistic spirit was indomitable, and that I could think of a lot worse ways to die!" Pete said with a guilty grin. "Dr. Kurtz took it as a direct challenge, of course. He stared hard at me and said, 'After the First World War, we Germans had to learn the *hard way* that there's a time for mutual respect and tranquility, especially during life's storms.' He said the German people hadn't believed that, and they had to reap the whirlwind."

Pete avoided looking at Colleen. "Maybe he was right about mutual respect and tranquility," he said a bit guiltily.

Unwilling to take sides, Colleen searched her mind for the right response.

"I think Dr. Kurtz never expected a *human* cyclone in a TB sanitarium!" she exclaimed. "He's frustrated by a situation that doesn't fit standard medical procedures."

"You mean me!" he laughed. "I'm not questioning Dr. Kurtz's good intentions, Colleen. I'll apologize, if it will please you," Pete said soothingly. "I just happen to think he's wrong."

Colleen looked fondly at Pete. He was irrepressible. "You're incorrigible, you know. You don't want to end up in a private room, do you? You're just letting bed rest get to you!"

"Things will be fine, Colleen," he reassured her.

Colleen didn't press the issue, but she was privately glad that Claire had begun to lock her apartment door. Without access to the piano, Colleen felt certain that Pete would be safe again. He was getting complete rest now, and his eyes had already lost some of their hollowness. His face had better color, too. Colleen felt he would recover quickly by strictly following the rules.

When they had come to the end of the hall and were alongside Colleen's locker, Pete pulled Colleen toward him. He glanced around to see whether Bret might be coming down the hall. "By the way, Colleen, I had temporarily given in to my death instinct and was hoping to go with you to the party as a vampire so that I could bite your neck," he exclaimed laughingly, "or at least until I was told that I couldn't attend." Pete bent down and placed his lips on the back of Colleen's neck. Instead of a bite, she felt a kiss.

"Was that the life or death instinct?" Colleen asked in surprise, feeling a flush come to her cheeks.

"That was this will have to do for now, because I can't go with you to the party," Pete said softly.

He held Colleen closely to him. Her cheek lay against his chest, and she could hear his heart beating rapidly from the exertion of walking. Because of the fear of contagion, how rarely had any of them felt the warmth of human touch during their time at Sherwood?

Pete was right, Colleen thought. They were like the dangling bird at the feeder that she had rescued back in Carlton. Each of them, in his own way, was hanging onto life and to the hope of escape from TB—but just barely, by the fingertips. By mere chance, some had more hope than others. But hope was what each of them clung to because it was all they had. The experience had driven a few of them to the edge of sanity. And Pete was holding onto hope in the form of Claire's piano.

"You complete me, Colleen," Pete said quietly as a patient passed by on the way to the dining room. Colleen felt Pete brush aside a strand of her hair that was partly covering her face. "I couldn't live without that charming and funny counterpoint of yours. Don't ever forget me."

Colleen was stunned. "Why would I do that, Pete?" she asked, not daring to look up.

There was no answer for a moment, and then Pete asked, "Do you trust me, Colleen? Or do you think I'm mad?"

"Of course I trust you, Pete!" she answered unhesitatingly.

She looked up into his face, and to her total astonishment, she saw both fear and tears in his eyes.

As the night of the Halloween party approached, Colleen and Abby spent their free time finishing their costumes. Abby had sewn hundreds of sequins onto her dress and wings. Emile had provided pajamas for Julie's clown costume, and Laura had found a jacket and pair of shoes for her George Washington outfit. Colleen would also be wearing a colonial costume. She planned to perform Beethoven's *Minuet in G*. Bret had finally decided that he would go as a colonial gentleman. It was agreed that Claire would play the Beethoven minuet a second time while Colleen danced with Laura. Bret was supposed to cut in and finish the dance.

When Halloween night arrived, everyone was dressed and ready to go except for Faith and Pete. Emile offered to stay with Pete, but Pete just waved him on telling him to enjoy himself. Emile was dressed as a pirate. His head was wrapped in a bandana made out of a tie, and he wore a black patch on his right eye. He had glued a wide black mustache over his upper lip. He had made a sword out of cardboard and had tucked it into a waist sash made out of two more ties. He looked very swashbuckling. Black pants and a black vest worn over a white shirt completed his costume. Emile lifted his eye patch and winked. "I'm a gonna take a very good care of Colleen and Abby, Pete!" Pete laughed and said he was not worried.

Emile looked relieved that Pete didn't mind being alone. He promised to bring Pete some treats and left for the party. Shortly thereafter, Colleen and Abby took the elevator upstairs to show Pete their costumes. Pete looked admiringly at Abby's gorgeous, sequined dress. "You're perfect!" he exclaimed. Abby beamed in delight.

"What about me?" Colleen asked. Colleen was wearing a long dress and a cook's apron over it. Her hair was powdered. She was wearing white gloves and a hat that she hoped looked colonial. She was also carrying a basket of fruit. "You look like Martha Washington, or maybe Marie Antoinette without a shepherd's crook!" he teased.

Pete coughed once, reaching for sputum paper. Colleen looked away, wondering how sick Pete really was. "Well," he said, "I guess you'd better get down there before you miss your cues," he said wistfully. "Bret and Emile left about ten minutes ago."

As Pete spoke, a piece of sheet music fell from his bed. Pete reached down for it. It was his own copy of the Mozart variations he had given to Colleen on her birthday.

"I was just looking this over again. I was going to play it tonight, but you know ..." Pete's voice trailed off regretfully.

"Mr. Olsen is going to take pictures," Colleen said encouragingly. "You'll get to see everything. Why don't you take a nap, Pete? The party will be over in a few hours, and I'll bring you some cookies afterward," Colleen promised. She didn't know what else she could say, so she simply said, "I'm sorry we can't go together tonight, Pete."

Pete handed her the music, trying to hide his disappointment. Colleen placed the music on the stand near his bed.

"Don't worry about me, Colleen," he smiled. "I'll probably read awhile and then go to bed early."

Colleen rejoined Abby, who was adjusting one of her wings at the entrance to Pete's porch.

"Let's go, Abby!" Colleen said. "Good-bye, Pete!" Colleen called as the elevator doors began to open.

The last thing Colleen heard before the elevator doors closed was, "So long, Colleen!"

Pete listened as the elevator made its descent. He turned onto his side and tried to read a book, but he could not keep his mind on it.

When the elevator doors opened at the first floor, Colleen and Abby followed a group of women patients down the hall toward the dining room. The women were dressed in various homemade costumes. One of them was dressed as an 1890s' girl. She wore a broad-brimmed hat tied under her chin with a bow and a long-sleeved blouse and floor-length skirt. Most of the women wore black or pink masks. It all seemed very magical to Colleen.

When they entered the dining room, Colleen saw Dr. Smith standing in front of a microphone. A curtain of sheets had been hung on a piece of rope across the front part of the room, and the staff had festooned the windows with crepe paper. Most of the patients were already seated and waiting for the show to begin. Colleen and Abby slipped behind the sheets and saw Bret, Julie, and Laura. The piano had been placed off to one side.

Claire arrived a bit later all out of breath. "I brought my fiancé tonight! It took us a while to get here! Are you ready, Julie? You'll go first with your juggling act, to get them laughing. Dr. Kurtz has volunteered to change the sets for us."

Colleen could see Dr. Kurtz dressed in black, standing in the wings by the first piece of scenery. It depicted a kitchen table with pies set on it. Claire peeked around the corner and nodded to Dr. Smith. Julie came running through the curtains with a whole stack of pie plates. Emile had taught her how to juggle three, but not four of them.

Two of the male patients pulled the sheets aside, and Claire began playing the piano. Julie was wearing a cook's hat and a clown outfit. She had brought out a tall stack of pie plates which she attempted to set down on the floor. As she did so, she tripped on Emile's shoes and went sprawling. Everyone laughed, assuming it was part of the act. Julie picked herself up and began playfully juggling just one. Then she picked up two plates. Someone yelled, "More, more!" Julie picked up a third plate and pretended to have a hard time as she ran from one side of the stage to the other in pursuit of them. She was amazingly athletic. She finally threw one of them very high in the air and whisked the other two behind her back, catching the third as it fell to earth again. She took a deep bow as the curtains closed.

Throughout Julie's performance, Pete had been lying restlessly in bed. He found it impossible to read or fall asleep. He got out of bed, paced restlessly, and then stepped out into the second-floor hall. A few women patients were asleep, and the library was eerily silent. When he opened the stairwell door, he heard laughter and the sound of Claire playing the piano.

He had chills and felt a bit feverish, but he stood listening to her piano music for a few minutes. Then he returned to the porch, put on his robe and slippers, and walked over to the elevator. He pushed the button for the third floor.

When the doors opened at the third floor, Pete glanced toward Dr. Edmonds's apartment. The landing was silent, and no one was around. He strode quickly to Claire's apartment door and turned the door handle. It didn't move. Instead, the entire door swung open. Claire had locked her door from the inside, but she had failed to draw the door completely shut. Unable to believe his luck, Pete went back downstairs and retrieved his copy of the Mozart variations. He took the elevator back up to Claire's apartment, sat down at the piano, and began to play. In his haste, he inadvertently left the apartment door open.

As Dr. Kurtz changed the set for Abby's number, Dr. Smith told some Halloween jokes. Colleen was surprised to hear the audience guffawing loudly. Pop Smith, obviously enjoying himself, told a few more jokes. Then he peeked through the curtains and saw that they were ready for Abby's skit.

Colleen began playing Chopin's *Butterfly Etude*. When Abby stepped onto the stage in her sequined gown, the men in the audience whistled en masse. Abby began to flitter about, pretending she was a butterfly. The overhead lighting suffused her sequined dress in a thousand points of light. Her tight black gown created the effect of a butterfly's body. For antennae, she had sewn two fronds of wild grass onto a small black hat that she had pinned to her hair. The effect was exquisitely real. Dr. Kurtz had painted a backdrop of a colorful flower garden so that Abby could flutter from flower to flower.

After Colleen had played the short *etude* three times, the lights went out, and Claire slid onto the piano bench next to Colleen. Colleen held a flashlight up to the music while Claire began to play the *Moonlight Sonata*.

Colleen glanced up, and through the gap at the end of the curtain, she saw a shadowy form outside the dining room window. The silhouette of a goblin-like figure in a short, black jacket hovered eerily behind the pane of glass. Colleen felt a shiver run up her spine. It was the Handyman. Pete had said that Halloween was a night for the death instinct and the destructive side of human nature, and now the Handyman had come back, perhaps for revenge, she thought.

The Handyman pressed his face against the glass, compressing it into a ghoulish leer. He seemed to be looking for someone. Colleen wondered if he was looking for Will. His eyes fell on Dr. Smith and then on Colleen. When he realized Dr. Smith saw him, he looked afraid, but when he saw Colleen watching him, he shook his fist angrily and then turned and fled. Colleen's hand shook as she tried to hold the flashlight steady. Claire looked questioningly at Colleen in the flickering light.

As Claire played the opening measures of Beethoven's *Moonlight* Sonata, Colleen watched Dr. Kurtz climb a ladder and begin to slowly raise a paper moon above the garden backdrop. They had all worked hard to make the night something special, and Colleen refused to let the Handyman's anger and hatred spoil it all. He *belonged* outside in the night—because it represented the way he had chosen to live as an outsider. Indeed, Colleen thought, he belonged to the deepest and darkest forests of the endless hills—and to the night itself.

Colleen tried to forget everything she had just seen outside the window. She listened quietly as Claire interpreted Beethoven's haunting theme. As Colleen listened, she felt that Beethoven had discovered a quality of moonlight that was quite unlike Debussy's interpretation of it. Debussy had captured the ethereal qualities of moonlight in his ballet-like sequences. His moonlight was delicate, yet highly sensual and evocative. Beethoven's moonlight seemed to convey inexpressible anguish over some secret loss. His moonlight was dark and brooding. Colleen thought that it was a fitting piece for Halloween. Poe's words, "Quoth the raven, 'Nevermore'" fluttered through Colleen's subconscious, like a startled bird in the night.

As Claire continued to play, Colleen listened carefully. Her sister Maureen had often played the piece at home in Carlton. In the middle of the composition, Beethoven seemed to abandon a moonlit, earthly realm and reach upward to the stars. As his sequence of broken chords cascaded back down to earth like falling stars, the music, perhaps aware that it had disturbed the heavens, became dark and brooding again. In the final measures, Beethoven's theme reappeared in the left hand as the insistent and stressed tolling of a single G-sharp. The single-note motif reminded Colleen of the repeated notes in the Chopin prelude that Pete had played for her. Although Beethoven reprised the upwardly flowing chords at the end of the piece, they seemed no longer capable of reaching the stars. Instead, they were trapped in the final cadence, which led inexorably to the somber, tonic chord. Beethoven deliberately repeated the final chord for emphasis.

To Colleen, those two chords felt like a hard bump with reality—like Icarus's fall to earth in Greek mythology. They seemed restless and unsettled, and Colleen wondered if all minor-key resolutions in the Romantic repertoire had a similar feeling of incompleteness. She wondered if they were a lament for something that might have been, but could be nevermore. Pete had said that there was nothing unlovely in sadness because music resolves all things, but Beethoven's final chords seemed as unsettled as grief and as restless as the human longing for Icarus's wings. The composition seemed to resolve into tragedy. She wondered if Pete's theory of music as Hope took that into account.

Suddenly, Colleen remembered that Pete said he would like to fly away through Claire's window. He had invited her to go with him. Her answer had only been an ambiguous, "Perhaps someday!" At the time, she had felt that her reply was a positive response, considering their health problems, but now her words seemed like a betrayal. She felt that she should have said yes. She remembered his stricken face in the hallway and his question, "Do you trust me, or do you think I'm mad?"

Colleen glanced up and looked out the dining room window. There was no one there. Dr. Smith had obviously recognized the Handyman. Dr. Smith's disapproving look had most likely frightened the Handyman away, perhaps for good.

Meanwhile, Dr. Edmonds had been shining a light on the rising moon held by Dr. Kurtz. As he did this, Abby pretended to be a moth, attracted first to the flowers and then to the moon and then to a lighted candle on a table near the right of the stage. When the music stopped, Abby extinguished the candle with her fingertips. There was a silence and then loud and appreciative applause.

The lights came up, and Abby turned and faced the audience. She smiled gaily and took a bow. Then she sat down in a vacant seat at the edge of the audience, hoping to have a good view of Colleen's skit. Her chair was very near the dining room doors, and Abby thought she could hear the sound of classical music coming from the stairwell. Curious, she stepped through the doors and listened. By the quality of the musicianship, she knew it must be Pete who was playing.

Claire slipped out from the edge of the curtains and sat down next to Abby. Abby took her out in the hall, and they both listened. Claire recognized the Mozart piece and immediately concluded that it had to be Pete. "I don't know how he did it, but it sounds like he's playing my piano!" she exclaimed.

Bret came out and joined them. He was supposed to jump out of the audience during Colleen's skit with Laura and take a turn dancing with Colleen. Bret also heard the music floating down from upstairs.

"It sounds vaguely like 'Twinkle, Twinkle, Little Star,'" he said, looking mystified.

Claire quickly replied, "It's Mozart's variations on it, Bret."

A look of recognition came across Bret's face. "And that would, ah, be Pete playing it, correct? He must be Houdini!" Bret marveled.

Claire said uneasily, "The question is what should we do about it?"

As the curtain opened and Colleen began playing Beethoven's *Minuet in G*, some of the other audience members had become aware of the competing strains of "Twinkle, Twinkle, Little Star" coming down the stairwell. They began to murmur in protest.

While Colleen continued to play the *Minuet in G*, Laura sat writing with a quill pen at a desk. She was dressed as George Washington. Dr. Kurtz had set up a backdrop of an American flag with its thirteen original stars. Out of the corner of her eye, Colleen saw Claire get up and speak to Dr. Smith. Then Claire joined Colleen at the piano bench. When Colleen had finished playing, Claire began playing the composition a second time. Colleen began to dance with Laura.

In the middle of the piece, Bret walked onto center stage and tapped Laura on the shoulder, cutting in on her. Bret's army of friends whooped in delight. Bret winked broadly at the audience and bent Colleen very gracefully over his arm. He leaned over her and whispered, "This isn't in the script, but they'll love it." He gave her a lingering kiss on the lips. It brought the house down.

Meanwhile, Pop Smith had rushed out of the dining room. He waited impatiently at the elevator and then decided to take the stairs. He took them two at a time. He could hear the strains of *Clair de Lune* floating down the stairwell. It was so beautiful that he paused a moment to listen. Suddenly there was a groan and the music stopped.

Dr. Smith could hear someone coming up the stairs behind him. It was Abby.

"Go back!" he warned her. "These are too many stairs for you to climb!"

Abby paused and saw Dr. Smith run up the remaining half flight. When she was almost to the top of the stairs, there was a moan, and she could hear Pete saying, "I'm dying, Pop!"

There was a short silence, and then another moan, and then Abby heard Dr. Smith say, "It's all right, Pete." Then there was what seemed to Abby an interminable silence.

Abby could hear the blood pounding in her ears. She stood still, paralyzed with fear. Dr. Smith came to the top of the stairs with a hopeless look in his eyes. "Don't go in, Abby. There's nothing you can do now," he said quietly.

Dr. Smith rushed down the stairs to summon Dr. Kurtz and nearly collided with Colleen in the hall. He rushed past her, not realizing that she was on her way upstairs.

Colleen took the elevator upstairs. When the doors opened, she could see Pete lying beside the piano bench on his back, his arms outstretched. He had obviously hemorrhaged. The window was open to the starry night. From down below, Colleen could hear the sounds of the revelers. The full moon had spread its light upon the carpet, and Pete's left hand was open, seeming to catch the moonlight in his hand. Abby was kneeling and weeping over Pete's lifeless body. The wings of her costume gleamed in the moonlight.

Colleen turned away as she reached out to press the elevator button. She stepped inside the elevator as she had so many times with him and began to cry. She rode the elevator back down to the first floor because she couldn't bear to see Pete dead.

Pete died playing the piano, she told herself. It was the same way that Victoria had died, except for one thing, Colleen thought.

Pete had known that he might die, but he had refused to let the music go out of his life. The piano had renewed his hope, had even offered him a glimpse of God, but it couldn't protect him against the ever-present reality of death at Sherwood.

Colleen felt the hard bump of the elevator as it reached the ground floor. The elevator doors opened, and the second floor patients began to file in. Colleen pushed past them and past her own emotional exhaustion and her need to sleep. She stepped out of the elevator and walked aimlessly toward the dining room.

She found Emile slumped in a chair, and she sat down next to him. A few remaining revelers, their masks removed, their faces shocked, glanced at Colleen and Emile and then moved on. Without looking at Colleen, Emile took her hand. "I promised him I'd look after you and Abby, Colleen," Emile said, "and I'ma going to do that! God bless Pete!" He took out his handkerchief and wiped his eyes.

"He told me I never wore a mask," Colleen said, looking at the Halloween mask that she held in her hand. She felt sick that she had left Pete alone to die.

The word "nevermore" seemed to shriek from the darkness behind the eyeholes of the mask. Or was it from some dark and hopeless place in her mind? She couldn't be sure which. In the end, perhaps it amounted to the same thing, she told herself. She tried to imagine Pete, still alive and still playing Claire's piano as only he could.

But there was only silence, and the terrible darkness at the top of the stairs.

Emile and Colleen sat huddled together forlornly for a while. A fire bell went off, breaking the stillness that enshrouded them, and Colleen was vaguely aware of confused shouts in the halls. Then they both looked up. Miss Marthe had found them. She looked sad, harried, and worn out. She told them they would have to go back to their porches and get some sleep.

The night was not yet over, however. Colleen gasped in horror as she noticed vivid red and yellow reflections on the windowpanes along the far side of the dining room. "Look, Miss Marthe!" she exclaimed, pointing to the windows in terror. "It looks like the whole forest is burning down!"

"It's all right, Colleen," Miss Marthe said, trying not to frighten her. "Ve haf already called the police and fire departments. Skippy found a burning cross in one of the trash cans, and the fire has spread to the trash area. Someone knew it vas the perfect place to start a fire!" she exclaimed angrily.

Colleen thought immediately of the Handyman. Emile ran to the window and looked out. "Skippy's out there with a garden hose. The whole hillside is on fire! Somebody musta have wanted to burn down the hospital!" he shouted.

"He is probably long gone by now," Miss Marthe exclaimed in consternation that the arsonist most likely had gotten away. She muttered something in German, and shook her head in outrage.

Dr. Smith had by then rushed into the room, and Miss Marthe jumped up to confer with him. There was pandemonium in the halls now, and the din of honking fire trucks was growing louder. The undulating shriek of their sirens sounded like the wailing of banshees to Colleen. She closed her eyes and shivered uncontrollably. For the first time since she had been at Sherwood, Colleen longed for the consolation of Sherwood's healing sleep

## Mummy Case

After Pete died, it seemed to Colleen that her whole world began to fall apart. At the end of November Abby and Laura were discharged, leaving Colleen feeling alone and dismayed by her indefinite prospects. Colleen had expected Abby's discharge, but she was surprised when Dr. Smith released Laura as well. Will was still in Chicago, and Laura's parting words were that she was going to find him. Abby promised Colleen that she would visit her in Carlton when Colleen had finally recovered. Abby gave her a pep talk about getting well soon, but Colleen knew this was unlikely. Dr. Kurtz was making no progress in keeping her lung down.

After Abby and Laura left Sherwood, Colleen would sometimes play Pete's music box, but the music never cheered her. If anything, it made her feel sadder. Faith finally suggested that Colleen write a letter to Pete's father, but Colleen didn't know what to say. When at last Colleen mustered enough courage to write the letter, she realized that she didn't even know Pete's last name. She had to ask Miss Marthe to look up his father's name and address.

"I'm glad you are vriting to him, Colleen!" Miss Marthe exclaimed sympathetically. "I think it vill do you good. Grief is not a good thing to keep inside you."

Colleen wrote a letter to Pete's father saying that she had known Pete well and that he had been a wonderful friend. She told him about the good times they had shared together, but she didn't mention Claire's piano. She wrapped the little music box and mailed it to Pete's father along with the letter. At the end of two weeks, a letter and a small package arrived in the mail for Colleen. Pete's father had sent back the music box, and his letter said:

*Dear Colleen,*

*Thank you for your kind words about my son. Pete often spoke about you in his letters. He told me that you were his best friend at Sherwood and that even though you were younger than he was, he found you mature beyond your years and quite artistic. He planned to see you again when you had both recovered.*

*I am returning the music box because I know he wanted you to have it. I believe it was the thing that started him on the path to music. I hope you will keep it and find inspiration in it, too.*

Sincerely,

Augustus Montaigne, DVM

Colleen placed Dr. Montaigne's letter in Miss Wilson's book so that she would not lose it, and then she wound the tiny key on the bottom of the music box. She listened to the familiar melody. In her mind's ear, she could hear Pete playing the Mozart variations, but the sound was very far away.

When the new wing on the Administrative Building was finally ready for occupancy, Colleen and her porch mates received word that they would be moved there within a day or two. Colleen was excited because Miss Marthe had told her that the porches in the new wing had windows that could be kept open in summer and closed in the winter. Miss Marthe told them that this was because year-round, open-air treatment was no longer considered necessary for recovery.

Bret reacted to the news with mixed emotions. "I understand the new wing is quite impressive," Bret observed during lunch on the day before the move. "Unfortunately, it's U-shaped, and a wide lawn separates the men's wing from the women's wing. What will we do if there are separate dining rooms over there too? What would life be like without the fair sex?" Bret exclaimed.

Emile said, "Don't worry, Bret, you could still crochet."

Colleen leaned her chin on her palm and studied Bret. In spite of his continued high humor, she wondered if Pete's death was weighing on him as heavily as it was on her. Bret had never spoken more than a few words about Pete's death to Colleen.

"I've heard that Dr. Kurtz wants the men and women to eat at separate tables because people have been meeting secretly on the roof and elsewhere," Colleen said.

Bret looked unhappy. He appealed to Julie and Faith for moral support.

"This isn't a convent!" Faith exclaimed. "Having our meals with the men is the only normal thing we do at Sherwood!"

Colleen laughed. "I just wanted to know how Bret felt about Dr. Kurtz's idea," she replied.

"I agree with Faith and Bret," Julie said. "It would be very dull without guys at Sherwood."

"Actually, so do I," Colleen agreed.

Bret shot Julie and Faith a triumphant grin. When dinner was over, Colleen walked slowly back to her porch, all the while thinking about Pete.

Pete's death had been like a massive earthquake that all of them had only barely survived. Colleen missed Pete's conversation and companionship. Meals were no longer the same, even though they all attempted to keep the conversation interesting. Claire felt responsible because Pete had died in her apartment. She continued to blame herself for not having closed the door securely. Colleen had tried to console her, but to no avail.

Colleen believed that only Bret had done the right thing by warning them about the danger Pete was placing himself in. She wondered if Bret regretted the stolen kiss as Pete lay dying. He had never mentioned it. For Colleen, the worst thing was that her conscience would not allow her to ignore the awful possibility that Pete might have lived if she hadn't told him about Claire's piano in the first place.

Colleen had never dared to ask Dr. Kurtz about the actual cause of Pete's death. She feared that Dr. Kurtz would blame her if he found out about Pete's visits to Claire's apartment. She thought again about Dr. Montaigne's kind letter. She wanted to write him a letter laying out the whole truth, but she recoiled guiltily at the thought of causing him any more grief.

When she got back to her porch, Colleen went to bed and rested, but she could not sleep. After the rest period, she started reading Miss Wilson's book. Since the book's pages had been almost completely separated from the binding, it was not easy. Each time Colleen opened the tattered book, she could feel the Handyman's wrath. Colleen wondered what had become of him, but in her heart, she didn't really want to know. She wanted to forget. He had boldly scrawled across the title page:

You were always looking down on me from your porch. From the beginning, you didn't show the proper respect! You, the Frenchman, and the cat got what each of you deserved.

Later in the evening, Colleen and the rest of her porch mates organized their things for the move to the new wing. Colleen removed Miss Wilson's book, Bret's little horse, Pete's music box, and the Mozart variations from her bed pocket. She packed them in her suitcase along with the clothes she had brought from home. Then she went to bed.

The wind had come up, and Colleen huddled under the covers. It was December 5. She had been at Sherwood exactly one year. Colleen placed her feet next to Will's foot warmer. The slats of the wooden cylinder were warm from the heat of the light bulb. She wondered if Will was sleeping with Mr. Mews in his Chicago apartment. Colleen felt that Laura was wrong in believing that she could go to Chicago right away. Dr. Smith's discharge advice to her had been, "Never stand when you can sit, and never sit when you can lie down. And don't drive a car!" And yet, Laura had seemed determined to go.

Abby had no extra money, but she had wanted to give Colleen a keepsake of their friendship. She had carefully removed all the sequins from her butterfly costume and placed them in a small box along with a card that said, "I'll come visit you in Carlton when I'm better. I'm so sorry about Pete. I think he loved you." That was the only thing Abby had ever said about Pete's death, except how beautifully Pete had been playing the piano the night he died.

Colleen woke up at midnight thinking about Pete. She took out Abby's box from under her pillow and reread Abby's note. Of all the women patients, Colleen had felt closest to Abby. She missed having her to confide in. Colleen needed to hear that Pete had loved her. She also needed to feel forgiven. She wanted to remember how he had lived and not how he died.

It was a beautiful night, and the stars were all out. Colleen tipped the box and allowed the sequins to cascade into her left hand. They glittered in the moonlight as they fell. They sparkled like drops of liquid moonlight. Colleen looked through the darkness outside the screen and toward the distant stars. It was like seeing through a glass darkly, Colleen thought, remembering the phrase Daisy's friend had quoted from Paul's letter to the Corinthians.

*Through a Halloween mask darkly!* Colleen thought sadly. All of the money and hard work that Pete's father had expended for Pete's care at Sherwood had not saved his son's life. Colleen reread Abby's note. Except for Emile and Faith, who had patiently crocheted and waited to go home, and Abby who had endured the bronchoscopies, in the end, each of them had challenged and defied Sherwood's rules.

*Including the Handyman,* she thought bitterly. In the end, Will had been made a scapegoat, and Pete had paid for his artistry with his life. And yet, how could it have been wrong to have known such happiness, given their bleak circumstances? Colleen slept fitfully, her unconscious mind struggling for an answer.

After Colleen moved into the new wing and had been there for two months, she finally began to feel her life settling down again into a familiar routine. In spite of the new surroundings, she still went for fluoroscopies and refills, and she still rested two hours a day.

In the new building there were more patients to get to know, and the staff was almost entirely unfamiliar. Most of the patients continued to crochet. Colleen, Faith, and Julie had advanced to quite intricate patterns. In spite of the endless time that had to be whiled away by crocheting, Colleen realized that she was one of the lucky ones. The advanced cases were forced to endure lobectomies or the rib, and some patients could not be saved, despite the most modern care available. Colleen had glimpsed a diabetic patient lying in a coma in one of the private rooms. Her lungs were being drained of fluid.

In Colleen's view, the worst thing about the move to the new building was that Miss Marthe had not been transferred there. Colleen had a new nurse named Miss Pringle. She was quite a bit older than Miss Marthe, and she was stern and wore horn-rimmed glasses. Miss Marthe had been like a mother to them. She had let them visit with Will and had even allowed Mr. Mews to come on their porch. Colleen was sure that nothing like that would ever happen under Miss Pringle's strict care.

*At least the new wing is modern and clean,* Colleen thought. She loved the crisp new sheets and shiny equipment. On the other hand, life in the other building had been cozier.

One evening, while her porch mates were in the bathroom, Colleen's eyes fell on the fire escape outside her window. Colleen knew that Daisy's porch was right below hers. She put on her robe and slippers, stepped out into the hall, and looked around. The hall was deserted. She opened the door to the fire escape and stepped outside. Daisy laughed when she saw Colleen at her window.

"Just out for a breath of fresh air, Colleen?" she joked as Colleen stepped inside.

"I'm completely out of fresh air!" Colleen exclaimed, sitting down on a corner of Daisy's bed. "Dr. Kurtz pumped 750 cc's of compressed air into me four days ago. Can't you tell?" she asked.

After they had chatted awhile, Colleen told Daisy that her mother didn't want her to become a Catholic. Deciding to make a clean breast of it, Colleen told her that she had mostly been interested in Bret.

"Why, hon, I suspected that all along!" she exclaimed. "I guessed it by the way you looked at him whenever he sat down at your table!"

"You did?" Colleen burst out laughing. "Do you suppose Bret knew?"

"He runs deeper than you think, Colleen, but he likes to think of himself as an actor in a romantic comedy," she replied. "Tragedy isn't his cup of tea. That might be why he was always at odds with your friend, Pete. I imagine he thought Pete took life a bit too seriously."

Colleen nodded her head, silently agreeing with Daisy's assessment.

Colleen still found it painful to talk about Pete, so she told Daisy about her brother's car accident over the Christmas holidays in Carlton. She described how Elliot had hit a tree during an ice storm and bruised his ribs. "My parents can't visit me until they have the car repaired. I'm pretty much on my own now," Colleen said.

Daisy patted Colleen's hand. "Then perhaps I could be your mother away from home. We won't talk about religion anymore if you don't want to."

Colleen studied the older woman and thought that Daisy, Pete, and Bret each possessed a deep spirituality, even if Bret did his best to hide it. *And so does Will,* Colleen thought, remembering the beautiful Langston Hughes poem about ancient rivers that Will had read to Laura.

Colleen's occasional visits with Daisy buoyed her spirits. They brightened the slow and soggy period of the winter thaw. Spring had been late in coming, but when the weather finally improved, Colleen listened for signs of life from the men's porches across the yard. Even though she couldn't make out the men's faces or activities, Colleen hoped to be able to hear Bret's Eddie Arnold cattle call at noon. Bret finally opened his windows as wide as possible one day at noon and cranked his radio up to full volume. Colleen could faintly hear the *Weeeeeooooooooooooooh!* Miss Pringle quickly found the source and put her foot down. There would be no cattle calling in the new wing.

Colleen had two new porch mates in the new building. One was an ambulatory patient named Carla, who had the bed on the end next to Faith. Carla had a good sense of humor, and when she introduced herself, she said, "Don't even think of calling me Carl. Ditto for Carlos!" Everyone had of course said, "Okay, Carl!" but she took it in stride. Carla worked three days a week in the operating room and seemed to enjoy it.

Colleen's other new porch mate was a girl named Suzie. Suzie had been assigned the bed next to Julie, and they had become good friends. Suzie had to undergo bronchoscopies periodically. Like Abby, she lived in dread of each session. Julie tried hard to cheer her up on bronchoscopy days, but it seldom worked.

Colleen happened to be walking down the hall when Suzie was being brought back from a bronchoscopy session one morning. She watched as Miss Pringle pushed her wheelchair briskly down the hall while Suzie stared straight ahead like a zombie. Her eyes were huge. She sat erect, looking neither to the left nor right, and she seemed not to see Colleen as she passed by. She had gone completely inward, a prisoner of her medical ordeal. Miss Pringle put Suzie to bed without saying a word and then came back out into the hall. When she saw Colleen, she said nothing and continued down the hall to the nurses' station.

Colleen was standing fairly near the nurses' station, and she could hear the nurses discussing Suzie. When they saw that Colleen was listening, they fell silent. Colleen had heard them mention a possible lobectomy. She knew that a lobe removal was serious business. When she went back to her porch, she said nothing about it because she didn't want to upset Suzie.

In order to reach the dining room, Colleen had to walk along the corridor where the private rooms for the sick and dying were located. It was always a relief to reach the comparative cheeriness of the ultra-modern dining room. The dining room was coed, and food was served family style. Bret and Emile also ate there.

One morning, a young woman named Angela joined them for breakfast. She was fastidious, prim, and proper. Colleen watched as she looked disapprovingly at Bret and Emile, who were wolfing down their breakfasts.

"A lady, or a *true* gentleman," Angela insisted rather loudly, "eats her or his toast just a little bit at a time."

To prove her point, she daintily cut her toast in half and spread a small amount of jelly on one of the corners. She took a bite and then repeated the process. To Colleen's astonishment, little by the little, Angela ate her toast in this fashion, until it was immaculately dispatched, with no jelly on her lips or face.

Bret had been listening attentively as he ate, and he insisted that they should all try out Angela's method of eating toast. Bret looked at Emile, who was oblivious to anything but the taste and amount of his food. "No, no, no, Emile! How gauche of you! Have you forgotten Mr. Pinkie?"

Emile looked confused and hurt. "I'ma no communist, Bret!" he exclaimed indignantly. "My second uncle many times removed in

Italy, maybe! But not me!"

Taking their cue from Bret's raised pinkie finger, Faith, Julie, and Colleen immediately lifted their little fingers on their coffee cup hands.

"Now, Angela, and I hope you don't mind me calling you by your first name, since we've not been properly introduced," Bret said, "there's one little thing I'd like to correct about your eating, if you wouldn't mind."

Angela immediately gave him a frigid smile. "What is that, Bret?" she asked.

Bret cleared his throat and looked down in his lap as if the worst possible faux pas had been committed. "It's about your little finger," he said, looking up with an angelic smile. "In high society, it's proper to crook your pinkie finger when holding your cup."

"You're joking, of course," she replied. She stood up and took her other piece of toast and her coffee to another table.

"I never joke about toast!" he called out over his shoulder to her, smearing his toast with as much jelly as he could and deliberately stuffing it into his mouth.

At this moment, Molly entered. Bret's eyes bugged out. Half a piece of toast was still hanging out of his mouth. She was perfectly proportioned and greatly endowed with Irish beauty and a mane of flaming red hair that fell gracefully to her shoulders. She was tall and utterly female. It was obvious that Bret was in love.

She gave Bret a dazzling smile. "You must be Bret," she said in a sultry tone. "I've heard about you."

*And her father is rich!* Colleen thought, a bit enviously. Colleen couldn't figure out how Molly had ever been admitted to Sherwood. Her father owned three small furniture stores. They had been hit hard during the Depression, but they had survived. Molly had become a Sherwood legend almost immediately upon her arrival. When she had been moved to the second floor, word had quickly spread that Molly had arrived. It had taken her just one smile to conquer Bret.

Bret hastily removed the toast and wiped his mouth with his napkin. His eyes followed Molly as she sat down at another table with a young woman named Betsy. Colleen knew that Betsy was also interested in Bret. She had summarized her philosophy about men in one sentence to Colleen, "Don't be coy, Colleen, just go for your man." Betsy was blonde and the same age as Bret. It was obvious that Molly would provide plenty of competition, yet the two women seemed to be good friends.

Colleen smiled sweetly at Bret and gently nudged the sugar bowl and creamer toward him.

"Will you take sugar with your coffee, Bret?" Colleen asked, looking innocently at Molly. "Or cream?" she added, nodding at Betsy. Bret's eyes twinkled with good-natured amusement.

"Very funny, Colleen, but I believe I'll have both!" he exclaimed as he helped himself to the sugar and cream. Bret seemed delighted by the challenge of becoming a mouse coveted by the two tigresses at the other table. "Isn't life grand?" he asked, leaning way back in his chair in utter contentment.

Emile raised his coffee cup and toasted life, which he always found grand.

Julie looked at Bret incredulously, but she said nothing. Faith smiled and patted Bret on the head. "It's been nice knowing ya', Bretie," she said fondly as she got up and headed back to her porch.

In addition to the meal rituals, the only other daily feature of life at Sherwood was the morning distribution of the mail. The nurses delivered the mail after breakfast in the new building. Colleen seldom received mail anymore. She had found it increasingly hard to write to her family from whose daily life she felt so completely separated. Colleen was therefore quite surprised when Miss Pringle brought her a large, padded envelope that bore her high school's return address.

"It feels like a very large book, Colleen," Miss Pringle told her.

Colleen's heart skipped a beat. Could it be a textbook? She quickly opened the package. Instead of a textbook, she discovered a copy of her high school yearbook. Colleen thumbed through the pages, pausing to read some of the captions, which were cute and brought back many memories. The happy faces seemed to be looking forward to graduation in June and to getting on with life.

A note slipped out of the back, and Colleen picked it up and read it. It was from Miss Wilson, who was the senior class advisor. It said:

Dear Colleen,

On the last page of the senior section, you will find a page dedicated to you. The senior class held a candy sale and raised enough money to make it possible. You have been greatly missed by all, and we wish you a speedy recovery. I hope to have the great pleasure of teaching you again when you return home.

Sincerely,

Dorothy Wilson

When Colleen came to the last page in the senior section, she saw a large picture of herself. It was the one she had sent to her mother back in September, although it had been printed in black and white. Colleen's eyes filled with tears, and she looked away so that no one would see. After a while, Colleen began looking for the pictures of her closest friends.

After about half an hour, Julie asked in a small voice, "Would you mind if I looked at it too, when you've finished with it, that is? It would be such fun!"

"Of course not, Julie," Colleen replied. "I think you'll enjoy what they've written about their hobbies and ambitions. Kyle wants to be a mortician! John, who used to explore all the local caves, wants to be a civil engineer. Lou Ann plans to be the first female admiral someday. Imagine that!" Colleen's eyes danced merrily as she thought of her old friends.

When Colleen had finished looking at the yearbook, she handed it to Julie. Julie opened the book and started reading the captions under each picture, trying to match the faces with the aspirations. "Do you think you can tell much about a person just by looking at him or her, Colleen?" Julie asked.

"After reading about my friends' plans for the future, I would say I hardly know them at all," Colleen replied, "but maybe that's because I've been away for so long."

"I think we've probably gotten to know each other at Sherwood better than the kids we would have known in high school," Julie said.

Colleen reflected awhile. "Maybe it's the things that don't change that make us what we are," she said.

Julie looked at the photographs for a while and seemed charmed when she got to a picture of a nice-looking boy named Walter. "He calls himself 'just plain Walt,' but he plans to make a million dollars someday. His favorite song is 'The Girl That I Marry.' I think he sounds romantic!"

Colleen smiled. Walter was intelligent and hardworking. He was the kind of person who was at ease with himself and other people. He had always been interested in the wider world, and it sounded to Colleen as if he was now ready to step out into it.

Colleen and Julie passed the hour before lunch talking about their hobbies and ambitions. Julie told Colleen that she wanted to lead an adventurous life when she got out of Sherwood. Colleen said she could fully understand the feeling, after having been confined to a porch for so long. They both had a good laugh dreaming up adventures they'd like to experience someday, and it felt good to Colleen to get her mind off the daily routine. It was the first time she had really laughed since Pete had died.

June arrived, and the weather turned hot. The lawn between the two wings was parched, and the porches were like ovens. Colleen's seventeenth birthday had already come and gone, and Bret had made her a bouquet of paper flowers in honor of it. She had also received a note from her mother, which described how the town had held a "card shower" for Colleen. Many people in Carlton had enclosed dollar bills to help with Colleen's support.

By the beginning of June, Bret and Angela's relations had degenerated into open warfare. The war began when Angela told Molly that Bret wasn't a gentleman. Betsy found out and told Bret. Bret complained vociferously to Angela, but she retorted that it was his own fault for getting himself in a *jam* with two women. She had walked off in a huff, secretly pleased with the pun. Bret had told her in no uncertain terms to stay out of his affairs. Angela, of course, had immediately exacted revenge by telling Betsy that Bret was having an affair with Molly. To Angela's surprise, this did not particularly disturb Betsy.

"God made the Brets of this world to be enjoyed, hon," Betsy told Angela in an unconcerned voice.

Angela gave her a pitying look. "He would never respect a *real* lady, you know. Molly would be better off with a gentleman."

In Betsy's view, Angela simply didn't understand Molly. In spite of her great beauty and regal presence, the real problem between Molly and Bret was that Molly had never really enjoyed being the subject of the hospital grapevine. Bret, on the other hand, was a showman and thrived on it. Betsy understood that Bret needed a star to play opposite him, but one who could not upstage him. She had known all along that Molly and Bret were not a fit, and that she was.

When Molly finally met a handsome patient her age named Dale, she gratefully accepted his discrete attentions. Dale was a tall redhead who was quiet and well built. Molly and he quickly became great friends. This left an open field for Betsy, just as Betsy had expected all along.

Angela's triumph and the loss of Molly rankled Bret. Bret was a straight shooter, and he didn't like women who didn't play fair.

"People who think they're high and mighty can be quite *petty*, don't you think?" he asked Colleen and Emile one morning, hoping that Angela was listening. "The French, God bless 'em, found a cure for that years ago in Madame La Guillotine." Bret placed his toast on his plate, slathered jelly all over it, and chopped it in half with one dramatic blow of his knife. Angela stuck out her tongue at him from her corner table.

Betsy laughed. "That girl is in for a big surprise the first time she goes out with a real man!" Bret looked at her appreciatively. Colleen thought that Bret had finally found a match, even if he still mourned the loss of Molly.

The hot weather continued through the month of June, but its initial dryness slowly gave way to oppressive humidity. The heat and humidity took a toll on the nursing staff. Colleen watched Miss Schmidt as she placed a new pitcher of ice water on the table around three o'clock one afternoon. Her nurse's uniform was drenched with perspiration. Miss Pringle came in and noticed her condition.

"Why in the world haven't you turned on the fan, Miss Schmidt?" she asked irritably. Miss Pringle reached for the electric cord and plugged it in. Colleen felt the fan's cool breeze evaporate some of the perspiration from her face.

"But Dr. Smith told us that we have to save electricity!" Miss Schmidt protested. She bent down and unplugged the fan.

"Save, the devil!" Miss Pringle hissed. "Turn on the fan!" Miss Schmidt made no move to plug it in. Miss Pringle reached down and plugged in the cord again. "See that it stays plugged in!" she said angrily.

Colleen felt the full blast of the fan. The two nurses stood there glaring defiantly at one another while Colleen, Julie, and Faith watched silently. Suzie continued to sleep peacefully through the row. Both nurses' curls flapped under their caps because Miss Pringle had turned on the fan as high as it would go.

Miss Schmidt finally acquiesced to Miss Pringle, but she added, "I won't be responsible if Dr. Smith sees this. He's supposed to be making rounds this afternoon!"

The two nurses stormed out of Colleen's porch. It was the only time Colleen had ever witnessed any friction between Sherwood staff members. Suzie woke up and asked Colleen why everyone was giggling. Colleen was about to explain when Dr. Smith and Dr. Kurtz appeared in the doorway.

Dr. Smith frowned at the use of the fan, but Dr. Kurtz gratefully moved to a spot where he could feel its cooling effect. He took out a handkerchief from his pocket and wiped his brow. Dr. Smith asked questions about each of the women's cases. Suzie had been scheduled for a lobectomy in Oakton. Dr. Smith wanted to know how she felt about it. Suzie said she thought it was probably for the best, especially if she wouldn't have to have any more bronchoscopies. Dr. Smith asked each of them a few questions more. He wanted to know how long Colleen had been at Sherwood. Dr. Smith also asked Colleen how she felt after the injection of 750 cc's of compressed air. Colleen told him it made her feel like she was almost suffocating.

When they had gone, Colleen felt that she was still in limbo. Dr. Smith had given no indication to any of them that they would soon be discharged. Colleen went to dinner feeling disappointed. Over dinner, Bret astounded them with the news that Dr. Smith was discharging him. Bret's father would be coming to take him home over the Fourth of July weekend.

"Why, that's in two more days!" Betsy wailed.

"Dr. Smith said he wanted to send me away with fireworks," Bret chuckled. "He must have found out about the firecrackers we tossed out the windows last year."

Julie's eyes opened wide. "That was you, Bret?" she said with awe in her voice. "But how—"

Bret leaned over and whispered in Julie's ear, "Mr. Olsen."

Bret had breakfast with them on his last morning at Sherwood. After breakfast, he took Colleen aside and stood talking with her for a few minutes. It seemed to Colleen that he was trying to get up enough nerve to ask her something. Finally, he asked if he could kiss her goodbye. Without waiting for her reply, he kissed Colleen on the forehead.

"You don't believe Angela's claim that I'm not a gentleman, do you, Colleen?" Bret asked anxiously. Colleen shook her head, trying to hold back her tears.

"I just want you to know that Betsy and Molly ... they're lovely women, but they were all just a game to keep me from going crazy. You were my only true friend at Sherwood."

Bret gave Colleen a piece of paper with his address and phone number written on it. "I've got to go now, Colleen, but if you would, write to me now and then. I really would like to take you to the races someday," he said quietly, almost shyly. Colleen promised Bret she would write. She watched him walk down the corridor to his porch. A man who must have been his father was standing there with a suitcase. Colleen walked back to her porch, feeling utterly empty.

After Bret left, Colleen experienced a sense of despair and desperation that she had never felt before at Sherwood. When September arrived, she thought the cooler weather might restore her spirits, but the change of season only reminded her that a new senior class was beginning another school year. She would sit by herself in the bathroom when no one was around and stare out the window, feeling that she had no future. She couldn't even play Claire's piano anymore.

Carla, who had seemed to have the best prospects of any of them, had suddenly collapsed in the OR that week. Her TB had come back, and she had to start her recovery all over again with complete bed rest. Colleen didn't know how she could stand it. She had been so close to getting out. Carla came into the bathroom when Colleen had been sitting there a long while one day. She put her arm around Colleen.

"What do you think you're doing?" she asked. "You know this won't do you any good. We all have to keep our chins up, don't we?"

"You're not discouraged?" Colleen asked. "You have every right to be."

"It's not a question of courage, Colleen. It's about faith in the future. If you don't believe you can get better, you'll probably never find the patience to try," Carla said. "I'm going to go back to bed, now. I just wanted to make sure you were okay."

Colleen sat for a long while in the bathroom, feeling forgotten and alone. Abby, Laura, Will and Mr. Mews, Pete, and now Bret, were gone. She tried to give herself a pep talk about keeping a positive attitude and waiting patiently for the new antibiotic, which supposedly held so much promise. She knew it was irrational to give up hope, and yet what progress had she really made? She had become TB negative very early in her treatment, but after that, nothing ever seemed to change.

Colleen thought of Pete reading *Robinson Crusoe*, and it made her cry. She had been his "Friday," but now she was alone. She felt shipwrecked and forgotten. She was beginning to forget what home, school, and a future meant. The daily monotony seemed to stretch around her like an endless sea. Her horizon was a flat line beyond which there was just more and more ocean.

Colleen pressed her forehead against the upper windowpane and looked down onto the grassy area between the men's and women's wings. It was like a small inland sea, like the Sargasso Sea that she had read about, also called the Devil's Triangle. The bottom half of the bathroom window was open, allowing a tiny bit of fresh air to pass through. Colleen felt the warm air lick at her ankles and shins like an incoming tide.

She remembered how Mr. Perkins had jumped off the roof of the new building. She was beginning to understand his despair. She could well understand his urge to escape the island of Sherwood, but she couldn't understand the desire to jump into the asphalt sea of the parking lot.

Pete had been reading *Moby Dick* on the day that Mr. Perkins had jumped. Pete had described to her how Captain Ahab walked the deck of the *Pequod* night after night while the ship was becalmed. He had mentioned that Mr. Perkins also had suffered many sleepless nights.

Pete said Mr. Perkins had wanted to go home and felt angry about his lack of improvement, but there was no one to blame his TB on except poverty, malnutrition, and overwork. If he went home, there would only be more of the same. He felt trapped.

Pete had also told her that Mr. Perkins wasn't a violent man, but he had let his anger go inward and turn to despair. Instead of fighting back, he had jumped off the roof. The nurse's rejection was his emotional tipping point. Pete said that like Ahab, Mr. Perkins had become the victim of his anger instead of a victor over it.

Pete had looked sorrowful and told her that Melville's story was a long poem about the futility of anger and revenge. He had said that Mr. Perkins must have known about TB's long and invincible history, and in his mind's eye the white plague of TB could have been transformed into something akin to the white whale.

In the end, Colleen asked herself, what is the difference between men like Mr. Perkins and Pete, or between Captain Ahab and the great white whale? What is the difference between the victim and the victor? She looked out the window and knew that she wished to be neither. She didn't want to be the hunter *or* the hunted.

But what *did* she want, beyond the assurance that she would one day get better?

*We are all hunting for something,* Colleen thought. She looked down into the sea of grass and then to the high brick wall of the men's wing. *Everyone has a tipping point,* she said to herself, and she wondered what hers might be. She thought about Pete and wondered if he had reached his own tipping point and if there might be a fatal tipping point toward the good too. She backed away from the open window and left the bathroom without an answer.

Colleen went to her locker and opened it, looking for anything that might lift her spirits. Miss Wilson's book lay on the bottom shelf. It was tattered and worn, but it was still intact. Then Colleen saw her white robe hanging with its sleeves twisted around itself among her dresses. The way in which it was wrapped around itself reminded her of a mummy, and the locker seemed like a mummy case.

One of her shoes had fallen on the floor, and Colleen knelt down to pick it up. She tried to think of better times. Her mummified robe seemed to laugh at her and say, "Foolish girl! TB was in Egypt when I was embalmed. It's what did me in! TB was there at creation. And God said it was good!" The words reverberated through her mind.

Colleen tried to concentrate and ignore her negative thoughts. She silently prayed that God would help science to find a cure. When she prayed, she didn't usually pray for things for herself, but this time she asked God to deliver her from her endless hospitalization. She felt at her wits' end. She heard someone behind her and jumped to her feet self-consciously. It was Miss Pringle. Miss Pringle looked at Colleen curiously but walked on by.

That evening, Colleen felt calmer. She ate a good dinner and went back to her porch and slept soundly.

By early December, Colleen felt that the first hopeful sign on her horizon had appeared. A package arrived in the mail from her parents. Inside there was a three-quarter length, dark green coat, which tied at the waist. Her mother had also sent Colleen a brand new white tam.

Colleen felt that her parents believed that she would soon be going home, or they wouldn't have sent her a new coat.

A second and far more hopeful sign followed soon after. The day that the patients and staff had long been awaiting finally arrived. Streptomycin had become available at Sherwood.

The first Sherwood patient to be given a dose of the new drug was a lady that Colleen knew. TB had escaped from her lungs and invaded her vocal cords. After treatment with the streptomycin, her voice became silky smooth, almost overnight. Colleen could not believe that the TB bacillus had finally met its match after thousands of years. It was the talk of the hospital. Drs. Smith and Kurtz were ecstatic.

Colleen lay in bed, remembering Pete's tale of the bubonic plague and the deliverance of London. Medical science, which Pete so admired, had not been quick enough to save him, but the advent of streptomycin meant that many others would now live. In the course of human history, it seemed that timing was all, and yet Pete had said that it was one's inner music, and not timing, which determined one's fate and happiness. He had insisted that the singing hand could *steal* time. Even when there was not much time left, Colleen thought sadly.

Just before Christmas, Dr. Kurtz came onto Colleen's porch with a big smile on his face. His eyes twinkled merrily. He was wearing a red shirt and a Christmas tie under his doctor's gown, and with his jolly smile, he looked a bit like Old Saint Nick. "Colleen, I have some wonderful news for you!" he said. "Dr. Smith says that you are well enough to go home and spend a week with your family for Christmas."

Colleen looked at Carla and then at Dr. Kurtz. Colleen thought of her green coat. "Do my parents know?"

Dr. Kurtz nodded. "You'll have to be careful though. Don't overdo!"

Colleen promised she would be very careful, and Dr. Kurtz patted her on the shoulder. "I'm glad for you, Colleen. Your hospitalization has gone on longer than any of us expected."

Colleen sat up and asked, "When do I leave?"

Dr. Kurtz told her that Elliot and a college friend would be driving up tomorrow. "Miss Marthe told me all about your family's trip to Chicago with Will, Colleen. I would like to meet Elliot before you go. I'll stop by tomorrow around ten o'clock."

Elliot and his friend Carl arrived promptly at ten o'clock. Elliot introduced him to Colleen. Elliot had invited him to spend Christmas with them because Carl's family was away on a business trip to Europe. Carl was a medical student, so Dr. Kurtz gave him a short tour of the second floor. When they were done, he told Elliot to make sure Colleen got plenty of rest. He gave Colleen some written instructions to follow while she was at home. Colleen thanked him, and then the three of them stepped into the elevator.

They were very surprised to find a patient named Gwen dressed in a street-length white dress and high heels. She was wearing a mauve coat and a matching hat with a veil. "What's the occasion, Gwen?" Colleen asked.

Gwen looked surprised. "I thought everyone knew! I'm on my way to the Justice of the Peace. I'm getting married to Jesse today. We're going to open a small store in Oakton.

"You mean, you're being discharged and getting married all in one day?" Colleen asked.

"What better way to start the beginning of the rest of my life?" Gwen grinned. "I've been ambulatory for some time, hon."

"I'm goin' home to spend a week with my folks at Christmas," Colleen said, after congratulating Gwen.

They reached the ground floor and stepped out of the elevator. "Good luck!" Colleen cried out as Gwen hurried past the nurses' station while signaling the cabbie that she was coming. Colleen watched Gwen get into the waiting cab.

"Good luck to you, too!" Gwen called as the cab sped off, carrying her into her new life.

Colleen's journey back to Carlton took three hours. Elliot talked nonstop about college, and Carl was full of ghoulish tales of medical school. Colleen fell asleep during the last hour of the trip. When she awoke, she looked out the window and saw the Green River and realized they were back in Carlton. Elliot directed Carl to turn onto the road that led up to their neighborhood. Carl parked the car, and Elliot helped Colleen get out. Carl carried Colleen's suitcase into the house while Colleen sank down onto the living room sofa and looked around. Her mother had decorated the house for Christmas, and the fragrance of freshly cut pine filled the room.

"I've got your room all set up for you on the porch, Colleen, so that you don't have to climb the stairs," Mrs. Reilly said. She was bustling here and there, anxious to make Colleen feel at home again. "I've made your favorite dinner! It's wonderful to have you home again!" She gave Colleen a huge hug.

Mr. Reilly was like a child who had found every present he had ever hoped for under the Christmas tree. The presents were his children. He gave Colleen some tinsel and asked her if she'd like to help finish trimming the tree. Colleen took the tinsel and placed some here and there while her father turned on the lights. It was beautiful, Colleen thought.

After dinner, they visited awhile, and then Mrs. Reilly reluctantly insisted that Colleen go to bed. Colleen changed into her pajamas. They reminded her of Sherwood, but she had to admit to herself that she was quite tired. She fell asleep to the sound of Carl playing carols on the family piano.

It didn't seem fair to Colleen that her week of freedom went by so quickly. The highlight of her visit was a shopping trip in Lockwood. Colleen bought a pair of snakeskin, black-and-white high heels, which added flair to her new coat and tam. While they were shopping, she saw an old classmate. He was older than Colleen, and he was wearing his military uniform. He gave Colleen a big smile and came over to welcome her back. He wanted to know if Colleen would be staying permanently in Carlton, and he looked disappointed when she told him she had to go back to Sherwood in a few days. He had evidently chosen to stay in the Army after the war, but he was posted for duty not far from Carlton. He was eager to resume old ties.

Colleen, her family, and Carl shopped for an hour and a half, and then they had lunch at a corner restaurant. Their table was next to a window that looked out onto Lockwood's festively decorated main street. The air was frosty, and a nippy wind had sprung up. There was snow in the air. Colleen wrapped her green coat around her and shivered as they came out of the restaurant.

By the time they got back home, Colleen felt that she had a slight fever. Her mother put her to bed and brought her extra blankets. Colleen slept fitfully all night because her chest felt tight and gave her some pain. In the morning, she told her mother that she thought she was getting a cold.

Colleen, Elliot, and Carl had to start back for Sherwood on the following day. Mrs. Reilly put an extra blanket and a pillow in the back seat so that Colleen could sit comfortably propped up in a corner. When they got to Sherwood, Elliot went to find a wheelchair because Colleen seemed so tired. Miss Pringle soon came out with one and wheeled Colleen up to her porch. Elliot and Carl waved good-bye and tried to seem unconcerned.

Colleen tried to ignore her cold. When she went to the dining room for breakfast the next morning, there was a commotion going on. Someone had saved an egg from breakfast, and on a dare, Dale was trying to break it open with his bare hands. He was in his pajamas, right arm fully extended, his hand holding the egg. His whole body shook with the effort of trying to crack it open. When he finally succeeded, globs of egg white and yolk flew across the room and hit Mandy, Colleen's friend from her first days at Sherwood, on the back of her head.

Mandy was furious. She was all dressed up, ready to leave on a pass. She stormed over to Dale. "That was no accident!" she exclaimed, her face red with fury. Dale looked at Mandy, but he couldn't think of what to say. He just hung his head and looked at the floor. Mandy ran off to the ladies' bathroom to clean the egg out of her hair.

Julie smiled and said, "Well, I guess some people just can't take a little practical yolk." Dale laughed, in spite of himself. "Mandy can take it. If she can fly a plane, she can get yolk out of that beautiful platinum hair."

Colleen went back to bed. On the following morning, she was sent for a fluoroscopy exam. Afterward, Dr. Kurtz noted that she had a cold, and he prescribed some medicine and told her to stay in bed.

Colleen's cold hung on for several weeks. By mid-February, Dr. Kurtz detected fluid on Colleen's lung. He looked very concerned and told Colleen that fluid on the lung was very serious.

"We will have to draw it off, Colleen."

On the following day, Colleen was sent to the treatment room. She was draped, and then Dr. Kurtz stuck a needle between her ribs. Dr. Kurtz was able to draw off a great deal of fluid.

Colleen was wheeled back to her porch and kept in bed. Over the course of a month, the fluid gradually went away.

By the end of March a totally unexpected thing happened. Colleen's lung stayed down for two weeks. Dr. Kurtz studied her X-rays with a happy smile.

"Colleen," he said, "the fluid on your lung has done something which medical science alone could not do. You see, we were afraid to put any more air in your lungs after we tried the 750 cc's and failed. The pressure and the fluid have stabilized your lung and let the cavity heal." Dr. Kurtz was jubilant.

"What do you mean, Dr. Kurtz?" Colleen asked, feeling a renewed sense of hope.

"I mean that Dr. Smith says you're ready to go home!" Dr. Kurtz smiled broadly.

Colleen was shocked. She had nearly given up believing that there was life for her beyond Sherwood. "Let me make sure I understand you," she said. "You're saying I can go home because I went shopping?"

Dr. Kurtz nodded. "In a way, yes, that is true," he said.

Colleen could hardly believe it. All of the years of tedious bed rest suddenly seemed excruciatingly and preposterously irrelevant. "I'm going home because I did what women love to do!" she exclaimed, still not believing it. "Mom always jokes that shopping is the answer to a woman's prayers!" she laughed. "I guess she's right."

"God doesn't save women by letting them go shopping. Colleen!" Dr. Kurtz said sternly, but his eyes twinkled with amusement.

"What happened to you, Colleen, was a bargain that may never be offered to you again. You will have to be very careful when you go home," he admonished her. "Your infection was a stroke of good fortune. You tempted fate, but you won, unlike—" Dr. Kurtz stopped speaking in midsentence.

*Unlike Pete*, Colleen thought.

"The body can cure itself, Colleen, when given the proper chance," Dr. Kurtz reflected. "It's too bad that Pete never got the same chance," he added regretfully.

An hour later, Dr. Kurtz notified Colleen's parents that she could go home. Her parents still didn't have a car. Luckily, Elliot was on Easter break from school. He found a friend in Carlton who was willing to drive him to and from Sherwood so that Colleen could come home.

Dr. Smith met with Colleen that afternoon and gave her the same advice that he had given Laura. He reminded her that she would have to undergo periodic refills of air during her convalescence, and later on, a phrenectomy. He explained that the crushed nerve would release her diaphragm, which in turn would compress her lung until it slowly reinflated during one last round of healing. Colleen would have to come back in about six months for the procedure. The phrenic nerve would gradually repair itself, the diaphragm would return to its normal position, and Colleen would be cured at last.

Dr. Kurtz, who had been passing by in the hall, poked his head in the door and wished her a speedy recovery. Then he continued down the hall to go take care of his other patients.

Colleen thanked Dr. Smith. He left to attend to other hospital matters.

The next morning, Colleen said good-bye to Julie, Faith, Suzie, and Carla. She gave each of them a big hug. She paused at Carla's bed and said, "Thanks for all the encouragement, Carla!" Carla gave her a great big hug. Faith cried when Colleen said good-bye, but she tried to make light of it. "There goes that merry-go-round, again, Colleen," she sighed.

Colleen bent down and kissed Faith on the forehead, in spite of the rules. She was worried about Faith, but she said, "You'll be out soon, Faith! I'll write to you!"

Colleen walked down the hall for the last time with Elliot. They took the elevator down to the first floor and walked out the front door. Elliot's friend was waiting for them in his car, which he had parked by the entrance.

Colleen saw that the gardens were blooming with spring flowers. She turned and took one last look at the porch she had first been assigned to. Then she smiled radiantly at her brother and said, "Let's go home!"

She was now almost eighteen years old.

# Part Three

## Summer Nights

The Green River was the first thing that greeted Colleen as they entered Carlton. It sparkled like a liquid emerald in the afternoon sunlight, and above it occasional cloud shadows floated lazily across the face of the hills. It seemed to Colleen that the river was the only thing that had remained unchanged during her stay at Sherwood. Except for the river, her memory of Carlton now seemed like a picture drawn by a kindergartner. The scale of things seemed all wrong. The shrubs around her house were taller, but that made the porch on her house, as she remembered it, seem too small. While she had become a young woman, her sister had become a teenager, and her parents had turned a little gray. Everyone's perspective had changed, and they all felt a bit awkward around each other now.

Colleen looked around her and was struck by the fact that everything had simply *gone on*. She felt a bit like the returning prodigal son. Only she had not been profligate with her life. Any profligacy was on the part of TB itself, which had thrown away two and a half years of her life.

Although her neighbors and friends had generously donated money for her care at Sherwood, Colleen quickly discovered that there still was a stigma attached to TB. Yet, in spite of lingering fears of the disease in the minds of many people, there was also great curiosity about the new drug, streptomycin. On their trip home, Elliot had stopped at a gas station, and a woman in a car at one of the pumps had recognized Colleen. She had come over to the car and asked, "You got that new drug up there at the hospital, didn't you?" Colleen said that she had not, and that it was possible to get better without antibiotics. The woman had merely shrugged and said, "I suppose time heals all things."

Colleen had wondered if the woman really understood or appreciated the gift of time. Pete had believed that we are all fools until we understand the beautiful potential of time, but his was a special view that was at odds with the natural world. That was the part of his philosophy that literally didn't fit. In Pete's world of stolen time that Colleen had experienced in Claire's apartment, time only flowed toward a beautiful conclusion. Pete had insisted that the human spirit dies without beauty. He had been drawn to Claire's piano because of his unquenchable need for beauty. Nevertheless, Pete's death had forced Colleen to face the fact that he had been unwilling and unable to make peace with an imperfect and diseased world where cleanliness and order were the *only* necessary and sufficient things if one wished to survive. And Pete had not survived; neither had Victoria and Frank. It seemed to Colleen that the woman at the gas station was wrong: time had not healed all things.

Colleen felt that her own life had somehow reached a critical point in time, and that everything was about to change forever. She had no idea what the change might be, and she had no evidence to justify this feeling, except the certainty that too much time had passed, and that major change was past due. Colleen felt that the longer her recovery lasted, the greater that change would be.

This feeling was neither confirmed nor denied by the languid motion of the Green River. It seemed in no hurry to reach the sea, and its unending flow seemed to deny that final resolution was possible. It would continue forever, its headwaters forever replenished by the rains, and the cycle of life. It had no beginning or end.

As time went by, Colleen would sometimes study the railroad tracks that ran alongside the river. The ties seemed to take the river's measure as they followed it on a parallel path. Colleen knew that the convergence of the rails at a point on the horizon was just an optical illusion, a trick of perspective. The human energy and planning that had gone into the laying of the tracks hid the fact that the ties were not evenly placed, that the bed heaved, and that whole sections sometimes needed to be replaced. Crews were sent out periodically to make repairs. Nothing was as precise and predictable as one thought. A free and easy stride upon the ties was not possible, in spite of the lovely view of the river.

Sometimes when Colleen studied the river, she remembered how Pete had invited her to wade in the waters of his music. He had been fearless, confident of their beauty and restorative powers. He had laughed at her need for physical safety, and he had urged her to join him. She was now faced with the boredom and frustration of a recovery that seemed to stretch out like the rails toward a vanishing point—toward a mere speck on the horizon, beyond which lay her postponed, and for the time being, unknowable future.

Colleen spent most of her time in the bedroom her mother had prepared for her on the first floor; her younger sister Katie kept her company in the afternoons. On school days, while Katie was at school, Mrs. Reilly often sat with Colleen and sewed skirts, which she would then deliver to neighbors and friends who had placed orders for them. Colleen slept or listened to the radio a good deal of the time when she was alone.

Her schedule varied only when Mr. Reilly took her to Lockwood for air refills every two weeks or on days when he came home from work to have lunch with them. Colleen had been ordered to rest and wait for the slow, healing changes that time and nature would bring about. She knew that these changes in her lung would be as imperceptible as the passing of the seasons. Colleen had been promised that her body, over time, would conquer the TB, wall it off, and knit the cavity in her lung, but without her Sherwood friends or her high school classmates, recuperation was as interesting as watching the grass grow.

Things changed abruptly, however, when Robert Carlson burst into her life. Colleen had met him at the corner grocery store, where he worked behind the meat counter, and soon discovered that Robert undertook everything he did, including his friendships, with tireless enthusiasm and attention to every detail. Colleen had at first felt he was not interested in her, but he had called shortly thereafter to ask if he and his brother could come over for cards. Since his brother and Katie were good friends, Colleen agreed to it.

Over cards, Colleen told Robert that she was determined to finish high school, whether she fit in or not. Robert was sympathetic because he had been held back one year in school. He was the son of a minister, and his family had been moved many times during Robert's elementary school years. The lack of continuity in Robert's math education had finally caught up with him. "It hurt my feelings to be held back, Colleen, because I'm basically really good at math," he had confided, hoping that she'd see that others had also been left behind unfairly by situations beyond their control.

Colleen thought Robert was handsome and smart as a fox. He was slim, with dark wavy hair, nice hazel eyes, and a musical voice. He sang in the school chorus, and when he sang, Katie said that he threw back his head so that his whole body and soul got involved. Robert played the trumpet—he and his four brothers all played instruments. Katie sometimes was invited over to their house in the afternoon, and she had told Colleen that there was always somebody playing a musical instrument somewhere in the house, including Robert's mother, who was a gifted pianist. "It's a very boisterous place!" she had replied, when Colleen asked what Robert's home life was like.

From the beginning, Robert, perhaps influenced by his father's ministerial example, had decided to help Colleen get out of bed and walk. In the interim, he tried to devise ways to keep her moving toward that goal. After a while, he came by almost every day to see how she was progressing. They quickly became close friends.

Robert immediately recognized that Colleen loved music as much as he did. Since he was a born mechanic and quite a good carpenter, he made a portable Victrola for Colleen on which he played his favorite records for her enjoyment. His favorite was "Don't Cry, Joe," and he would sing along with the vocalist in a pleasant tenor with so much drama and gusto that he invariably made Colleen laugh. The more she laughed, the more he sang. At those times, Mr. or Mrs. Reilly would usually poke a nose in the doorway and laugh, "Oh, it's you again, Robert!"

For Colleen, college had never been an option because her parents couldn't afford to send her. College wasn't an option for Robert for the same reason, and this created another bond between the two of them. Robert wanted to be an engineer, and Colleen wanted to study everything from the universe on down to the smallest microbe.

As the weeks crawled by for Colleen, April turned into May. Colleen was glad that the school year was coming to an end because she knew that Katie and her friends would be around more often, making life more normal. In the meantime, she maintained her connection with the world by listening to the news on the radio. There was a nationwide coal strike, and Truman was keeping the trains running by sending in the Army. Colleen wondered if the coal trains that made their runs up the holler and down into coal country had soldiers on board. She wondered if there was labor trouble down in Abby's hometown.

Toward the end of the summer, the 1948 presidential campaign heated up. Colleen followed it closely on the radio. Mr. Reilly favored Truman. Mr. Reilly strongly disapproved of Strom Thurmond, who had broken with the Democrats and formed the States Rights Party in retaliation for Truman's legislation designed to end segregation in education and employment. Negroes were organizing to bring about historic changes such as an end to the Ku Klux Klan's long reign of terror through lynching. Mr. Reilly was also against Wallace's Progressive Party, because he feared it might draw votes from Truman and give the race to Dewey. Mr. Reilly favored the way Truman had handled the economy, which he considered wise and fair to all sides. Although the idea of the atomic bomb scared him the way it did Mr.

Wallace, Mr. Reilly felt that it had ended the war and saved lives.

A new technology called television covered the conventions, but few Americans had seen it, including the Reillys. Largely ignoring TV, Harry Truman took his case directly to the people in a cross-country whistle-stop tour. He won by over two million votes. Colleen listened to the early returns on election night, but she fell asleep without knowing who the winner was. The next morning she learned that Truman had overcome Dewey's lead in the wee hours of the night. The Chicago Daily Tribune had rushed to print too soon with the banner headline "DEWEY BEATS TRUMAN!" Truman had made them eat crow by holding the front page up at every stop of the train in his triumphant return to Washington.

By November, Colleen's doctors felt that she was doing well enough to participate in a Christmas play at the church. Although she couldn't have a speaking part because of her collapsed lung, she enjoyed being out among people and doing something in her community again. In the third week of December, her doctor in Lockwood told her she no longer needed refills. A phrenectomy had been scheduled for Colleen at Sherwood just before Christmas. This would make Colleen's fourth Christmas at Sherwood.

On the morning of the surgery, Mr. and Mrs. Reilly drove Colleen back to Sherwood. As they came up the drive, the enormous oaks filled the chilly December sky, just as they had four years ago when Colleen had first arrived.

Although Sherwood had never really become home, Colleen felt that it had become a place that would always be a part of her. It had become her parallel life, with nonparallel friends and nonparallel problems. As her father parked the car, Colleen worried that she might always live in two separate worlds, and that she might never fully recover. There were times when she wondered if she would live to be forty. No one understood the other world she inhabited. She tried to put on the best face possible, but these different worlds were like two trains carrying incongruent thoughts and feelings for delivery to an unknown destination. To Colleen, they were like a modern diesel and an old steam-driven freight train, each barreling down the tracks of her mind, ignoring the other, and pursuing a river of memories from opposite directions. They were headed for a collision.

Once they were inside the hospital, a nurse whom Colleen did not recognize wheeled her down the hall to the fluoroscopy room and left her there while she went to speak with the surgical nurse. To Colleen's surprise, she found Bret sitting there by himself in a wheelchair.

Bret looked as surprised as Colleen when they saw each other. "I'm just back for a checkup," he reassured Colleen as he reached over and squeezed her hand affectionately. "What brings you to these parts, if I may ask?"

"I'm here for a phrenectomy!" she exclaimed.

"Well, just be ready for the big *whoosh* when they crush the nerve and the air goes out of you!" he exclaimed. "But six months after the surgery, your nerve will heal, your lung will have reinflated, and no more cavity! It's great to see you again, Colleen!" he said, grinning.

"You too, Bret!" Colleen replied.

Colleen and Bret looked at each other for a moment, each assessing how the other looked.

"How long have you been out?" Bret asked.

"Well, they finally discharged me because I went shopping over Christmas last year and caught a cold. The fluid compressed my lung long enough for them to release me. Otherwise, I think I'd still be here," Colleen replied.

"I never thought of goin' shopping as a way of getting released, but you were always the creative one, Colleen," Bret quipped admiringly. "Pop Smith probably threw a party when he sent me home; and to think that all of us patients could have saved him a lot of time and effort by just goin' shopping," he marveled jokingly.

"How *are* you, Bret? And be serious for once in your life!" Colleen exclaimed, once again charmed by Bret's ability to take facts to their logical conclusion and then some.

"Actually, I've had a slight relapse, Colleen, but nothing serious, I hope. Too much going on at home, I suppose," he replied. "I developed some infiltrate on the lung when I tried to help out around the house," he said. "The doctors think I'll be fine now. I've had plenty of time in which to figure out how to get my life back on track. I've even thought about becoming a priest."

Colleen stared disbelievingly at the least likely candidate for the priesthood she could think of. "You're joking, right?" she asked.

"Not really," Bret answered calmly. "I finally realized one day that amusing everybody in my role as comic hero wasn't making me feel like a part of the human family at all. During these past months, I've had plenty of time to realize how lonely I was. I finally figured out that a comic hero can be a tragic and foolish one, too."

Bret flushed self-consciously and tried to change the subject. "Have you heard anything from Abby, or anything from Laura and Will?" he asked. He paused and added, "Or maybe from Dr. Montaigne?" Bret looked curiously at Colleen, afraid to ask the unasked question that his eyes could not hide.

Colleen shook her head sadly. "I haven't heard from any of them."

Bret shot Colleen a serious look and pulled her wheelchair around so that she was facing him. "Maybe this is none of my business, Colleen, but there's something I never got to tell you. Pete lived in a very different world than the rest of us because of his extraordinary talents, but he needed to be a real Pete, too. I think you brought that out in him. When he went upstairs with you to Claire's apartment that first time, it was to be with you—not with the piano. You understood him when nobody else did."

"He loved music so much that he made it into a god that destroyed him, Colleen. But that had nothing to do with you!" Bret exclaimed.

"Sooner or later, he would have found out about Claire's piano. We could sometimes hear her playing it in her apartment, even when she shut the door."

"Do you think Pete was tragically flawed, or just lonely and afraid like the rest of us?" Colleen asked. "He said he wanted to give me hope. Maybe he wanted to give himself hope as well."

Bret was about to say that it takes two to make hope, but he didn't get a chance to answer, because at that moment, Colleen's nurse came back and told her it was time to go into surgery. Bret took his rosary beads out of his pocket and pressed them into the palm of Colleen's hand.

"Take these, Colleen! You were always a better Catholic than I was," Bret said, a bit self-consciously.

"I was never a Catholic, Bret," Colleen confessed guiltily, looking at the rosary.

"I know! Pete told me! You were a great Catholic, in spite of yourself. Please, take it," he said. "You can be an honorary member of the club."

Colleen looked dubiously at the beads and then accepted them.

The nurse looked at her watch and insisted that Colleen had to go. She pointed Colleen's wheelchair in the direction of the operating room and started pushing Colleen through the doors.

"Wait a minute, nurse! I was just hearing this young woman's confession!" Bret shouted as he pulled alongside the nurse and cut her off. "Don't forget that your penance, Colleen, is a date for the big race!" he said, ignoring the determined nurse.

The nurse brought Colleen's wheelchair to a very sudden halt and looked angrily at him. "You're blocking the way! Is there anything else you want to say before I report you to my supervisor?"

Bret's eyes gleamed. "Why, yes, I believe there is!" He picked up Colleen's hand and kissed it. "Farewell, Sherwood's prettiest and cleverest escapee! We shall meet again, my child! At the races!" he added, glaring at the officious nurse.

"At the races!" Colleen promised over her shoulder as the operating room door closed behind her. "You're a good man, Father Bret!"

As Bret wheeled himself back to the fluoroscopy room with a pleased grin, Colleen's nurse helped her climb onto the operating table. The doctor looked displeased with the commotion that Bret had caused. The procedure seemed to go well, however, and he looked relieved and satisfied when it was over. A sudden quiet had settled over the room as he crushed Colleen's phrenic nerve. The surgery's purpose was to crush but not sever the nerve controlling the diaphragm. Just as Bret had said, Colleen felt the air suddenly forced out of her lung as the diaphragm jumped higher into her chest. She quickly inhaled. The surgeon finished stitching up Colleen and left her with a nurse to recover.

Within a week, Colleen was back at Sherwood to have her stitches removed. This time, she was taken to the fluoroscopy room. Colleen looked around for Bret, but he was not there. She was the only patient in the room. Dr. Smith greeted her and had her stand behind the fluoroscope so that he could study her lung. Then he directed her to lie on the exam table so that he could remove her stitches. He turned his back to Colleen and said to the assisting doctor and nurse, "That lung will never re-expand!"

Colleen lay there, mutely trying to assimilate the fact that she would live the rest of her life with only one working lung. She said nothing, but she felt that she now understood the looks of horror on Abby's and Suzie's faces after their bronchoscopies. The nurse squeezed Colleen's hand sympathetically and wheeled her back to her parents.

At first, Colleen hoped that she had perhaps misunderstood, and so she decided to say nothing to her parents. However, as time passed and her lung failed to reinflate, she told no one about her fears, except Robert. When she eventually returned to school, she told none of her teachers, not even Miss Wilson.

At the beginning of the second semester of the school year, Colleen was allowed to return to school on a half-time basis. She took English and economic geography. Neither involved the standing that was required in laboratory sciences. On the first day of school, Miss Wilson welcomed her back and assigned her a seat by the window. Although several boys from Colleen's neighborhood gathered around her desk to talk to her before the bell rang, some of the girls eyed her suspiciously. Only a few gave her friendly smiles. As time passed, Colleen discovered that her presence posed no threat to the male hierarchy; indeed, it interested them. But her maturity upset the girls' cliques and internal hierarchy. Since she was too old to fit anywhere into it, Colleen resolved to simply be herself.

The remainder of the winter passed slowly. At the end of her short day, her father would pick her up in his car and take her home. Colleen received a letter from Bret in March in which he explained that he was driving a taxi so that he could help pay his father's medical bills. He wrote that his father had a chronic illness that made him miss a lot of work. Bret was afraid that his father might lose his job because of his health problems. He concluded his letter by saying:

Colleen, I hope you will forgive me when I tell you that I can't take you to the races after all. I never knew things would be this hard when I got out! I've sapped my strength by caring for my father and working nights. It's awfully discouraging, and doubly so since I was really looking forward to taking you to the Oakton Stakes. Unfortunately, my plans for the priesthood will have to wait until my father's situation is resolved. With love, Bret

Colleen put the letter down with a sigh. In truth, she had never thought Bret would actually follow up on his offer. It pleased her that he had meant to, however. She sat down and wrote him a note telling him not to be discouraged and that she understood.

That same week, Colleen received a letter from her friend Edith at Sherwood. Edith wrote,

> I wanted you to know that Faith passed away this week. I'm so sorry, but I knew you would want to know. I've asked Dr. Smith if I could have the rib surgery, and he's given me some hope. I've been here so many years that I fear it is my last chance for recovery. I'll write you if I hear anything positive. Love, Edith

Colleen put the two letters away in a drawer where she kept Bret's little horse, Abby's box of sequins, and Pete's music box and the Mozart variations, and then she cried.

At school, Colleen's English class had begun a study of Keats's *Ode to a Nightingale* and *Ode on a Grecian Urn*. Colleen listened silently as her classmates analyzed the poetry of a man dying of tuberculosis. They seemed sympathetic to Keats's plight, and they understood his wish to die in peace while listening to the nightingale's song. They debated whether or not the two poems showed that Keats believed in the lasting consolation of beauty and whether history showed that a Garden of Eden or heaven on earth was possible. They argued about why beauty and a happy state can be imagined, but never come to full or lasting fruition in human society. They felt that when Keats seemed to awaken from his dream of the nightingale, he felt forsaken and forlorn, cheated like a child who had believed too long in a fairy-tale world. Some of them thought, at least in the case of the nightingale, that beauty exacerbated the poet's awareness of his own mortality. Others disagreed that the beauty of art is a coldly immortal thing. They said that it flowed from suffering and compassion for others. They felt that it could be inspiring and a source of hope for the world. Some suggested that Keats was half in love with death, but the other half of him wanted very badly to live, and it made him bitter toward death.

With regard to the truth, one student wondered if Keats meant that the price of truth was sacrifice—and whether a sacrificial lamb, like the calf depicted on the urn, was necessary in the process of the revelation of the truth. Some students felt this was unfair and unbeautiful and that the image of the calf being led to slaughter was violent. They found no beauty in the truth side of the urn. One student pointed out that Keats had not talked about truth and power except to say that the song of the nightingale was free to emperors and clowns. He wondered if Keats believed that the great masses of humanity were mere clowns to emperors. The class also talked about what growing old meant, and whether the need for truth and beauty increased as death approached, and why that might be.

Colleen said that deceit and vanity were the opposites of truth and beauty, and she thought the design of the urn might be fundamentally flawed, but no one seemed to understand, except Miss Wilson.

At the end of the class, Miss Wilson reread *Ode to a Nightingale* out loud and pointed out the lines which she found reminiscent of Hamlet's soliloquy on suicide and death. She reminded the class that they would be studying Shakespeare the following year. She also read them the lines that F. Scott Fitzgerald had borrowed as the title of his book, *Tender Is the Night*. She explained that artists are influenced by each other's thinking and writing. Then she said that when Keats realized that he was dying of tuberculosis, he requested that his epitaph be, "Here lies one whose name was writ in water." She asked them to think about that. For homework, Miss Wilson assigned them a theme on either truth or beauty as depicted on the Grecian urn or as depicted in *Ode to a Nightingale*. They would share their ideas together in class the next day.

Colleen decided to write about beauty.

She reread Keats's *Ode on a Grecian Urn*. It was a poem about the truth of beauty and the beauty of truth. On the beauty side of the urn, Keats had imagined a wedding party in which a musician played his flute beneath a tree as the groom was about to kiss his bride. Keats had described the mad pursuit, desire, and ecstasy in the scene, but he had also written that the *truth* about beauty is that it is a fleeting thing because we must all grow old and die. Keats had found cold comfort in the fact that beauty could be captured forever on the urn. *And forever in a photograph, too!* Colleen thought. She remembered Mr. Olsen's pictures and wished she had a picture of Bret—and Pete.

In the scene of truth, Keats had imagined a priest leading a sacrificial calf to slaughter. The streets of the town were deserted, and Keats wrote that the truth was that no soul had ever returned to affirm the truth of the resurrection. But where was the *beauty?* Colleen presumed that Keats saw nobility or humility in the beauty of sacrifice, but it only made her think of the calf's suffering. *What constitutes a proof?* The poem seemed to offer no answer. She tried to imagine a tinkling bell on the calf's neck put there by a shepherd so that the animal would not be lost from the herd. Miss Wilson had said that poetry is supposed to show the invisible in the visible. Colleen hoped that Keats had heard that little bell through his own pain and suffering, but she knew that Miss Wilson would never accept an invisible bell as a proof of the beauty in sacrifice.

So she turned instead to Keats's *Ode to a Nightingale.* She began her composition by asking, "What *are* we without beauty?" She remembered that Pete had said that people revolt when society fails to provide cleanliness, order, and beauty, and so she wrote that down. Then she added, "Without beauty, life would be a robotic kind of existence. We may be machines, but we are thinking and feeling machines. We ignore truth and beauty at our own peril. Truth and beauty are both essential to our health." She remembered Miss Marthe's words and added, "Great harm and ugliness come about when people live with lies, as during the Nazi regime of Adolf Hitler." Colleen reread the last lines of Keats's *Ode to a Nightingale*, trying to understand what he meant when he wrote:

Adieu! Adieu! Thy plaintive anthem fades

Past the near meadows, over the still stream,

Up the hillside, and now 'tis buried deep

In the valley glades:

Was it a vision or a waking dream?

Colleen suddenly realized that her dream of the lark had been the same as Keats's dream of the nightingale. The meadows, streams, hillsides, and valleys of Keats's poem were the same endless hills that her lark had flown over to find the secret place where music begins.

She wondered if perhaps Keats had misunderstood that place because a lark does not bury itself in the gloomy depths of the forest. She tried to write about that. Colleen felt that she understood Keats's feeling, even though his tuberculosis had advanced much farther than hers. Night had fallen over his life, but it had not yet fallen over hers. She still had hope because of her one good lung.

Then she wondered sadly whether Pete might have felt like Keats. She put down her pen, lost in thought. She felt that both odes were about leaving home for the unknown. Keats longed to leave the world on the wings of poetry and for his life to dissolve peacefully in the nightingale's song. Pete had also believed in the final merging of one's melody with God's. She wondered if loving something or someone too much made leaving easier or harder, especially if it wasn't possible to come home again or if the ultimate destination seemed meaningless and cruel.

Colleen reread the *Ode to the Nightingale* one last time, trying to capture the mood of a dying artist contemplating his vision of pure beauty.

She finally wrote:

All the wordless things of this world require metaphor. They always have, and they always will. They will always be elusive. As a poet, Keats longed for something he could not have and hold. He could only experience it. It seemed as free as a bird to him, and as happy. Its song seemed to resolve all his problems, or at least make them bearable, but he forgot the most important thing! The nightingale would come back to him, even if it seemed to fade with the dawn, because its purpose was to sing through the night. And there was a lark, by day. In his pain, Keats forgot that the nightingale was eternally free to all. As free as a bird.

Colleen's second spring back home passed quietly. The nicest part of her day was when she and Miss Wilson would talk together while Colleen waited for her father to pick her up at school. Miss Wilson had a free hour in her teaching schedule, which provided time for them to talk alone, provided that Miss Wilson wasn't too busy with her planning.

When the semester was finally over, Colleen and Robert began spending their summer evenings together with Katie and Robert's brother, John. Robert still had his job at the small grocery store during the day, but at night the four of them usually played Rook and then went to the soda shop. When the weather was especially sultry and oppressive, Robert would drive them up the holler for a drink of cold water from the spring in the mountainside.

From the holler, they could see all of Carlton, including the Green River, which on clear nights always glittered in the gathering darkness. They could see the O&S railroad and the main road into and out of Carlton.

On a particularly hot evening in July, Robert stayed with Colleen in the car while Katie and John walked farther up the holler in search of wildflowers. "I'm going to leave this place someday and make something of myself," Robert said, almost to himself. He was too busy studying the railroad tracks and the road out of Carlton to be completely aware of Colleen.

"Why would you want to leave? It's so peaceful and quiet," Colleen objected, looking down into the valley.

"You can't eat the scenery, Colleen," he laughed, finally looking over at her. "When I've saved enough money, I'll go to college and study math and physics so that I can become an aeronautical engineer someday. That's where the future of the country lies, and I want to be a part of it."

"I'm not sure if I even have a future," Colleen sighed. "How far can I go in life without even a simple skill, like typing?"

"Some folks have too much money and not enough brains, and others have enough brains or skills, but not enough money. Something's wrong there somewhere, wouldn't you say?" Robert asked. "But we'll both make it, Colleen, because we won't take no for an answer," he added, with a determined look in his eye.

Colleen smiled. "Everybody deserves a chance to be really challenged, Robert, and to see what he's made of, but that doesn't always happen, I suppose."

Robert laughed hollowly. "Didn't Miss Wilson tell you about F. Scott Fitzgerald yet? 'The rich are not like you and me,' and all that? They get a runnin' start, Colleen, but then, what do they do with it?"

Robert asked a bit sarcastically. "Not like you and me, I'd say! They like their running start, and they don't mind leavin' you behind in the dust! Gatsby's dream girl killed someone with his fast and fancy car!" Robert added, with a mischievous grin.

"But we all have things in common!" Colleen objected. "When the chips are down, we have to face our common humanity."

"That's what my dad's always sayin'," Robert laughed, a bit sardonically. "Last year, when I told him Miss Wilson had us reading *The Great Gatsby*, he just laughed and said, 'It just proves that money can't buy happiness, Robert!' So I told him that our 'common humanity' is all well and good, but what about our common inhumanity? He said that what we call 'evil' is merely temptation—one choice among many. He said if we pray not to be led into temptation, things will take care of themselves. He didn't explain how we will be delivered from the choices of those who *don't* pray to be delivered from evil!"

Robert shrugged, as if he was having an inner debate with himself, and then he finally said, "But like I said before, Colleen, you can't eat the scenery!" Robert looked down on Carlton again, lost in his own thoughts about the future.

Colleen's eyes followed his gaze. The sight of the O&S railroad tracks again reminded her of the two trains that seemed to be barreling down the tracks of her mind. She shook her head, trying to dispel the feeling. Just then, Katie and John returned from their walk. Katie was holding a handful of wildflowers they had gathered as a surprise for Mrs. Reilly. Colleen looked at Robert, who had not noticed them because he was still ruminating on his future. Colleen tapped him on the shoulder and pointed to the wildflowers that Katie and John had collected in the holler.

"Maybe your dad just meant that the lilies of the field are more beautiful than Solomon in all his glory. They grow in hollers, too, Robert."

"I *know* that, Colleen," he muttered in frustration. Then he grinned and added, "Just don't try to boil them and have them for your supper!"

Summer passed quickly, and by the end of August Colleen was finally beginning to feel the pulse of her life in Carlton returning to normal. Just before school started, Robert found a job with the railroad. In September, Colleen had to go back to school for her final year, which meant that she and Robert could only see each other on weekends or in the evening. When he could, Robert would hurry home, wash the soot off his hands and face, have a quick meal with his parents, and go over for a visit to see how Colleen was doing.

Neither Robert nor Katie had given up on the idea of getting Colleen to walk. Since Colleen was now going to school full time, Katie had been encouraging her to walk more during the day to build up her strength and stamina. One day they took the bus uptown to buy some pharmacy items, and Katie suggested that Colleen try to walk at least part of the way home.

"Let's not take the bus, Colleen! It's only a half mile. You can do it," she insisted.

Colleen very reluctantly acquiesced. She had barely used her leg muscles in three years. She began to walk along the sidewalk very slowly, but she soon felt a burning in her calves. She paused at a street bench and leaned on it.

"I don't think I'm going to make it. We'll have to take the bus," Colleen said.

Katie sat down on the bench with Colleen. When Colleen stood up again and almost fell over, Katie jumped up to catch her. Colleen just laughed.

"Let's keep going. I feel I have my second wind!" she said, smiling tentatively.

Katie looked dubious, but Colleen insisted that they continue.

When they finally arrived back home, Katie took Colleen's arm because she looked like she might collapse in a heap on the lawn. "Just a few more feet!" she whispered.

Colleen dragged herself up the walk, wobbled through the front door, and staggered into her bedroom. She threw herself on the bed and said, "Don't you ever tell Mom! Not ever! She'd kill us if she knew about this!"

Mrs. Reilly was busy making dinner. Katie brought Colleen a glass of water from the kitchen and then took off her shoes and socks for her. She shifted her into a more comfortable position on the bed, and after a while, Colleen felt her legs stop burning.

Katie stayed awhile with Colleen. She felt very pleased with Colleen's achievement. When she was satisfied that Colleen was resting comfortably, she went into the kitchen to help her mother make dinner so that Colleen could rest. Katie came back to check and found Colleen fast asleep. She had to wake her up for dinner.

Colleen had been invited to lunch with Robert's family on Thanksgiving Day, but Robert had deliberately not told her what he had in mind for "dessert." Dessert was a suggestion that they walk home instead of taking his father's Chevy. "But that's a mile!" Colleen protested.

Robert smiled and said, "I know! And it's a perfect day for it! The leaves are all comin' down, and the sun is shining. Let's go!" he said with a grin.

They started out slowly. When they were about halfway home, they saw Lindsay Patterson driving by. All the teachers knew about Colleen's situation, including Miss Patterson, who taught home economics and history. When she saw Colleen and Robert walking together, she flashed a big smile of encouragement.

Colleen began to waver as they got closer to her home. Robert was watching her closely, hovering over her protectively, while trying to appear nonchalant. From time to time, he would simply say, "You can do it, Colleen!" When they reached her house, Colleen gave a tired sigh of relief.

Robert joked, "You know what this means, don't you, Colleen? You're ready for a ride in Gertrude! You've just proven that we can walk home if she breaks down on us." This appeared to be a likely event, in Colleen's view. Gertrude was an old, square-shaped jalopy, which Robert and his friend Keith had jointly purchased secondhand, or probably tenthhand. It regularly broke down and seemed to be on its last wheels. This did not daunt Robert. He had recently installed a water pump and cooling system in Gertrude that he had improvised out of plumbing materials from his father's shed. No one at the local garage had believed it would work. Robert knew it would. And it did.

As soon as Carlton's pre-Christmas business activity began, Robert lost no time in augmenting his income by selling Christmas trees at a local Christmas tree lot. He was still working hard on the railroad, and he worked well into the evening selling the trees.

Robert surprised Colleen on Christmas day with a pretty wristwatch. He stayed for lunch, and Colleen baked him his favorite chocolate cake. Her present to him was a warm, knitted cap which he wore home.

The holiday's festivity was shattered when Robert's father collapsed after dinner one evening with a severe heart attack. He survived, but he could only work part time from the house. He was reassigned to a new church position pending his recovery. Robert applied for work at a light bulb factory in a nearby town in his search for a better income. He was offered a position on the assembly line, and the pay was very good. Robert was able to drive Gertrude to work because Keith worked locally and could take the bus.

Because Robert was gone most of the time, Colleen focused on her studies. She had watched Robert struggle to make his way in the world, and she was worried about her job prospects after graduation. She tried to persuade the counselor to allow her to enroll in typing, but her doctors wouldn't allow her to take more than the minimum credits for graduation.

Colleen was exasperated. When she exerted herself, she could feel a pain in her back below her shoulder blade. She wondered if there was any kind of job that she could do when she graduated.

During her school's Easter holiday, Colleen went to the movies with two classmates, but during the movie, her friends mostly talked about people in the class that Colleen didn't know. Colleen watched the movie. The film was titled *The Keys of the Kingdom,* and Gregory Peck played the starring role. Colleen kept visualizing Bret in the part of Father Frances Chisholm.

When the movie was over, they left the theater. The two girls lived on the other side of town, but they offered to walk Colleen home. She smiled and said she'd be fine. She watched them walk away, chatting gaily about their plans for the holiday. Colleen went home by herself. Along the way, she stopped at the library to borrow a copy of A. J. Cronin's book upon which the film had been based. She had been greatly touched by the movie and wanted to read the original work. She liked how the story came full circle when Father Chisholm returned to Scotland and went fishing with the child he thought of as a grandson. She liked the idea that one could come home again and be happy being a fisherman, especially with a child at one's side.

The week seemed to pass quickly. Colleen finished reading the book and wrote a note to Bret, highly recommending it and urging him to read it since he wanted to be a priest.

On Good Friday, Colleen went to church with her parents and Katie. When they entered the sanctuary, they took seats in an unfilled pew along the right wall. Colleen's place at the end of the pew was directly under a stained glass window, which portrayed Jesus praying in the garden of Gethsemane. Everyone was sitting quietly, waiting for the service to begin. A few people were whispering greetings to one another, and Katie was trying to get the broken clasp of her pocketbook to stay shut.

Colleen looked around her, and finding nothing to do, let her gaze fall on the stained glass portrait of Jesus. Sunlight poured through the panes of colored glass, but beyond the quiet of the sanctuary, a deeper silence somehow seemed to fill the busy, outside world. Colleen tried to imagine the pure and distant melody of Pete's God, but instead, what she thought she heard was the song of a lark. It was nearly lost amid traffic sounds and the busyness of the world. It seemed to be singing in a minor key, the way the lark in her dream had sung on Sue Ann's windowsill. Then, its song faded away.

Colleen studied the portrait of Christ and tried to imagine the long-forgotten sounds of the scene at Golgatha—the groans of the crucified, the rumbling of the earthquake, the ripping sound of the curtain being torn in the temple.

After the opening prayers and hymns, the minister stepped into the pulpit, which was higher than the choir loft and off to one side, and he began to read from Ecclesiastes.

Its message was that everything is meaningless. "Or so it seems!" the minister added in solemn tones. Colleen listened as he read:

There is a time for everything … a time to kill and a time to heal … a time to mourn and a time to dance … a time to be silent and a time to speak … a time to love and a time to hate …

and then, The wicked do not fear God … God made mankind upright, but men have gone in search of many schemes. Men are full of evil and there is madness in their hearts … the quiet words of the wise are more to be heeded … The race is not to the swift or the battle to the strong … but time and chance happen to them all

... so men are trapped by evil things that fall unexpectedly upon them ... Wisdom is better than weapons of war.

and finally, "Meaningless! Meaningless!" says the Teacher. "Everything is meaningless!" ... here is the conclusion of the matter: Fear God and keep his commandments ... For God will bring every deed into judgment, including every hidden thing, whether it is good or evil.

The minister bowed his head and said, "Perhaps this is how life seemed to the disciples when Jesus was betrayed and taken away for torture and trial by mob."

A hymn followed, and then the minister rose into the pulpit a second time and read from the Gospel of Matthew:

Then Jesus went with his disciples to a place called Gethsemane, and he said to them, "Sit here, while I go over there and pray." He took Peter and the two sons of Zebedee along with him ... Going a little farther, he fell on his face to the ground and prayed, "My father, if it is possible, may this cup be taken from me. Yet not as I will, but as you will."

The minister turned to the crucifixion scene and read Jesus's dying words from the Gospels of Luke and Mark:

"Father, forgive them, for they do not know what they are doing." and then, "My God, my God, why have you forsaken me?" ... The curtain of the temple was torn in two from top to bottom ... Jesus called out with a loud voice, "Father, into your hands I commend my spirit."

Then the minister turned to the Gospel of John and read:

*"It is finished."*

The minister turned to the congregation with tears in his eyes and said, "Not so! God will not abandon his world or his suffering servants! In the resurrection, he shows his love and redeeming power over the Empire of Man!" He then invited the congregation to take communion.

Colleen studied the stained glass window, mentally trying to piece together the minister's themes: a time to love and a time to hate, meaninglessness, and the hidden things of life, the good and the bad. When she reached the communion bar, Colleen knelt and listened to the minister's words, "Take, eat. This is my body that was broken for thee." Colleen looked at the pieces of bread and thought of Pete. She wondered if he had found peace in the "God in music" that he had been looking for in Claire's apartment, or whether he had only found betrayal as he lay dying. Colleen took the bread and said a prayer for him.

The minister then said, "Take and drink. This is my blood that was shed for thee." Colleen took one of the tiny glasses of grape juice. The purple juice in the bottom of the glass was like a quiet pool, like David's pool of still waters. Pete had said that David sang his songs to God over those still waters. The tiny pool in the bottom of the communion glass was royal purple, its color produced by the red in Jesus's arteries and the blue of the blood in his veins. As Colleen drank, she remembered Pete's blood, and she felt that she was choking on it. Katie looked up in surprise when she heard Colleen coughing.

Colleen looked into the now empty communion glass. Her church did not use a common cup. Colleen thought that if the church ever acquired one, its silver, outer surface would reflect the light of God's truth and beauty. The inside would be stained with the blood and wine of human vanity and lies. It would contain more worldly dissonance than Pete had ever believed possible. The natural tendency was to recoil from the brim of the abyss and to miss hearing the pure and distant melody hidden within. *Fools all, until we understand the reality and beautiful potential of time.* Isn't that what Pete had said?

"*It is finished!*" echoed in Colleen's ears. Within her private sanctuary, behind the drawn curtains of her prayers, she felt that something had been irrevocably torn. She knew it was her heart.

Too late, she knew that she had loved Pete.

She tried to remember and understand. He had known that he was in danger. Of that, she was certain. She had seen it in his eyes. Even so, he couldn't forsake his music because the gift in him had been too perfect all along. He had believed others could discover the same gift in themselves, and that it would change their lives *forever* if they would only try. He had wanted passionately to help her find that gift as well, because he recognized and loved it in her.

"*It is finished!*"

But *how* had it finished? Colleen had to know. Colleen thought about Pascal's wager. Bret had said that Pete refused to live his life that way. Colleen now perceived that Pete had made a different kind of bet: that if he was dying, there was salvation and consolation in his music; if he lived, there was everything to be gained in continuing to play Claire's piano. He had made his wager, believing that Eden could be now.

And what had she believed? Too young to fully understand, she had let the possibility of love remain a distant mirage, an ever-receding *something* beyond her reach at Sherwood. He had been telling her all along exactly what it was and that he loved her. Without understanding the most essential thing in herself, she had lost Eden. By the simple act of not remembering to move back Claire's chair to its proper place, they had been locked out of Eden. At least until Pete had found a way back in.

"It is finished!"

But *how* did he die? On the night that Pete had died, he had begun to play *Clair de Lune*, most assuredly in the hope that she would hear it, but she had been unable to hear him downstairs. She would never know exactly how he had played it, except that Abby said it had been exquisitely beautiful.

She didn't need to know. She knew what his music had been saying. It had been saying, "I love you."

He had *not* been taken away by foolish bravado in the face of TB and death. He had understood that nature weeds out the good with the bad, and not just the weak from the strong. He had gone to Claire's apartment in spite of that, because to him music *wasn't* a risk. It was the one true and beautiful thing. Life was *meaningless* without music.

He had found a piece of eternity in the upstairs room as he played Debussy in the moonlight. Pete had dared to imagine a different world, and Colleen wondered if she had also been a part of it. Perhaps he had glimpsed a bit of eternity in her as well.

In the apartment, time had stood still. Colleen had always believed in God the Creator, and in God-among-us in his son, Jesus, but for the first time, Pete had shown her that there was more to God; there was God *in* us. That was how Pete had regarded music. It was more than the gift his mother had given him and more than a way to remember his mother forever; it was a consolation that nature could never give anyone; it was paradise restored; an end, and a symbol of the reason for living. It was an eternity with purpose and beauty, and one that made sense of all things. Its eternity reached beyond nature's eternal present. He had shown her that this inner consolation existed in music but also in the voice of a child and in the *trust* between two people. *It was the way to lead one's life,* Colleen thought sadly, *but no longer with him.*

"Do you trust me, Colleen, or do you think I'm mad?"

No, Colleen realized. She had not thought he was mad. She had thought that he was the incarnation of truth and beauty. She simply had not believed that anyone like him could love her that much.

As to whether he had sacrificed himself on the altar of the god of music, as Bret believed, or to a trust in the real God, why, that would depend on which kind of wager a man thinks life really is.

When school resumed after the holiday, Miss Wilson announced that they would be studying *Macbeth* and *Hamlet* for the remainder of the year. The class would be going to see a production of *Macbeth*, which was coming to town in a month. By the time they had finished *Macbeth,* Colleen was eager to see how the director would stage the Birnham Woods scene. Miss Wilson told them to watch for Lady Macbeth's descent into madness, because the question of insanity would recur again in *Hamlet.* Colleen sat up straight in her chair when Miss Wilson said this, remembering Pete's question, "Do you trust me, or do you think I'm mad?"

After the play, Miss Wilson immediately launched into *Hamlet,* which she said was her favorite of Shakespeare's plays. There was a paper due, and after that Colleen would graduate. It would be the last time Colleen would write a composition for Miss Wilson, and she wanted to make it a good one.

Colleen chose the element of music in *Hamlet* to write about. She tried to trace how the music slowly went out of Hamlet's life by showing at what point it had become only "words, words, words," and at what points the music seemed to reappear. She tried to understand how a young man so full of nobility and grace could come to such a tragic end. Colleen wrote that in spite of the odds, Hamlet had hope until the very end. He had also finally made peace with death and recognized that "readiness" for it was all. She wrote that Hamlet's last words, "the rest is silence," represented the final fading of music from his life amid the havoc of a treacherous world without music and love.

Colleen closed by observing that the King had his comeuppance because he had not factored in the chance that the Queen, out of motherly love, might drink from the poisoned goblet. Colleen wrote that the King had understood the "beau" in beauty, the "pow!" in power, but not the "love" in loveliness. He had failed to discover the other side of the Grecian urn. He would not repent and sacrifice his ill-gotten crown. His failure brought about the fall of Denmark.

Colleen wrote that the things a person focuses on or ignores determine events, not fate. She added that "the ignorant present," which Macbeth had rued, favored the chances of the rational man—a man such as Horatio—and not a ruthlessly ambitious man. Colleen concluded, however, by saying that a *totally* rational man, who lived a life without music, was also a tragedy—and might never have imagined the ghost and exposed a king. No one, she wrote, had been true to himself in the play. Only Ophelia had truly understood that the music had gone out of their lives, and she had gone mad.

On June 30, 1950, a month after Colleen had graduated, President Truman committed US ground forces to Korea. Robert received his draft notice on the day after the Fourth of July. It was the *coup de grâce* as far as Colleen was concerned. Robert was her best friend. When he called with the news, Colleen was left feeling alone and desolate.

Robert came to Colleen's house with his draft notice and put it on the kitchen table.

"Well, there you have it. Uncle Sam wants me!" he said, frowning at the form. Robert's expression brightened, and he added, "With some luck, they can use me as a mechanic, Colleen. I'm a fast typist, too. Maybe I'll even qualify for intelligence work."

"I'd like to see you off at the bus station," Colleen said forlornly.

Her parents offered to drive Robert to the draft office. When they got there, Robert got out of the car and entered the building. Colleen and her parents waited in the car. Once inside, Robert took a seat next to some other young men his age. A door on Robert's left opened, and an Army sergeant appeared in the doorway and called out a name. A tall and freckled blond fellow stood up. He followed the sergeant into his office. The door on Robert's right opened and a Marine sergeant said, "I need two more! Anderson and Carlson!" Robert and the fellow sitting next to him looked up in surprise. They stood up and followed the Marine into his office.

When Robert came out to the car, his face was pale and grim. "The Marines took me! Can you believe that? I've been ordered to report immediately to Parris Island for basic training."

Mr. Reilly shook his head and looked worried.

Robert simply said, "I have to sign some forms. The bus will be leaving as soon as they process the rest of the fellows inside. You can meet me at the station at two o'clock."

Colleen and her parents went to the bus station and sat in the waiting room. In a little while, a small, military bus arrived with Robert and the rest of the recruits in it. A sergeant ordered them to go inside and wait. Robert came over and sat with Colleen and her parents while he waited for the bus that would take him to Parris Island. Robert seemed preoccupied, so Colleen and her parents carried on a one-sided conversation with him.

When the bus arrived at the station, Robert stood up and shook hands with Mr. Reilly. Colleen gave him an encouraging smile. He gave her a quick hug, and then without a word, he jammed his hat on his head and walked resolutely toward the waiting bus. He didn't look back.

*Robert has never been one to look back*, Colleen thought. The future had always been everything to him, even the unexpected future. He would make the most of it as he always had. She saw him take an unoccupied place in the aisle of bus seats opposite the platform. A few recruits stood up in the aisle just as the bus pulled out of the terminal.

They blocked Robert's last chance to wave good-bye to Colleen.

"Do you think Robert will survive boot camp?" Colleen asked, not knowing whether to laugh or cry. Robert was a free spirit, a renaissance man, and a self-reliant man, all of which, at least in Colleen's mind, seemed the antithesis of what Uncle Sam might be looking for in a Marine.

"I'm sure he'll figure out a way to survive Parris Island, Colleen," Mr. Reilly reassured her, "but I don't envy him the experience."

## David

As soon as Colleen and her family arrived back home, Colleen went into the living room to read the newspaper in order to get her mind off of Robert. A small advertisement in the Help Wanted section caught her eye. It said:

SUMMER POSITION. No experience needed. Must like music and children.

Free room and board if desired. Reply: Richard Erikson, PO Box 105, Carlton.

Colleen went out in the kitchen and showed the advertisement to her mother. "I think I could do this, Mom! What do you think?" Colleen asked excitedly.

"It sure sounds like they're describing you, Colleen. You could always try," her mother said encouragingly. Mrs. Reilly found a pen and stationary, and Colleen sat down at the kitchen table to compose a reply. When she had completed it, Mr. Reilly took it to the post office and put it in the afternoon mail.

Within two days, Colleen received a phone call from Richard Erikson. He told her he was looking for a person to help him care for his developmentally disabled son. "There's no lifting, and he's easy to be around because he's very quiet and fairly undemanding," he explained. "I need someone to watch him while I'm getting my mother's house ready to sell." Colleen agreed to come out the next morning for an interview.

Since Elliot was now home for the summer, he volunteered to drive Colleen out to Mr. Erikson's house the next day. Elliot had been offered a teaching position in Chicago, which would begin in the fall, and he had managed to buy a used car.

Richard Erikson's house was situated along a country road outside of Carlton. Elliot spotted the Erikson mailbox without any difficulty. He turned into a drive that led to an old wooden farmhouse with enormous Victorian windows. Through the open windows, Colleen could hear someone playing a Chopin nocturne. When they knocked on the door, the music stopped. A tall, strongly built man in his late twenties answered the door. He had a red beard and piercing hazel eyes. "You must be Colleen! I'm Richard. Please come in!" His voice was welcoming and gentle.

"This is my brother Elliot," Colleen explained.

"Why don't you come this way, and we'll meet David," Richard suggested. He led Colleen down a center hall, which opened onto a large living room. It was a sunny room furnished with a desk, a sofa, several stuffed chairs, and a grand piano. A little boy of about four or five was sitting by the piano and repeatedly spinning a globe. He had tousled, unruly black hair and dark brown eyes. He was wearing socks, but no shoes. Each time that the globe came to a stop, he would spin it again and say, "Here we go!" He seemed oblivious of anyone's presence.

They sat down together, and Richard asked Colleen to tell him about herself. After a while, he excused himself and went into the kitchen. He came back with a graham cracker.

"His name is David," he said. Richard offered his son the cracker.

The little boy smelled it, touched it with his tongue, and then laid it on the floor. "Good-bye, don't want." Richard tried to offer David some noodles on a spoon, but he turned his head away and said, "I don't." Colleen noticed that he didn't seem to look his father in the eye.

David then took Richard by the finger and led him into the kitchen. Colleen noticed that the little boy walked on his tiptoes the entire distance.

"Come with us, Colleen," Richard called over his shoulder. Colleen followed Richard and watched as David carefully made Richard's hand open the refrigerator door. "He wants his juice. He prefers it in this blue cup. He doesn't like bright colors." Richard gave David his drink. Colleen watched the child take the cup and drink from it.

They returned to the living room. As Richard and Colleen talked, Elliot sat quietly in a stuffed chair by the bookcase. The bookcase was tall and reached nearly to the ceiling. It was full of toys. Elliot was mostly watching David and only half-listening to the conversation.

After a while, David went over to Elliot and crawled into the chair with him. Elliot smiled at him, thinking the boy wanted to make friends, but David silently climbed over him and tried to reach the upper shelf. He stood precariously balanced with one foot on Elliot's shoulder in an attempt to reach a ball. Elliot quickly pulled the boy off his shoulder, and the child shrieked as piercingly as a parrot. When Elliot handed him the ball, David took it into a corner and finally went and hid in a closet.

From inside the closet, Elliot heard David say, "Don't look!"

"Leave him in there, if you don't mind," Richard requested when Elliot made a move to coax the boy out of the closet. "He doesn't want you to look at him. He'll stay in there until he feels safe. He doesn't like changes in routine and he doesn't understand what strangers want if they approach him too quickly. As you've probably noticed, he has a very limited vocabulary. He's also still in diapers."

Elliot reached involuntarily for his shoulder to feel for wetness. He looked at Colleen with a shocked look on his face.

"He probably won't talk to you for a while, Colleen, but he'll learn to play alongside you if you take the job," Richard continued.

"I desperately need a second pair of eyes to watch him for his own safety. If you'll agree to live here, there's a large bedroom downstairs that you can use. I usually lie down with him at night in his bedroom to get him to settle down, but he sometimes comes downstairs and plays around the house at night. Two older women have already quit because they couldn't take it," Richard said. "I would just need you to alert me if he does that. He can't ever be outside on his own alone, especially at night."

Colleen seemed to be wavering.

"I can pay you well, Colleen!" Richard pleaded. "I hope to sell this place by the end of the summer. It belonged to my mother until she died this past spring. After I sell the house, I'll take David back to Maryland to see a specialist. A Dr. Kanner at Johns Hopkins has described a disorder that fits David's symptoms. It's called autism."

Colleen looked at the grand piano by the window. "Was your mother a musician?"

"Actually, I am!" Richard said. "I play French horn in the Baltimore Symphony Orchestra. That was the piano I grew up with. If you play piano, you're welcome to play it anytime you want. David is very musical, and he might enjoy that. He appears to have absolute pitch. His favorite key is F major, but when he says, 'No thank you!' he sings it in the relative D minor!"

Colleen asked about her salary. Richard offered her much more than she had expected. She told him she would like to think about it overnight, and then she and Elliot left and drove home.

As soon as they were out of earshot, Elliot said, "I think you'd better think this over! Did you hear him scream?"

"If you were afraid, or if you were in pain and couldn't tell someone, wouldn't you scream?" Colleen asked.

When they got home, Colleen described the situation to her parents. They left the decision up to her. Colleen immediately called Richard and accepted the job.

On her first day, Mr. Reilly drove Colleen out to the house and was impressed with Richard's intelligence and warmth. He had no qualms about Colleen working there in the evenings. He kissed her good-bye and drove off to work.

Richard was very pleased that Colleen had accepted the position. He showed her the first floor bedroom and a closet for her belongings, and then he said, "If there's anything else you need, please let me know."

They went into the living room where David was playing. He was busy arranging and rearranging some storybooks in a long line across the carpet.

"When he hears conversation, sometimes he'll repeat a word he's heard before, Colleen," Richard said, watching his son. "He doesn't really play with things, but he likes to feel textures and put things in order. His speech therapist swears she heard him say, 'What a beautiful sight!' one time. That's an expression he might have heard me use, but he doesn't normally talk in full sentences."

Richard sat down at his desk and went to work on entering credits and debits into the ledger of his mother's estate, leaving Colleen on her own to interact with his son. Colleen watched David and sometimes offered him toys from the bookshelf. He would feel their texture or sometimes carry several around in his hands. She put his things away and brought him some juice.

Colleen went over to the piano. She played "Twinkle, Twinkle, Little Star" and watched his reaction. He did not look up from play. She went into the kitchen and brought back a handful of spoons, a few of which she put on the floor beside him. She clinked her own spoons together in a simple rhythm. The boy paused, picked up the spoons and repeated what Colleen had done. Colleen changed the rhythm, and David again repeated the new one. With her back to David, Colleen tried the melody again on the piano, but she heard nothing. Instead, she felt David's arms embrace both of her legs and hold on tightly. Richard looked on in astonishment.

Colleen said, "There must at least be some remnant of music in him. Somehow. Somewhere. Maybe we can build on that."

At lunchtime David ate a grilled cheese sandwich. Richard said there were many tastes that David wouldn't accept. After lunch, Richard took him out in the backyard and chased him around. Then he picked up his son and threw him into the air several times.

"He loves to be tickled, and he loves to smell people's hair, Colleen. Sometimes when we're outside, he'll run in a straight line across the yard and back. He always runs in a straight line. He never dodges if I try to play chase with him." Richard tickled David, and he giggled.

Colleen bent down so that David could smell her hair.

In the afternoon, Colleen watched David walk around the house feeling the textures of different household items. He seemed to prefer slightly rough surfaces. When the ceiling fan made a high-pitched, metallic sound as a sudden breeze caught it, David covered his ears and screamed. "We'd better turn that off until I can fix it," Richard noted. "He can't stand loud, high pitches."

Colleen sat on the floor and read books out loud to David while she pointed to the pictures. He didn't seem to be listening, and he never looked up from whatever object held his interest. She couldn't get his attention by pointing to things and naming them, nor could she get him to look at her. One time when he had thought she wasn't watching, she had caught him looking at her with one eye shut, his head cocked, and mouth pulled up at an angle toward the closed eye in an effort to study her, like a painter. He had looked away when she looked at him. She had also seen him purse up his mouth and study it in the bathroom mirror as if trying to figure out how it worked.

Colleen left the books on the floor, and David arranged them in a row. She counted the books over and over. "One, two, three!" she exclaimed, but David said nothing. Before dinner, Colleen watched him pour marbles from one jar to another for over an hour.

At dinner, Colleen asked Richard how it was possible to get David's attention.

Richard answered, "In reality, I think he's the one who gets my attention, but only indirectly and in his own way—and only when he wants something. His psychologist says it's as if he doesn't have a 'person center.' You saw him climb over Elliot. Sometimes he seems completely unaware of other people, and yet he's hyperaware of noise, texture, and smells."

"How do you know what he wants? How can he tell you if he's sick or where it hurts?" Colleen asked in dismay.

"He either leads me by the finger, or he screams," Richard said with a hollow laugh. "When he screams, I can only guess what he wants. He's been taught to say, 'More, please!'"

In the evenings, Richard usually worked on an oratorio that he was composing, while David would sit on the sofa making little noises. Colleen wondered how Richard could hear the notes in his head through David's interruptions. Occasionally David would join their conversation by repeating a word or by making loud, squawking noises.

Richard had given Colleen a copy of *The Magic Mountain* to read. He had found it in his mother's library. "Considering your experience at Sherwood, I'd be interested in hearing how you think it compares," he observed.

When Colleen finished it, she told Richard that there were no posh lounges at Sherwood, and that she had not gone out for hikes. No one had become involved in a duel. Richard laughed. He seemed to find her witty, which pleased Colleen a good deal because she had come to greatly respect his thoughts. His clarity of mind and rare gentleness were the two virtues Colleen most admired.

One evening, after Richard had put David to bed, he sat down at the piano and played the Chopin nocturne that Colleen had overheard on the day of her interview. Colleen had been practicing on weekends and had made great progress at the piano. Richard was aware of this and offered to teach her the piece. Colleen sat down beside him on the piano bench and Richard explained some of the more difficult passages to her. Then he pointed out aspects of the piece that he found original and beautiful. With some difficulty, Colleen managed to play the first page all the way through.

"You play very expressively, Colleen!" Richard said approvingly. He patted her hand and allowed his hand to remain on hers. Colleen did not take her hand away. She felt totally comfortable with her hand in his. He smiled at her and said, "You are a most extraordinary young woman, Colleen."

They talked awhile, and then Colleen excused herself and went to bed. She lay in bed thinking about Richard and wondered if he was thinking of her. In the middle of the night, she heard David playing in the upstairs hall. She could hear Richard talking to him and trying to coax him back into bed.

In the morning over breakfast, Colleen suggested that she keep a log of David's behavior. "Perhaps Dr. Kanner will find it useful," she suggested. Richard agreed to the plan.

For the next two months, Colleen kept fastidious notes, but she couldn't solve the mystery of David's autism. It was frustrating, but the child's basic sweetness made the effort worthwhile. Richard was worried that she was working too hard and worrying too much about David. He usually sent her home early on Friday afternoons so that she could rest. On those days, as she gathered up her things to leave for the weekend, he would look at her wistfully. He seemed to want to go, too—not just to get away from David's constant care, she thought, but to be with her. When she would return on Monday morning, Richard would always look tired.

Colleen worked hard trying to devise ways to help David. As they were sitting down to breakfast one morning, David took their hands and said, "God is great, God is good!" Richard finished the blessing and then said to Colleen, "His mother always said grace. You must remind him of her."

"Am I like her?" Colleen asked curiously.

"You're quite like her, but much younger. And just as lovely," he said. "She died a year ago. It has been hard raising him alone." Richard changed the subject. "What will you do today?" he asked.

Colleen took out some hollow reeds that she had pulled from a bed of day lilies in the front yard. "We're going to blow bubbles!" she exclaimed.

"I don't know if he can, Colleen," Richard said doubtfully.

"Well, it's a beautiful day, and it's worth a try. Maybe he'll chase them and pop them. May I take him out on the front lawn?" she asked. "The back yard is too shady in the morning."

Richard seemed deep in thought and a bit distracted. "That's fine," he answered.

Colleen took David outside and blew some bubbles. She popped some and let others blow away. David watched the bubbles float in the air, and then he started running after a big one. When he reached the end of the drive, it burst, and he started running down the road. He began to run along the center stripe and seemed unaware of Colleen's frantic shouts.

Colleen ran inside. "Richard! Come quickly! David ran away!" she cried.

Richard was already at the door. "Which way did he go?" he asked worriedly. Colleen pointed, and Richard started running up the road. He disappeared around a bend. Colleen waited, hoping there were no cars on the road. In a few minutes, she saw Richard coming back with David held tightly in his arms. As they walked back up the driveway, Richard suddenly took Colleen's hand in his and held on tightly to it.

When they reached the front porch, David ran up the stairs and into the house. Colleen started to follow him in, but Richard stopped her. "There's something I need to tell you, Colleen," he said. "When I came back down the road just now and saw you reappear around the curve, I knew it wasn't just David that I had been looking for. It was for you, too." Colleen looked up at him in surprise. Then Richard bent down and kissed her.

Toward mid-September, Richard was getting ready to move back to Baltimore. The house had been sold, which was very good news and a relief for him. The symphony orchestra's fall season would soon begin, and David needed to see a specialist.

Colleen loved being with the two of them, and she was not looking forward to his departure. In her heart, she knew that she had fallen in love with him. She believed he loved her too, though he had never explicitly told her so. But sometimes in the evenings when they were alone together reading or just talking, he would stroke her long brown hair meditatively and say, "What would I do without you?"

Only yesterday, David had knocked nearly all his toys out of the bookcase as he reached for a ball on the top shelf. The sound of the avalanche of toys had brought Richard and her running into the living room, where they found David sitting unhurt in a heap of toys in the middle of the rug. They sat down with him and put David's finger puppets on their fingers, laughing like children at play who could go on forever that way. But Colleen knew that this idyllic state could not continue indefinitely. Time had finally caught up with them, and Richard would soon return to Baltimore.

This morning, however, Colleen had her own news for Richard. She had received two phone calls that morning from Elliot while Richard had been at the bank. Robert had completed his basic training and was home on leave before going on regular duty. He had qualified for intelligence work and had been assigned to a nearby base. He wanted to see Colleen before he left. Colleen had received many letters from Robert during basic training and was very much looking forward to his visit. Elliot had called a second time to say that Laura and Will had met Abby in Oakton while she was in the city visiting relatives. They were bringing her back by car following a visit with Miss Marthe. All of them, including Robert, would be at the Reilly house by afternoon.

Richard suggested that Colleen invite them to dinner that evening at his house. "Let's invite Elliot, Katie, and your parents, too, Colleen!" he suggested. "I'll cook, and you can keep track of David."

At four o'clock in the afternoon, two cars pulled into the driveway. Colleen went out on the porch and saw Laura, Will, and Mr. Mews sitting in the front seat of an old Studebaker. Her parents had parked behind them. Robert was squeezed into the back of the car along with Katie, Elliot, and Abby. Colleen invited everyone to come in, and she heard Abby say, "Now don't hang back, Robert! Make way for the Marines, ya'll!"

They all went inside, and Colleen introduced her friends to Richard. Mr. Mews ran around the room while David retreated to the closet. Richard remarked casually, "You can meet David in a little while."

Richard was cooking, so after the introductions he excused himself and went into the kitchen to check on the dinner. He had prepared several vegetarian dishes as well as a huge pot roast.

Robert sat down on the sofa next to Colleen as the rest of the party waited for Richard to announce dinner. Colleen gave Robert a big hug. "I've missed you, Robert! You look as if you've lost some weight," she said with a concerned expression.

"I got pneumonia toward the end of basic training," he replied. "They put me in the hospital and promised me a position in the Marine band if I would take basic training all over again." Robert grinned and said, "I told them there was no way I would do that! I finished up half-dead, but I survived. Besides, I doubt that repeating boot camp would have made me a better trumpet player. It would probably have finished me off," he laughed.

Colleen wanted to hear all about Parris Island. Everyone listened in varying degrees of horror and amusement as Robert described it. Colleen was proud of Robert's accomplishment and his grit. She asked him if he thought it was worth it and he said, "They say they made a man out of me, Colleen. *Semper Fi* and all that! Even though I turned them down on the Marine band, I hope they'll forgive and forget and make an engineer out of me."

At that moment, Richard came into the living room and called everyone to dinner. Colleen had created a centerpiece out of wildflowers with paper birds nestled among the blossoms. Robert sat down between Abby and Colleen, and Richard remained at the head of the table to carve the meat. Laura and Will were discreetly holding hands. David came out of the closet, so Richard made up a small plate for him. He set it on the table corner next to him where he could keep an eye on David.

"We're on our way to Mississippi, Colleen," Laura announced. "We couldn't get jobs with any newspapers except as stringers. We asked a Chicago editor if we could send him a few stories about race relations in the South before Will goes back to Haiti. It was Will's idea to do the stories from both a black and a white perspective. The editor thought it might work. He said we would be on our own if we got in trouble!"

Mr. Reilly wondered whether it was safe for them to travel through the South together.

"Laura will be perfectly safe with me as her 'chauffeur.' Don't you remember, Mr. Reilly? It was you who gave me the idea, during our trip to Chicago. No one will ever suspect what Laura and I will be up to until we've left town and our stories appear a month or so later. Once we are back in my own country, things will be much easier. If all goes well, we are hoping to write news stories about the conditions in Haiti as well."

"What did you do while you were in Chicago?" Mrs. Reilly asked.

"I worked in a French restaurant and Laura eventually found a job as a concierge not far from where I worked. We saved all our earnings, and now we have enough to return to my country."

"By way of Mississippi!" Katie exclaimed with wide eyes.

Will nodded. "In Haiti, we will write about the extremes of wealth and poverty and about the disease the white man brought to my country, which has spread very virulently."

David offered Will Pete's music box. "More please!" he asked.

"That's Pete's music box!" Abby exclaimed.

Colleen took the music box from Will and turned the key. David carried the music box around the room as it slowly wound down.

There was a lull in the conversation as everyone watched David. When the music box finally stopped playing, there was a momentary silence. Colleen had left the radio on in the living room. Through the dining room entrance, she could see the "always faithful" listening dogs, RCA's cute logo for the fidelity of their sound systems, and beside the listening dogs, the phrase, His Master's Voice, embossed on the woven material that covered the loud speaker. The dinner party listened as the radio announcer reported that a B29 had crashed into a California trailer park, causing 17 fatalities. The B29 had been carrying an atomic bomb, but fortunately, the bomb had not detonated.

Everyone looked at Robert, but Robert just laughed and said, "I'd say that that was *very* fortunate! Don't look at me! I'm not to blame for what the Pentagon does!"

Katie said, rather solemnly, "Do you know that stars are really suns which are constantly exploding like huge atomic bombs in outer space? I learned that in science yesterday." When no one said anything, Katie filled the silence by adding, "The words to Pete's music box song should really be, 'Twinkle, Twinkle, Little *Bomb*!'"

Colleen was upset by her sister's remark because it didn't fit the spirit of the Mozart variations at all.

Mrs. Reilly sighed and said, "When I was a little girl, we made wishes upon the stars."

Abby looked horrified, her lovely image of the stars in the night sky suddenly shattered.

Richard just laughed and told Colleen, "I forbid you to teach my son those lyrics!"

Colleen laughed, and then she answered, "What would Dr. Kanner think if David came out with that?"

After dinner, the guests went out on the porch. Colleen went into the kitchen to help Richard with the cleanup. Then she went to rest a moment in the living room before rejoining the party on the porch. Will had just come out of the bathroom, and he crossed over to the piano and sat down without realizing Colleen was in the room. He opened a hymnal that was on the music rack and played a few spirituals. Colleen had not known that Will could play so well. She took the chair nearest the piano so that she could listen. Mr. Mews immediately jumped into her lap. Colleen laughed and began to pet him.

Will looked up and smiled at Colleen. "I hope you do not mind, Colleen. A priest taught me how to play when I was a little boy in Haiti. I have not played in many years. It is a great pleasure to play on such a beautiful instrument," he said admiringly.

"It was the piano Richard learned to play on," Colleen said with a smile.

"Laura and I plan to marry, when we go home to my country," Will said, a bit too casually.

Colleen was not totally surprised. "That's wonderful, Will. I hope you will have a happy life together," she murmured.

"It will be easier for us to live as a married couple in Haiti. If America ever changes its attitude toward interracial marriages, perhaps we shall return one day," he said. Will thumbed through the hymnal and began to play "Lift Every Voice and Sing!"

"This song is sometimes called the Negro's national anthem, Colleen," he said as he continued to play. Then he stopped for a moment and said, "It begins by talking about the harmonies of liberty. I wonder what beautiful country this music is describing."

Colleen remembered all the trouble the Handyman had caused Will. "But at least Laura understands, Will. I want to understand, too!"

"Of all the white people I have met, only Laura truly understands. She doesn't fear change. She lives for it!" he exclaimed.

Will began to play once again until he had finished the refrain. "The music speaks of bitter bygone days when hope unborn died, Colleen. That happened in my own land, my Haiti!" he exclaimed passionately. "Its history is written in black blood! In Haiti—and in America—we will have to *make* white people listen by asking them to sit down at the table with us as friends and equals."

"So, change will begin by listening!" Colleen exclaimed.

"It is only in the doing of a thing that any of us ever truly understands," Will said. "One must clean one's own house before telling another man how to clean his!"

"You mean we must clean up the stain of race," Colleen said.

"I do!" Will exclaimed. Will played "Lift Every Voice and Sing!" one more time and looked intently at Colleen. "No child should grow up feeling that he doesn't count, Colleen.

"I wrote some short tales about race while I was living in Haiti. Children in many parts of the world have read them. Their success allowed me to enter this country. When I tell a white man that I have written books, at first he is pleased and interested; later, there is a malignant desire to know who I really am; then, when he has read one or two of my books, he believes that he could have written them better—more to his *liking*."

"If you let me read your books someday, I promise not to do that, Will," Colleen said.

"You don't have to promise me that, Colleen. I wrote my books for children, but I know you will enjoy them because you are as innocent as a child in your spirit. I see that in the way you treat David."

Colleen and Will continued to talk for a while, and when they finally went out onto the porch, the daylight was beginning to wane. It was nearly the last day of summer, and the evening had turned chilly. The cool dampness made Colleen shiver, and she went and got a sweater for David and for herself. When she returned, the talk turned from the movies to politics, and finally to old times at Sherwood.

In a corner of the porch, she saw that Abby had taken a seat next to Robert and was avidly listening to him recount his experiences at Parris Island.

Richard listened to the conversation for a while and then went upstairs to stay with David until his son fell asleep. When he finally came back downstairs, everyone was getting ready to go home. Colleen's family and Robert were already out in the car.

Will, Laura, and Abby thanked Richard for his hospitality. They would be staying at Colleen's house overnight before departing in the morning. After that, Laura and Will would head south toward Mississippi, dropping Abby at her home along the way. Colleen urged them to be careful on the back roads.

"We have the *Green Book*, Miss Colleen!" Will reassured her.

Colleen gave Will and Laura a worried look. She wondered whether the *Green Book* would work in Mississippi and whether Will's role as chauffeur would protect a black-and-white couple traveling together by private car through the South. But she said nothing, hoping that Will was right, because she had no answer to her questions. She doubted that there was any answer except to find out.

When everyone had left, Richard and Colleen went outside, and they sat down beside a small pool that his mother had always enjoyed. Its far edge was bordered by chrysanthemums and the dying remnants of lilies and faded summer flowers. The pool contained several large goldfish.

Colleen studied Richard. It was the first time she had seen him relax since the sale of the house. A page had turned in his life, and for the moment, he seemed content to watch the goldfish glide serenely and gracefully around the pool.

"I sometimes think about the story of Narcissus when I look at this pool," Richard said.

"And David is Echo," Colleen said, guessing his thought.

Richard nodded his head. "I wonder what the future has in store for him in Baltimore. I hope to get some answers when we go up there. When I take him anywhere, people usually pretend he's not there. You're the only one who isn't put off by his behavior."

"But I know he's more than an echo!" Colleen exclaimed.

"Dr. Kanner has discovered four qualities that make an autistic child different. The most important is aloneness, but there's also the preference for routines and sameness. He says autistic children always have some unusual ability. In David's case, that's probably music."

Richard tossed a handful of fish food into the pool, and circles began to spread across the water's surface. He watched the fish come to the surface and feed.

"David's psychologist says he is a very musical little boy, but what good is his musicality if it's bottled up inside him?" Richard said. He touched the water and watched the expanding circles collide with the edge of the pool and reverberate as liquid echoes. "If I try to reach out and touch him through words, they only come back to me in echoes."

"I wonder if the melodies and rhythms in his voice *can* flow freely into words," Colleen mused. "Maybe something interferes with that flow. Words and music should go together naturally. They should grow and grow, together! Speech should be as free as a bird. Conversation isn't just about reasoning, Richard. It's about two melodies listening to each other. Words contain more than logic!" Colleen exclaimed.

"Listen to what I'm about to say very carefully, Richard," Colleen said.

She spoke the words, "Where is David's soul?" and "Who is David?" as naturally as she could.

"My words didn't come out in a flat and robotic way because there's *music* in them," she continued. "The music was the emotion I felt when I spoke them. Our voices express the full range of our emotions because that's what music does. David doesn't speak like a robot, either, because music is still in him. Maybe we can help him make it grow, until it just *has* to flow out of him."

"He may be too filled with music when we speak to him, Colleen. The music in our voices may overwhelm him just as much as the noise of the living room fan. Maybe that's why he needs to be alone. It might be another way in which he can't be touched," Richard said dispiritedly.

Colleen felt dashed by this possibility. "When will you be leaving for Baltimore?" she asked, almost afraid to find out. She and Richard had grown very close.

"Tomorrow, or possibly the next day, Colleen," Richard replied. "That's what I want to talk to you about. I have to leave for Baltimore immediately, or I'll miss the opening of the symphony season. The buyers of this house have agreed to take all its furnishings. Now that the contract has been finalized, there's nothing left to do except to pack our clothes."

"Will you leave your mother's piano as well?" Colleen asked in surprise.

Richard nodded, and then he added, "Will you come with me to Baltimore, Colleen?"

Colleen was taken by surprise, but after hesitating a moment, she agreed. A life without him seemed inconceivable now.

"We'll have to ask your folks, of course. They might want to know my … intentions," Richard added.

"They'll be happy that I've found meaningful work …" Colleen started to say.

Richard turned to face Colleen and with a smile said, "I meant, Colleen, isn't that what a man does when he asks for a woman's hand in marriage?"

It took a second for Colleen to absorb and process the meaning of Richard's words. She said nothing, and Richard feared that he had been too bold. She finally said, "You're asking me to marry you?"

"Yes," he answered. Then he took her hand and said, "I love you, Colleen. Will you marry me?"

Colleen looked down at her hand in his and nodded.

Richard drew Colleen to him, held her tightly in his arms, and then he kissed her.

As it was getting dark, they went back inside to sit on the porch and talk awhile. Richard offered to make Colleen some tea. When he returned with the tea, they talked about the symphony orchestra's fall schedule and David's scheduled round of appointments with doctors at Johns Hopkins. At ten o'clock, they both went to bed, but not before Richard kissed her good night.

Colleen went into her room, put on her nightgown, and got into bed. She could hear a mockingbird singing somewhere outside her window. It sounded so loud that she thought it must be singing at Richard's upstairs window. *It's like David,* she thought, and she wondered where its own song had gone.

Colleen lay in bed thinking. She was very happy that Richard had asked her to marry him, but she was still worried about David. The mockingbird was singing so loudly now that she found it almost impossible to sort out her thoughts.

She heard the old clock in the living room chime ten o'clock. It had belonged to Richard's mother, and so he had kept it. It no longer kept perfect time and was always out of sync with the rest of the clocks in the house. It didn't really matter because its chime was so lovely.

At what point did a person being out of sync with the events of everyday life become something more than the aging and wearing down of a lovely old clock? *she asked herself.* At what point did a person's separateness become something more serious and uncontrollable, like autism? *Colleen did not know.*

She wondered what David *really* meant when he sang, "No thank you!" in D minor. There were things about David that seemed beyond comprehension, like his lack of a person center. She felt that this missing piece of him contradicted Pete's belief in the melody of God that gives hope to every child.

Richard had told her that the full text of Schweitzer's remark had been, "We must listen to this voice … as to a pure and distant melody that comes across the noise of the world's doings … *that we may become the children of God.*"

Without a person center, how could there be any hope for a child like David? It took *time* to compose the swirl of one's thoughts and feelings. When someone was emotionally overwrought, wasn't he often told, "Try to *compose* yourself!"? She presumed that amid life's noise and busyness, there was little time for people to compose their true feelings except with clichés. Most people might be far more scripted than they realized, and so they failed to say what was really in their hearts until it was too late. Perhaps the gap between their real feelings and their thoughts never closed, and only poets and musicians took time to compose their true feelings. She was so glad that Richard had said what was in his heart before leaving for Baltimore!

Colleen lay in bed, wide awake now. It seemed likely that David could neither compose his true feelings nor close the gap with words. She recalled how words had failed her when Frank had asked, "Why didn't they tell me I'm dying?" Had David's autism taught him to say "No thank you!" to an incomprehensible world in the same way that

Frank had turned wordlessly away to face the blank wall and loneliness of his approaching death? She couldn't bear to think that a little boy could feel that way about his life.

The moon was full. Its silvery light had created long, gray-green shadows that extended all the way across the front lawn. The mockingbird was still singing songs that were not its own. Colleen glanced at the clock. It was past midnight.

She covered her ears with the blanket and then with the pillow. How could anyone understand a child like David? If anyone could, she thought it might be Miss Wilson. After all, she had taught thousands of students to speak and write well. Colleen decided that she would ask Richard if they could see Miss Wilson before leaving for Baltimore. The thought comforted her, and she finally fell into a deep and dreamless sleep. She didn't wake up until eight o'clock the next morning.

In the morning, as Richard was packing, Colleen called her parents to let them know her plans. Mrs. Reilly answered the phone, and after briefly chatting, Colleen told her mother that Richard had proposed marriage. There was a long silence on the other end of the phone, and then she heard her mother say, "Oh, Colleen, I'm so happy for you! He's a wonderful man." Then there was another silence. She finally heard her mother call out loudly and excitedly, "Elliot, come here this very *minute*!"

When Colleen hung up, Richard took a last look around the house and then closed the windows and locked the front door. They drove back to Colleen's house so that Colleen could pack her clothes, too. While Richard and Mr. Reilly talked over Richard's plans for the future, Colleen went upstairs, with her mother alongside talking nonstop. They went into Colleen's room so that she could collect the things that Colleen wanted to take with her to Baltimore. Katie and Elliot joined them and gave her big, excited hugs. Elliot was also packed because he had to leave immediately for his new job in a private school in Chicago. Laura, Will, and Abby had already left very early that morning.

"Now you mustn't overdo, Colleen!" her mother admonished her. "Make sure Richard helps out with David."

"He always does, Mom," Colleen said, smiling. When they came back down, they had coffee together, and then Richard and Colleen said good-bye.

When their car reached the main road, Colleen asked Richard to turn off and follow a back road so that they could enjoy the open countryside for as long as possible. She had never lived in a big city like Baltimore, and she needed time to say good-bye to the countryside. The sudden change in her life had been too abrupt. David was in the backseat playing with Pete's music box.

As they were driving along, they came upon the small airpark located on the outskirts of Carlton. There was a small, country fair going on, and at the far end of the field nearest the hangar, there were some airplanes on display.

"Could we stop for a while, Richard? Neither of us has had lunch, and David might enjoy a ride on the carousel," Colleen suggested.

Richard parked the car in the shade, and the three of them walked over to the amusement area. Richard was feeling a bit tired because he had been kept awake the previous night by all the excitement and later on by the mockingbird that had sung for two hours outside his bedroom window.

"Why don't you take David over to the carousel so that he can take a ride?" Richard suggested. "I'm worn out from all the excitement, and a short nap under a tree will restore me before we get back on the road. We can get lunch here before we go. I noticed a homemade baked goods and lunch pavilion that looked promising on the way in."

While Richard stretched out on the grass under a large maple, Colleen and David walked toward the carousel. As she waited in line for tickets, she noticed that the ticket vendor was dressed in a black velvet suit with a dancing skeleton on his shirtfront. The man wore a long silk cape over the suit. A crowd of children had followed him like a pied piper from the tent where he had been giving a magic show. She heard a little boy come up to him and ask how he had made the rabbit disappear.

"Mr. Death never reveals his trade secrets, sonny," she heard him say irritably. His face was glistening with perspiration because the day had grown warm and the temperature had climbed into the eighties. His voice sounded familiar to Colleen.

When she and David got to the head of the line, the man scowled at David, who was making little noises. He looked up at Colleen, and a look of sudden recognition crossed his face. It was the Handyman.

"Well, hello, Colleen," he said in an unfriendly tone. "What's wrong with the kid?"

"He's autistic," Colleen said, trying to ignore his rudeness.

A young woman dressed in a gypsy outfit came up to the Handyman and whispered something in his ear.

"I have to go back and check something in the machinery. My sister Magna will sell you your tickets. Parents are responsible for their children's safety, so you'd better stay with him on the ride. He don't look quite normal, and I don't want him scaring away my fan club."

Colleen barely heard what he said because she had been taken aback by the young woman's name.

The Handyman strode away, his cape swirling after him, while Magna sold Colleen two tickets.

"He's my half brother," she said, obviously embarrassed by his behavior. "I work with him during the summer. He does the magic act and runs the carousel. I tell fortunes. I'm sorry he was rude to your child."

"That's all right," Colleen replied. "I know your half brother. He used to work in a place where I was staying. I'm curious about your name. The only place I ever heard it before was in a book I read."

Magna looked startled and replied, "It's funny you should mention that. I think I've heard of that book. My brother gave it to me as a present. Then it mysteriously disappeared. I never got to read it. I've always wondered if he took it back. He's not quite right in the head. Even when he was a little boy, he was fascinated by death and magic." Magna shuddered. "I do run on, don't I?" she said, and she moved away hurriedly when she heard her half brother returning.

Colleen helped David onto the platform and then helped him get onto a white stallion that David had been attracted to. It was a most unusual carousel. Colleen thought that the carved animals looked European. They created a strange menagerie composed of ferociously real, wild animals that seemed to stalk the domesticated cats, hounds, and horses.

*It was a most unusual carousel. The carved animals created a strange menagerie of ferociously real, wild animals that seemed to stalk the domesticated cats, hounds, and horses.*

Magna and her brother were passing through the assorted animals, checking to see that each child was secure. A little girl had been frightened by the menacing leer of one of the tigers, and the Handyman roughly moved her to a Persian cat. It was designed in the shape of a coach, and it didn't move up and down. The little girl looked disappointed and sat glumly by herself on the hard bench. Her coach was beside David's horse, and they were both seated in the inner circle of animals. The little girl couldn't see her parents. "There's a nice, tame, kitty cat for you, little girl," the Handyman growled scornfully.

When the children had all settled down, Magna and the Handyman jumped off the platform. The Handyman pulled the lever, and the platform began to revolve. Colleen felt the Handyman's eyes following her malevolently.

*He remembers, and he's looking for revenge,* Colleen thought.

Halfway through the ride, David dropped Pete's music box. It fell onto the platform and began to play. David uttered an unearthly scream, and the other children now looked frightened of him. The little girl in the Persian cat began to cry for her mother. Pete's music box had rolled between the poles of the outer horses, causing Colleen to lose sight of it. She could see some of the children trying to reach down and catch it.

The Handyman, fearing that pandemonium was about to break out, raised the lever and stopped the carousel. He jumped onto the platform and strode over to Colleen and David.

One of the parents retrieved the music box and returned it to Colleen. Colleen had already taken David off the stallion and was holding his hand tightly.

The Handyman glared at Colleen and said in a low, threatening tone so that none of the parents could hear, "Get that kid off my carousel right now. I knew the moment I laid eyes on him that he wasn't normal. Get out!"

"For your information, he's a little boy who has a communication problem. He can't tell anyone in the usual way when something frightens him. At best, he can only echo."

The Handyman's eyes bugged out of his head, and he looked incredulous—as if he were looking at two alien species.

"The trouble with you, and people like you, Colleen, is that you don't know what normal is, but you insist on telling other people what it is and ought to be. And all the while you keep thinkin' that we'll see things your abnormal way. To add insult to injury, you and your abnormal friends got me fired for no good reason."

"That's a lie," Colleen said angrily.

He ignored her, then smirked and said, "Now, why don't you just take yourself and that kid elsewhere, or I'll have to call the cops because little Mr. Sir Echo is disturbin' the peace!"

He inched closer to Colleen until he was right in her face. She felt his hot breath and was forced to look into the narrow, reptilian slit of his eyes. Beneath the mask-like slits, his eyes smoldered with hatred. They were like dying coals in a winter hearth, fading to a cold death. Then they flashed into a sudden explosion of heat and fire.

Colleen drew back involuntarily, but he grabbed her roughly by the arm and pulled her back toward him.

He had thrown off the mask now. There were no more shadows to hide in, and he didn't care. He had Colleen where he wanted her at last.

He released her arm and hissed, "You'll figure out someday, *Colleen*, that there are *plenty* of Handymen out there just like me, from the lowest to the very highest parts of society, and we've all figured out something that you haven't. In this world, it's use and be used, or lose. Your kid's an obvious loser! You're working for the wrong side, *Colleen*." Again, there was the insidious familiarity that Colleen detested.

A malicious gleam came into the Handyman's eyes, and he reached into his pocket. He pulled out his card and said, "Here's my card, Colleen! I only do magic in the summer to practice my sleight of hand and as a vacation from my work during the rest of the year. Maybe someday, you or one of your friends, or the *kid* here, could use my regular services."

He disdainfully and victoriously flicked a business card at Colleen's feet. Colleen bent down beside David and picked up the card. It read:

## MAN OR MOUSE

## VERMIN REMOVAL SERVICE

Mice, Rats, and Other Pests Removed—Permanently!

Satisfaction Guaranteed.

Colleen read the card and started to put it in her pocket, intending to ignore the insult, but then she handed it back to him. "I don't think I'll need your services, but I'll tell you something my Irish grandmother always told me," Colleen said.

"What's that, Colleen?" he asked curiously, the venom in his voice replaced with smug, self-satisfaction.

"Life kicks you in the pants, but you still win," she replied. "Take a good look! He's just a little boy! What are you afraid of?" Colleen turned on her heel and didn't wait for his reply.

By the time Colleen and David had reached the end of the arcade, she felt a little better, but the Handyman's insulting words about David had stung her. "He thinks he knows what he's doing!" she muttered to herself as she was approaching Richard. "And he feels no remorse. He thinks it's okay to be cruel as long as it's considered normal!"

Colleen found Richard sound asleep under the tree. She woke him and told him what had happened on the carousel. "He said I should call him if I ever need his services!" Then Colleen started to laugh. She laughed so hard that tears ran down her cheeks.

"Maybe he thought I was crazy when I told him 'life kicks you in the pants, but you still win'," Colleen finally managed to say.

"Maybe he thought he had met his match," Richard observed quietly.

As they walked slowly toward the lunch pavilion, Colleen and

Richard discussed what they needed to do when they reached Baltimore. He would have to make calls to confirm David's appointments and begin rehearsing for upcoming performances. At the lunch counter, they ordered a hot lunch as well as a bag of sandwiches and fruit to eat in the car later on.

While Richard studied the maps of West Virginia and Maryland, Colleen amused David, but her mind was elsewhere as she thought about living in a city as large as Baltimore. Richard showed her a map of Baltimore and pointed out the street where they would be living. "The place where we perform," he said, tracing out a path from his town house to the Lyric Opera, "is about 15 minutes away." Colleen had never heard Richard play with the symphony orchestra, and the thought of it thrilled her. Richard pointed to a green square on the map which was a park only 5 minutes from his townhouse. "The three of us could take walks there and not have to ride the bus," Richard added.

When they had finished lunch, they got in the car and arranged the pillows and blankets in a makeshift bed for David to sleep on overnight during their long trip to Baltimore. Richard had included two pillows, in case Colleen wanted to sleep in the back seat with David. They drove through the night and arrived in Baltimore shortly before 8:00 a.m. Colleen had slept during part of the trip, but had kept Richard company during the middle of the night. When they arrived in Baltimore, Richard immediately went to bed and slept for 12 hours. Later in the afternoon, David curled up with him and also fell asleep.

Left to her own devices, Colleen looked around the apartment and was enchanted by the dining room which looked out upon the garden through French doors. It was large enough for David to play in. Sunlight streamed into the dining room from the garden. It would be a cheery place to eat in throughout the year.

When she went into the living room, she found two floor-to-ceiling bookcases full of books. A stack of music occupied one corner of

Richard's desk. There were stuffed chairs upholstered in a beautiful rose floral pattern. Sheer ruffled drapes were hung at the two large windows that looked out onto the street. Colleen sat down in a chair by the windows and watched passersby for a while before falling asleep.

When Richard awoke, they had a hot meal. He was famished after the long drive. After dinner they discussed where and when they should get married. They finally decided to get married at City Hall and have a more formal wedding when Richard could get time off. They were married the following week, with Richard's two best friends from the orchestra acting as witnesses.

The following three weeks flew by with a round of appointments for David and rehearsals for Richard. Richard had been able to get a ticket for Colleen for a matinee symphony performance on the day after Halloween. Since tonight was Halloween, Richard went to a local grocery store and bought some candy. When the first goblin appeared at the door, however, David went into his bedroom and hid. It took some time to coax him to bed. And then, finally, all was quiet.

Colleen rose early the next morning. She had heard a neighbor's car start up, and had awoken with a start, thinking it must be late. It was only daybreak, but she was too excited to sleep. She also wanted a little time by herself to think about everything that had taken place in the past month. It had been hectic, but everything was finally in place, including David's schedule of appointments and the details of his planned treatment.

She went into the kitchen and poured some ground coffee into the percolator, and then sat down at the small kitchen table and waited for the coffee to brew. She wondered what one wore to a concert in a big city. Richard had told her that the performance was sold out and that there would be a large crowd. This pleased him. The orchestra would be playing Beethoven's Fifth Symphony, which was a favorite of most of the members of the orchestra as well as the public.

When the coffee was ready, Colleen put on a coat over her nightgown, and then balanced her cup of coffee in her left hand while she pushed open the French doors that led into the garden. The pre-dawn air, crisp and autumnal, jolted her awake. Richard and David were still asleep, warm in their beds.

The garden was as quiet as the house. Frost had lightly coated the roses and grassy places along the flower beds. The flagstone walk glistened with melting frost. Daylight was just beginning to spill over the garden wall. It was the magic moment of the day; the change of state that came with the dawn. It never failed to thrill her. It was like the moment before the conductor's baton fell.

Avoiding puddles, she tiptoed to the small patio table that Richard had bought for her. A crescent moon was shining through the branches of the dogwood in the center of the garden. Nestled in the web of branches, it looked like a nest for the migrating birds that were beginning to fly south. "Perhaps they are on their way to Kentucky," she whispered to herself, thinking of her parents and friends back home. The last three weeks had gone by so quickly in the blur of appointments for David, Richard's rehearsals, and the mess of moving in that she had barely had time to miss them.

She sipped her coffee and listened as birds began to twitter in her neighbor's hedge.

The city was also awakening. She wasn't used to the early rush hour and people rushing everywhere toward the possibilities that a big city offered. She sat down on one of the wrought iron patio chairs, which grated as she pulled it under her. The sound startled the birds in the part of the hedge beside her. They flapped their wings in protest. She told them, "I will bring you some coffee, if you like."

As she said this, she noticed two rats raiding her neighbor's garbage cans in the alley at the end of their yard. God had created snakes and rats and declared them good, but they were still her least favorite things. When the rats saw her, they moved soundlessly down the alley.

Richard had told her that all cities had rats, and it was likely they were there to stay.

Colleen sighed. It had taken them two hours to get David to bed last night. He had been overstimulated by the Halloween ghosts and goblins. Somewhere around 9 pm, the last trick or treater had come and gone. She and Richard had collapsed into bed early, knowing that Richard would have to rise fairly early to get ready for the performance of Beethoven's most famous symphony.

As the sun rose higher, the remainder of the birds began to twitter. Their first few peeps soon swelled to an excited chatter. It lasted until the sun rose high enough for them to take flight and abandon the garden. The last chirp rose on the breeze, then fell to earth, dissolving like time and melody, into what was only a lovely memory.

It was All Saints Day, a day to follow Halloween. It was a day dedicated to remembering those who had led truly good lives. A time to honor their passing in the past year. A time to remember Pete. Her thoughts of Pete brought back a day when she and Richard were still living in Kentucky. It had been a lovely day in late summer, and she and Richard had been wandering through a meadow near his house. The tall grasses whispered in the wind, and far overhead they had heard the song of a lark.

"He's up there, somewhere overhead," she had said, pointing to a patch of blue sky between billowing clouds. But she could see nothing. "He must be above the clouds!" Colleen had cried out, shading her eyes against the sun.

"I heard him too," Richard said.

He squinted his eyes, trying to spot the elusive bird. He, too, saw nothing, but he heard the call again. It was so far away that he wondered if he had actually heard it.

He smiled at Colleen. "Back in Shakespeare's day, the farmers working their fields would hear a lark, but when they looked up, they most often saw nothing. But they could still hear the lark singing high above them. It seemed to fly impossibly high. It was so beautiful and mysterious that it inspired Shakespeare to write, "Hark! The lark at Heaven's Gate is singing!"

Colleen continued to listen intently, but she heard nothing more. "What a lovely idea!" She thought it was a perfect metaphor for Pete.

Colleen stared wistfully through the branches of the dogwood tree. She doubted there were any larks in Baltimore. A mate would not hear its call above the noise of the city. She thought it a pity that modern life did not include the notion of a Heaven's Gate.

And to think how far autism was from Heaven's gate! It seemed incomprehensibly far from that beautiful place. According to David's psychologist, autism had robbed David of his "person center." He couldn't catch a ball like an ordinary child. He even placed Richard's hand on top of his to open the refrigerator, as if he felt that his hand couldn't do it. He sometimes repeated bits of conversation, and though he could see and hear, most of the time he couldn't or wouldn't listen. He seemed to prefer his own world. It would be a struggle to bring him out of it. The psychologist thought David's mind was like a tangled switchboard where incoming phone calls rang in all the wrong rooms, and he could not tell who was calling him and what the message was.

Colleen had recently witnessed what she felt might be a clue to David's mysterious condition. While visiting a cousin with a two-month-old baby girl, Colleen had noticed how the baby repeatedly reached for her ear and touched it, as if mapping its exact location and the time it took for her hand to reach it. It seemed obvious that the infant had begun to map her own body – her own self – and was beginning to form a picture of herself in space and time. This would eventually enable her to walk and talk as her knowledge of herself moved down her body. Was this the map of a "person center" that David had failed to form?

Colleen compared what the baby had done with the way she had learned to use her hands and fingers to find notes on the piano keyboard. The first thing her teacher had taught her was to feel how the black keys were arranged in groups of twos and threes. "Let your fingers and ears be your guides, and not your eyes!" her teacher had warned her. At first the piano music only included notes in the octaves adjacent to Middle C. The white keys were not merely nooks and crannies between and among the black keys: they had names. It was the beginning of music literacy. The black keys were sharps and flats. Gradually, she learned how to pick up her hands and move to the black keys of other octaves. Eventually, she was rewarded with a complete picture of the keyboard. After much practice, she could find all the notes of a piece while keeping up with the tempo.

It pained her to realize that her cousin's baby had begun to map her body on her own, while David could not. The infant would soon begin to make sounds while interacting with her mother. The sounds would eventually combine into meaningful words. Why hadn't David been able to do that? Later, her mother would read poetry to her and she would learn about rhythm and rhymes. Without help, David would not. When she went to school, her teachers would introduce her to music through simple songs and the handling of kindergarten musical instruments. She would learn to keep time to the teacher's piano playing. Colleen's piano teacher had said, with a straight face, "In piano, you learn that rhythm is in the seat of your pants." It was like jumping rope while seated.

It was child's play. The play of the child was the child's natural work. But not for David.

Language and music were supposed to develop in tandem, one expressing thought, and the other, emotion. By the time her cousin's baby was five, she would learn that her speech contained words, rhythms, punctuation, and sentences, and she would begin to read. Her private music teacher would introduce her to parallel structures of chords, rhythms, cadences, and phrases. Or, if she didn't take music lessons, she might unconsciously absorb these things when she sang.

And when she grew into adulthood and thought more abstractly, and if she had talent, she might even reach the level of Beethoven or Shakespeare. Colleen knew that Richard was disappointed that David might never develop real musicianship. He wanted to share all that beauty with his son.

Richard had been working hard to get ready for the Baltimore Symphony Orchestra's performance of Beethoven's Fifth Symphony, surely one of the most complex pieces ever to arise from a simple motif. "Dit, Dit, Dit, Dah!" Its opening notes were as bold as the "V" for Victory Churchill had flashed to the world during the darkest hours of World War II. During the war Richard had admired Churchill's foresight. "All his life, he felt he was swimming upstream, but he never gave up. Never, never, never!" Richard had shouted those words, and two nights ago she had learned why.

He had told her that David's original doctor had never disclosed his true suspicions about David's condition. By "protecting" Richard, he had made things worse. Two years had been lost. "They didn't want to tell me the bad news! Couldn't they see that he is my son, and I love him. I will always love him no matter what! I will never give in to it. Never!"

He had sat down in a chair, buried his head in his hands, and cried. Colleen had never seen Richard cry. She had rubbed his shoulders and tried to reassure him that David would improve. She told him about a poem written by Emily Dickinson that Colleen often thought about when her spirits sagged.

"She called Hope a 'thing with feathers.' She said it is perched in the soul, and that it sings a wordless tune, and it never stops singing at all." She looked pleadingly at Richard. "Don't you see? The 'thing with feathers' is God telling us he never gives up on us. The thing with feathers' tune is like a pure and distant melody coming to us from afar, like Pete said. God is always there and believes in us." It had only made Richard cry harder. But she understood his bitterness and sorrow that nothing had been done to help David.

Colleen's greatest fear was that it WAS too late for David. He was past the age when most children had achieved relative fluency in their speech. Richard also feared that the costs of David's care might be financially ruinous. Fortunately, David's great aunt had promised to help them as much as she could.

Now, at least, David's psychologist had come up with an educational plan that would build associations between the visual, auditory, and spatial parts of David's brain. The psychologist thought he might learn to read someday. At least at an elementary level. He planned to bring in a speech pathologist to correct things that David's tongue could not do. David would resist, but it could only be done in a set order, week by week. He had physical and emotional deficits that also had to be addressed. That was the theory, and that was the hope.

In spite of it all, Colleen thought that David had shown signs of progress. Without professional help, Richard had managed to teach David a few songs with words. David always sang the words in his favorite key of F-major. It showed he had musical memory. She felt that that he took pleasure in simple things like the sweet smell of her hair, or the fun of saying "Here we go!" when he spun his world globe. When he said "God is great" before a meal, he seemed to feel the pleasure of being with his parents and his awareness of their love. On the other hand, he sang "No thank you" in D-minor, when he didn't want to disappoint Richard. "No thank YOUUUUU." Short, short, long. Sung sweetly and sadly. In his own unique way, he had found ways to express the pleasures and pains that made David, David. He had an emotional map of himself and others. There was certainly hope in that. It seemed obvious that "the thing with feathers" existed in David!

She went inside and told Richard about her thoughts. He was awake and already shaved and dressed. He suggested that she might like to work with David's psychologist in carrying out the educational program being devised for David. It would give her something to work on as they raised David. He knew that Colleen hoped to go to college someday and learn a profession that might help his son. She also wanted to continue her piano studies. "Why not combine the fields of psychology and music?" Richard suggested.

"Could I do that?" she asked.

"I don't see why not," Richard said. "I think our son would like that."

It was the first time that Richard had ever called David "our son." She was immeasurably touched!

After an early lunch, Richard went into the living room where he made a call to a friend whose wife was willing to babysit David so that Colleen could attend the orchestra's matinee performance. Then he gathered up his things, kissed her goodbye, and went out the door. Colleen could hear David playing in his bedroom, so she finished washing the dishes and then got dressed to go out. She had been waiting about 15 minutes for the babysitter to arrive when the phone rang. The wife of Richard's friend was too sick to come due to a stomach virus. She expressed her regrets and hung up.

Colleen decided she would have to take David with her to the performance. She bundled him up against the chilly day, and then they went out to the street corner to catch a bus. When the bus came, they both boarded without difficulty. David had never been in a bus before or seen so many people. But the passing scenes outside his window kept him occupied. So far, so good!

Colleen watched him and wondered if someday he might be well enough to catch a bus on his own and work at a job that might be repetitious, but not beyond him. For instance, he might be able to work at one of the city's hospitals and fold towels and linens. She hoped there would be a place in the world for him someday.

It was late when they arrived at the concert hall. She decided it might be a disaster to try to find a seat for David when the performance was about to start. The concert master had given the indication for the orchestra to tune up. When David heard Richard's horn, he sang "AAAAAAAAAAA." Colleen smiled at him and hoped all would be well. He seemed to recognize the sound of Richard's horn.

She found a place in an alcove off the main entrance where they could listen, unobserved and without distractions. David had brought a new music box with him. It once had two dancing figurines on its top. The ceramic figurines represented Cinderella and the prince. David had deliberately pulled them off the lid of the music box. Instead of playing the music, he preferred to twist the figures back and forth as they danced silently and rhythmically between his thumb and fingers. He kept the dancing figurines locked in a quarter turn, never allowing them to complete their waltz. He seemed fascinated by the moment when Cinderella stepped back, following the prince's lead, just as they began their first turn. David sometimes repeated this movement for such a long time that Colleen found it alarming. She would usually try to distract him into doing something else. Today, she thought it might be a useful way for him to bide his time through the lengthy symphony.

The doors of the concert hall remained open for any late comers. The lights went down, and the first movement began. Dit, Dit, Dit, Dah! Was there anything more electric and exciting than Beethoven's genius? It went on and on, "con brio" and "allegro", but it dropped to quiet moments too, but always insistent that there was more. Beethoven had ten minutes of repetitions up his sleeve. It was like electricity pulsing through the brain in pursuit of the motif, from woodwind to string to horn. And then it was Richard's turn. Her body could barely contain the joyous tension of the music. She wanted to throw back her head, and what? Laugh? Or cry for joy? As one might cry when finding something indescribably beautiful that one had longed and waited for? Here was the mind of a genius unfurling in unpredictable and fantastically new ways. It made the classical perfection of Mozart's music seem formulaic. Here was sheer audacity and joy! Beethoven did not work in the way that Mozart or Hayden worked. Instead of following the rules for writing a sonata that a genius like Mozart could create and turn out in weeks, Beethoven worked with infinite patience until he found the totally new structures through which his melodies and harmonies would move. He wrote with precision and in the way that he wished, and not in the dignified way the aristocratic eighteenth century prescribed. His was a new day, free from the tyranny of wealth, power, and musical tradition. It was an exhilarating new day for the entire world!

David knew nothing of this. But at points, when the horns came in, he would look up. Throughout the first movement, a custodian had been methodically cleaning the entrance area. He had finally reached the alcove and was surprised to find Colleen and David there. Colleen explained her predicament and showed him her ticket. He was sympathetic and said that as far as he was concerned, they could stay. David seemed oblivious of the custodian, and kept playing with the figures.

All was well. The second movement was performed "andante con moto." But at times, Colleen could hear the short, short, short, long motif presented in totally new ways. And she also thought she heard notes that resembled a heartbeat. Beethoven's genie was totally out of the bottle. His heart and mind were revealed.

She heard the same heartbeat in the third movement, which was a scherzo, rather than the traditional minuet and trio. David was getting restless. Was it David's heartbeat that she heard, or her own fear that he might scream or disrupt the performance in some way? It was a fear that never left her. If only they could be free of autism and as free as Beethoven. She tried to think of a way to distract him. She opened her pocketbook and let him sort through it. He was too restless to be distracted. There was no way he would last through the fourth and final movement.

She told the custodian that she would be leaving and gave him a note written for Richard that explained why she and David had to leave. The custodian said he would be sure that Richard got the message.

When she and David arrived home, she gave him a snack and then let him play in the garden. After washing up the few dishes, she went outside to watch him and to rest before dinner. At times, she still became fatigued because of her partially collapsed lung. The tension of worrying about David during the concert had taken its toll. She seldom told people that she'd had TB because so many people were still afraid of TB. Their fears persisted even though antibiotic therapy was now understood and available. However, the fear and shock that people felt when they encountered David was deeper and darker than the stigma of TB. Fortunately, the custodian had not been like so many other people.

Nevertheless, she could hardly blame most people for reacting fearfully to David. The first time she had ever seen David lost in repetitive actions, it had felt like a body blow. It was so unlike anything a caring person would want to see in a child…so alone and meaningless, and so far from the normally happy life of a child that one expected.

Because of David, she had begun to understand the Handyman's behavior. She looked around their pretty little garden. If life was a garden, then the Handyman was lost in the thorns. If he would only look up and see that the thorn protected the rose. A rose always hid a thorn. One must be grateful for its beauty, but nonetheless careful in its care. She believed that it would be a long time until he understood this and healed. Perhaps he had reached out too many times and been pricked. At Sherwood, he had been willing to burn down the beauty of the garden in order to smite the thorns. He found no beauty in his own suffering or in the suffering of others. He had become a thorn and a predator through his own violence. Suffering was fine for others, but not for him. His own humanity had drowned in a toxic stew of hate.

In the end, he had missed the Truth and Beauty in the garden. She believed that the Handyman had not learned that there are as many varieties of Beauty as there are beautiful children in the world, including David. Each one would only grow and thrive in a garden full of love. "That includes OUR son, as well!" she whispered to herself.

Then she looked over at David and knew that there was only one certain Truth: Year after year, autumn and winter would enter the gardens of our lives. As time passed, the masks of lies and deceit would fall onto the fertile soil, like spent leaves. Spring would follow winter. The beauty of the garden would return for all. And meanwhile, "the thing with feathers" would be singing its wordless tune of hope, filling the garden with beauty. More of the Truth would be learned, and we would grow. There was only one rule that must be unfailingly followed: Though the rose always comes with the thorn, we must mend what is broken.

She told herself, "This is the place where music begins." Pete had found that place at Heaven's Gate. But it was also only as far away as a child playing in one's own garden.

# Afterword

I would like to thank my friend Helen for her help in making this book possible. She experienced many of the story's events personally and provided the details of medical treatment of TB during the late 1940's that are described in this book. The compression treatment of that era did not work well on her still young, elastic lung, and she almost lost hope that she would ever be discharged. Her memories of the friends she made at the sanitarium formed the basis for many of the main characters except Pete, who was my own invention.

Helen did survive TB and went on to become a piano teacher and composer. In later life, she was married to a member of the Baltimore Symphony Orchestra who played French horn. I got to know him through Helen. They met at our local community college where he taught her music theory and composition. He is a voracious reader, and his character, Richard, reflects his deep knowledge of literature.

After finishing junior college, Helen eventually earned a degree in music and psychology. Most of the chapter titles in this book are titles of compositions that Helen wrote for her students. Helen used her knowledge of psychology to figure out a way to teach an autistic teenager to play the piano. I attended a recital by her piano students and saw how well they played under her guidance. She passed away after a long life of helping others. I will never forget how she said in her pure Kentucky accent, "Hi there, Bette!"

Because Helen had a severely autistic grandson, and because she loved him so much, she asked if I would also write about him. In order to include him in a story that ended in 1950, I imagined her grandson as being one of the first handful of cases of autism that were discovered at this time. I had Helen become mother, and not grandmother, of an autistic child, and I used Helen's second husband as the model for Richard. The techniques that are used by the psychologist to treat David were developed later than 1950, but they were moved into an earlier time to further illustrate autism.

My descriptions of David were from my observations of Helen's grandson when she invited me to come talk to him at her house. By then, it was 2005. I wanted to use all the things I discovered about her real-life grandson because he is such a good child and makes a very appealing character who has musical promise but is afflicted with autism. Colleen says things that she could not possibly have known in 1950, but I needed a way for her to try to understand David from her present musical knowledge and intuitions, as well as through her high school studies of literature.

In real life, Helen's high school teacher hugely influenced Helen's life. Helen told me that her teacher inspired a love of learning that no other teacher had brought out in her. Helen wrote about her teacher and her struggles to get an education on her college application many years later. Her teacher was the one who made the lovely gesture of including Helen in her class's yearbook in June of the year she would have graduated, had she not still been in the sanitarium. Helen was deeply moved not to be forgotten by her teacher and classmates.

If the concluding scene of Colleen's story moved you to want to learn more about autism, I would suggest *Nobody Nowhere*, and *Somebody Somewhere*, by Donna Williams, as well as the books of Temple Grandin as a place to start.

In Donna Williams's story you will be able to feel what it's like not to recognize yourself in the mirror, because that's what autism did to her. Also, you will experience emotions out of sync with events because your brain is too densely packed with neurons and has emotional processing delays. Your emotions will not be paired with events as they happen to you, but instead crash over you much later in an incomprehensible avalanche that literally knocks you out. You will also feel what it's like to have a job sewing buttons onto garments when you don't understand buttonholes. Or maybe you will sew buttonholes all the way up the sleeve. You will know what it feels like to be really lost:

to be "nobody, nowhere." You will experience what it's like not to be whole. You will learn as a child to cross your eyes and make the world disappear. In desperation, you will adopt someone else's personality and use his or her phrases, while pretending to understand what's going on. You will become even less "you" with such a coping strategy, but it will hide from others how different you are. And then one day, you will touch a mirror and realize that the person in the mirror has cold hands, while yours are warm. You will begin to understand that the reflection is you, and not another person. With the help of a psychologist, you will learn to listen and follow another person's speech. But following a three-way conversation will remain very, very hard. You will be be taught to understand the spectrum of emotions that other people express, until you finally begin to be "somebody, somewhere." However, your brain's fundamental delays will never go away, no matter how well you came to understand them. This is the way you will feel when you walk in Donna Williams's shoes as a "mono channeling" autistic person.

On the other hand, you will find that Temple Grandin's autism lies on a different place of the autism spectrum. She is a high functioning visual thinker. If you lived a life like hers, you would have a brain that holds an endless file of pictures of previous scenes and events, and things to say about them. You would think visually and understand the life of animals. You could quickly scan your files and know where you are. But you would need a very short list of things to remember to do, in order to fit it in your crowded, visual memory bank. Your speech would be scripted to fit the scene you find yourself in. However, you would be able to give a lecture and take questions afterwards, but in a scripted way.

There is an ever-increasing amount of literature on autism and its related neuroscience. Besides the books by Williams and Grandin, there are a few articles or portions of books I would like to recommend that discuss the physical underpinnings of speech. Many are music related. The reader can find out more about rhythm and speech in Malcolm Gladwell's *The Tipping Point*. You will find an excellent article about prosody (the intonation in our speech) if you Google "Prosody and Linguistics." There are many articles under that heading that will come up, but the one I found most relevant to this story was the Wikipedia entry.

Also, I would like to recommend two articles in Scientific American published in 2010. One is called "Mirror Neurons". Mirror neurons are involved in imitative learning and are implicated in autism. The other article, "Programmed for Speech," is about our "speech center" and a possible "speech gene," which we share in common with songbirds. Without it, a bird cannot sing and will only chirp. A related article in Penn State's Science Journal, Fall/Winter 2010, titled, "Songbirds Provide Insight into Speech Production" reported that songbirds acquire their songs in orderly syllables and with syntax. It is not yet known if song birds communicate in a code with "words." This unity of speech and song in the brain is enticingly close to Keats' Truth/Beauty paradox, which some readers may enjoy thinking about. Such readers might also enjoy a book by Rodolfo Llenas called *i of the Vortex*, in which he describes the amygdala as the "conductor" of the complex geometries of the "instruments" of the cortex. Llenas believes that the brain evolved in animals as a means to navigate through space and time. (Plants do not move, and they have no brains.) The hand, he points out, is shaped like the tongue, and different areas of the tongue are used to form various phonetic combinations. This, too, seems rather like coordinating notes through time and space as one does in performing piano music with the hands and fingers.

If, ultimately, we better understand "the map" of the brain, will that enable our autistic children to succeed and be happy in their daily lives? If we can "mend" them, should we? I ask this question because things have changed quite a bit since Helen's grandson was young. In recent years, science has developed machines that enable autistic children to communicate through an iPad, and some of these children can now succeed in college level and post-graduate programs by learning and communicating in their own way. A neurodiversity movement has sprung up which encourages movement away from demanding "normal" behavior or "passing for normal" from autistic children. Making a child think he must "pass for normal" creates anxiety. Children learn best when they are not anxious. Instead, "neurodiversity" advocates emphasize meaningful jobs and joyful relationships for those on the autistic spectrum. Maintaining eye contact for example, takes away energy that could be better employed in learning skills. The motto of the movement is "Nothing about us, without us." All of this is discussed in "Rethinking Autism Therapy," by Claudia Wallis in the Dec. 2022 issue of Scientific American.

Before closing, I should mention something about Helen as a teacher. Her concern for children went beyond her grandson. Her piano recitals were truly joyful events. Each child walked up happily to the piano and played his piece. She had taught them, I think, that when you count the notes, they are like all the different children in the world, and each one counts. And if you concentrate on not losing even one, it is a most wonderful thing. I think her students absorbed that, and they were very happy children because of that knowledge.

There was one key quality that defined Helen, and this is what I found so compelling about Helen and her grandson: She went the second mile, after already suffering in the first mile. She had what it takes to be truly human.

Below is a poem which I learned in a high school French class and used as inspiration for the last scene in this book. Over the years I have forgotten the poet's name. It may have been Eugene de Langlais or perhaps Eugene de Lanley. I couldn't find either name on the internet. The translation is mine. My thanks to good teachers everywhere, including Helen!

Friendship

On Earth, everything shares its portion of sun. Each thorn has its rose. Each night, its dawn. For the meadow, God made the grass. For the field, the harvest. For the air, the superb eagle. For the nest, the bush. In this world where everything bends toward a better center, the flower is for the branch; the friend is for the heart.

# Figures

"Sherwood" TB Sanitarium as it was in the 1940's. Colleen began her stay in the main building and was moved to the building in the background when she became ambulatory. A long, tree-shrouded driveway ran down to the main road. It was where the "Handyman" attacked "Will."

Yearbook graduation portrait of Helen, who was the inspiration for "Colleen." After 3 years in "Sherwood" she returned to high school and graduated at the age of 20.

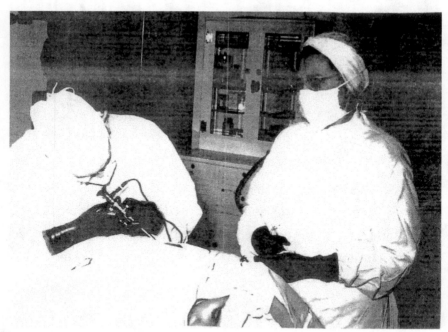

Compression therapy at "Sherwood" for a TB patient, performed before the discovery of streptomycin.

Willy, a grounds keeper, brought kittens to visit with "Sherwood" patients. He inspired the character of "Will," a Haitian intellectual and writer. "Laura" named one of the kittens "Mr. Mews" after the poet and short story writer, Langston Hughes.

"Dr. Smith" acts as master of ceremonies for the fateful Halloween party. "Sherwood's" real Medical Director was Dr. Turner. He worked actively to integrate "Sherwood." The patient dressed as a pirate inspired the character of "Emile," Colleen's friend and fellow patient.

## Author Bio

Bette Hurst earned a BA in philosophy from Penn State and a teaching certificate in French and Spanish from Towson State University. She likes to play the piano and go for walks with her husband and their two dachshunds. She and her family live in Maryland.

Ms. Hurst's friend Helen grew up in a TB sanitarium in the 1940's and provided many memories about the realities of TB treatment during that era. Helen, a composer, piano teacher, and grandmother of a severely autistic grandson, provided the author with many heart-rending observations about the challenges facing an autistic child.

Kitty McNaughton is a commercial artist and muralist. She created the interior black and white drawings in Sherwood.

Printed in the USA
CPSIA information can be obtained
at www.ICGtesting.com
LVHW011601260923
758034LV00008B/122/J